COOGAN'S BREAK

SIX PACK TWO : BOOKS 7-12

HOPE MALONE

BAD BIRDS
Squabbling Sparrows Press

IN THIS

SIX PACK

Lindsey is hiding out at the crumbling mansion she's inherited from her great aunt. After taking the fall for a crime he didn't commit, Ethan has decided the view from a prison cell isn't to his liking. Will this pair escape together?

ONE

ETHAN

On looking around the rundown summerhouse I currently call home, my mind is elsewhere. Prison, to be exact.

Three years for grand theft auto, all while pretending to be someone else, stays with a man long after the sentence is over.

Sure, I'd gone along on joy rides when I was young and stupid, just not the one they locked me up for. Lucky for me, was Scott Latham only ever stole the one. Luckier for him was he'd been outside when the cops busted the hovel we were living in.

Scotty and I were always being mistaken for each other. This coupled with me sitting next to his backpack when the cops smashed in the front door and they'd assumed that's who I was. I'd gone along with it thinking that anything Scotty was guilty of would be child's play compared to what they were after me for.

I'm not sure what the penalty is for assuming someone else's identity, and I hope I never find out. That means keeping clean from now on. Difficult when I still have to prove I'm innocent of the crimes they originally accused me of.

Until such a time as I can, I don't dare use Ethan Hunter, my birth name.

Flat on my back on the large bench in the middle of the summerhouse, I stare up at the boards that line the ceiling of the octagonal structure. The peeling aqua paint is probably all that's holding the building together. It's a far cry from how it had looked when I'd used it as a make-out spot when I was a teenager. The same goes for the condition of Eagle's Nest, the main house.

I'd been sleeping rough when I read that Bella Sanderson, the old girl who owned the place, had died in her sleep. If not for that gust of wind ruffling the newspapers I'd been using to keep warm, I'd never have known.

It hadn't taken long to see Eagle's was unoccupied with no lights at night, and no other signs of activity. While it would have been a simple matter to let myself in, I'd opted for the safer option of crashing in the summerhouse.

When a woman turned up a couple of days back and moved in like she owned the place, I knew I'd made the right call.

With her arrival, I'd thought briefly about moving on. That was before I'd seen that she rarely left the main house. With me tucked away in a far corner of the property, the chances of her accidentally stumbling upon me were slim.

Add to this, my plan is to be gone early each morning, only returning late at night, and I should be okay. Despite the austere nature of the summerhouse, it's safer than sleeping rough at the park in the middle of town.

More than once I'd had trouble from kids who got their kicks harassing those supposedly weaker than them. Apart from them, the public wants nothing to do with me, thanks to my filthy clothing.

Filthy enough that I'd been able to watch my brother and grandfather walking through the park on their way to lunch and they'd not looked at me twice.

I still can't believe my little brother is a bounty hunter, doubtless, so he can have the privilege of arresting me himself. I'll be damned if that's happening before I've cleared my name.

My thoughts once again on the woman living in the main house and I indulge in a lazy grin. To call her a 'woman' is a misnomer. She's a goddess that I'm sure would have done it for me, even without the three years' enforced abstinence.

The other thing I'm sure of is that she's not a local. She looks to be a similar age to me, meaning we'd have been in high school at the same time. There isn't a chance I'd forget those riotous dark curls. Nor would I be likely to forget a body that lush.

Her curves are the sort that don't quit. The sort a man can bury himself in, surrendering to their raw sensuality.

It's a shame I can't have anything to do with her, with this being two-fold.

First off, I can't risk anyone seeing me other than in disguise. While I might be older and a hell of a lot wiser, I'm still Ethan Hunter, so far as the locals are concerned.

Second, and more important, is I can't afford to get involved with a woman of her caliber, not now, potentially ever. And anyway, no woman like that would want anything to do with a guy like me. I'm too rough and definitely too ready.

Hell, I may as well have BAD tattooed across my forehead as a warning to the innocents of this world. It's something my old cellmate would have been more than happy to take care of.

Mind you, that doofus would have spelled bad D.A.B. While I'd been okay with him inking tribal patterns on my shoulder and arm, that was as far as I'd trust him.

I shake my head to clear it of my time in prison, instead replacing it with how the woman had looked on clearing the mailbox the day before. It was because I'd checked it earlier that I now know her name.

"Lindsey Abbott." While her name is unfamiliar, simply whispering it has my mind flooded with images of exactly how hot she'd looked in that flimsy dressing gown. It's also enough to have my cock straining for release, and more.

It's been too damned long since I was close to a woman. The quality of my erection is testament to this, and I know from experience it won't go away on its own. It's not just my arousal that needs attention. I'm also in desperate need of a bath.

LINDSEY

After hitting the save button for the third time in the past half-hour, I sit tall in my expensive ergonomic office chair. I twist first to the right, and then the left, the resultant crackle telling me I've spent far too long hunched over my computer.

I've never worked this hard on a novel before. However, following the disparaging comments from the critics on my last book, I'm out for redemption. If not for the sales of my "Abysmal piece of writing," being through the roof, I'd have given up on the writing altogether.

Instead, I've removed myself from society. I'm determined to have those critics eating their words when it comes time to review my next book. For that to happen, my life needs to be free of distractions, making Eagle's Nest perfect.

I stretch my arms above my head, hoping to unlock further knots, for all the good it does. Much as my head is still in the scene I'm working on, I need to move, to get the blood flowing, and to send any stiffness, packing.

Despite choosing the turret room at the top of Eagle's Nest as my study, when the words are flowing, the world around me ceases to exist. I've been writing for what must be four or five hours, with no sense of time.

After spinning my chair to the side, I lurch to my feet, having to steady myself on the side of my desk. Yep, I doubt I've moved an inch since I first sat down at three this morning. What was it about my creativity that it froze during the day, only to come to life in the middle of the night?

The scene I'd been struggling with just the day before had hit me, fully formed when I should have been sleeping. It had been too good to resist, and so after dragging on leggings and a hoodie, and making a coffee, I'd headed for my study.

Only once I'm steady on my feet do I wander over to stare out of the windows that encircle the room. Many a realtor will say a room has three-sixty-degree views when they're more like one-eighty-degrees. However, this room truly lives up to the description.

As tempting as I find the view out to sea, I'd deliberately set my desk up so my back is to the ocean. My ploy hasn't exactly worked, because when the wind whips through those redwoods at the back of town, they're every bit as mesmerizing as the waves.

My gaze then drops from the horizon, and I see something that has the beauties of nature taking a back seat. "Who on earth are you?"

With my words quiet and the windows closed, there's no reaction from the man currently luxuriating in my late aunt's outdoor tub. He continues lathering his very naked form, leaving nothing out, and I mean nothing. My mouth suddenly dry, I reach out for my cup of coffee, only to remember I'd finished it earlier.

A quick check of the clock on my computer and I can see it's just after eight. Could this be the man from the job center? They said they'd send someone over as soon as they found them, but I hadn't expected one this soon. Apparently handymen are few in this backwater.

However, there's nothing of the *handyman* about this guy. He's more like the hero in the romantic suspense I'm currently working on.

And wow, does he fit that tub, or what? This shows me he's tall and broad, with muscles to match. There's also more than a hint of the bad boy about him, thanks to the tattoo that snakes over one shoulder and down his arm. I'm sure if I opened a window I'd be able to smell the pheromones.

It's as if he's leaped off the pages of one of my novels, rather than simply turned up to cut the grass. And if that is what he's here for, then what on earth is he doing helping himself to the facilities?

It makes a mockery of the job center telling me they'd background check anyone they sent over. "Why, of all the nerve?"

I'm flying down the stairs soon after, ready to reprimand him and then send him packing.

On walking behind the brick wall that protects the bathtub from the prevailing winds, I realize he'd have thought the structure hid him from the main house.

This also means I've got the element of surprise. The question is, how best to use it?

It might be because my head is still partly in the story I've been working on, but rather than act like myself, I act like my heroine. This sees me marching around the end of the wall and snatching up the pile of clothes atop the tree stump next to the tub.

"What on earth do you think you're playing at?"

As I hug his clothes to my chest, I'm immediately engulfed by the raw, earthy smell of the man. This coupled with his sheer male beauty, and it's a wonder I can breathe at all. If I thought he looked hot from my eyrie, up this close he's blowing my fuses.

I'm about to drop his clothes back on the tree trunk and retreat when he rears up out of the tub and grabs at them. This has me instinctively gripping them like my life depends on it. It's also what sees us landing in a tangle of limbs in the old tub, with water sloshing everywhere.

I'm not sure what shocks me the most. That the water is freezing, or that it appears to have done nothing to dampen the erection poking me in the tummy. My eyes flash open and I wish I'd kept them shut when I'm lost in a pair the color of the sea on a cloudy day.

Only on closer inspection do I see the laughter lurking in their depths.

"I am so sorry, ma'am. I didn't mean to, um, I'm, ah."

To a background of the world's most disjointed apology, I desperately try scrambling out of the tub for all the good it does. It also has me putting my hands in places they've no right being, before he grabs me around the waist.

"Hang on, I've got this." He then twists me around before propelling me up and over the side of the tub like I'm as light as a proverbial feather. While done for efficiency, it also had him putting his hands in places they've no right, but that felt oh so good.

Once more safely on my feet, there's nothing I can do to stop from looking at his cock, my eyes widening of their own volition.

He appears bigger than he had earlier. It must be something to do with the refraction of the water. I narrow my gaze. Hmmm, maybe not.

Only his brief snort of laughter has me aware I'm licking my bottom lip. A peek at his face shows his eyes are sparkling with humor, and something else indefinable.

TWO

Not until he hides his manhood with his sodden clothes does my ability to speak return.

"You're from the job center. They ... they said they'd vet anyone they sent over and yet..." I wave my hand to encompass him, his state of undress and the tub.

I then have to swallow again.

His behavior is hardly appropriate when he's here to work.

What if that's not why he's here?

This thought alone has me taking a big step back. *What if, despite the brutal haircut, he's a homeless person?* I take another step back. This has me in amongst the branches of one of the many lemon trees that dot the property, the citrus tang tickling my nose.

After some initial confusion, he eventually answers. "Sorry about that. Got sweaty on the walk over. Anyway, yeah, I'm here for the, ah, em, job?"

I'm not so sure of this, with his last sentence being more a question than a statement.

And all that aside, how on earth is he supposed to work in wet clothes? This has me checking out his chiseled abs. Only another snort of laughter has my gaze returning to his handsome face.

"That's okay. It's a beautiful day. They'll dry soon enough," he says, as if I've voiced my question aloud. After sucking briefly on his bottom lip, he continues. "What would you like me to do first?"

Oh my, what if you told him exactly what that was?

I know I'm blushing, but there isn't a chance I'm putting my hands up to my face. Instead, I center my thoughts, shouting, "The lawns!" at him, before following this up with, "There's a mower in the garage at the front of the property."

Unable to face his knowing gaze any longer, I get out of there as fast as my jelly legs will allow me. The first thing I'll do once it hits nine, is ring the job center and find out what the story is with this one.

And what happened to them having trouble filling the post? For someone to arrive the very next day, means they've sent any old person over.

Well, not just any old person, with the man I'd left in the tub, less handyman and more strip-o-gram.

I'm running when I hit the steps at the front of the house. I'm also unable to stop myself from locking the door after me. Then I chide myself for my overactive imagination.

He just wanted to clean up. To make a good impression, for goodness' sake.

Oh, he did that, alright!

Only after I've made peace with myself about why he's here, do I look at the polished wooden floor and the puddle forming at my feet. I'm not the only one to get wet this morning. Just thinking about the man whose name I don't even know, and I'm on my way to being wetter still.

———

Despite trying, I don't get hold of the job center, with their answering system sending me to more dead ends than a drive in the country. However, watching the man I now know as Scott Latham, mowing the lawns, my fears subside.

I briefly step away from the windows, grab a pen and notebook off my desk, and open to a fresh page. There's something so fluid about the way Scott moves that I'd be a fool not to make a note of it.

If not for this, I wouldn't have seen how particular he was in the simple task of mowing the lawns. Straight lines, slightly overlapped, no blade of grass missed. These are hardly the actions of a vagrant or someone wishing me ill health.

It's for this reason I make him a mid-morning snack with cheese, crackers, and a cold drink. As tempted as I'd been to join him on the front porch, I'd been too self-conscious. This had been two-fold.

First, he wouldn't want someone like me hanging around, drooling over him.

Second, I don't enjoy eating in front of others with them often too quick to judge what, or how much, I consume. Instead, I take my snack back up to the turret room.

Soon enough, the mower roars to life, reminding me of the notes I'd made earlier about how Scott moves. I've got just the scene to use them in, with me soon immersed in the story.

Until I hear the unmistakable sound of water running on the second floor. Talk about cheeky. First, he uses the outdoor bath, now he's using the bathroom inside the main house?

I'd showed him the utilitarian bathroom behind the garage. Why isn't he using that?

I've come to no conclusions when I encounter water on the second floor landing. A quick look to my right shows no sign of my gorgeous handyman. It does, however, reveal an overflowing basin in the bathroom.

After paddling through the water in my stocking feet, I remove the plug from the sink. It's only on trying to stop the trickle from the antique faucet that things escalate. Instead of turning, the whole thing comes away in my hand, with water shooting straight out of the exposed pipe and hitting me in the stomach.

I'm unaware I'm yelling and screaming until Scott turns up next to me, quickly dealing with the issue. He slams a hand over the end of the protruding pipe, wincing.

"Do you know where the shut-off valve is?"

Do I? No, I haven't done so much as look for it, never mind know where it is. "No, I'm sorry, I don't."

He frowns in response. "Well, one thing is for sure, I can't stand here holding this and go look at the same time." He must see something in my expression, because the next thing he does is grab the towel off the rack above the old-fashioned tub. I'm thinking there isn't a chance it will stop the water, but he has another plan. He replaces his hand with the towel and then, taking mine, jams it hard against it.

"I'll go find the valve and shut it off." He's halfway down the stairs when he yells out, "Hold tight! I'll be as quick as I can."

He finds it sooner than I've expected, with me no longer required to apply pressure to stop the water spraying all over the bathroom.

Only then do I have time to take in my current state. What is it about me constantly being wet since this man came into my life?

SCOTT

After turning off the water, I sprint across the lawn, through the front door, and back up the stairs. There I'm stopped in my tracks. What is it about this woman being wet whenever I'm around?

Temptation like this is the last thing I need, with her gloriously disheveled. Were life less complicated, I'd offer to help her out in that department. Thankfully, the perfect distraction arrives soon enough.

I'm drying my hands on my shirt when she gasps. If not for this, I wouldn't even have realized I'd cut myself on that rusty pipe. With the water still switched off, I don't even have the option of cleaning it up.

"That looks bad. Let me grab my first aid kit."

Without waiting for my agreement, she marches out of the bathroom and downstairs. There's no option but to follow, something that's nowhere near as mundane as it sounds. That is one peach of an ass. Round, succulent, juicy.

On entering the kitchen and finding her rummaging in a large bottom drawer, I have to look away. There's only so much temptation I can take, and this doesn't get any easier when she sets to work on cleaning the jagged cut on the palm of my hand.

Apart from a couple of disastrous hook-ups after I got out of prison, this is the closest I've been to a woman in years. If not for my out-of-control libido, I could view her actions as maternal.

And yet being mothered is the last thing on my mind with Lindsey.

After cleaning the wound with antiseptic, which hurts more than the cut, she applies a dressing. When she's finished, I flex my hand experimentally. "Hey, it's good as new."

It's certainly good enough for me to fix the broken faucet. This is preferable to her calling in a plumber, because the fewer locals who see me looking like *me*, the better. "Do you have anything I could use to fix the faucet?"

She puts her knuckles against her lips as she ponders this. When she remembers, her eyes widen, and she starts across the kitchen. "I saw a box of stuff down in the basement on my walk-through with the lawyer. It mightn't be any good, though. Most of it looked to be as old as the house."

She opens the door leading to the basement and stands back. "It's in the far corner. You should be able to find it easily enough."

That she's not leading the way tells me that like a lot of women, she's not a fan of basements. It's that, or she doesn't want to be alone with me down there. I'm hoping it's the former, because the idea of a woman fearing me doesn't sit well.

While I might have skirted the law as a teenager, I'd never lay a hand on a woman unless she wanted me to. And most of them were as keen on that as I was.

Despite her directions being vague, I have no trouble finding the box she'd talked of. Even better is that I spot a few plumbing fittings in the mix. And she wasn't kidding about the age of the pieces. Definitely old enough that you could tell people they were vintage if you wanted to get rid of them at a flea market.

I've got the faucet reconnected in no time. Given the age of the parts I've used, I then show Lindsey how she can turn the water back on, allowing me to stand guard in the bathroom. The last thing she needs is more water on those real wood floors.

I know the second she turns the water back on. The pipes in the old house make their presence known by banging and shuddering in response to the increased pressure. It gets bad enough that I shrug out of my t-shirt and throw it over the faucet just in case. The towel I'd used earlier is nowhere in sight.

At least this way, if the faucet explodes again, it'll stop water from spraying everywhere. But miraculously, my repair holds. Who knows if it'll mess with other faucets in the place? I guess time will tell.

By the time I've checked the house from top to bottom and fixed the third major leak of the day, it's after six. I need to get into town, and soon. Unable to afford top-of-the-line surveillance gear, I'm stuck changing out the batteries on my budget models more often than I'd like.

There's no way I want to miss out on any of the evidence I need to prove myself innocent of selling Class-A drugs. Failing because of flat batteries would mess with my head and potentially see me back inside for a very long time.

After returning my borrowed tools and parts to the basement, I catch up with Lindsey in the kitchen. "Hey, you should be all good for now. Nothing else can go wrong. I'll make sure I'm here early in the morning, though."

I'm ashamed at how easily this lie comes. Of course I'll be there early; I will have spent the night in the summerhouse. A quick glance in Lindsey's direction and there's nothing I can do to stop the errant thought about where I'd rather be spending the night.

My physical reaction has me shoving my hands in the front pockets of my jeans. With my innocence still on the line, the decent thing to do is hide my interest in the woman standing wide-eyed before me.

But screw me, it's no easy feat. Not by a long shot.

THREE

LINDSEY

He's leaving? Strange that he appears loath to do so. What if another pipe bursts, or there's an electrical fire, or I need him to drill something?

Like you?

I can't stop a nervous giggle at this thought and that has him peering at me as if looking for loose screws.

And maybe I have got a loose screw. There isn't a chance of my attracting a guy this hot.

We don't match.

We don't even go together in the traditional sense.

Heck, we'd end up going viral, mostly because people couldn't believe a girl like me could attract a guy like him. I'd be first in line on that assumption.

It then takes all my self-control to stifle another nervous giggle. What is it about this man that brings out the bad girl in me? Could it be the bad boy in him?

I've given up trying to convince myself why I don't want him to leave. The only thing left in the house that needs attention is me. And I know exactly how. My fevered mind has been working overtime on that front.

"Why don't you stay for dinner? I've got plenty to go around."

I'm unaware of the ambiguity of my words until he lifts an eyebrow. That he's fighting a smile is obvious. The only thing I'm unsure of is what's amused him. I know I'm curvier than a lot of girls. I always have been.

However, that's not what I'd meant with my 'plenty to go around' comment. That this might be the cause for his amusement has me stiffening.

His simple, "I'd love to," should have been enough to put me at my ease.

Instead, I hold my breath, waiting for the 'but' that is surely coming, and that leads to an awkward silence.

"I'd better go wash up."

I'm now so on edge that it's a relief when he disappears off to the half bath at the end of the hallway. This gives me time to splash some water on my face at the kitchen sink.

After this, I frantically wave my arms and legs around. I hope to disperse the sexual energy that's close to crashing my system. On hearing the creaking of the floorboards in the hall, I stop immediately. I've embarrassed myself enough for one evening.

While I go about getting something ready for dinner, I'm conscious of him watching my every move. He's sitting at the large kitchen table in what must have been the 1920s equivalent of an island. He's taking his time drinking the beer I'd grabbed out of the fridge.

"You're welcome to go outside and sit on the porch. It's lovely watching the sun go down."

"Thanks, I'm good where I am. I've got all the time in the world to watch things go down."

This casual remark, coupled with the glint in his eye, has me dropping the whisk I'd been holding aloft like a microphone. After this, I come close to burning the gravy while behaving like a fifteen-year-old girl with her first crush.

Surely I'm imagining it? I must be. Things like this don't happen to me. Even that online tarot card reader said if I wanted to find a man, I'd have to get out of the house more.

Despite a flurry of internal rebukes, my arousal continues to build. It's been ages since I spent any amount of time this close to a guy, especially one as hot as this.

Actually, it might be the first time on that front.

After serving up the meal, much as I want to take my plate of food upstairs, I can't. Instead, we sit across from each other at the table. There's no hiding from him now. No way of pretending to give something an urgent stir, or grabbing something out of the fridge.

There's nothing separating us but a slab of wood.

Would you rather the wood was underneath you?

Or even in you?

This last thought has me close to needing the Heimlich maneuver. The heat in my cheeks starts out gently, before flaming into something incendiary, as I imagine Scott in the intimate scene I'd been struggling with earlier. While still not right, it's plenty hot in my books.

Or it could be after a hard edit.

He's close to finishing his beer and I'm pouring myself a much-needed second glass of wine when I ask him if he'd also like a glass.

"I'd better not."

His gaze caresses me; leaving me wondering what would happen if he had that wine.

I'm doing my best to jam the cork back in the bottle when he swallows the last of his beer in a loud gulp. He stares briefly at his empty bottle before looking at me. "Maybe I will have a wine, after all."

Such is my haste to get him a glass, that I come close to sending my chair flying when I stand.

Steady on, girl. He's not going anywhere.

On reaching up to grab a glass from the overhead cupboard, I'm conscious he's following my every move. It's something that has me holding his glass with both hands for fear it'll slip from my fingers.

Soon enough, the meal is over, with it nowhere as daunting as I thought it would be. Perhaps this is because I've nearly finished my third glass of wine. Across the table, Scott puts his own glass down, carefully. "So, you're a romance author."

Despite the brevity of his words, I get the distinct impression they're somehow loaded. What the heck is it about people and romance novels? They're difficult to write, and they're what people want, with my sales a testament to this.

For a second, my mind is full of the nasty things the critics had said about my last book, but I soon quash them. To deflect any potential criticisms he has, I raise my glass in salute. "I am, and proud of it." I follow this up with a steely gaze that says he'd better not question my choice of genre.

His eyes widen perceptibly in response, and he swallows deeply before speaking. "Hey, there's nothing wrong with romances." He makes sure he's made eye contact before adding, "Love makes the world go around."

I'm waiting for the *BUT*, when he adds, "It's just that printout sitting on your desk. It's..."

By now I'm leaning over the table, my wineglass all but forgotten, ready to defend my words with all my heart. Mesmerized by his hypnotic gaze, it takes a moment to remember which scene it was I'd printed out.

I slam back into my chair, no longer ready to defend, or even discuss my work. How am I supposed to pull apart a sex scene with a guy like the one opposite? Even thinking about it has me damp. Nope, make that damp-er.

However, I grit my teeth. I need all the help I can get if I'm to avoid more vicious reviews of the sort my last book got slammed with. I never want to be put through that again, my throat constricting as I think back on how devastated I'd been.

It's for this reason my "What about it?" comes out squeakier than I'd like.

SCOTT

There's no missing when Lindsey realizes which scene I'm talking about. Without that glass of wine on top of the beer, I'd never have had the nerve to bring it up, but it's too late to back down now.

My cock sure as hell isn't showing any sign of backing down.

It was while tightening the windows in her study earlier that I'd seen the printout. That she'd been struggling with the scene had been obvious, with the half-dozen pages littered with red notes.

The last time I saw something like that had been back in high school, any time I actually got around to handing in a paper. I'd even written one using a red pen just to save Miss Morrison, my history teacher, the trouble.

She'd been annoyed enough that she'd given me a D without bothering to read it.

Now, while I don't know a lot about history, biology is a whole different story. With that subject, my misspent youth had me putting in the effort I should have made at school. Yep, in practical skills, I was a straight-A-student all the way.

I know Lindsey's writing is good. I'd read enough romances while inside to know this. Books weren't always easy to come by. You read whatever was at hand; even if this had you stuck with the consequences of an erection with nowhere to go.

Rather, it was as if the scene she'd written was being viewed from a distance. If I didn't know better, I'd think she feared getting too close to the real action. And yet there's a sensuality to her that tells me this isn't the case.

No chance of her escaping the notice of any guy who loved losing himself in a real woman's curves.

The other thing I'd noticed in that printout was that the main character's tattoo bore a marked resemblance to my own. Here, her description exploded off the page. If I didn't know better, I'd think she'd watched when I was mowing the lawns earlier. And damn it if that thought doesn't ramp up my arousal even more.

As I take in her expression of dread with hints of anticipation, I kick myself for even bringing it up. It's not my responsibility to help with her sex scenes. If the number of books in her study that bear her name is anything to go by, she's plenty successful on her own.

There's also the minor point of me needing to get into town to change out any batteries that need it. I can't afford to tell her where she's going wrong, or worse, show her.

Hmmm, maybe not worse, just longer; a lot longer.

"Nah, it's nothing." After getting carefully to my feet, I'm surprised to find the alcohol has affected me more than I'd realized. Since my release, I've spent all my spare cash on electronics. "I need to get going, but I promise I'll be back early tomorrow." Again, the lie comes more easily than I'm comfortable with.

What isn't as easy to deal with is Lindsey's obvious disappointment. Is that because she doesn't want me to leave or because I've held back on what was wrong with that scene? I suspect it's the latter, because why would a woman like her be interested in a deadbeat like me?

In my haste to leave, I'm out on the porch before she's even stood. That she wrings her hands once she's done so, not boding well. Am I about to be sacked from a job I don't even have?

"I've been thinking ... Would it be okay if you stayed here tonight?" Her words tumble over each other, and her color is high. "Only, if anything else goes wrong, and I'm on my own..."

If I'd thought she was scarlet before, this is nothing compared to the color of her cheeks now. "In ... In one of the guest rooms. Not in my..."

Unable to get the rest of her words out, she instead waves her hands, no doubt in hopes I'll catch on.

"Hmmm. That might not be a bad idea." As if to confirm this, there comes a banging of pipes from somewhere deep in the house. Both of us hold our breath, waiting for the unmistakable splash of water that usually follows, but none does. "Of course I can. I'll need to head home and grab a few things. I should only be an hour."

Without waiting to find out if this is acceptable, or whether she's brave enough to give me a key, I get out of there while I can. I can't afford to lose sight of the true reason I'm back in town.

Distractions like Lindsey Abbott, while mighty appealing, shouldn't be my sole focus.

The cool night air is welcome, going a long way to clearing the lust from my system. At the bottom of the front steps, I turn to find Lindsey regarding me through the still open door.

She swallows deeply, before calling out, "I'll leave a key under the mat." She points down, showing which one, although she makes no move to step back and close the door.

Damn, her watching me like this means I'll have to fake leaving the front way, only to double back when it's safe. There isn't a chance I'm walking into town looking as I do now. Instead, I'll be dragging on the set of filthy clothes stuffed under the floor of the summerhouse.

Even thinking about putting these on has me fighting the urge to scratch. I'm glad I haven't given into this when at the end of the driveway; I turn to face the house. Damn it, I can see her silhouette at a window on the second floor. I'll have to walk to the end of the lane and wait before I can safely retrace my steps.

I'll be okay coming home when it's fully dark. Again, I'm assailed by guilt. I've got no right abusing her kindness like this. This isn't her fight; she doesn't deserve me involving her like this, even if this hadn't been my initial plan.

And yet part of me is very glad I've met her, even if the timing isn't great.

I'm unable to stop my grin as I shoot down the lane, all the while keeping to the shadows.

FOUR

LINDSEY

After watching Scott disappear through the narrow gate that leads to the driveway, I get the spare key and place it under the mat.

There's then nothing I can do to stop myself from racing out into the hallway, flicking on the lights, and flying up the stairs. Who'd have thought a guest room with a view of the lane would come in handy?

As I watch from the darkened room, my breath quickens. There's something about the way he moves that does it for me. A confident swagger and a heap of sex appeal is a powerful combination.

Only after he's disappeared around the corner at the end of the lane, do I give thought to fixing up the guest room I've said he can use. There aren't even sheets on the bed, something that will require me looking through a lot of boxes if I'm to find any.

There's one slight problem. Those boxes are in the basement, a place that unsettles me in the middle of the day, never mind this late. It's a good thing my role as hostess overrides any misgivings I have about going down there.

Luckily for my nerves, I find a large box marked 'linens' soon enough. The other thing in my favor is that the basement is dry, and it's not long since I packed up in Seattle. A quick sniff says I don't need to wash and dry them before putting them on the bed.

There's something intimate about making up a bed for a man I'd happily share it with. My hands run over the cool white sheets, smoothing them, stroking them in a poor imitation of my heart's desire.

The room looking presentable, I head back downstairs to finish tidying up. Doing the dishes takes me no time at all, neither does sweeping the floor. It's only on using the dustpan that I notice the small medallion tucked in amongst the debris I've collected.

Holding it up to the light, I can see the initials EH on the front, and some Latin inscription on the back. Squint as I might, I can't make the words out, with them too small to read without daylight or a magnifying glass.

That the piece belongs to Scott is obvious, with me having swept the floor that morning. There are drawbacks to living this close to the beach, with sand finding its way inside the house even when I keep the doors and windows shut.

On placing the medallion on the table in front of the seat Scott had used earlier, I give thought to whose it is. It has to belong to a girlfriend, surely? This has me rubbing my chest to help my heart process the disappointment.

Idiot, why are you surprised? Hot AND single?

Yeah, that's so not happening.

"What if he's married?" My question rattling around in the kitchen tells me I've asked this aloud. It's a good point, though. What if he is? I close my eyes long enough that I can see him as he'd been eating dinner. Nope, there hadn't been a wedding band or even a strip of faded skin, so I doubt there's a wife on the scene.

Surely if that was the case when I asked him to stay the night, he'd have said something. And wouldn't the same be true if he had a girlfriend? Maybe that's why he had to go back to his place? So he could check on his little woman and tell her he'd be keeping a spinster company that night.

It's a sad thought that has me once again realizing how little I know about the man I've invited into my home. Could my intuition about him be wrong? It's never let me down before, but there's always a first time for everything.

The last thing I do before heading up to my study to work on *that* scene is to scribble a note on the kitchen calendar. This hangs next to the back door, a leftover from my Aunt Bella, which I've continued using in her memory. Silly, but it's true.

I should really have persevered with getting hold of the job center today, but with all those leaks and whatnot, it had slipped my mind.

I won't forget tomorrow.

SCOTT

On reaching the end of the lane, I scoot around the corner, blending in with the hedge that fronts the neighboring property. There's no one around that I can see, but I'd be a fool to let my guard down.

I give it a couple of minutes before I look around the corner and back to the house. The silhouette at the window is no longer there. This tells me I'm okay to retrace my steps, having wasted enough time already.

After hot-footing it up the lane and then the driveway, I edge around the side of Eagle's Nest, away from the sea. My footfalls as I make my way down to the summerhouse are as quiet as possible. ensuring Lindsey won't hear me.

Safely hidden by the rickety structure, I crouch down, reach underneath and drag my disguise free. It's even filthier than when I'd stuffed it under there on getting back in the early hours of the morning.

I don't have a problem with the state of it. The more disreputable I am, the less chance of anyone giving me a second look. If anyone gets too close, all I need to do is put my hand out and mutter something about being hungry. This soon has them on their way.

After stripping off in the summerhouse, dressing in my rags was every bit as disgusting as I knew it would be. The clothes literally make my skin crawl, even though I know there's nothing to cause this.

It's while putting my good clothes in my backpack that I remember I won't be sleeping here tonight. I'll be in the guest room of the main house. Guilt, an emotion I've not experienced much over the years, assails me.

Would Lindsey be as quick to give me a key if she knew I was fresh out of prison while still on the run for another crime? I doubt it.

My backpack safely tucked under the bench in the summerhouse, I jump over the wall and onto the cliff path that fronts the property. The batteries that are the best I could afford rattle in my pockets.

After jamming my cap down on my head, I turn toward town, my mind already on my destination. As I settle into a slow trot, my thoughts stray to other places, lots of them, with all of them to be found on Lindsey's delectable body.

I should never have given into my desire and talked about that damned sex scene. I should have shut up, taken advantage of her hospitality, and then got the hell out of there. That's what the old Ethan would have done.

This new Ethan is a revelation. Could it be my time inside has helped my conscience? Or is that all down to the woman waiting for me back at Eagle's Nest?

I guess you'll find out when you go home later, won't you?

Home?

Despite my promise to concentrate on the task at hand, my mind has other ideas. How would life be if I truly was going home later tonight? Back to Lindsey, back to her bed. There's no forgetting how good she'd felt all over me in the tub this morning.

Imagine if she'd been as naked as I was, the water hot, and her as willing as my cock? Such are my fevered imaginings that when I skulk across a patch of open ground on the edge of town, I'm packing wood.

My destination in sight, I put a lid on my erotic musings. I've got work to do, and unless I want to get caught while I'm about it, I'd best concentrate. Get in, change the batteries and the memory cards, and leave without being caught.

Yeah, a piece of cake, with the place crawling with the very people I'm trying to get the evidence on. That some of them are on the police force is the biggest challenge of all.

It had been a surprise, and yet it hadn't, to learn on my return to Coogan's Break that Roger Sutton was still the local Chief of Police. Being as the guy was a combination of inept and corrupt, the local criminals made sure of his re-election.

It was also the reason I'd taken the blame all those years ago.

I hadn't been alone the night the cops caught up with me. Craig Sutton, the chief's son, had been with me. Strange that he never made it to the holding cell alongside me. There wasn't a chance the chief would stand by while his son got locked up.

It had been far easier to pin the crimes on the local delinquent—yours truly.

It was time for payback. But, and it was a big but, I wanted a life after that took place.

Even a life with someone like Lindsey?

Yeah, why not?

It doesn't matter that I've known her next to no time. When I'm with her, I feel worthy. I want to look after her, and I want to be part of something bigger than myself. Nuts, but I already feel closer to her than I ever did to my family.

Apart from my deadbeat parents, I love my family. But will my brother and grandfather complete me in the same way Lindsey does? No, they won't. The only thing I'm unsure of is whether she feels the same way about me.

Now that'd be a rare thing, but a man can hope, can't he?

FIVE

LINDSEY

Despite putting a key under the mat, as I told Scott I would, I can't settle. Knowing he'll be spending the night has me on edge. I doubt sleep would be possible even if I went to bed.

This sees me curled up on the squishy couch in the living room, the printout of that blasted scene lying crumpled in my lap. I don't know what he thought was wrong with it. Nor do I understand how a handyman can pass judgment on a romance, even if it is romantic suspense.

I've come to no conclusions when I hear movement outside. I've even given into some 'What if it's not him' panic, when Scott calls out, "It's only me," before turning the key in the lock. Now I don't know whether to be relieved or nervous.

While I'm relieved it's him, I'm nervous that his criticism of my work still clouds the air. I know I won't be able to stop myself from asking about it. And who knows what can of worms that will open?

Do I really want to hear his criticisms about why my sex scene doesn't work? Undecided and unable to remain sitting, I shove the printout down the side of the couch, jump up, and scoot through to the kitchen.

"I'm making a hot chocolate if you want one?" Then I beat myself up for offering one of the sexiest men I've ever met, a toddler's bedtime drink.

His backpack dropped just inside the door, he shrugs out of a jacket he wasn't wearing when he left, and sits at the kitchen table. "Actually, that'd be nice. My Grammy used to make those for me when I was little."

Then, as if sensing he's already said too much, he swallows any further comment. His shuttered expression says there's no point asking him to expand. And I don't know him well enough to push for more information.

The same goes when his hand slides out and covers the small medallion. However, when he takes his hand away, the medallion is no longer there, palmed as expertly as any playing card in Vegas.

While I can't question him on this, I can say something, so he at least knows I know he's in a relationship. "I dare say your girlfriend will be pleased to have that back."

His head snaps up, revealing eyes that are stormier than ever. And then, just as with a summer storm, his expression lightens. "I don't have a girlfriend." He falls silent for a second, before adding, "Or a wife."

His tightly fisted hand back on the table, he turns it over and then unfurls his fingers to reveal the monogrammed piece. He then examines it as if for the first time.

"It belonged to someone I knew a long time ago." And then, as if expecting what I'm about to ask, he adds a bald, "He's dead."

Even with the mystery surrounding Scott's background, I trust him implicitly. If not, I wouldn't have given him a key. Heck, I wouldn't even have allowed him inside the house. To help calm my thoughts, I get on with preparing our hot chocolates the old-fashioned way, from scratch.

As when I'd been getting dinner ready, he watches my every move.

I wonder what he'll make of the level of ceremony I attach to preparing the hot drink. There's no instant powder for me; it's Belgian chocolate, cream, and a pinch of chili all the way. When he doesn't comment, I wonder if this is how his grandmother used to make it.

After sliding his hot chocolate across the kitchen table, I dither about joining him or saying goodnight, and heading upstairs for bed. I've not decided when he says, "Hey, it's been a long day. Is it okay if we sit in the living room? My body's screaming out for a soft spot."

I freeze as I analyze his words. His first sentence had been straightforward enough. However, there's an ambiguity to his second that, taking in the glint in his eyes, I'm sure is on purpose.

"Of course, of course we can."

I then point with my mug to the double pocket-doors in an invitation of sorts. He wastes no time getting to his feet, picking up his hot chocolate and walking into the living room, leaving me to trail behind.

After some hesitation, he walks straight over to the couch. He then places his drink on the coffee table before sitting in the seat I'd just vacated. There's no missing the resultant crinkle of paper, with him immediately rocking to the side to check what he's sat on.

I'm still standing just inside the doors, unsure which seat to take, when he retrieves the printout. After smoothing it out on his lap, he none-too-subtly looks at the couch next to him.

Dare I sit beside him when he's effectively holding a guide to seduction that's specific to my desires?

Hey, missy, you wanted to know what was wrong with it. Now's your chance.

Despite having decided I'll join him, my movements are slow, something that appears to amuse him.

"Come on, it'll be my way of saying thank you for that wonderful dinner."

Sitting next to him, I feel awkward, unsure of myself, and so very nervous. It's one thing to work on sex scenes in the privacy of my head, or my study. It's quite another to sit and discuss them with the sort of man I envisage playing the male lead.

After a couple of fortifying sips of hot chocolate, I put my mug down on the coffee table. The suspense of waiting for his feedback is hideous, something that has my tone less than conciliatory when I ask, "Okay, what's wrong with it?"

He doesn't answer immediately; too busy taking a sip of his own hot chocolate. His sigh after he swallows is one of raw pleasure, my body reacting as if he was licking me, and not the rim of his mug.

On him turning to face me, it's obvious he knows exactly what I'm thinking. As caught up as I am in the moment, I don't have time to hide it from him. Heck, I haven't even had time to hide it from myself.

"That! That right there is what's missing from your scene." He reaches out and runs his knuckles gently down the side of my face. "You get *that* on the page, and you'll have it made."

"I can't put *that* on the page." My voice drops to a whisper before I add, "What if people think it's ... What if they think it's about me?"

His nonchalant shrug as he puts his mug back down is no help at all.

"Hey, it's okay for you to shrug like it's no big deal. It wouldn't be your name on the cover. It wouldn't be you having to answer embarrassing questions at launch events."

Rather than sympathize, he bursts out laughing. "What? Questions like, do you like it when a guy has his cock buried so deep inside you he gifts you his soul?" His storm gray eyes capture mine before he continues.

"Or do you love it when a guy's mouth closes over your bud and he draws a climax out of you by using his tongue?" He briefly lifts an eyebrow, before innocently adding, "Those sorts of questions?"

When he follows this up by slowly licking his lips, I can't move. I'm frozen, although I'm not cold. Nor is my lack of motion all down to embarrassment. Oh no, it's down to being so turned on that if I move, I'll have a spontaneous orgasm.

I'm damp and on the edge, and his smile says he knows it.

SCOTT

Lindsey's arousal is coming off her in waves, engulfing me, leaving me harder than ever. Unless I do something about it, and soon.

What was it my grandfather used to say during those horrendously awkward talks of his about the birds and the bees? That's right; don't look for consent, check to see if she's eager.

"Unless she's eager, you back away. You have no clue what sort of upbringing she's had. She could be too scared to say no."

Then he'd hit me with that thousand-yard stare of his to make sure I was 'listening with both ears'. "A lack of no doesn't make it a yes."

His words rang true, and I've stuck with them ever since. Unless a woman is begging for it, I keep my cock in my pants.

Just as well, I've learned a lot about what makes women *eager* when on my way to becoming a man. Exhibit A is Lindsey, looking at me as though she could eat me. And trust me, I wouldn't turn her down.

And yet, I can't go there. It wouldn't be fair. Also not fair is her moving closer under the guise of making herself more comfortable.

When she nibbles on her bottom lip, I have to think back to my time in prison to stop myself from giving into temptation. I'm not sure I can hold out much longer.

I need to get upstairs and away from her. Even if mankind marks me as being sub-human, it's not true. "Ah yeah, I really should call it a night. There are a lot more repairs to attend to in the morning." I then marvel at my stupidity when I add an asinine, "Gotta get my beauty sleep."

Who the hell are you, and what have you done with Ethan Hunter?

Oh, that's right; you killed him off when you became Scott Latham.

When I shake my head at my having said such a lame thing, Lindsey stills. It's as if I've just chucked a bucket of cold water over her. As tempting as it is to make use of this cooling of her ardor, I'm wracked with guilt at her, thinking I mean something I don't.

I open my mouth to offer assurances, but the words stick in my throat. Meanwhile, the distress on her face continues to build. This has me sliding across the couch and dragging her into my arms. After a second's hesitation, she melts against my side, fitting me as well as my skin.

If not for us both turning toward each other at exactly the same time, I doubt I'd have kissed her. And yet, I'm so very glad I did. If I'd thought she felt right tucked up against my side, my lips moving across hers have us closer than ever.

I could lose myself in this woman. Forget who I was, and what I needed to do. With her, time ceases to exist; my slate wiped clean. I'm back to being an eighteen-year-old before my life started its downward spiral.

If only life was this easy, this pleasurable, this hot.

And just like that, I forget about analyzing what a mess I've made of my life, and instead concentrate on the woman I'm doing my best to devour.

Soon even this isn't enough. My hands roaming over her curves, I make a list of places I want to explore later with tongue, teeth, and cock. I want to bury myself in her, exactly like I'd said when I was coming up with all those pretend questions.

She hadn't been the only one affected by me voicing my desires. Funny, but I'd usually be circumspect about laying myself open like that. I'm still thinking about this when I undo the last button on Lindsey's blouse. I slowly spread it to the sides in imitation of what I'll do later when I expose her very core.

The blouse soon lies over the back of the couch, my sole focus now on a pair of stunning lace-covered breasts. What is it about creamy flesh being viewed through a veil of black lace that has them all the more enticing for the concealment?

They're not concealed for long as I slide first one strap, and then the other, over her shoulders and down her arms. I dip my head to lick her nipples, blowing on them and watching them pucker in response. Her guttural moan heads straight for my cock, with no deviations on the way.

If the rest of her body is as responsive, we're in for one hell of a night.

SIX

LINDSEY

Scott takes his mouth away from my breasts and I'm immediately bereft, although not for long. His callused fingers roll my nipples, with the shooting sensations rushing down my body and between my legs.

After a brief kiss to the end of my nose, his lips once again close over mine, his tongue poking at the seam, asking for permission to enter. My lips part on a sigh and his tongue fills my mouth in a poor imitation of coitus.

A poor imitation it might be, but it overloads my senses all the same. He's still not as close as I'd like him to be. Lost as I am in the haze, I take a second to understand his hands are no longer on my breasts.

Instead, one hand rests on the top of my thigh, while he runs the other up and down the front of my jeans. His nails rake the zipper in a way that has vibrations hitting me in all the good bits.

When he makes no move to undo the zipper, I take matters into my own hands. I don't want him holding back because he thinks I'm not into this. I am. I've never wanted something—no, make that someone—as much as I want this man right now.

Slapping his hand out of the way, I'm rewarded by him straightening. However, the moment I undo the button, and then the zip of my jeans, his attitude changes completely.

Damn it, if he doesn't have the sexiest smile I've ever seen. His lips curl up, his eyes twinkle, and his laughter lines are more pronounced than ever. And it melts me every bit as much as his lips on my nipples had earlier.

Then I come to my senses. We can't make love here. It'd be a disaster.

While the vintage couch might have been up to my late aunt entertaining the local ladies, it's not up to what I've got in mind. If Scott's smile is any indicator, we'll break it.

This has me pulling up the zipper on my jeans, although I don't bother with the button. Only on my third try do I get the words out, time in which the intensity of Scott's gaze has me fizzing with want. "Shall ... shall we go upstairs?"

His smile turns into a broad grin. "I thought you'd never ask." He gets to his feet before turning to help me stand. "Your room or mine?"

This gives me pause. While the bed in his room has clean sheets, for me, it would be like hooking up with a guy in a hotel room. I want this man in my life, and that means my bedroom, not the guest room I'd prepared for him.

"My room might be better, the bed is ah..." How am I supposed to explain that the vintage bed in that guest room is about as substantial as the couch? However, the bed in my room is up to the challenge.

Rather than waltz through the house half-naked, I drag my blouse back on. I'm simply not that comfortable in my skin. When we stagger into my bedroom, thanks to us not wanting to let go of each other, this is the least of my worries.

When I'd said we should make use of my room, I'd forgotten about my dog-eared copy of Fanny Hill on the bedside table. I'd been re-reading it, purely for reference.

There's no missing his spotting it, nor the dirty grin that says he's familiar with the title.

I'm still absorbed in how that could be, when he starts a strip-tease that has me wondering if he's done so professionally.

His movements are slow, sensual and designed to have my arousal at a fever pitch. Even if this isn't his goal, that's what's happening. I'm so engrossed in his performance that it's not until I spot the gleam in his eye that I realize I've been unconsciously aping his every move.

I've never stood naked in front of a guy like this, always preferring to strip in the dark and get myself under the covers as soon as humanly possible. One look at Scott's face, and I know I don't need to hide from him, ever. Liberating doesn't come close to explaining the sensation when I slowly turn, allowing him to see me from all angles.

On turning back to the front, he's closer than he had been. Another step and our bodies slam together as neatly as two halves of any whole. His lips claim mine and we fall back onto the bed. I'm unable to squelch my laughter at wondering what would have happened if we'd tried this in his room.

We'd be back downstairs in the living room in a pile of plaster by now. When I tell him this, his burst of laughter has me giggling, although not for long. Keeping eye contact, he slowly licks his thumb before running it through my cleft. It's something that has me arching my hips to increase the pressure.

I've yielded to Scott's devotions when I hear something buzzing. It must be my phone. I roll my head languidly to the side, my anticipation of what's about to happen close to overwhelming me.

However, my phone isn't on the bedside table, it's upstairs on the charger in my study. Rather, the buzzing I can hear is coming from the floor next to the bed.

I know to the second when Scott hears it, his thumb stopping its lazy back and forth over my clit. "Sorry, babe, I need to check that."

"Now?!" There's nothing I can do about the element of whine in my question. I'd been so close.

He nods briefly, while reaching down beside the bed. "I only get alerts when it's urgent." His expression, when he checks his phone, says the news isn't good. "Sorry, babe, I have to sort this out."

To add weight to his apology, he rasps his tongue slowly across one of my nipples before drawing it into his mouth. He then sucks on it to the point of pain, such delicious pain.

The look on his face when he finally lifts his head says he's as frustrated as I am that he has to leave. When he's once again dressed, he gives brief attention to my other nipple, as if this will somehow help.

All it does is leave me hornier than ever.

SCOTT

Sheesh, my erection makes walking down stairs a challenge. That sensor had to be triggered right then? It would have been so easy to dismiss it, to lose myself in Lindsey. But, if I was ever to have a future, then I had to sort this out.

I'm letting myself out the French doors onto the porch when I hear the unmistakable sound of running water. I doubt very much it's Lindsey. This has me racing part way up the stairs, and yelling, "I'll turn the water off and fix it in the morning."

As much as Lindsey speaks fondly of her late aunt, the old lady really should have kept up the maintenance of the house. I can't complain, though. The decrepit state of the place is what's given me a roof over my head and something to fill my days.

And someone to fill your nights?

As I cut through the trees to the summerhouse, I can't help but grin as memories of Lindsey laid out on her bed come back to me.

As bad as the timing had been for that alarm to be tripped, I'm also relieved. The grainy image via the app on my phone shows Craig is at the warehouse. It's seeing who's standing next to him that gives me pause.

It would certainly explain how easily I broke out of the local jail. The only way it could have been any easier would have been if Chief Sutton escorted me out personally.

He knew I'd run when things got hot. And like the idiot I was, I'd taken off without a backward glance. So much easier for his son to avoid notice if the cops were busy chasing me down.

As I once again don my disguise, I run through other inconsistencies around my original arrest and events in the days that followed. Looking back on it, I can see Chief Sutton's anger wasn't being fired in my direction. It was being directed at the cop who'd been stupid enough to arrest his son along with me.

I'm skulking across the open wasteland toward the warehouse when I catch movement at the back of the enormous building. Dammit, what's he doing here? The last thing I need is my younger brother potentially finding some of my surveillance equipment.

Even worse would be him finding me. While the police chief might have been able to organize my escape the first time around, I doubt it would be as easy a second.

Exactly how close to the action do I want to get?

On the one hand, I need to confirm that the guy who was with Craig Sutton is who I think it is. On the other, I don't want to risk my stupid, do-good brother getting close enough to slap cuffs on me.

As tempting as it is to involve him when the time comes to bring the true criminals to justice, it's not a risk I'm prepared to take. It's bad enough the Suttons have ruined my life. I don't want them doing the same to my annoying brother.

The only unknown in my carefully thought-out plan is how I'll spring the trap without showing my involvement. If there's even a hint I'm behind it, my life won't be worth living.

Not here, not anywhere.

Despite having known Lindsey for the blink of an eye, I want to stick around to see where things go. It's a thought that warms me as I lie there watching Chase scoping out the building.

He's bulked up since I fled town, something I'd noticed when I saw him cutting through the park with Gramps. Despite this, his movements are confident and sparse, as though to conserve energy. Even when I hold my breath, I'm unable to hear him.

What the hell are you up to, brother?

I've come to no conclusions when the side door of the warehouse opens and light spills across the wasteland. It's only brief, with the guy who's leaving immediately killing the lights.

He's not as quick to lock the door, with my brother jumping him before he's had a chance. Other than a brief shout, all is silent.

It's only broken when Chase hefts the now unconscious guy up off the ground with a grunt and tosses him over one shoulder. He then straightens and walks nonchalantly away. On reaching a beat up truck parked at the end of the alley, he stuffs the guy in the back. He then roars off into the night without a clue how much he's just helped me out.

As annoying as the delay has been, at least now I know there's no one inside, and that the warehouse is unlocked. Add in that there had been no telltale wail of the alarm being set, and I know the idiot Chase just arrested didn't get around to arming it.

After getting to my feet, I start across the open area, all the while fighting the desire to whistle. The one thing I don't fight is my smile as I think back on how I'd left Lindsey. I hope she's having more fun than I am.

SEVEN

LINDSEY

This morning my fingers fly over the keys, struggling to move as fast as the words are coming. As I commit my memories of last night to paper—make that screen—I'm hit with a yet another ping of arousal.

Despite his assurances that he'd be back, I'd woken alone. That had been at three am thanks to my mind running the scene we'd been discussing before things got hot and heavy.

Scott had been right that it lacked something, even if he hadn't been able to articulate what that was. Might the scene be distant because that's how it's always been between me and any guy I've dated?

Maybe that's the reason I've never gotten close to a guy, other than in a purely physical sense? Too busy trying to protect myself from being hurt.

My head down, I work away on the scene, borrowing heavily from the foreplay action with Scott last night. The eroticism of the scene is enough to have me fanning my face, with my arousal getting away on me.

Where the heck is he when I really need him? I can't even have a cold shower with the water still not back on.

A quick look at the bottom of my screen and I'm surprised to see it's already after eight. If he doesn't show up soon, I might have to head into town and actually pay to go to a gym for a shower. Not my usual habitat, but needs must.

After standing, I wander over to the top of the stairs and listen. Other than the general creaking of the old house, there's no movement downstairs. If he was back, he would have let me know. I'd even checked the guest room when I'd first got up, but the bed remained as tidy as when I'd made it the day before.

Nope, I'm alone. Conscious of how stiff I am, I arch my back and am rewarded with more clicks than is healthy for someone my age. However, the relief is instant, reminding me yet again that I really do need to remember to sit up straight.

I'm getting rid of yet more kinks when I look out of the window and am surprised to see Scott lying in the outdoor bath. His head hangs over the edge of the tub, and he looks to be asleep.

That's weird; surely if he'd turned the water back on, then that leak from last night would have started up again. It's then I remember the old tub gets filled courtesy of a rainwater tank.

I grab the binoculars I'd finally found yesterday, but then have trouble getting them to focus. What I'm checking out now differs from trying to spot the whales that often play offshore.

"If I said you had a gorgeous body, would you hold it against me?" I then have a giggle at this oldie but goodie. "Is that steam?"

It is steam! Now that I think about it, I vaguely remember him saying something about an on-demand water heater in the basement. I guess he must have gotten it working.

I continue scanning his body at my leisure, only moving onto his face once I've had my fill.

This reveals he's not asleep anymore, his dirty grin letting me know I've been busted.

I come close to dropping the binoculars in my haste to get them away from my eyes and me away from the window.

Despite that, there's no hiding what I was up to, demonstrating my level of desire has me feeling vulnerable. What if he somehow takes advantage of this?

This, more than anything, has me reassessing my attraction to Scott. I need to play it cool and hide some of this, if I'm to avoid scaring him off. The last thing I want is to come across as needy and pathetic.

SCOTT

It's a flash of light against my eyelids that has me looking up at the turret window. I'm unable to stop my broad grin when I catch Lindsey checking me out through binoculars.

Sure, I could cover my cock with the washcloth I'd picked up at the charity shop, but let her have her fill. At least in that department, I've got nothing to be ashamed of.

I'm tired after running around half the night; with me not home very long. *Home?* It has a nice ring to it, but I've got no right to call it that.

I really shouldn't be staying here. The less Lindsey has to do with me, the safer she'll be. I'd never forgive myself if she got hurt because of my digging up the evidence required to convict the true criminals.

After I'd snuck inside the warehouse, I made quick work of swapping out the memory cards and batteries on my equipment. From there I'd moved onto a couple more locations, relieved to have done so without being caught.

A quick check of the footage on my return to the summerhouse had me pleased with my progress. I'd then uploaded everything to a drop box while I ditched my disguise.

Lindsey really should have that blisteringly fast Wi-Fi of hers password-protected. I guess the house is far enough from the neighbors that it's not a problem.

The water rapidly cooling, I get out of the tub, dry off, and gobble down a couple of granola bars. From there, I head to the basement to grab some tools. My priority of the day is to fix the latest leak and turn the water back on for the main house.

Then, all going well, I want to catch up with Lindsey. She's been taking up head space since I left her on the brink of an orgasm last night.

I fix the plumbing in no time, with practice definitely making perfect. The one problem I'm facing is that I'm running low on parts, having used most of the odds and ends stored in that old soda crate. I tidy everything away for next time, before walking up the stairs and into the kitchen.

There I find Lindsey bustling about making coffee.

I don't even try to fight my grin. "Spot any whales this morning?"

She goes scarlet and I decide I like it, imagining her color would be this high if I found myself buried balls-deep in her juicy bits. Another look at Lindsey and I quash this thought. She's all business this morning, despite her spying on me earlier.

Nope, she doesn't look *eager* at all.

Late afternoon finds me working on the windows in one of the guest rooms on the second floor. On hearing movement behind me, I turn to find Lindsey looking at me with an interesting mix of nerves and embarrassment.

I'm surprised to see her, with her having made herself scarce for most of the day. She hadn't even kept me company at lunch. Instead, taking hers back up to her study mumbling something about being on deadline.

Eventually, she stammers out that she needs my help with another scene.

"A sex scene?" I'm unable to keep the hope out of my voice, especially not when I'd just been thinking about how great it would be to plumb her hidden depths.

She hesitates enough that I suspect I'm right.

"Ah, no. This is a fight scene. I usually skim over them, but with your help..." She falls silent for a beat before adding, "I write romantic suspense."

She's about to say more when I hold a hand up to stop her from speaking. "Why the hell do you think I can help with that?"

There's no stopping the hard edge to my words. The reason I'd gotten into so much trouble as a kid was because I'd looked like I was up to no good, even when I wasn't. They'd labeled me a criminal before I'd even considered stealing a candy bar.

In the end, I'd decided that if that was all people saw, then I might as well live up to my reputation. I've changed a lot since being inside. Being locked up with men who are evil to the core and who live up to their reputations had been an eye-opener.

Sure, I can take care of myself with the best of them, but I don't actively seek violence.

And here she is labeling me a low-life. Damn it, I thought I'd moved on from that. My hands fisted at my sides, I grit out, "I am not a criminal!"

with every minute of my miserable life injected into the simple statement.

Of course, Lindsey knows none of this, nor can she. Instead, she appears stunned. Yeah, well, I know exactly how she feels. It's seeing the hurt in her eyes that stops me from saying anything else. Hell, that's not what I wanted, not at all. So much for all that anger management they had subjected me to when I was inside.

Before I can apologize, she backs out of the room, fleeing for her study in the turret. Damn it, what chance do I have of rejoining mainstream society if I go off after being asked such a simple question?

EIGHT

Back in my study after my altercation with Scott, I sit staring at my computer screen, unable to focus. I'm in shock. I don't understand it? Why on earth would he think I thought he was a criminal?

His over-reaction gives me pause, though. After slowing my breathing, I think about his reaction. Really examine it, rather than simply react to it.

My hands fly up to cradle my face as realization hits me. I'd hurt him, deeply. Why, or how, I don't have a clue, but what I'd taken as anger had in fact been pain.

While it had been unintentional, I've hurt him when he's only been kind to me. And yet there's something off about his reaction. For a person to protest their innocence to that degree, they have to be hiding something, don't they?

Sure, I've got a wild imagination, something I think most authors have. But Scott has definitely been light on background details. Thinking back on it, whenever our conversation strayed to family, he'd change the subject.

And he's good at it, with me not even noticing. But I sure do now. It doesn't matter that the job center said they'd reference-check anyone they sent over. Something about Scott doesn't ring true.

A quick look at what time it is, and I berate myself for forgetting to call them today. Rather than rely on my remembering to look at my aunt's calendar, I make a note in my journal. This way I'm more likely to see it. I've just put my pen down when I hear footfalls on the stairs leading up to the turret.

"Lindsey?" Scott doesn't sound sure of himself, and yet he has to know I'm up here.

"Yes?"

"I'm really sorry. I should never have spoken to you like that." He keeps apologizing while making his way up the rest of the stairs.

After a quick look at me, he squeezes his eyes shut, and then shoves his hand in the front pocket of his jeans. A moment later, he carefully places my spare key on the newel post at the top of the stairs. "I'm sorry things worked out the way they have. I'll be off."

Without another word, he turns and disappears down the stairs, with me right behind him. I watch in silence as he grabs his backpack from the guest room, before making his way downstairs and out through the French doors.

All of this time, I stay quiet, even though inside I'm screaming for him to stay.

After closing the door behind himself, he kisses his fingers and places them briefly against the glass. Then, without a backward glance, he races down the porch steps and disappears.

Despite not having said anything since acknowledging him earlier, my throat hurts, as if I've been screaming at the top of my lungs. After dropping onto the couch, I collapse back and stare at the wall while trying to deal with what's just happened.

My thoughts are tumultuous, full of *what if* scenarios? Not all of them are about Scott blowing up earlier. I've only got to close my eyes to remember how his tongue pebbled my nipples, how his lips felt on mine.

And I've let him go, without even trying to find out what the issue was. I'm such a wimp about confrontations.

I need a cup of tea with a lot of sugar.

A quick check in the fridge and I know that's not happening. Not without milk. And that won't be the only thing I'll be looking for when I'm in town. He can't have gotten far on foot.

SCOTT

After leaving via the front drive, I circle back as I had last night. I'm still not sure if I'll sleep in the summerhouse. I doubt my conscience would let me sleep, anyway.

The hurt in Lindsey's eyes as I'd closed the door will stay with me for a long time. My grandfather would give me grief if he ever heard about it.

And I wouldn't blame him. I'd deserve that and more for the way I've treated her. Even worse is how I've taken advantage of her good nature. I used the state of her home to move in and insert myself into her life and other places.

Wrong, wrong, wrong.

In the end, I decide against staying in the summerhouse, instead packing all my clean clothes into my backpack and stuffing it under the floorboards. Without a safe place to stay, I'll be in disguise from now on.

I'm in town, staggering along Seaview Road while playing the part of a drunk, when Lindsey drives slowly by. Five minutes later, she drives by again. What is she up to?

Don't tell me she's out looking for me?

I'm unable to fight the hope that flares deep in my chest. However, I ignore it. I'd had no right taking advantage of her.

Thank goodness I'm back to being dressed as a vagrant. I'm not Scott Latham, I'm not Ethan Hunter. I'm just some random homeless guy. Nothing to see here, move along.

However, after passing by me the third time, Lindsey's driving becomes erratic, and she comes close to mounting the curb. Too busy looking in the rearview mirror would be my guess.

Head down, I complete a U-turn, marching away as fast as I can. While the way I'm moving is enough to blow my cover of being drunk, it's a risk I'll have to take. The moment I round the nearest corner, I revert to staggering and pretending to argue with someone who isn't there. This puts most people off getting close to me.

With no sign of Lindsey for half-an-hour, I sit down in a doorway. Once as comfortable as I'm likely to get, I take a battered cardboard sign out of my coat pocket. If muttering to invisible friends isn't enough to put busybodies off, asking for money seals the deal.

The other thing that is deliberate is where I've chosen to sit. I haven't had time to settle in for the long haul when someone stops next to my old pizza box.

I'd recognize those embroidered sneakers anywhere. A second later, a handful of coins lands in the box, followed by a note. She then walks off without saying a word. Not until she's well away do I retrieve the note and slowly unfold it.

I have to angle it toward the streetlight to read it, the words as surprising as anything. *She's sorry?* But I was the one who exploded.

She wants me to go back home, to discuss things.

Damn it, that's the last thing I can do. To tell her anything is to put her in danger. And that's not happening. Not if I can help it. But neither can I leave her hanging. I need to explain things to her.

Do you, Buddy? Do you really?

I get back to Eagle's Nest in record time, sprinting along the cliff path, and hoping like hell no one sees me out this late. If I'm stopped, I'll just say I'm being chased by zombies. If I freak out enough, it's guaranteed whoever it is will leave me well alone.

A quick change at the summerhouse and I jog up to Eagle's Nest. Every light on the first floor appears to be on, and stepping up onto the porch, I see Lindsey sitting at the kitchen table, a drink in front of her.

More telling is that there's a mug on what I think of as my side of the table. Alongside of this is the key I'd so recently handed back to her.

You'll tell her enough to ease the hurt, and then you're outta here.

Despite this promise to myself, on entering the house, all thoughts of leaving flee. The sense of home-coming is enough to have tears threatening. I've not felt this in a long time; a very long time. I'd be an idiot to throw it away.

On sitting, I'm conscious of her watching my every move. As tempting as it is, I don't pick up the key. Instead, I grab my hot chocolate and take a sip, the memories of my long-dead grandmother flooding me as they had the night before.

After a couple more sips, I put the mug down. "I can't tell you much. It wouldn't be safe."

Her dark blue eyes widen in alarm over the rim of her mug and she appears to change her mind about taking a sip. Instead, she lowers her mug carefully to the tabletop, her hands wrapped around it as though taking comfort in the warmth.

"Why?" Her voice cracks enough on this single word that she clears her throat before continuing. "What have you done?"

"Nothing illegal!" My words are louder than I'd intended, marking them patently false. Okay, so I'm definitely no angel, but for the supply of Class-A drugs, I'm as innocent as she is.

The same isn't true of Chief Sutton's son. He'd been up to his neck in it from the get go. Compared to him, I'd simply been a bit player, hanging around with the bad guys, hoping to pick up some street cred.

Dumb, young, and gullible.

And that's my biggest challenge. For me to prove my innocence, I have to pin the blame squarely on Craig Sutton.

His father got him out of trouble once. The chances are high that the chief will do it again.

NINE

LINDSEY

Scott tells me only enough to convince me he's not a criminal, but not so much that I'll start nosing about.

The one mystery his confession had cleared up was how he'd turned up so soon after I'd been to the job center. I guess I'd better tell them I don't need anyone after all.

"I can't tell you any more than that. If anything were to happen to you, I'd never forgive myself." Following this heartfelt declaration, his stomach rumbles loudly, somewhat ruining the mood.

Only when my stomach answers back am I reminded I've had no dinner, either. "Let me rustle up some mac 'n' cheese." His look says it all. "Not the packet stuff, the real deal."

I waste no time getting on with preparing the simple meal, with Scott even helping me out by grating the cheese and setting the table. Busy as I am stirring the cheese sauce, it's only on turning back that I see there are candles on the table.

This romantic notion surprises me. There's been no hint of passion between us, since I cooled things after he caught me spying. I'd even shut down his attempt at flirting when he'd teased me about my *whale watching*.

. . .

Later that evening and I'm having a few regrets about uncorking a second bottle of wine. However, my thought process had been that if Scott had a few drinks, he might open up a bit more.

Instead, it's me who's opening up, thanks to Scott peeling me like a grape to allow him to run his tongue over my clit. Over and over, he repeats the action until my body burns for release.

As I arch my hips off the bed to give him better access, my keen of longing fills the room. He licks me once more, before he lifts his head and smiles at me along the length of my body. "You like that, do you?"

Control of my body balanced on a precipice, my nod is wobbly,

"What about this?"

I'm wondering what he's talking about when he slides a finger deep inside me, then two.

"Oh, oh, that's soooooo gooooood!" My words are breathy and insubstantial.

There's nothing insubstantial about his fingers when he presses the little pip inside me. When his mouth once again closes over my clit and he sucks hard, it's too much.

I scream his name as my body shatters like glass.

Lost as I am in a sexual fog, it takes a second to realize he's frozen. Sure, his mouth still covers me and his breath warms my skin, but he isn't moving.

"Scott? What's wrong?"

He lifts his head, pulls his fingers free, and slides up next to me on the bed. Rather than say what the problem is, he pulls me into an embrace tight enough that breathing is difficult.

He then kisses me like his life depends on it, easing my fears somewhat.

And yet there's something wrong. There'd been no missing his strange expression a second before he kissed me. If I didn't know better, I'd think it was guilt. But how can it be? He'd told me as much as he could earlier.

What else is he keeping from me, supposedly for my safety?

The following morning I'm in town picking up more paper and toner when, on a whim, I grab a copy of the local paper. There's something so quaint about this when I'm more used to reading the news online.

On arriving back at the house, I find Scott trimming the edges. The place is looking so much better than when I took up residence just over a week ago. I still don't know why my aunt stopped caring for the place. It could have been down to poor health, but I guess I'll never know.

Sometimes when a person's eyesight went, they just didn't notice that sort of thing. Thankfully, the inside of the house was in better condition, except for the plumbing, that is. After getting my supplies out of the car, I give Scott a brief wave and head inside. I'm hanging out for a coffee.

After dropping the newspaper on the kitchen table, I call out to Scott to let him know there'll be coffee in a few minutes. Soon enough, the French press is on the table with coffee cups, milk, and sugar. Meanwhile, Scott is still working away outside. In the end I tire of waiting, plunge the coffee, and pour myself a cup.

I'm flicking through the newspaper, keeping an eye out for Scott, when something catches my attention. There's an image of him staring back at me, with a dollar amount attached to it.

Ten thousand, to be exact.

"What the?"

It doesn't take me long to read the article and, while some of it ties in with what Scott told me last night, there's so much more.

The biggest shock is that he's not Scott, he's Ethan Hunter, and he's wanted for the supply of Class-A drugs. My coffee forgotten, I reread the article. It's no better the second time around. It explains one thing though, and that's why Scott, I mean Ethan, had frozen when I'd called out his name in the throes of passion last night.

According to the article, people are sure they've seen him around town, with the public told to be on the lookout. We're also told not to approach him, as he's deemed dangerous.

On hearing Scott—Ethan—making his way up the porch steps, I've got two options.

I either hide the newspaper, or I confront him.

In the end, he arrives sooner than I've been expecting, and I don't have time to turn the page, let alone hide the newspaper. Instead, I spin the paper around so that it faces his chair.

He drops in a boneless heap, dry washes his face, and then leans forward, resting his forehead on the newspaper. His sigh is heartfelt, his, "I can explain," muffled with him keeping his head down.

"Oh, you think?!"

ETHAN

I lift my head to speak, but am lost for words. What the hell do I focus on?

That Lindsey thinks I'm some sort of drug runner?

That she knows I've been lying about my name?

Or that I've somehow been spotted despite being in disguise whenever I was in town.

The reporter behind the article had even called on Chase, my younger brother, to see if he knew of my whereabouts. By reading between the lines, my brother sent the reporter packing.

Another thing I know is that I'll have to bring things forward. Not what I want, but then I can hardly prove my innocence from inside if I get that far. Chief Sutton might have helped me escape last time. This time I doubt I'd be as lucky. Even if the police chief called it a nasty accident, it's one I'd rather avoid.

Lindsey slams her hands down on the tabletop, the coffee cups, and French press rattling and me subjected to every ounce of her rage. "Well?!"

"It's ... I'm... That is..." I tap the newspaper. "It's not true. None of it is."

She glares at me. "And you can prove this, how?" Her eyebrows shoot up to show that she expects an answer, and it had better be good.

I've got nothing, nothing that will suffice. Not without telling her everything. I'd rather she thought me the most odious man alive, than she be hurt because I've involved her.

"It might be better if you found somewhere else to stay." She holds her hand out for the key, beckoning with her fingers to hasten this. "I won't turn you in, but you can't stay here."

There's no point arguing. Instead, I drag the key out of my pocket and slide it across the table. "I'll go grab my backpack and be on my way." It's with a heavy heart that I walk upstairs to my room, for all I've never actually slept in it.

Damn it, I've finally had a glimpse of the sort of life I've always longed for. And it's being taken away from me, all thanks to the Sutton family. I still don't know how they knew I was back in town. I've been so careful.

It's then I have an 'ah ha' moment. What if they've found some of my surveillance equipment? If they had, then the newspaper article could simply be a fishing trip. It would be a simple thing for Chief Sutton to tip off the reporter and then leave him to it.

Back downstairs, Lindsey stands rigid next to the kitchen table, staring straight ahead with tears streaming down her face. I take a step toward her, desperate to take her in my arms and kiss away her sadness. Her reaction says this isn't a good idea.

"Thank you for everything." I think about saying more, but the best I can come up with is, "We all make mistakes."

Color flares to life in her cheeks and she sucks in a lungful of air that has her choking.

"No, that's not what I mean!" I step over and gently pat her back to help her catch her breath. "There was no mistake with you. You're the best thing that's ever happened to me."

I then give her shoulder a tender squeeze, but don't wait to see if she's accepted my words as truth. Instead, I walk over to the door, out onto the porch, and leave.

This time I don't bother faking an exit via the driveway. I turn and make straight for the summerhouse. No point hiding my movements from her any longer. However, I need to get into disguise before I head for the park in the middle of town. This time I won't be leaving my backpack behind. I'll be taking it with me, wrapped in a threadbare sack.

I've still got a few key pieces of evidence to collect if I'm to prove my innocence of the historic charges. The identity of the true criminals has to be in no doubt. They framed me once, but I'll be damned if I'll let them get away with it a second time.

I'm older, wiser, and a hell of a lot tougher.

My biggest regret is that once I hand the evidence to the authorities, I'll have to leave town and not look back. If there was even an outside chance of staying and having a life with Lindsey, I'd go for it. Unfortunately, I don't see how that's possible.

TEN

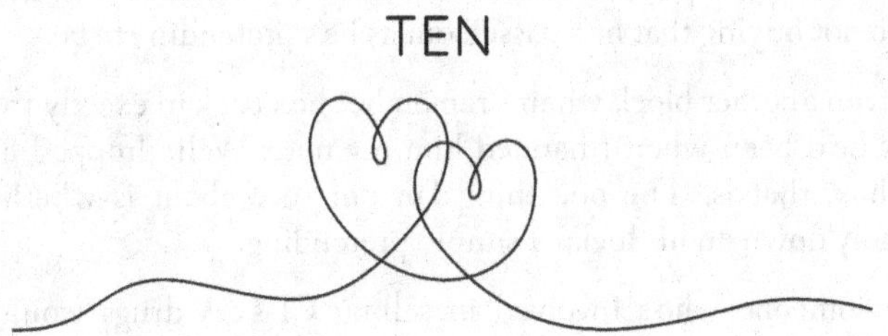

LINDSEY

It's been a week since I saw Ethan, although I'm still getting used to calling him that. My writing has proved a distraction, with me surprised at progress on my manuscript given my disordered mind. If only the words came this easily all the time.

Not everything has been going well in my life, though. I've had to call the emergency plumber on three occasions, with him not impressed by the state of the pipes. The job center hasn't been able to replace 'Scott', and my meals have all been of the microwave variety.

It's the same again tonight, although when I open the freezer, I find it's empty. Even my emergency pint of mint chocolate chip has mysteriously disappeared overnight.

"Blast it!"

I don't want to go to the supermarket, not this late, but if I'm to eat, I'll have to. Rather than simply jump in the car and drive into town, I take the time to write a list. If I were to hit the supermarket *hangry* as I am, who knew what I'd come home with?

This simple task has me remembering Ethan's eyes lighting up when he found out I was making mac 'n' cheese from scratch.

This has me remembering what had been on the menu for dessert that night. It doesn't matter that he was a lying ratbag, I miss him. I felt we had something together and then he had to ruin it by being a career criminal.

I've finished my shopping and am driving home when I see what at first glance looks like a pile of rags in a doorway. Only I know this isn't true. I'm also not buying that he's passed out as he's pretending to be.

I've driven another block when I remember he's back in exactly the same spot as he'd been when I handed him my note. Well, dropped it in his pizza box, that is. The one thing I'm not sure about is whether he's genuinely down on his luck, or simply pretending.

Surely someone who's involved in selling Class-A drugs wouldn't be broke. Could it be he's as innocent as he'd said? Okay, so he can't stay at my place. This doesn't mean I want him spending tonight on the streets. With rain threatening, it would be a miserable prospect.

This has me completing a U-turn, driving by his doorway and parking around the corner. I'm soon standing in front of his grubby pizza box where, as before, I drop a handful of coins in. I then follow this up by handing him the pastries I'd bought at the supermarket.

"Thanks, lady." Is all I get in response to my charity, but it's enough. I'm not here to blow his cover, something that would be at risk if I were to take any more notice of him. I can only hope he'll be okay.

Strange that he's sticking around when there's a reward being offered for his capture. It'd be easy enough for him to move onto the next town and disappear. No one took any notice of the homeless for fear of getting dragged into their messy lives.

Back home, I'm at a loss about what to do with myself. Even my writing isn't calling to me tonight. Maybe those critics were right about my lack of talent?

The house feels so empty without Ethan to distract me. For the first time, I'm conscious of rattling around in the place. However, there's one place where I know I'll feel close to him, and that's the one place I'll always associate him with.

ETHAN

Despite promising Lindsey that I'd stay away, I'm back, although only to make use of the bath. I hate being dirty, and I especially hate wearing filthy clothes.

There are no lights on in the house, so I know I'll be able to sneak in, have a bath, and leave without Lindsey knowing. And I could have, too, if not for her already being in the bath. Damn if she isn't a sight to bring a man to his knees.

Her skin glistens under the full moon, with this being helped by the candles flickering on the tree stump. Bubbles cling to her delicious curves, with my body responding in a heartbeat. I want her so badly that it hurts. And it's not all down to sex. I want to hold this woman, to care for her, to look after her until she's old. I want her to have my babies.

It's a thought that has me sucking in air. Never have I felt this way about a woman before, it being both exhilarating and frightening.

"Ethan, is that you?" She stares into the dark and tries sitting up in the bath, but slips and splashes back into the water. The old cast iron tub is big enough that even I'd wallow in it when it's as full as it is now.

"Yeah, I'm sorry. Needed a bath, and I didn't know where else to go. I'll be on my way."

I'm walking away when she calls out "No, wait! Come back. I want..."

I'm not sure what it is she wants, her words having faltered. It's not until I'm right next to the bath looking down at her I know exactly what it is she wants, and she's not alone.

This has me shedding clothes like a madman a second later. I'm naked and ready to climb in behind her, when she motions I should sit in front. "Your hair, it's um."

She doesn't need to say anything more. Days spent wearing that disgusting wig, has my scalp crawling to escape. Soon enough, I'm in the tub in front of her, the water scalding after the cool night air.

A moment later and she's filled an old yogurt container with water and has upended it over my head. She then grabs some shampoo and starts washing my hair.

And it's the most sensual thing I've ever experienced. It's erotic enough that I'm rock hard before she's rinsed. The discomfort of the past week is but a memory as I surrender to Lindsey's ministrations. With her, I'm not a criminal; I'm just a man, like any other.

I'm also one who is going to lose it if he doesn't bury himself in her depths and soon, and that's not happening in the bath. Not enough purchase for what I've got in mind. Even better is that I'm not alone in my desires.

After handing me a towel and wrapping one around herself, she picks up one of the two candles. "Let's go to the summerhouse. There's a surprise."

After grabbing the other candle, I cup my hand around it to stop the cool breeze from blowing it out. "I might have a surprise of my own." My laughter then rings out, with me happier than I've been in days, maybe even longer.

Despite everything hanging over my head, when I'm with Lindsey, I can forget all about that. I keep pace with her on the walk to the summerhouse, although my steps slow when we cross the threshold.

"Someone's been busy." To the casual observer there wouldn't be much difference, but to me, the improvements are huge. The best of all is the plump cushion on the bench in the middle of the structure.

I'd have slept better if it'd been here all along. Now it'll provide comfort for something else entirely. After putting my candle on the window ledge, I take my towel off and drop it to the ground for want of anywhere else to put it.

Lindsey matches my actions, with both of us now naked. This is different to the bath, or even Lindsey's bedroom. Here it's just the two of us, and that damned bench. After a second's thought, I decide it should be Lindsey who sets the pace.

This sees me lay down on my back in the middle of the cushion, doing nothing to hide my erection. "Darling, I'm all yours." I then put my hands behind my head, all while grinning. "Do with me what you will."

ELEVEN

I stare wide-eyed at Ethan, lying shamelessly back on the cushion, waiting for me to have my way with him.

I'm not even aware I'm sucking on my bottom lip until I see Ethan take a deep breath, reach down and squeeze the tip of his penis.

"Darling, you keep biting your lip like that and the fun will be over before it's started."

I take a step closer, and even go so far as putting one knee on the bench. "It's just that I've never, um, taken control like this."

His smile is tentative at first, although he's soon grinning. "Just imagine we're enacting that scene from your book."

There's nothing I can do about my snort of laughter at this. It does, however, tell me exactly how I should proceed. Climbing up onto the bench, I straddle him. When he takes his hand away from his cock and puts it back behind his head, I know I'm on the right track.

This sees me confidently taking hold of his shaft. Then, after a bit of shuffling back and forth, I position it just so. Going off script, I then drop, claiming his full length in a move that leaves us gasping. There'd been no need for foreplay, with me as wet inside as I was out after that bath.

It's not long before we're overtaken by climaxes that rock both our worlds. And it's okay that our first time has been fast. We've got all night. I'd like to think we've got our whole lives ahead of us, but I don't think this is so.

Despite the fun we have trying every position imaginable—and a few that aren't — there's an edge of sadness to Ethan tonight. One I've not seen before, his melancholy adding a bitter-sweet note to our coupling.

Back up in my room, we fall asleep with arms wrapped around each other, wanting to stay close as we'd been in the summerhouse. My last thought before sleep claims me is how unfair life can be.

Just how unfair hits me between the eyes when I wake not long after dawn and find a note from Ethan on the pillow next to me.

Still half asleep, I have to read it twice to make sense of it. According to the note, 'tonight's the night'.

What this actually means, I'm as in the dark now as I had been yesterday. I just wish he'd share everything with me, rather than throw cryptic half-sentences at me.

However, there's no missing the meaning in the last few sentences of his note.

If you don't see me tomorrow, I want you to get on with your life. Don't hide away in this crumbling house. Live life like it's one of your stories. Have fun, have adventures, find love. EH xxx.

"Like hell I will." After tossing the note to one side, I throw back the covers and drag on my sweats. I'm darned if I'll stand by while the man I love throws his life away.

Downstairs, I dig that newspaper out of the recycling, flicking through it until I find the article on Ethan. Yep, sure enough, there at the bottom is a classified ad for his brother's bail bond service.

After punching in the number, I listen to it ringing, hoping like heck his brother is an early riser, because I've got work for him to do.

ETHAN

I know leaving Lindsey a note was a cowardly thing to do, but it was also the right one. If everything goes to crap tonight, I don't want her wasting her life waiting for me to get out of prison. Something I think she's more than capable of.

With me getting ready to take on Craig Sutton, Chief Sutton, and any rotten cops in their employ, my chances of being captured are high. I don't want Lindsey caught up in that. I don't want her seeing me led away in chains, or worse.

Better we remember each other as we'd been last night.

Lying amid the crap strewn across the wasteland bordering the warehouse, I'm as good as invisible. Even if it weren't nighttime, the rags I'm wearing would have me blending perfectly with the surroundings.

However, I'm blind to all that, my sole focus being what I can hear through the earpiece hidden under my dirty blond wig.

Despite writing that *tonight would be the night* in my note, the extent of what was going down hadn't been obvious. While tempted to stop the drugs currently in the warehouse from being shipped out, I can't. Not on my own.

Busy as I am listening to events unfolding inside, I'm unaware of my brother's presence, until he drops beside me, scaring the crap out of me.

Even in the dark, I can see his face is every bit as dirty as my own, his outfit as hideous. "How in the hell did you know where to find me?"

Without taking his eyes off the large truck that's pulled to a stop at the back of the warehouse, he whispers, "I got a call from some woman called Lindsey. You're lucky she could put two and two together from what you let spill." He then holds up a pair of night-vision goggles to further clarify how he found me out here in the dark.

He stills for a second before adding. "You dumbass. Why didn't you say something to Gramps all those years ago instead of taking off like you did?"

I don't immediately answer, busy listening to the conversation I can hear through my earpiece. "I ran because of who I was up against. The same people I'm *still* up against."

I jerk my head toward the warehouse. "Chief Sutton is in there right now, brokering the cocaine deal of the century. What chance do you think I'd have had of proving my innocence with him involved?"

"That incompetent piece of ... Are you serious?"

"Yep, deadly serious. He's in there, along with that idiot son of his and at least half-a-dozen cops that I know of."

Chase's only response is a brief whistle.

As we watch people turning up at the warehouse in ones and twos, the true scale of tonight's operation makes itself known. I twist my head to the side, squinting at my brother through the gloom. "I hope you're as good in a fight as people say you are."

"Yeah, about that. Bro, next time you upload something to the cloud. Make sure it's your cloud and not someone else's."

"What do you mean?"

He shakes his head slowly before he answers. "Lindsey was downloading some documents from her cloud this morning when she came across your files. She rang me back to tell me what she'd found and so I kinda called in the reinforcements."

I've not asked him what he means by this, when half-a-dozen black SUVs scream up to the side door of the warehouse. A similar number covers the roller door at the back. That truck's not going anywhere tonight.

I then watch in disbelief as four or five heavily armed guys get out of each vehicle, the reflective DEA visible on their vests even at this distance.

There isn't a chance the chief will talk his way out of this. Not with the evidence I'll be sending in, although that's not happening tonight. As soon as I can, I'm heading home to say thank you to a very special lady.

On my stepping up onto the porch, Lindsey flies out of the door and into my arms, crying and laughing. "I'm so sorry. I had to bring your brother in on this. I was so afraid."

"No, don't be sorry. You did the right thing." My lips claim hers and I pour all my heartache, longing, and love into that one kiss. It's still not enough; I doubt it ever will be. With Lindsey, I'll always want more. "Come on, let's go to bed."

Soon after, we lay in bed, a tangle of arms and legs. But for once, it's not about sex. Well, at least not yet.

"Lindsey, I know it's still early days, and I don't want to rush you, but it's just that—"

I have to take a deep breath, rushing the words out before I lose my nerve. "I love you."

She goes to speak, but I put my finger on her full lips.

"I've loved you from the moment I saw you walking around the garden in that summer dress. From the time you made me mac 'n' cheese. And definitely from the first time we got close."

I used my thumb to swipe away the tears running down her face. "Baby, I'm sorry, I thought..."

Who was I kidding? Why would a woman as wonderful as Lindsey be interested in anything permanent with a no hoper like me? Even if I prove the Suttons were behind it originally, I'll still have to go to court to face jumping bail. There's also my having assumed someone else's identity for three odd years. This is hardly the stuff of dreams.

I'm doing my best to disentangle myself when Lindsey's hold on me tightens.

"Where do you think you're going, Ethan Hunter?"

On hearing her use my full name, joy springs to life in my chest with an effervescent fizz. I can't remember when I last heard a woman use it with such love in her voice.

She strokes my face gently, before continuing, "Yes, it is early days, but I also know you're the right man for me. You're like my favorite book hero come to life. You're everything I've always wanted, and more. I love you, no matter what your name is."

To reinforce her words, her hand disappears under the covers and she wraps her fingers tight around my cock. When she rubs her thumb back and forth across the tip, I give up fighting it. Instead, I roll her onto her back and bury myself as completely as I've always wanted to.

That she loves it is clear by her breathy gasps, timed perfectly with each of my balls-deep thrusts.

EPILOGUE

LINDSEY

Steam rolls off the water filling the bathtub, the scent from the rose petals I'm scattering wafting up to embrace me. Six months have passed since Chief Sutton and the others got arrested. He'd done his best to say the DEA had interrupted *his* bust, but the evidence provided by Chase Hunter said otherwise.

Despite Ethan's innocence no longer in doubt, he'd still had to lie low for a few months to avoid being connected to the take-down. No point in him being free if the criminals who escaped arrest that night were gunning for him.

Three glorious months of what amounted to house-arrest. We'd made the most of it though, getting to know each other better, our life together, solidifying, and settling.

Of course, he'd then had to face charges connected to his jumping bail. A separate issue so far as the authorities were concerned. In his favor had been the judge who'd presided over the case being lenient. According to Chase, the woman had never been a fan of Chief Sutton with his reputation as a sexist, incompetent jerk, well-earned.

Either way, Ethan received three months of community service, along with a one-thousand-dollar fine. A slap on the wrist compared to what they could have hit him with.

I've just turned the water off when Ethan walks up and slings his arm around my shoulders, pulling me tight against his side. It's a gesture I love. I also love that we're now free to get on with our life together.

As we climb into the tub, I lean back against his chest and we just lie there for a moment, enjoying the water. All that changes when he grabs the soap.

He's soon lathering my breasts in a manner that has nothing to do with getting clean, and everything to do with getting dirty. As I arch my back, my moan of pure need tells him more than words ever will.

I'll never get enough of this man, never. But, I'm willing to try my hardest. This has me grinding my ass into his erection, my actions being met with delighted laughter.

He drops his head and kisses the top of my ear before whispering, "Summerhouse?"

I giggle before answering. "I thought you'd never ask."

We don't bother with towels, both of us knowing exactly what's about to happen, our lives having fallen into a rhythm in more ways than one. On stepping inside, I'm brought up short. I spin to face Ethan, who's right behind me. "It's beautiful."

As I look around the structure, I'm also confused. Usually we'd only have a couple of candles, enough to see where we're going, but nothing more. Tonight the space flickers with the light cast by dozens.

It's then I notice the small box sitting in the middle of the large cushion that tops the bench. My eyes widen, and I take a step closer. Could it be?

ETHAN

As I watch Lindsey circling the bench, I'm unable to stop grinning. My smile is wide enough that my cheeks hurt, and if not for the joy bubbling out of her, I'd be getting worried.

As it is, I know it's only a matter of time before I ask, and she says yes.

Never has something felt so right, with Lindsey closer to me than my family, although I'm working on that. Certainly Chase collecting the reward for helping shut down one of the largest syndicates on the West Coast has helped. There'd been enough to not only reimburse my grandfather for the money lost when I jumped bail, but to help with the set-up of my new business.

It had been Lindsey's idea, with her *still* not having heard from the job center about a replacement handyman. And she'd been right. Once word got out that I wasn't a drug runner, the work came in thick and fast. If it keeps going how it is, I'll have to employ an assistant.

Deciding I've waited long enough, I step over to the bench, stopping Lindsey's latest lap. After reaching down and collecting the ring box, I get down on one knee and open it.

"Lindsey Abbott, would you do me the honor of becoming my wife?"

She doesn't say yes. She's too choked up for that. Instead, tears of happiness stream down her face and she nods repeatedly. Then she holds her hand out and I slide the ring onto her finger, sealing the deal with a brief kiss to her knuckles.

Back on my feet, I drag her into a tight embrace and swing her around, our delighted laughter filling the space. Then I lower her to the bench and show her yet again how much she really means to me.

BOOKS

Congrats to local author Lindsey Hunter for hitting The New York Times Best Seller list with her latest romantic suspense, Love Lies Lost.

LLL is a huge hit with readers, with critics also raving about the complex storyline and believable characters.

Help Lindsay celebrate making the list with drinks at Maddigans this coming Friday night. All welcome.

Angie is a lawyer who is questioning the toll her career is taking. Drew has already faced the consequences of an all-consuming profession. Will these two learn that love beats work any day?

ONE

DREW

I'm not sure what has me glancing up and through the one-way-glass to reception, but I'm glad I have.

She's back, and just as gorgeous as I remember. While not the type I'd usually find attractive, my body reacts as it had when she was in yesterday grabbing brochures.

It had also reacted last night when she'd invaded my dreams. Thinking back on it, she'd more than invaded them. She'd taken them over; seducing me as surely as if we'd actually shared my bed.

As I continue watching her, the state of my cock tells me last night's response wasn't a one off. Her luscious curves and tumble of auburn curls have me as hard now as I'd been on waking this morning.

Strange when you consider I've been more used to dating professional dancers, women with bodies like those of Olympic athletes. They hadn't exactly brought me happiness though, with none interested in me these days. I'm no longer famous enough to stroke their egos, or more likely, to help their careers.

Despite the woman out front not having a dancer's body, she moves like one. More than that, she moves like silk. Nothing catches, nothing jars. Her every curve is perfection.

I don't realize I've grabbed my coffee until I feel the top of the takeaway cup against my lips. I take a sip before putting it back down and flicking the switch on the intercom. Despite being connected to Natalie, my receptionist, I don't speak. I simply listen without moving.

With the intercom open, it's all too easy for my receptionist to hear what I'm up to, and the same goes for the woman she's speaking to. I even take up shallow breathing as I listen to what our visitor has to say.

"I'm here to book a few one-on-one sessions. Is that possible?"

She then holds up one of our Latin American dance leaflets, and my heart drops. The thought of this luscious creature being alone with Juan Alcaraz doesn't sit well with me.

The guy's a predator with one hell of a reputation for bedding his mature students. I'd tried reprimanding him about it, but as Juan took pride in pointing out, none of his students were complaining.

Anything but, with his schedule and bed, never empty.

I'd replace him if it was possible. Unfortunately, he's the only teacher of Latin dance in town. Unless I take the classes myself, I'm stuck with him.

Of course, I doubt the woman in reception knows any of this. Or perhaps she does, and she's after Juan's bed as much as his self-proclaimed mastery on the dance floor.

Not until Natalie books the first session, do I break my silence.

"Hold off Natalie, I'll be out in a second."

That she doesn't react tells me she's known I was listening in. However, our visitor's mouth is a wide 'O' as she looks around, trying to work out where the voice has come from.

Despite promising myself I'd never interfere with any of the teachers' bookings, I'm about to go there, and then some.

I've not taken more than a couple of steps into reception when I see that the woman has recognized me. And yet she's a stranger and not from around here. Her air of sophistication firmly marks her as being from the city, although which one, I'm not sure.

Rather than give her time to gush about my career, I extend my hand. "Drew Morton. I'm the owner." As subtly as I can, I tip my head in Natalie's direction.

I haven't used Andrew Morton-Huxley since that horrific night in New York, the night my Achilles gave out on me in spectacular fashion. I've built a new life for myself here. The last thing I want or need is my old life gatecrashing.

There are some arts reporters who'd take great delight in blogging my spectacular fall from fame. It wouldn't matter that they'd only done so to boost the click rate on their blogs. The reminder of what I'd lost would have the wounds as fresh as the day I collapsed on stage.

The woman quirks a meticulously groomed eyebrow, telling me she won't use my stage name, even if she's not sure why. After this I'm at a loss. How do I go about finding out if she's truly here to book one-on-one dance sessions, or if she's after Juan's other services?

Damn it, I hate that he's got me pimping him out. Perhaps it's down to these thoughts muddying my brain that my, "I'm afraid we don't have any availability," comes out louder than I've meant.

A quick glance at Natalie and I can see I've taken her unawares. Her mouth hangs open in response to my blatant lie. Of interest is that our visitor appears as surprised.

"But your receptionist said you had plenty of availability." She scans reception, as if to emphasize that it's empty but for the three of us. She then stares at me. "You can't have filled spaces that quickly. You don't even have an online booking system."

"I'm really sorry we misinformed you." Another peek at Natalie and I know I owe her chocolates or a bottle of wine for this. "We really don't have any spaces left. You could try back next month."

I fall silent. It's only then I become aware there's now someone behind me. The merest flare of my nostrils tells me exactly who it is. The only man around here who douses himself in Pour Homme to that extent is Juan Alcaraz.

ANGIE

What on earth is Andrew Morton-Huxley up to? Or should I call him plain old Drew Morton as he's introduced himself? While I'd seen the name on the signs and promotional materials, I hadn't put two-and-two together.

Thanks to my years of practicing law, I'm convinced Drew is lying. The incredulous expressions of his receptionist and the guy behind him back this up.

Juan Alcaraz himself. When I'd decided on one-on-one sessions to avoid the crush of a class, I hadn't actually met the guy. His photo in the brochure, airbrushed to the max, had failed to convey how truly awful he was.

He's sleazy, fake to the core and has had *work*. While I don't have a problem with this per se, I do when it's try-hard and of poor quality. It looks like the surgeon used a wind tunnel rather than a scalpel. Ditto the guy's hairdresser.

What annoys me the most is that I've had some wonderful Latino colleagues in the past. Honorable men, who were proud of their heritage, rather than two-dimensional caricatures like Juan Alcaraz.

Much as I want to lose myself in a solo session, that wasn't happening with this creep. All I want is a break from the monotony of living in someone else's home, of sitting around with too much time to think.

I'd met Sally, the homeowner, at a Lawyer's Association conference where we'd hit it off immediately. We had similar jobs, and both being curvy, could offer each other moral support at the buffet lunches. It had been nice to sit with someone who wasn't second-guessing every morsel I put in my mouth.

I'd phoned her the day my boss told me I was on three months' sabbatical. He'd said unless I rediscovered my killer instincts in the courtroom, I should reconsider my career choices.

I'd therefore needed to talk through my options with someone who understood the situation, and who wasn't my parents.

She was the one who'd suggested that I house-sit for her with this solving problems for both of us. She was between tenants in the home she managed for her brother, and I needed the space to think things through. According to her, the cottage at Coogan's is perfect for rational thought.

And while I'm supposed to be thinking about my career, I've been avoiding it. I'm not ready to decide anything yet.

Could Alcaraz be why Drew had been trying to put me off the one-on-ones? Drew's reputation as a nice guy had remained intact right up to the moment they carried him off stage.

Of course, I don't have a clue what a failed career could do to a man's psyche.

Another glance at Alcaraz tells me dancing with him would be a nightmare. I'd spend all my time moving his hands back to where they should be rather than where they were. No way do I want to deal with that, at least not with Alcaraz.

Now, if it were Drew, that'd be a different story.

He could put his hands wherever he liked and you wouldn't hear me complaining. Engrossed as I am with my dreams, I miss what the Latin teacher has said. Rather than ask him to repeat himself, I lock eyes with Drew.

This is a big mistake, with my breath catching in response. He's even more gorgeous in the flesh than in the framed posters I have at my apartment back in LA. To say I'd been an ardent fan was an understatement.

The night he collapsed on stage in New York, I'd left the theater in tears. Having been involved in the dance community since I was a kid, I'd known the impact a ripped Achilles would have on his career.

I knew I'd probably never get to see him dance again. It was this, as much as the physical and emotional pain he had been in that night, that had me sobbing my heart out.

As I think back on his cries of pain echoing around the theater, my tummy flips in response. I've even put my hand up to my mouth when Drew says, "Are you okay? You don't look good." He quickly follows this up with, "Ah, I mean, come into my office and I'll get you some water."

As unintentional as this has been, it's also the perfect excuse to get away from Alcaraz. While Drew is ready to comfort me, Juan is backing away, happy to distance himself from a woman with the potential to faint, or worse.

"Please, this way." Drew motions to the open door at the side of reception, before walking in that direction himself.

After a couple of fortifying breaths, I follow in his wake. This, more than smelling salts, has me back in my body. The way this guy moves is, is... Hmmm, like a cat? No, a cat is too tame.

He's more of a Jaguar and not one of the zoo varieties, either. Nope, we're talking wild beast, with his sheer animal magnetism mesmerizing me.

After I've entered his office, he places his hand gently in the middle of my back to steer me toward one of his visitor's chairs.

There's nothing sexual about it, but my body doesn't realize this. A flash of excitement flies from his palm to the apex of my thighs. On arrival, it explodes in a shower of tingling heat that has me rushing to sit.

He's hardly touched me and yet I'm damp and confused.

I've never reacted to a man to this extent, and especially not after such a simple gesture. What would happen if he was really trying?

After closing the door, Drew fills a glass from the small water cooler in the corner of his office.

Meanwhile, I'm still fighting to get my arousal under control, my wiggling not helping at all. Honestly, I'm a grown woman; I shouldn't be reacting as if I've recently hit puberty.

And yet here I am squirming in my seat, exactly as I'd been the last time I saw him dance. If I'd thought he was hot through opera glasses, it's nothing compared to him being in touching distance.

If I'd known he would be here today, I could have mentally prepared myself.

Hah, who are you fooling? If you'd known he was here, you'd have been too chicken to step foot in the place.

"Here you are." He places the glass of water in front of me before making his way around the desk and sitting down.

After realizing he's waiting for me to drink, I pick up the glass and take the smallest sip possible. The last thing I want is to choke because I've taken too much.

That an unknown emotion constricts my throat isn't helping. A moment's thought and I realize what it is. Despite no longer wanting one-on-one sessions with Juan Alcaraz, I still want to dance. I want to dance so much that it hurts.

I fake a few more sips to give myself time to think. Only then do I admit to myself who I want to dance with. On my libido yelling that it wants more than this, I shut it down. If I'm to argue my case convincingly, I'll have to concentrate.

Sure, I'm rusty after not having danced in years, but I still know my way around a dance floor. The trophies stuffed in a cupboard at my folks' place are testament to that.

What I don't know is whether someone of Drew's caliber would deign to dance with me. I guess there's only one way to find out.

TWO

ANGIE

Thanks to all those years in court, I'm used to thinking on my feet, even when I'm opposite a man like Drew. He really rattles my thoughts and other places.

"I'm not after lessons. I only decided on one-on-one sessions so I could relax and simply enjoy the dancing."

After he nods slowly in response, I continue. "So, if Alcaraz isn't available..." I have to swallow deeply before I can continue. "What about you?"

I don't give him a chance to answer. I rush on. "I've followed your career enough to know your Latin American dancing is amazing."

Whoa, cut the stalker fan girl gushing, will you? You'll scare him off.

Rather than risk exposure, I shut up and wait.

I don't have to wait long. "I'm afraid I can't help you with that. My Achilles..."

There's nothing I can do to stop the lawyer in me from jumping straight in with, "... was operated on immediately. You then received a year's physio. We're not talking competition dance here, merely a salsa or two."

While he's looking at me, I doubt he's focused. How deeply has he buried that part of his life, that my reminding him of it has him... traumatized?

What if he hasn't danced since that fateful night?

I can't imagine giving up something I loved like that. And I knew he'd loved it. No-one could dance with such abandon unless they were fully into it.

I wish I could say the same about my career. While it was shocking to hear I was on an enforced three-month sabbatical, it hadn't exactly distressed me. Would it devastate me if I never went back?

It wouldn't be easy to give up the way of life I've known for the past seven years, to throw it all away. And yet this is exactly what I'm considering.

Drew had a career that spanned ten years, and he'd had no say in when it ended. That doesn't mean he can't dance again, or that he shouldn't.

I can't believe what I'm about to do. It was the sort of ploy some lawyers used in court, but was it something I'd try in real life? Apparently it is.

After my ultimatum, Drew stares at me open-mouthed. Meanwhile, I sit silent to avoid taking my words back. Part of me feels bad; another part of me wants to dance with him so much that it doesn't care. Not one jot.

Eventually, he stutters out, "So let's see if I've got this right. I either dance with you, or you'll book sessions with Señor Alcaraz and sue me when he hits on you?"

I nod briefly.

"But... but... that's blackmail."

I tilt my head to the side briefly. "Well, technically, without a physical threat, it would be closer to coercion. But in this case, it's neither. Either I dance with Alcaraz, or I dance with you."

My hands hidden by the desktop, I cross all my fingers, hoping he'll go for it. There isn't a chance I'd dance with Juan and I'd certainly never litigate against him. All I need is for Drew to believe I would.

I also need to be right about his drive to protect me from that man. My lawyer's gut has never let me down before.

If not for my experience in court, I'd fold under Drew's steely gaze. He's furious, which I'm okay with. I wait, and soon enough, he speaks.

"But you're a beginner, you're not... you can't expect someone of my experience to dance with..." Rather than say anything further, he waves in my direction.

Ooooh, he did not go there. Despite not stating it implicitly, I know exactly what he's getting at. If he thinks Latin American dancing is too fast and furious for someone with curves, I'll show him.

I respond as if he's actually voiced his unspoken objections. "Well, there's only one way you'll know for sure, isn't there?"

I subject him to my version of his steely gaze, one that's had many a witness blurting out more than they meant to. "One dance, and if I can't keep up with you, you'll never see or hear from me again."

DREW

Damn this woman and her *just one dance*. She could have two left feet and I'd still accept her challenge. Better I suffer through one dance than Alcaraz adds her to his ever-growing list of conquests.

Of course, I'll let her down as gently as I can. The only thing I'm not sure of is whether my bed will be under her when this happens.

"And you'll keep your word. Just one dance?"

She bristles at my questioning her. "Mr. Morton, I'm a lawyer. Despite our reputation, we don't lie. My word is good."

A lawyer, well, that explains her ability to tie me in knots with her words. I'd feel manipulated if not for me finally admitting to myself that I want to dance with her, too.

Strange, but I did not see today turning out like this. I certainly didn't see it ending with me dancing with a partner. I never expected that to happen, ever again.

Even after I was back to full health, there wasn't a professional company prepared to take me on. Once you've damaged your Achilles, there's always the chance it can happen again.

While I'd been pushing my body to the limit with my physio, younger men had been successfully filling my roles, taking my place.

These days, so far as audiences are concerned, I've simply ceased to exist. My professional pride being what it is, I'm unwilling to try again, for fear of being viewed as past my prime. My ego has taken enough of a battering.

I only notice my surroundings when the woman opposite huffs at my lack of response. She's not the only one who's annoyed.

"I'm sorry. Where were we? That's right. You were forcing me to dance with you." I immediately feel terrible about speaking so sharply, her eyes having widened in response. Much as I try to work through my frustrations in the gym, sometimes it's not enough.

Fine, she can have her one dance, but it's not something anyone is going to know about. If I can keep my true identity under wraps, I'll do it. "Tonight. It'll need to be after the evening classes."

She has a peek at the leaflet she's still holding. "Would nine-thirty work?"

I nod in response rather than speak, as thoughts of being alone with this woman clamor for my attention.

After putting her glass on my desk, she stands, her movements as fluid as ever. "I'll see you then." Without waiting for any other response from me, she opens my office door and leaves.

I'm not alone for long, with Juan Alcaraz appearing soon after the mystery woman had disappeared.

"What the hell was that about? You know I've got availability. And for a hottie like that, I can definitely fit her in." Alcaraz snorts, before adding, "Almost as well as I can fit IN her."

I stare at the guy, unable to comprehend what the local ladies see in him. The reaction from the woman who'd just left is what I'd expect.

And just like that, I realize I don't even know her name.

"You've got more than enough students already. I won't have you trying your bull on out-of-town visitors." As tempted as I am to add, "Especially not when they're a lawyer," I think better of it.

The less he knows about the woman, the better. I especially don't want him aware she'll be back later tonight to dance with me. It's a thought that has me again reaching for my coffee, not worried that it's now stone cold.

"If that's all, can you please close the door on your way out?" I put my coffee down and grab my phone to emphasize my request.

Only after he's left and made his way upstairs, do I call Natalie. "Do we have a name for the woman who was after the solo sessions?"

If I'm being forced to dance with her, I want to learn all I can.

"Sure do. Angela Bennington. LA address. You want that?"

I think about it for a second. "Yep, give me whatever you've got." I'm finishing up my coffee when Natalie places a print-out in front of me.

She grabs the bottle of wine I'd put on the corner of my desk on her way out.

Despite us not having an online booking system, I know my way around the internet. It therefore doesn't take long for me to know more than enough about Angela—Angie—Bennington. It would appear she's quite the mover and shaker in LA legal circles.

And if so, why is she in Coogan's Break for the next few months, as she'd told Natalie? If she's trying to book dance classes, I doubt she's here on business.

Unless she's trying to dig up dirt on something, or someone. Then I shake my head. Of course she isn't. Lawyers don't dig up dirt, only dish it out.

A check of my watch and see I've got twelve hours until Angie is back at the school. Twelve hours until we're alone, and I get to dance with a woman for the first time in three years.

After leaning to the right, I open the bottom drawer of my desk. My last pair of stage shoes reminds me to never take life for granted. I'd learned the hard way that it can change in a split second.

THREE

ANGIE

Only on leaving Dynamic Five Dance does it dawn on me that the dance shoes I'd ordered online the day before have yet to arrive. The site had promised 'overnight delivery' to anywhere in the country, so I hope this proves to be the case.

The last thing I want after forcing Drew into dancing with me is to have to cancel, because I don't have the right shoes. There isn't a chance I can dance properly wearing anything else.

It's a shame mine are in storage. If they weren't, I could have arranged for them, and a few other things, to be sent to me. I honestly hadn't thought I'd need anything while in Coogan's Break.

Little did I realize how quickly I'd become bored without twelve-hour workdays. I'd done my best to stay busy, although obviously not enough.

I'd even considered learning to surf, with the beginner classes through the Surf Shack looking easy enough. However, it was on leaving Skye High Pies that I'd stumbled across the dance school. In this, I knew I'd found the perfect solution.

Even better, had been the online shopping necessary, because I hadn't packed dance gear. This involved ordering the sort of shoes and outfits I'd always wanted to. The sort I'd been unable to afford as a college student, but that I could now.

I might have gone a teensy bit nuts with the number of items I'd put in my cart. The Supadance Latin shoes, in particular, had been quite the splurge. Of course, now I'm glad about it. I'm also pleased I hadn't known I'd be dancing with Andrew Morton-Huxley when I was shopping.

Who knew how much damage I would have done to my credit card if that were the case? Sure, I'd had great dance partners in the past, but none in the same league as Drew.

And none of them had me frothing with arousal like he had when I was in his office. Heaven help me when we were actually dancing together. I can only hope my nerves won't have me stepping on his feet.

This gives me second thoughts about this evening. If I've got a hope of having more than the one dance with my idol, I'll need to be on form. As I unlock my car, I'm focused on the need to get some practice in, plus I'll have to check online to see where my packages are.

If I'm lucky, they'll be there when I get back to the house.

Never in the history of packages have some taken so long to arrive. Not until three in the afternoon is there a knock at the door. On opening it, there's no sign of the delivery person, but there is a rather large package sitting on the front porch.

While I shop online a lot, it's usually for boring work-clothes from brands I'm familiar with. This package is in another league.

As well as being unfamiliar with some brands, I'll be wearing these clothes in front of Drew. That makes one heck of a difference. If nothing fits, I'm not sure what I'll do, but it will involve at least one pint of ice cream.

As I stand in front of the full-length mirror in the hallway at Sally's place, I'm stunned. While the outfit looks good, would it have been something I'd have chosen if I'd known I'd be dancing with Andrew Morton-Huxley?

Ah, that'd be a heck no. I feel on display as never. The wraparound skirt was mid-thigh on the model on that website. On me, it barely skims my cheeks. The woman mustn't have been much above five-foot. At five-foot-eight, I get to show a lot more thigh than she did.

Ditto on how low-cut the scoop neck of the top is. The only plus in all of this is that the tights are a brand I've bought before. They, at least, fit as I've been expecting.

Will it still feel as though I'm as good as naked when I'm dancing with Drew? There's nothing I can do about my nervous laughter as I realize I'm okay with this.

Who knows what Drew will think of my ensemble? What if he thinks I've chosen everything with Juan Alcaraz in mind? Even giving consideration to this has me shuddering.

Thanks to the flocks of butterflies in my tummy, dinner is coffee and a couple of rice thins with cream cheese. Less than I'd usually have, but enough to stop me fainting mid-dance.

The butterflies continue fluttering as I wait in my car for everyone to leave Dynamic Five. They then come crashing down when I see the lights inside turned off.

The last person to leave is the receptionist, with her locking the door behind her. Surely Drew hasn't changed his mind? He'd better not have.

As if knowing tonight has to be kept quiet, I've parked down the street a little. I also turn up the collar of my coat before getting out of the car.

After knocking on the front door of the dance school, I look around nervously while waiting for the door to be answered. That's if it is.

I'd laugh at my fantasies, but I can't ignore the sensation that I'm being watched. However, a quick look up and down the street shows that I'm on my own.

A last-minute check above the front door doesn't reveal a security camera.

I'm still looking up when Drew wrenches open the front door. Such is my surprise that I'm unable to stop my squeak of alarm. A glimpse of his dark expression, and all my brain can come up with, is crickets.

Incapable of speech, I simply nod in greeting and, after another check of the street, I scuttle inside.

With reception only lit courtesy of the security lights outside, it's still too dark to get a proper look at him. I only know he's no longer in the button-down shirt and chinos he'd been wearing earlier.

He's dressed from head-to-toe in unforgiving black.

It's what he was renowned for wearing on stage, with the memories of performances I'd attended coming back in flashes.

The impact on my libido is instantaneous. Oh heck, if I'm aroused when he's standing glowering at me, what will it be like when we're dancing? It's enough to make my hands clammy.

Tonight will either be heaven or hell.

DREW

In part, I'm annoyed she's turned up. Attraction aside, I'd still hoped she'd lose her nerve, and think better of forcing me to dance with her.

But no, here she is, knocking on the door right on time.

On my swinging it wide, there's no missing her unease. She's on edge, glancing up and down the street, before rushing inside.

In response to her obvious nerves, I also check around outside before closing the door. There'd been no one around that I could see, thank goodness.

I don't want a hint of any clandestine activity in a place this small. It'd be all over the front page of the local newspaper before you could say EXCLUSIVE.

After securing the front door, I take a moment to savor the familiar sense of peace that settles when I'm locked away from the world.

And then I remember I'm not alone; rather, I've got Angie to contend with. One dance and she is out of here. "Come on, we're in the studio upstairs, at the back." Without waiting for her agreement to this, I start up the stairs, our way lit by small lights on each tread.

I'd been fortunate to find the place when I first opened the school. An old city building that was no longer needed; I'd got it for a great price. Even better is that thanks to the tall ceilings and vast windows, the studios are flooded with light during the day.

On reaching the top of the stairs, I find Angie is right behind me. Damn, but she's light on her feet. The studio we're in tonight isn't one used for classes, but where I work on keeping myself fit, although for what, I'm no longer sure.

After punching in the key code, I open the door and stand to the side, allowing Angie to enter the brightly lit room. As when I'd shown her into my office this morning, I'm unable to stop myself from touching the small of her back. This time, rather than quiver under my touch, she shies away.

Hmmm, seems as if the country's top dancers aren't alone in wanting nothing to do with me. In which case, why the hell is she so determined to dance with me? Is it to cross it off some dance bucket list? Or does she simply feel sorry for me?

Either way, I take my hand away in short order. I'll touch her only as much as required to dance, and no more.

One dance, that's all she's after.

I can do this.

"I'll change my shoes." She immediately drops to a chair next to the door, her bag on the floor in front of her. Head down, she concentrates on the task.

I'm pleased she's got more appropriate footwear with her. There'd been no missing her sneakers when she arrived. They're hardly the correct footwear for Latin, or any kind of dance other than hip hop.

While she swaps out her shoes, I walk over to the sound system and have a quick scroll through the music. As much as I want this to be over quickly, I veer away from anything too up-tempo.

I don't want to kill her love of dance by choosing a challenging track. Much as she's backed me into a corner over this, I'd never be that cruel.

While she moves like silk when walking, she could be a terrible dancer. Her being an amateur is one reason I'd been reticent about us dancing.

To me, dance is sacred.

On the plus side, one dance will be enough to show her I'm way out of her league.

And from my point-of-view, there's nothing like someone stomping all over my feet to snuff any sexual attraction in minutes.

No, it's easier to forget my past if I'm with a woman who knows nothing of it. No constant reminders of what I've lost. Angie has already had me remembering things I'd rather forget.

I'm struggling with the direction of my thoughts when I hear footsteps behind me. On turning, her beauty steals my breath and holds it for ransom.

I'd be a fool to deny I'm attracted to her. However, nothing could have prepared me for her body being on display like this. Her top, tights, and wrap skirt leave nothing to my imagination, and believe me, I've got plenty.

The black ensemble starkly outlines her curves. The wrap skirt barely skimming the tops of her thighs. And, wow, what thighs? They're the sort that could squeeze an erection out of me, no matter how bad my day had been.

After roaming south, my gaze heads north again. This has me faced with a pair of magnificent breasts that are doing their best to escape the low neckline of her top.

How the hell am I supposed to dance with those beautiful orbs squashed tight against my chest? The chances of her popping a nipple are right up there. That I can visualize exactly this doesn't help.

At this rate, it'll be me who'll be treading on toes. Unable to concentrate, thanks to my cock doing its best to make first contact. Never, in all my years of dancing, have a wanted to bed a partner as much as I want to bed Angie.

Oh, you want more than that, much more.

It's true. I don't just want to bed her. I want to make love, to screw, to fornicate, to have her every which way I can think of.

To get my mind out of bed and back into the studio, I drop my gaze to her shoes.

They're not only black; they're brand new, firmly marking her as an amateur. Sexual attraction to one side, I suspect tonight will be dance hell for me.

FOUR

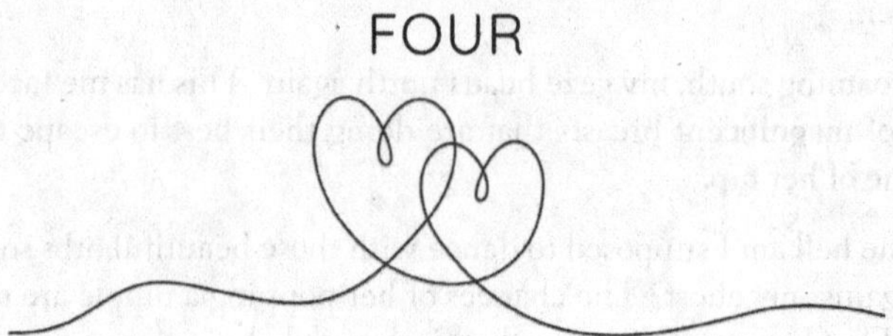

ANGIE

While Drew was busy sorting out the music, I change my shoes. Not until after I've buckled them do I stand, turn my back to him, and shrug out of my coat.

I know I was delaying the inevitable, but honestly, this outfit has me feeling as good as naked. It doesn't matter that I'm encased from head to toe in Lycra. Well, mostly, because on looking down on my way over to join Drew, I encounter an eye-watering amount of cleavage.

Thinking of him seeing this has my chest blooming in response. To take my mind off what he'll think of this, I instead take in the small studio.

It's very different from the larger studios the receptionist had shown me yesterday. The keypad lock on the door, a pile of gym equipment at one end, and no mirrors on the walls say this is his personal space.

If I were dreaming, this would be because he wanted to be alone with me. Sadly, I suspect it's because he wants to keep our dancing—make that dance—a secret from the world.

While expected, it's a letdown all the same.

Rather than stay rooted to the spot, I pace quietly back and forth, all the while taking sneaky peeks at Drew. This both warms my muscles and rids me of my nervous energy. It also goes a long way to desensitize me to how hot he looks in those black Latin pants and fitted t-shirt.

For all the good it does, because when he turns and faces me, I know I'm in trouble. While it's not the first time I've seen him dressed like this, it is the first time I've been this close. It has an incendiary effect on my libido.

I'll be lucky if I can stay upright, let alone dance.

Apparently, I'm not the only one affected, with his eyes widening as they take in my new outfit. Rather than settle on my boobs, his gaze plummets to take in my shoes and belt-like skirt. Honestly, the model in that image online gave entirely the wrong impression as to the skirt's length.

To my growing embarrassment, his gaze then moves back up to my chest. His nostrils flare in response to my girls being on display as they are. Modest scoop neck my ass. The neckline plunges enough that even a shallow breath has me flashing my black lace bra.

Never have I felt as on display in front of a man. And never one I'm as attracted to as Drew. He oozes a natural confidence that has me desperate to get my water bottle out of my gym bag.

Not to take a sip of water, but to douse the arousal that's threatening to overwhelm me. Damn, he's hot.

Despite not having danced professionally in close to three years, he's sure kept himself in shape. I guess that's what the gym equipment is for. You could bounce coins off that taut butt of his. I then have to bite on my lips to stop my nervous laughter at what would happen if I tried.

Hah, reality-check! Who am I kidding? He'd never be interested in someone like me.

If I hadn't put the pressure on, he'd never have agreed to dance with me. Not in a million years. I'm therefore making the most of it, and that means doing my best not to disgrace myself on the dance floor.

To me, it would be like performing badly in bed, with dancing a close cousin in that department. Me and Drew in a tight embrace, moving in sync, and moving as one. It's coitus with your clothes on, for sure.

I'm nervous. Of more interest is that he looks to be equally ill at ease. Without thought, I take five slow belly breaths to regulate my heart rate and center my thoughts. It works in court, and I'm pleased when it works here, too.

Despite my rampant imagination once more being under control, I still react when Drew places his hand on the small of my back.

While he's done so to steer me to the middle of the small studio, I arch my back to keep the distance between us. Not because I don't want him to touch me, but that I do. Oh, so very much.

I'll need to concentrate tonight if I want to avoid looking like an idiot. He's only agreed to the one dance. I'm not messing that up by tripping over my own feet. This is a possibility, because thanks to my reaction to him in dance gear, all my blood is now hiding behind my ridiculously short skirt.

Sure, dancing is a physical thing, but you also need to concentrate if you're to avoid missed steps, or worse, stomping on your dance partner. While I'd love to get physical with Drew, this wouldn't be my first choice.

As if sensing I'm finally ready, Drew points a remote toward the sound system, and then slides it into the back pocket of his trousers. Music fills the room, letting me know what our dance will be, even if this comes as a surprise.

What I'm unsure of is whether he's chosen a tango track on purpose, or by accident? On seeing his frown, I suspect it's the latter and disappointment fills me.

Will he change the song?

Or will we dance?

Tossing caution to the wind, I quirk a brow in challenge. I'm a great believer in synchronicity and to change the track would be to ignore that. Instead, I go with my gut instinct.

When he doesn't move to change the track or move at all, I throw down the gauntlet. If I'm only getting one dance, this is a hell of a dance to get.

"I'm game, if you are, Drew."

Only after he's retrieved the remote from his pocket and pointed it at the sound system, do I get my answer. While I'm expecting another track to play, the same track starts up again.

OMG, I'm about to perform the ultimate dance of seduction with a man I've fantasized over for years. And all in a skirt that's nothing more than a glorified belt. If ovaries could sing, mine would currently be belting out show tunes.

DREW

I can't believe it. I'd cued up a track suitable for a beginner-friendly salsa, not the tango. While outwardly simple, the tango is one of the more complex dances.

And damn if she hasn't challenged me on it. Sure, I could wimp out and change the track, but part of me is dying to see what we'd be like in bed.

The only thing that'll kill my arousal will be if she's got two left feet she introduces to mine as often as possible. Nothing kills an erection quicker than that.

Sixteen bars in and I know I'm in trouble. As she walks, so does she dance, her body moving in sync with mine as no partner before her. With the slightest pressure from my fingers, she moves as I want, as if aware of my desire before I am.

This is tandem with her full breasts flattened against my chest, and I'm soon sporting a cock hard enough I could hammer in nails. It's also a challenge not to put my hands in places that even the tango aficionados frown on.

Despite its base origins in the brothels of Buenos Aires, they've sanitized it over the years.

Lost as I am in the dance, it comes as a surprise when the track finishes. Only then do I see Angie is as stunned as I am. Could it be she felt the same as I did?

Her rapid blinking before she's finally able to focus on my face, says yes. Her words, for all that they make no sense, back this up.

"That was... that was. I've never. It was." She then shakes her head as if to center her thoughts. "I mean, was it always like that? For you I mean?" She then bites on her bottom lip in a manner that has me longing to bite it myself. "It was never like that for me, ever."

I'm now faced with a choice. Do I admit our dancing was out of this world? Or do I deny I'd also found it mind-blowing. Hard to do the latter and then stick with one dance.

And just like that, I don't want to stop at one dance. Tonight has brought home in a big way how much I've missed it. Even if our joining hadn't been as spectacular as it was, simply dancing with a partner has shown me what I've been missing out on.

And why? Because I'm no longer able to dance professionally? What a fool I've been.

Have I been avoiding something I love because of misplaced pride? Unable to put all of this into words, I instead take the remote out of my pocket and point it at the sound system. I don't care what track is next, so long as I'm dancing with Angie, I'll be happy.

As I once again take her into my arms, the only thing that'd make me happier would be if we were in bed. If we're this in sync dancing, our lovemaking would be spectacular, the sort to have me forgetting life's low points and regrets.

The music is slow to start, but when it does, it tells me that the universe is looking out for me. With no chance of this woman joining me in my bed tonight, a Lambada is the next best thing.

There's no such thing as a tame Lambada. No holding back, no acting like your grandma is in the room. It's a dance that will see her straddling my thigh, her core warming my leg as she rubs herself against me and I drop her back in my arms.

Halfway through the track, and if there were any octogenarians on the premises, they'd have passed out by now. While the dance calls for me to run my hand down the center of Angie's chest when I dip her, I might have strayed a bit.

And she might have twisted slightly in my arms to make this happen. Either way, my hand runs back and forth over her breasts, her nipples responding as I knew they would.

Am I about to discover if playing with the hem of that super-short skirt will see her even more pliant in my arms? As I swing her up after a deeper dip than I'd have thought possible, our lips mash together in a kiss that takes my breath away.

I lift my lips only long enough to work out where we are in the room. I'm then kissing her again and spinning us over to—and through—the door to my apartment.

We're about to dance the ultimate dance.

The oldest dance known to man—and I hope this woman—because I want her in my bed. It's realizing I want more than this that affects my erection the most.

FIVE

Never has dancing felt more like foreplay.

While the sexiness of Latin American dancing is often down to artifice, my interactions with Drew are all too real.

What I'm having trouble believing is that it's affected him in the same way. And yet, we've had a second dance after his insistence there will only be one. That has to mean something, doesn't it?

Despite all this, I don't care. So what if tonight is a one-off? I'm in a town where no-one knows me, and what are the chances of having an opportunity like this again?

Zero would be my guess. I'd be a fool to pass it up.

On Drew opening the door to what I soon realize is his apartment, I'm again surprised. Rather than something sensual as I'd expect, the space is a virtual monk's cell. Clean lines, white walls, minimal furniture.

Other than a couple of doors, the entire space is open, with the kitchen merging with dining, and then living. The most dominant thing about the room is the large windows. With it being dark outside, these work like mirrors, showing me tight in Drew's embrace.

I hope it's not all a dream and that we look as good together as we feel. Dancing with him has been like nothing I've experienced with any previous partners. There'd been nothing perfunctory about the way we moved.

Even before he'd signal with his fingers which move was next, I'd known what was to come. Would it be like that if we were making love?

As he cradles my face and leans in for another kiss, I abandon trying to make sense of it.

Tonight is my Cinderella moment, except that I have no intention of fleeing into the night and leaving a shoe behind.

I've danced with my prince, now I want more, so much more. And I need him to know this. I've wasted enough of my life already. That's not happening tonight.

After his lips eventually leave mine, I peep at one of the other doors. "Where does that lead?"

After brushing my hair back from my face, he smiles. "That's a storage cupboard."

I'm well on my way to feeling like an idiot when he adds, "But that one is to my bedroom."

He then tilts his head to the side in question and I respond with a jerky nod.

After another brief kiss, he squeezes my hand and leads the way. On him opening the five-panel door, the room beyond is dark and I'm relieved.

The idea of shedding my belt-skirt and dance gear with him looking on would be enough to have me hyperventilating. Next to him, I'm self-conscious of my body. While he's a study of finely honed muscle, I'm soft in all the wrong places.

Drew steps into the dark, taking me with him. He also hits a switch just inside the door. A glance around the room, and I see it could have been worse.

The lights on either side of a king-size bed are middle-eastern in design, their carved brass shades throwing shadows over the dark blue walls.

On closer inspection, I see dark blue is a recurring theme and the perfect match to Drew's eyes. This room is such a contrast to the public spaces of the apartment. Here the furnishings are lush and carnal, as if to arouse the senses.

And they're doing a stellar job with my body buzzing with arousal. The only thing I'm not sure of is how we get from fully clothed to naked under that sumptuous blue velvet coverlet.

Drew's hands settle on my hips, although they don't stay there for long. Instead, he pulls on the tie that holds my wrap skirt in place, with it falling away soon after. As minimal as it's been, I hardly notice its removal.

"Damn it, Angie, but your body is the sort to bring a man to his knees."

If not for my habit of thinking before I speak, I'd have blurted out "Why?!" Instead, I wait for more. I don't do well with half statements, having incorrectly finished them myself in the past, with disastrous results.

Better I hear his thoughts in his own words. It's with this in mind that I simply say, "And?"

"And... I think we're both wearing too much." His hands run all over my body, leaving trails of fire in their wake.

"I want to graze your nipples with my teeth before drawing them into my mouth and tonguing them." He massages my buds gently through my Lycra top with my back arching to give him better access.

"I want to slide a finger, or two, deep inside you while I thumb your clit."

He backs this up by covering my mons with his hand and again squeezing for emphasis.

"When a climax is close to overwhelming you, I'll slide slowly into your depths. I'll fill you again and again, all the while moving faster and faster."

He pulls me closer, his thigh jammed between my legs as it had been during the Lambada. "Angie, I want to hear you scream my name as I shout yours."

Following this erotic checklist, I have to hold on to him to stay upright. If not for me riding his thigh, I'd be a puddle on the floor.

This surely has to be a dream?

In reality, the dancing was below average, and now I'm at home tucked up in bed with my imagination running riot. But, if it's all a dream, there's no limit to how badly I can behave, is there?

DREW

As good as this feels, I won't be happy until Angie's skin is tight against mine, until nothing separates us but our thoughts. Meanwhile, she's covered from head to toe in Lycra. And as sexy as this is, it's also in the way of a good time for both of us.

After dropping a gentle kiss on her neck, I whisper, "We need to get naked, and soon. I can't wait much longer."

Despite having said I can't wait, it's a lie. I'd wait a long time for a woman like Angie. I have waited a long time. She's the first woman I've entertained in this apartment, and the first I've invited into this bed.

I'm careful about who I let into my life these days. And someone who shouldn't be on the list is a woman who knows of my accident. The less involvement I have with women like that, the fewer reminders I'll have of my old life.

With Angie, I'm risking it all, and I'm not sure why. Maybe it's that dancing with her was one of the most natural, beautiful, and yet surreal experiences of my life.

Rather than a partner who's scoring points to look good, dancing with Angie had been a true partnership.

It's then I notice how quiet the room is. When Angie joined me in my dreams last night, there had been music, adding a cinematic quality to our lovemaking.

On remembering the remote is still in my pocket, I point it at the sound system on the other side of the wall and press play. As thin as the partition wall is, I know it'll work. What I'm unsure of is which track will play.

It's a gamble, and one that pans out. The opening bars of La Cumparsita, the tango track we'd danced to earlier, drift through the wall into the bedroom.

It's the perfect soundtrack, perfect for what I've got in mind.

Much as I want to peel Angie's clothes off her a layer at a time, I instead remove my t-shirt. I follow this up by holding my arms out to the side in open invitation. And she accepts with alacrity, her top soon lying on the floor next to my t-shirt.

And repeat.

Soon enough, we're both naked and open to each other's gaze. As fitted as dance clothes are, our stripping like this, while not exactly sexy, has been practical.

There had been elements of the tango about it, with both of us unable to stop ourselves from moving to the music.

On my pulling Angie back into my arms, I'm disappointed when the track ends. But then the Lambada track fills the room, my cock jumping in response.

If I'd thought it was hot when Angie rode my thigh with clothes on, it's nothing compared to now. When she drops back, rather than run my hand down the middle of her chest, I make the most of her arched back and naked breasts.

They're stunning, like the woman herself.

As I roll her nipples, my breathing hitches. I want so much from this woman, and yet if asked, I couldn't tell you what that was. When I try putting it in words, all that comes out is, "I need more..."

"More of what?" She then answers by squeezing my leg with her thighs and, after standing tall, she rubs against me. "More of this?" When she kisses me, I can feel her smile against my lips. It's something I return, joy making itself at home deep in my chest.

Unable to wait any longer, I collapse on the lush velvet coverlet, taking Angie with me. My thigh still being wedged between hers, a gentle nudge is all it takes to have her legs splayed in open invitation.

Wanting this to last as long as possible, I slide down her body to kneel on the floor at the end of the bed. She's now spread out before me as a picnic for the senses.

I run my hands up over her body, exploring curves that, in reality, are every bit as erotic as they'd been in my dreams. They're familiar, and yet they still surprise me.

On running a finger through her cleft, there's no doubt she's as ready for me as I am for her. While swirling my finger around her clit, I lean forward and drop a kiss on her belly. "Slow and steady or something more up-tempo?"

When she doesn't immediately answer, I gently squeeze her clit between my thumb and forefinger. She lifts off the bed, with her cry of pleasure filling the room.

She still hasn't answered when a Shakira track blasts out of the speakers next door, answering for her. It would appear our first time together will be fast, furious, and a lot of fun. Certainly, there's no foreplay needed for either of us to be any readier than we already are.

Rearing up off the floor, I settle between her thighs, poised, ready, and waiting.

"Drew, don't make me wait. I've wanted this from the first time I saw you dance."

And if that didn't give me permission, her breathy, "Please," speaks to me.

Her nectar coats the tip of my cock. We don't have to take it slow. Instead, I fill her in a heartbeat, every inch of her with every inch of me.

I'm in, right up to my balls, with her ecstatic moan the best welcome ever. When she follows this up by clenching her muscles around my length, I come close to losing it.

"Steady, babe, I want us to finish this dance together."

I don't make it easy on myself, or her, when I withdraw almost completely and then slam back home. And repeat. As when we'd been dancing, Angie is with me every step of the way, meeting me with hip thrusts of her own.

Never has making love been like this. It's as if she can read my body, knowing exactly when, and how, to move. We last through the end of the track, although we laugh when another up-tempo number follows.

Neither of us can slow at this point. Rather, we drive to a climax that's worthy of a standing ovation. I've not experienced anything as powerful since I was last on stage.

As we collapse in a heap in the middle of the bed, I do my best to wipe my tears without Angie seeing them.

SIX

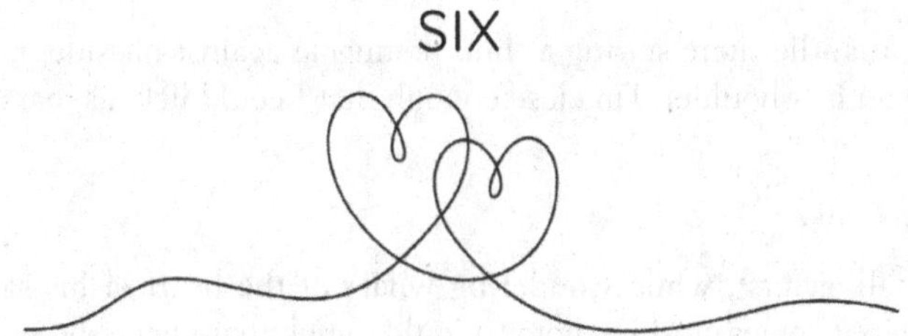

ANGIE

Spread out on blue velvet, I luxuriate in the aftershocks of a climax like I've never experienced.

Sure, I've climaxed in the past, although it would be like comparing backyard fireworks to a full-on 4th of July display. It had been spectacular. Take your breath away, worthy of a YouTube video.

And then I notice the sheen of tears on Drew's cheeks and my delight dies. I thought he enjoyed himself, too? Then I berate myself for such an idiotic notion.

Of course, he'd enjoyed himself; there'd been no hiding that.

But what emotion had set him off like this?

And will he be like most guys and not want to talk about it? He'd done his best to wipe his tears on the coverlet before I could see them. Was this simply down to it not being 'manly' to cry in front of a woman, or was there more to it?

Much as my legal career took it out of me some days, it also taught me how to ask questions; the right questions. There isn't a chance I'll open with, "Would you like to talk about it?"

Instead, I blurt out, seemingly at random, "That was kinda 4th of July, wasn't it?"

Often the trick with talking things through was starting somewhere. If nothing else, I've got his attention.

"Fourth of July?"

His question, while short, is croaky. It's as if he's holding back tears, but about what? My heart stills for a second. Or was it about whom?

Rather than lie there staring at him, I snuggle against his side, my face resting on his shoulder. I'm close enough that I could lick his tears if I so chose.

Rather, I talk.

Small talk at first, while wondering what's at the heart of his sadness. And then it comes crashing home. Could tonight have been the first time he's danced with someone since that disastrous night in New York?

If it was me, I'd also be shedding a tear or two. Actually, I'd be a blubbering mess. Of course, our dancing together would remind him of what he'd lost.

"When I saw you collapse on stage that night, I cried."

Next to me, Drew freezes, as if hewn from marble, and not flesh and blood. Eventually, he softens. "You were there?"

Rather than answer, I simply nod against his shoulder. I don't want to interrupt him. I want to give him the space to talk, although when he does, it's not what I've been expecting.

"What are you doing for lunch tomorrow?"

"Lunch? Tomorrow? Uh, nothing." My response is staccato, to match my thoughts as they pinball around inside my head. I gave him a chance to spill, and he's changed the subject, not trying to hide it, either.

"Let's head up the coast. There's a vineyard a couple of hours north, and the food is great. We can make a day of it."

There's nothing I can do to silence my lawyer's brain about what he's up to. He's avoided talking about his past, for sure. Is he also trying to get me to leave?

To go home so I'm ready for tomorrow, only for him to cancel in the morning?

There's only one way to find out for sure. "Ah, that'd be great. Since I got to town, I haven't explored much. I guess I'd better get home so I can get some sleep."

While waiting for him to agree, I hold my breath. However, he pulls me even tighter against him. "No need for that, unless you want to, of course. I can set the alarm for five."

Okay, so I was wrong about that. What else have I been wrong about? On Drew twisting me in his embrace, and his lips claiming mine, I stop compiling lists. Rather, I concentrate on returning his kiss.

Even with the alarm set for five, it's after six-thirty when Drew lets me out the back door of the dance school. An hour-and-a-half of glorious lovemaking, with each climax somehow more spectacular than the last.

On walking to my car, my legs are wobbly enough that it's as if I've been dancing all night. And I have, the only difference being I wouldn't be smiling this broadly if the tangos had been of the upright variety.

DREW

I manage an hour's fitful sleep after showing Angie out the back way. This hadn't exactly left me with a good feeling. While I'd be proud to be seen out and about with Angie, it's better I keep my private life under wraps.

The town is a hotbed of gossip, something that had come as a shock when I first moved here. I'm still not even sure why I chose the place. Maybe it was that it was as far from civilization as I could get, while still civilized.

Sadly, it's also small enough that if you so much as sneeze, half the town will hear of it before the day is out. There isn't a chance I want the gossips dissecting what Angie and I have together.

Too many of the women would be ready to compare her body to theirs and find it wanting. I won't expose her to that; I'd seen the damage that sort of spite could cause when I was dancing professionally.

It's for this reason I pick her up from where she's house sitting rather than have her meeting me at the dance school. This will also mean Juan Alcaraz doesn't see. There's something about the guy that makes me think he'd use our going out for lunch to his advantage.

Only then do I concede it's more than just lunch. It's actually a date.

Our first date? I don't see how it can be after the intimacies we'd shared last night.

As I pull up outside the small Victorian Gingerbread cottage where Angie's staying, I'm whistling along to the tune on the radio.

When she opens the door, I couldn't whistle if I tried. Other than in appreciation, that is. There'll be no trouble removing this outfit. In fact, thanks to the flowing skirt, I might not have to.

Steady on, you've got a two-hour drive ahead of you. You want to do that with a boner?

It's a sobering thought. Of course, it is only nine; we've got plenty of time.

This must show on my face, because next thing I know, Angie has grabbed my hand and is pulling me inside.

And I was right about her dress.

It's another hour before we're on the road heading north, both of us grinning broadly, our hands joined on the console of my classic Jaguar XJS.

Angie strokes the walnut trim with her free hand. "This really is a gorgeous car."

"Thanks. I picked it up when I was dancing in London for a season. I had her converted to left hand-drive when I got home."

While it had been a pain in the ass, watching Angie's simple enjoyment of the vehicle makes all that paperwork worth it.

There's nothing random about the music that plays on the trip north, with me having carefully curated every track. I've gone for easy-listening tunes that are great to drive to and a perfect foil for the white-capped sea off to our left.

Because it's mid-week, the restaurant at the vineyard is quiet. I'm therefore surprised when the waiter puts us at a small table out amongst the vines and away from anyone else.

Do we really look that ready to resort to heavy petting before the entrée is served? A check of Angie after we're seated, and I see the waiter has the right of it. Even after we've eaten, I know I'll still be hungry for more.

Dessert comes, and I'm pretty close myself, with Angie's foot firmly lodged in my groin. Thank goodness the snow-white tablecloth is as long as it is.

Despite all this, we need more privacy for what I've got planned. We're finishing up dessert when I decide to test the waters. "Are you in a hurry to get back to town this afternoon?"

As casual as my question has been, Angie's toes gripping my cock tell me she knows exactly what I'm talking about. Rather than answer immediately, she leans to the side and gets her purse off the ground.

After setting it on her lap, she opens it.

"I'm all good." She reaches inside her purse and grabs something. "I packed." She then stretches across the table and drops whatever it is in my lap. Before I've unfurled the small bundle, the waiter arrives to clear our plates.

On straightening the scrap of fabric, I see it's a black lace G-string.

"Can I get you folks anything else to eat? We've got a great cheese board. Perhaps some coffee?"

I'm waiting for him to ask if we want a room, but he doesn't. Unable to talk, I simply shake my head. I can't speak and fight coming at the same time.

We make it to a nearby motel, only just. Minutes after stumbling into our room, I'm buried deep in Angie with her holding me tight in the ultimate embrace.

Only after I've got myself under control, do I start a slow-and-steady pumping. With the friction having every nerve ending screaming for release, it takes all my control not to lose it.

The faster I move, the better it gets for both of us, with her soon wrapping her legs behind my back. It's a move designed to take me deeper, and it works exquisitely.

My balls are getting quite the hammering and yet I couldn't be happier. Under me, Angie writhes and moans, her breath quickening, her skin flushed.

When her body surrenders, her muscles ripple along my length, milking a response out of me. A couple of extra hard drives, and I give into the orgasm I've been holding back on.

Every muscle in my body screams in ecstasy as I shout my release. It's warmed me as no rave review ever did. Rather than pull free, I drop forward and lay along Angie's length.

Only then do I see an unknown emotion swirling in her cool gray eyes. It's not something I've seen before.

So many of the women I've slept with in the past have treated sex like a competition, or performance art. Never able to forget they're artists. With Angie I get that I'm in the presence of the real woman and this has me nervous.

Not about my performance because it's obvious she's enjoyed it as much as I have. My worry is that she might see what lies beneath my physical scars.

SEVEN

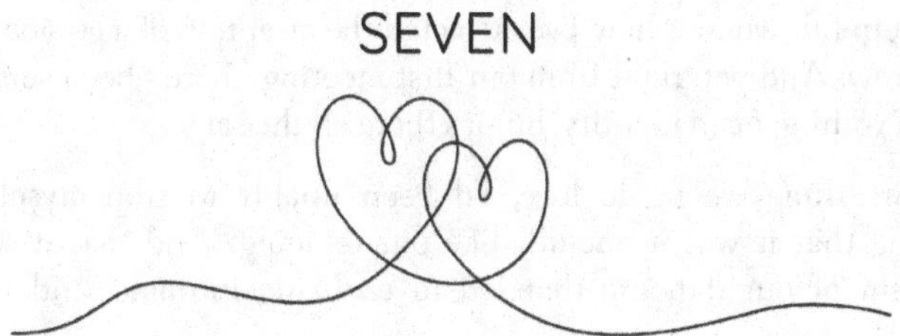

ANGIE

On parking down the side street next to the dance school, excitement bubbles through me. I can't think of a better way to spend an evening than dancing with Drew in the private studio, followed by mind-blowing sex.

It's getting better every night, too. Our dancing is more intuitive than ever, as is our lovemaking. I never have to spell out what I want, because he knows, almost before I do sometimes.

And it's the same for me with knowing what drives him wild. Even better is that when he's having a good time, I get to go along for the ride. Had it been something I instinctively knew when I'd watched him on stage all those times?

Or is he like this with every woman? Then I shake my head at my foolish musings. Hah, of course he is. He'd trained for years on how to move his body, to use it as a tool of visual and physical pleasure.

Sadly, I don't see my time enjoying his company lasting long, so I'm making the most of it while I can. I'm risking heartbreak for sure, but it would hurt as much to walk away.

I tap on the back door twice and Drew opens it, with light spilling out into the alleyway, leaving me feeling exposed. A moment later, I'm inside and in Drew's arms, with the back door slammed shut. His lips claim mine in a kiss that feeds my soul.

Never in my life had I thought I'd be happy to be unemployed, but I am now. If I was spending tomorrow in court or going through case notes, there wasn't a chance I could spend the night dancing and making love.

Despite my intention of making the most of it, as we dance that night, I can't help but wonder how I've attracted the attention of a gorgeous man like Drew. And yet, right from our first meeting, there's been something there. Nothing I can identify, but it's there all the same.

The first time we made love, I'd been unable to stop myself from thinking that it was a one-off, like our dancing. And that it was the eroticism of our dancing that led to us being intimate, and nothing more.

The more I think that he's chosen me because I'm an outsider, the worse my dancing gets. As if a man this gorgeous, and who's had his pick of dancing partners, would be content with me.

Lost as I am in this downward spiral of self-loathing, I miss a step, and the unthinkable happens. "Oh, oh, I'm so sorry. I'm not sure what happened."

Well, I do, but it's nothing I'll admit to.

I'm left dealing with Drew's pained expression as he reacts to me stepping on the arch of his foot with my full weight. I've only done this once before, and that was when I first started dancing as a kid.

Mortified doesn't describe how I'm feeling. Drew, not mired with negative thoughts, simply says, "Hey babe, if you're not into it, shall we call it an early night?"

My worst nightmare playing out in real time. I'm left to nod mutely in response. I guess I should be lucky that I've had four nights with the man of my dreams. Four nights of absolute bliss, each night better than the one before.

I'm devastated. To wake cradled in Drew's arms is a habit I'd happily enjoy for a lifetime. Four nights of bliss that will ruin any other man for me. I smile wanly, thinking about how to say goodbye without sounding too pathetic.

I twist in his arms, ready to grab my overnight bag, fly down the stairs and out into the night. But he won't let go of my hand.

"Hey, where do you think you're going? Even if you don't feel like dancing, that doesn't mean we can't spend the evening together. There's bound to be something on Netflix we can check out."

I'm so confused. That he wants me to stay is obvious, his words having a pleading quality to them I've not heard before. I have to swallow deeply before I'm capable of speech. "That sounds lovely." While I've outwardly agreed, my mind is still a muddle of scenarios about how our night will play out.

I'm definitely in uncharted territory, not understanding where I stand, or lay, with this gorgeous man. Am I fooling myself? Or is he fooling me? Am I opening myself up for more heartbreak than I can deal with?

Am I prepared to risk it all for a few more nights of bliss?

Yes, yes, I am.

With this in mind, I follow Drew as he leads the way over to the door to his apartment and my temporary Nirvana.

There's nothing Nirvana-like about it on waking the following morning. It's far lighter than it should be at six o'clock. Half asleep, I roll onto my side, reaching out for my phone on the nightstand.

A second later, my eyes snap wide open. Nine-thirty!!!

I could have sworn I'd set the alarm, so I'd be up and away before the school opened at ten. Another look at the screen and I can see I'd set it; it's simply failed to ring.

I need to move if I'm to avoid running into the receptionist or one of the dance teachers. Not because I'm ashamed to be with Drew, but that he wants to keep our relationship quiet.

On finally scrambling free of the tangled sheets, the word relationship rings loud in my head. Is that what we've got? Or is it more of a casual hook-up? "Drew, wake up. It's after nine-thirty. We slept in!"

In my shock, I've shouted. This sees him sitting bolt upright in bed, looking gloriously disheveled. I can see when my words cut through the sleep that still clouds him.

DREW

Sheesh, this is not how I saw this morning panning out. Usually we wake around six and then spend a leisurely hour or two making love before Angie leaves.

There'll be none of that today. Not if I want to keep our relationship quiet.

Do we have a relationship? She's not in town for long and has made no secret of the career waiting for her in LA.

Does she even have time for me in her life?

Do I want to make space for her in mine?

Our dressing this morning is every bit as frantic as our undressing had been last night. I hope there's no-one around downstairs because given the state of us, there's no hiding what we've been up to.

We both appear well bedded, meaning we can't even fake an early dance session.

Despite wanting to hurry, I stop Angie at the top of the stairs to listen out for anyone moving downstairs. Only when I'm sure the coast is clear, do I race down the stairs, with Angie right behind me.

I don't want her to leave in what equates to a walk of shame. Without a kiss, without us making plans for tonight as we usually would. While not ready to go public, neither do I want her to think I'm embarrassed to be seen with her.

And yet this is exactly how I'm behaving.

Her hurrying away with head hanging low has me wondering if I'm not alone in wanting to keep our liaison quiet.

Is she yet another dancing diva who wants to crow they've had Andrew Morton-Huxley? And maybe this had been part of her appeal for me, at least initially. Was it down to my still wanting to be lauded and revered as I had when at the height of my career?

Is our relationship really all about me stroking my ego, of reliving my glory days?

It's a sobering thought. It's also one that has me aware there's more to Angie than someone to bolster my flagging ego. My thoughts solidify slowly, to the point she's about to disappear around the corner of the alleyway.

Only then do I call out, "See you tonight?"

She slams to a stop.

Her saying yes should have been a given, but there'd been something off about her last night and again this morning. I hold my breath while waiting for her to respond. Her nod is so brief and non-committal that I'm left in doubt.

I'm about to close the back door when Juan Alcaraz appears from the other direction. His knowing smirk says he saw Angie leave.

"Well, well, well, so much for you saying we shouldn't fraternize with the students."

He then keeps walking to follow Angie, and I see red. I don't think twice. Leaving the door wide open behind me, I follow in his footsteps. I'll protect Angie, no matter the cost.

Out on the side street, I watch Alcaraz cross the road, making for Angie's silver BMW parked opposite. What is a surprise is that Angie's simply sitting there, the engine running, staring straight ahead.

She's obviously startled when Juan knocks on the window right next to her head.

What is of interest is that she also appears surprised by what he says after she opens the window. I don't hear all he says, but his, "Don't be late. I'll be waiting for you, baby," is damning enough.

As shocked as I am, I don't hear her response before she stomps on the gas and roars away. Was this because she spotted me and didn't want to be caught hooking up with another dancer?

Alcaraz turns, and on seeing me, smiles broadly, although this doesn't make it as far as his eyes. "We can't have you keeping all the candy to yourself."

Rather than watch my rival sauntering back to the dance school, I follow Angie's progress down the road. It's seeing her brake lights and indicator go on soon after, that reminds me how close her house-sit is.

Rather than waste time getting my car out of the garage down the alleyway, I take off. Some things are worth chasing.

I haven't run this fast since my injury and despite a solid year's physio, I'm nervous about doing damage. It doesn't help that I haven't warmed up or that I'm wearing loafers.

Because of this, I slow from a sprint to a steady jog. I'd rather get there a couple of minutes later with my Achilles still intact. As I plod toward where Angie is staying, I have time to think things through.

She wouldn't have agreed to meet up with Juan, would she? No-one could fake repugnance as Angie had when talking of the Latin dance instructor. There was also how she'd responded to me last night to consider.

When an orgasm overwhelms Angie, there's no hiding it. Her arching against me, desperate to get closer, is all too real. Even an award-winning actress couldn't fake a response like that.

As I get closer, I see she's sitting in her car in the driveway, staring straight ahead. She's exactly as she was when Alcaraz knocked on her car window earlier.

I hope she's okay?

My worrying about her brings it home to me how much I care for her. Despite wanting to keep my past fame a secret, I want to shout my feelings for this woman from the rooftops.

The one thing I have no way of knowing is how she'll react to that. What if I am just another dance bucket list item for her? What if she is meeting up with Juan later today?

EIGHT

ANGIE

After parking in the driveway at Sally's house, I don't immediately get out of the car; my mind is whirring too much for that.

I replay the voicemail from my boss in LA, listening to it properly this time. As distressed as I'd been after leaving Drew, I'd only heard half of it the first time around.

It was because of this that I'd recorded some notes. This was what I'd been doing when Juan Alcaraz knocked on my car window, scaring the life out of me.

And then there's the Latin teacher's nasty offer to consider. Hideous enough, I hadn't even responded. Instead, I'd stomped on the gas without looking back, desperate to get away from him.

That aside, my biggest dilemma is whether Drew had meant it when he'd asked me to return tonight. Does he want me back for dancing, or simply sex?

I wouldn't be averse to either if it weren't for how cool he'd been this morning. He'd been intent on hustling me out the back door as fast as he could. Worried people would see me leaving.

It was hardly the fairytale ending to yet another night of loving words and actions. While Drew's behavior has left me feeling rejected, the voicemail from my boss in LA has me feeling something else altogether.

Isn't a partnership in the law firm what I've been working toward? So what if it's because the firm's largest client had insisted on it?

A partnership was a partnership, wasn't it?

Unless it was a romantic partnership, that is.

But I'd be a fool to turn down Collins, French, and Brown's offer on the slim chance I might have something with Drew. After finally turning off the engine, I grab my overnight bag off the passenger seat and open my door.

I then get my second fright of the morning when I find Drew right next to me. He's out of breath, as if he's been running for his life.

"What are you doing here? What's wrong?"

He takes a couple of deep breaths before responding. "Please, don't accept that offer. I'm sorry I acted like an idiot before."

"But how did you..." Then logic takes over. There's no way Drew can know about the partnership with the law firm. The only other offer I've received this morning is Juan's.

But how could he know about that? He wasn't there. Or was he?

Then I remember that after looking briefly at Juan, I'd gone back to staring straight ahead. Anything was better than being that up-close and personal with him. Because of all this, Drew could well have been there and I wouldn't have known.

And if he was, how much did he hear? Juan's head was almost inside the car when he hit me with that offer, and a healthy dose of garlic breath.

The other thing I'm unsure of is why Drew doesn't want me accepting. Is it down to jealousy? Or is it because he's worried I'll say something to Alcaraz about his past?

Unaware of my internal machinations, Drew's brow wrinkles in response to my saying, "Relax, I wouldn't say anything to him about your past."

I then hold up my phone and waggle it about. "And anyway, they want me back at work." I have another look at the text. "Tomorrow!"

Rather than be pleased, as I've expected, Drew's shoulders drop. He bites his bottom lip as if to stop from saying anything, but does anyway. "I thought you hated that job. Didn't you say it was slowly killing you?"

Of course he's right, I said exactly that. But, having devoted a sizable chunk of my life to law, I can't simply leave it all behind, can I?

My parents, both lawyers, would flip, especially when I was turning down a partnership.

Then I simply shrug, before throwing out a flippant, "Hey, we all like to feel wanted."

He steps forward. "What if I want you?" There's a pause before he adds, "Need you?"

He looks down briefly in response to my overnight bag having slipped from my nerveless fingers. He then drags me into a tight embrace. His lips find mine and I return the kiss like a drowning woman. All thoughts of my career momentarily wiped clean.

When a passing car beeps, Drew smiles against my lips, but rather than pull away as I've expected, he holds me even tighter.

He eventually breaks the kiss and looks down at me, his eyes dark with passion. "I know this is super-fast, but I'd like to give it a shot. "That is, I'd like to give US a shot."

Super-fast? Is he kidding? It's supersonic, and yet it's not. Despite having only met him less than a week back, I've known Drew for most of my life. Well, not known him, but known OF him, which counts for something. Doesn't it?

There'd also been the sense we'd already met when he walked out into reception, when I knew we hadn't. Was I ready to throw all that away for a career I'd have to give up if I ever wanted babies?

And I do, so very much.

DREW

Despite having asked Angie to stick around on a whim, I have no regrets.

Never has a woman felt so right in my arms. I want to see if the same is true of having her in my life. And no sneaking around in the dark, either.

"But what about the partnership? My old firm..."

She waggles her phone again, as if this explains everything.

I've got a bad feeling about this, but ask anyway. "Your what?"

"My firm in LA has offered me a partnership. I'll be the youngest ever, and the only female."

Her eyes widen as the enormity of the offer makes itself known, and with good cause. Even I'm aware a partnership is a big deal; I've watched enough legal TV shows to know.

That aside, there's nothing soap opera about the offer for Angie. This has me holding her even tighter. I care about her. I want to protect her, and comfort her when she needs it, which she obviously does right now.

What I don't know is whether she'll find my offer the more tempting of the two, or is that three? I still don't know what Alcaraz was offering back at her car.

Whichever one she chooses, it has to be her decision. If she turns me down, of course, it'll hurt like hell. But what was that saying? That's right, if you love something, set it free.

Until such a time as that happens, I'm hanging on as tight as I can.

"I can't help you with that decision, Angie. All I know is that I want to give us a shot." I pull back enough that we once again make eye contact. "And not behind closed doors either, but out in the open."

And I mean it. No more keeping a low profile. With this woman at my side, I'm prepared to take on the world.

Only she doesn't appear to be in step with me on this.

She dithers, something I've not seen to date. She then eases out of my embrace.

"It's just that Juan...".

She doesn't need to say anything else, although her choosing him over me comes as a shock. It's because of this blow that I don't even say goodbye. I simply turn and walk away. I don't have it in me to speak, let alone beg as I want to.

She's decided, and I've lost. She'll soon find out she's one of many where that sleaze is concerned. Will I be around to pick up the pieces?

I'm not sure. While my love for her is stronger than I'd have thought possible, is it up to a test of that sort? I just wish I'd had the nerve to tell her I loved her before it was too late.

As I trudge back up the street, my mind swirls with thoughts of how I could have gotten it so wrong. How I could have mis-read Angie as badly as I have.

Was she choosing Juan over me because I was no longer world famous?

It sure feels that way.

It had taken longer than it should to realize my glory days of dating were over after my forced retirement. I didn't realize the pulling power of stardom.

Of course, it's only now I'm also realizing that every single one of those relationships had been shallow.

The other thing I'm now ready to admit is that I'd been just as shallow. Basking in the adoration rather than getting to know any of those women properly.

Where else have I gone wrong in my life?

NINE

ANGIE

What is up with Drew? After saying he wanted us to give it a go, he didn't even say goodbye. He simply turned and took off. Was it something I said?

My mind muddled, I have to go through everything up to his abrupt departure multiple times, before I understand. My hand flies to my mouth, but there's no way to take my words back now.

"No! No, no, no!"

I'm ready to kick myself. If the partners at my law firm could see how badly I'd just messed up, they'd be rescinding their partnership offer, pronto.

Meanwhile, Drew's hurt is clear by how he's marching up the street, back to Dynamic Five. There's nothing cat-like about his movements now. Every step is jerky and full of pain, and it's my fault.

Such has been my confusion over his abrupt departure, that he's gotten quite the head-start. His legs being as long as they are, he's certainly moving too fast for me to catch up on foot.

Rather than leave my overnight bag in the middle of the driveway, I toss it back inside the car. I'm reversing out of the driveway seconds later.

I pull up just as he turns into the alleyway at the rear of the dance school. When he slams the back door in my face, I'm hoping it's because he hasn't seen me, rather than because he has.

I think about thumping on the door, but then realize I hadn't heard it being locked. Maybe it's kept open during the day for students to come and go?

Despite this, I consider walking around to the front entrance to avoid sneaking in the back way. Then I decide the longer I leave Drew alone with his thoughts, the worse they'll get. At least this is how it would be if it were me doing the thinking.

Sure enough, when I push on the back door, it opens silently. After inching inside, I'm greeted by the sight of Juan Alcaraz and Drew facing off. The receptionist stands transfixed next to them.

It takes a second to realize Drew's rigid stance is now down to anger rather than pain. On catching the threats the Latin teacher is firing at him, I'm soon just as angry.

No, make that incandescent with rage, with every ounce directed at Juan Alcaraz. The creep is about to be hit with a combination of this anger, my years in court and me protecting the man I love.

And just as in court, here evidence will be paramount.

This has me grabbing my phone out of my jacket pocket. I then find the notes I'd been recording when Alcaraz knocked on my window. As tempted as I am to march over and insert myself between the two men, I wait.

Soon enough, Alcaraz shuts up just long enough for me to push the play button. Before this, I'd made sure the volume was up as loud as it can go.

Let's see if Drew thinks as little of Juan's offer as I had.

DREW

As inward facing as my thoughts have been, I'm back at Dynamic Five with little recollection of the walk.

I'm shocked to find Juan Alcaraz with his arms wrapped tight around Natalie. He's doing his best to kiss her. However, this is no loving embrace, with Natalie struggling to be free.

It is exactly the diversion I need. Rather than slow, I stride the length of reception and slam my hand down on Juan's shoulder.

"Get your hands off her, now!" My voice is low, my words full of menace. Enough is enough. He's already messed things up with Angie. I'll be damned if I'll stand by and see him effectively cheating on her by forcing himself on Natalie.

Even though Angie's chosen him over me, I won't see her hurt. Neither woman deserves to be treated that way. My determination to be rid of him has me acknowledging I'll take the classes myself if I have to.

Not my first choice, but I don't want Natalie leaving because of Juan pestering her. I also want all reminders of Angie gone from my sight. Juan's personality is such that he'd take every opportunity to remind me I'd lost out to him.

After helping Natalie free herself, I'm seething with rage, but being a lover, not a fighter, I simply say, "Get your stuff, Alcaraz, and get out of here."

Juan's shock is over in a second. "Hah, and what are you going to do for a teacher of Latin? There's no-one of my caliber in this godforsaken place."

His smirk when he adds, "Is there?" all while peering at me intently, tells me he might know my true identity. I have nothing to hide. It's just that life is easier without constant reminders of what I'd lost.

Of course, Alcaraz doesn't know any of this.

His spitting out, "I'll start a school of my own. I'll ruin you," has me reconsidering the lover, not a fighter part of my personality. I've worked hard to establish the school.

"You'll end up with nothing, not even the delectable Angie. Why do you think she's so tired when she visits you at night? It's because I've had her every which way during the day. Sure, I've had better, but she'll do for now. Why only yesterday afternoon..."

The asshole is lying about this, with Angie and me having spent the day together. How dare he talk about her like that? I want to wipe the smile off his face, and then some.

Once again, Juan's voice reverberates around reception.

There's then a moment's confusion when I see his lips aren't moving. Only then do I realize the voice is coming from behind me and has a tinny quality to it.

Angie is there, holding her phone up, making it easier for us all to hear Juan's threat.

Unless she sleeps with him regularly, he'll tell every arts reporter in the country how to find me. He'll tell them how I'm reduced to teaching dance to snot-nosed kids and middle-aged women.

Natalie is the first to react to the recording. "But, but that's blackmail."

Angie and I answer in concert with, "No, it's coercion."

Angie is on her own when she glares at Juan and adds, "And it's illegal."

TEN

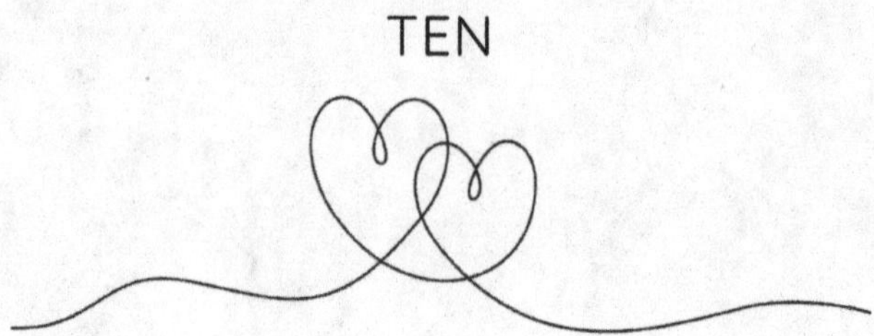

ANGIE

Despite my alluding to Juan's activities being illegal, the guy stands tall, arms folded, belligerent in the face of the damning evidence.

I'd seen it in court many times, and it hadn't worked then, either. It was as if their bravado would somehow make everything go away.

Well, it wouldn't work today, either. Not with me, and definitely not with Drew if his expression is anything to go on. Shock and anger mar his usually handsome face.

"Do you want to press charges, Angie?"

I shake my head vehemently. "I wouldn't waste the court's time on this creep."

Rather than leave as told to, Juan glares at Drew. "And what about your dirty little secret? What about that? I've got footage of you, and this one, dancing."

He looks slyly in my direction and mouths, "And more," causing my blood to run cold.

He again scowls at Drew. "What would the arts community do if they learned you were hiding out in this backwater?" He narrows his eyes and continues. "If this cow won't sleep with me, how much are you willing to pay to keep it quiet?"

My eyes widen in response to this. Has he just threatened Drew with two witnesses present? Not only is he a lowlife, he's an idiot. I'm having second thoughts about not pressing charges. I'd have a field day in court with this guy.

He's the sort to admit to his crimes simply because of how cool he thought it made him look. Juan looks anything but cool when Drew's fist connects with his jaw.

In between rubbing his knuckles, Drew shouts, "Get out of here! We are through!"

Juan's botoxed visage does its best to sneer before he grinds out, "You're making a big mistake, Morton. You fire me and I'll ruin you, because I can, you know."

I've had enough of him and his threats. I step forward and force myself between the two men. Rather than face Drew, I give Juan my full attention, shoving back on his shoulders with every ounce of my anger.

I then take delight in running through the charges I'll be pressing. That I do so in legal terms has Juan looking at me twice.

Never underestimate an angry woman, particularly not one with an honors law degree. Drew squeezes my shoulder before dropping a kiss on the back of my neck. Well, a law degree, and a good man backing her up.

Rather than skulk away as I've expected, Juan pushes me to the side and gets right up in Drew's face. "You've not heard the last of me, Huxley. Not by a long shot."

He twists around and makes for the front door. The last thing he shouts on leaving is, "You'll regret firing me, big time!"

It's only after he's left and I'm being hugged by Drew that I'm able to think back on his various threats. By now, my lawyer's brain is firing on all cylinders.

It doesn't take long to realize Drew and I only ever danced in the private studio upstairs. And what was it Juan had mouthed about 'more'?

"He said he'd filmed us?" I point up toward Drew's private studio before swinging my finger toward his apartment.

Thanks to the warehouse on the other side of the alleyway, there was no way for Alcaraz to film us from outside. That means...

I see when Drew comes to the same conclusion. His expression saying he'd happily smack Juan again if he were around. He'll have a fight on his hands on this front, because I've never been as angry—or violated —ever.

My dancing with Drew was magical. Knowing Alcaraz had been spying on us, has taken the shine off somewhat.

DREW

I still can't believe the lowlife has left. Sadly, I doubt this is the last I'll see of him. There's no way he'll up and disappear. Guys like him never did.

I've not given voice to this when Natalie starts a slow clap behind me. "Bravo! He's been asking for that for a long time."

It turns out the rumors around town are rife about Juan targeting women. Specifically, older married women with secrets, and a healthy bank balance. Lucky for Angie is her having had her phone set to record when Alcaraz tried it with her.

We don't get to discuss it further thanks to a gaggle of women rushing in the front door. The subject of their animated discussion is none other than Juan, who they've just passed.

"Does this mean there's no class today?" is the most common question, with all eyes on me. I don't even think twice, instead I nudge Angie with my shoulder.

"What do you say, feel like a dance?" A moment later, and she's walking toward the back door. How could I have gotten it so wrong?

"I need to grab my things out of the car."

The local ladies take some convincing as to my abilities to teach their Latin dance class. Thank goodness for Angie at my side, because after some of our flashier moves, our little audience is gushing.

"Juan was never that good!" says one. "He said in order for him to shine, he needed a world-class partner," adds another.

After class, we hear more of Juan's extortion, with a few women opening up after Angie had shared her experience.

Meanwhile, I've been on the other side of the studio pretending to select music for the next class. Nothing could be further from the truth, with me doing my best to listen in.

Damn the man, I've been lucky not to have the school shut down because of his behavior. I feel responsible for the women who've been his victims. While two or three have declared they're ready to press charges, the majority simply nod in support.

Who knew what Alcaraz had on the quiet ones that they're unwilling to talk? Letting him go is no longer an option.

It's something Angie and I discuss in bed that afternoon, but only after we've scoured the room for hidden cameras. On none coming to light, we breathe a sigh of relief.

The same hadn't been true of my private studio next door. I'd wanted to smash the half-dozen cameras we'd found. However, Angie had been adamant we remove them carefully, all while avoiding fingerprints.

To her, it was yet more evidence of Juan's nefarious activities.

Cameras aside, I'm relieved we're going public, with no need to scuttle around in the dark anymore. Making love to Angie with the sun streaming in through the windows above the bed had been sexy as hell.

Every glorious inch of her on display, every inch as wonderful as I'd imagined in the subdued light of evening. Even more of a turn-on had been her loving glances as she returned the favor.

And then I had to ruin it all by asking, "So, the partnership, are you going to take it?"

Next to me, Angie stills, before she stutters out, "Have... you changed your mind? About us?" As well as hesitant, her words are low. I need to think about what she's said to be sure I've heard her right.

"What? No! Hell no! I meant every word I said this morning about you and me."

After rolling onto her side, Angie smiles at me. "Thank goodness, because I've already told my old company they should've thought about the partnership before forcing me to take a sabbatical."

"So you're staying?"

Her smile fades, and her brow knots, causing a lump to form in my stomach.

"I am, but I'll need to find somewhere to live. From the little I've heard, the property market here is tight thanks to people wanting second homes at the beach."

This doesn't surprise me. It was part of the reason I'd converted half the second-floor into an apartment. "Well, you could always stay with me here."

I can't believe I'm asking a woman to move in with me after knowing her for all of a week. And yet, as when I'd said I wanted her in my life, I know it's the right choice.

Being with Angie is as easy as breathing, perhaps even easier.

Her blinding smile is answer enough. It would appear I'm not the only one who knows when something is right.

And just like that, my years of hiding from life are over, and I've got Angie to thank for it. However, rather than feeling exposed as I've always thought I would, I feel loved and accepted.

Despite no longer being Andrew Morton-Huxley and simply Drew Morton, I couldn't be happier.

EPILOGUE

ANGIE

On looking out at my students, I can't believe how far my life has come in a few short months.

My sabbatical from my old firm ended without me returning. Instead of being run into the ground by demanding clients and bosses, I've got a whole new life, and a budding career as a dance teacher.

While I'm not fully qualified, I have enough experience to teach, with my women-only Latin fitness classes, a big hit. The nicest thing about those was looking out and seeing a few curvy girls dancing like no-one was watching.

Gone are the courtroom performance anxieties and constant worry of impressing my parents. While they were furious about my decision to quit the law, when they'd seen how happy I was, they couldn't argue.

After finishing the house sitting, I'd moved in with Drew. This had made little difference with me spending most nights at his apartment, anyway. However, I'd promised Sally I'd stay at her brother's until the new tenants arrived, and so I had.

Rather than sell my old apartment in LA, I've put my belongings into storage and am renting it out as an Airbnb. I've been working on Drew's reluctance to enter competitions. If I'm successful, we'll need a place in town now and then.

I'd had to get quite pushy to get him to see a local physio for regular treatments, with this already paying off. Any twinges in his Achilles are a rare thing these days.

While no longer up to the punishing demands of a full-time professional career, he's up to competing at a state level with me.

How many competitions had I entered with lack-luster partners only to be beaten for the top spot? Too many to count, that's for sure. With Drew at my side, we'll be unbeatable.

Any other thoughts of competitions flee when I see Drew through the glass panel in the studio door. He's impatiently tapping his watch.

Much as I want to stop the music and send my students on their way, I allow the track to end. I wrap things up as quickly as any woman can with a passionate man waiting for her upstairs.

Only this isn't the case today, with Drew waiting for me outside in reception. However, his smile says he's still got a surprise for me. After wrapping his arms tight around me, he rests his chin on top of my head, waiting for the students to leave.

They take their own sweet time, booking more classes, and indulging in some retail therapy at our new shop. After the debacle I'd had with the things I'd bought off the internet, I knew the importance of being able to try items on first.

I didn't toss the skirt though, because Drew loves it when I wear it, especially when that's all I wear. Well, that, and a smile. I smile a lot these days.

Only after the last student has left, along with Natalie the receptionist, do I turn to Drew, excitement bubbling in my chest. "So, what have you got planned?"

I'm in love with a very imaginative man, something that has nothing off-limits in the bedroom when he puts his mind to it. Anyone who's capable of award-winning choreography will never bore in bed.

DREW

The expectation on Angie's face is enough for laughter to bubble deep in my chest.

"All in good time, darling, all in good time. First, I want to show you something..." I pause for dramatic effect before adding, "Something else, that is."

This has her laughter matching my own. "Well, show me then." She pulls a cheerleader pose and taps her toe, all while grinning.

"Hah, impatient much?" After hooking my arm through hers, I steer her toward the end of reception closest to the front door. We come to a stop in front of a large glass cabinet that hadn't been there when her class started an hour ago.

While the case is new, the trophies and awards it contains are not.

And they're not all mine either, with Angie well represented with silverware.

She takes her gaze off the case long enough to stare at me. "You have been busy."

Her words are neutral and so I'm unsure if she's pleased or not. "Hey you should be proud of your achievements."

Funny, but my saying this has me realizing I'm proud of my own.

Okay, so short of starting a dance company, I'll never dance professionally again, but that doesn't mean I can't dance. I squeeze Angie to my side. "Until I went through all that stuff your mom sent, I didn't realize what a stalker you were."

And it's true; Angie owns more promotional posters of me than I do myself. When she attended one of my performances, it had been a big deal for her, whereas for me, it was just another night. Even if I had bothered to collect them, I wouldn't have thought to get them framed.

It never occurred to me that my career would end so quickly, and certainly not as dramatically as it had.

"Come on. Let's lock up so I can show you that other thing."

Upstairs, Angie is in as much of a hurry as I am, keen to strip and get in the shower. I love this part of our day, when we've got the building to ourselves.

It had been quite the shock to find Juan's cameras. After locating the first half-dozen, I'd had a security company come in to check we'd gotten them all.

A bigger shock had been the two recording devices found in the ladies' changing room. It must have been these that garnered Alcaraz the means to extort my students.

That had been a step too far for Angie, who'd insisted I press charges. She'd pressed charges of her own regarding coercion. While a lot of the other victims refused to come forward, Angie had no such compunction. She'd been more than happy to step up for the other victims.

Even if Alcaraz avoids prison, he'll never teach dance again. I've made sure of this, putting the word out on the sly. Nothing in writing, with a word in the right ears being more than enough.

We've got quite the lather going when I pull Angie tight against me. "Have I told you lately how much I love you?"

She smiles up at me shyly. However, there's nothing shy about the way her slippery hand tightens around my cock. "You might have. Have I told you how much I love you?"

She squeezes harder, before sliding her hand up and down my length, my pulse thumping in my ears, deafening me to all else.

I'm not missing out on all the action, though. "Angie, have I shown you?" I run my hand down her front, before sliding my fingers in amongst her curls. No resistance, just heat, and her dancing in my arms and opening herself to me fully.

As sexy as her dancing is, I put a stop to things. "Wait. If I take you in here, we'll both need to see the physio."

After turning off the water, we stumble through to the bedroom, neither of us caring that we're still wet and soapy. Nope, definitely no complaints from me on that front, or the back, and sides.

I slide inside her seconds after we come to rest on the bed, my cock slick from her earlier ministrations. And damn, it feels good. Not just physically, but also emotionally. All those years I thought my life was full, when really it had been missing the most important thing of all.

Heart and the love of a good woman.

This woman.

My Angie.

DANCE

Locals, Angie Bennington and Drew Morton have done it again, taking out the top Pro-Am award for Latin at the California Open.

The co-owners of Dynamic Five Dance have also added Latin for Seniors to their already packed schedule.

As Angie Bennington says, "Dance is fabulous for your overall health no matter what your age, or shape."

Bettany is a doggy daycare owner who's being run ragged by her charges. Dax is a personal trainer who loves a challenge. It will be anyone's guess who'll be the first to lie down and roll over when they get together.

ONE

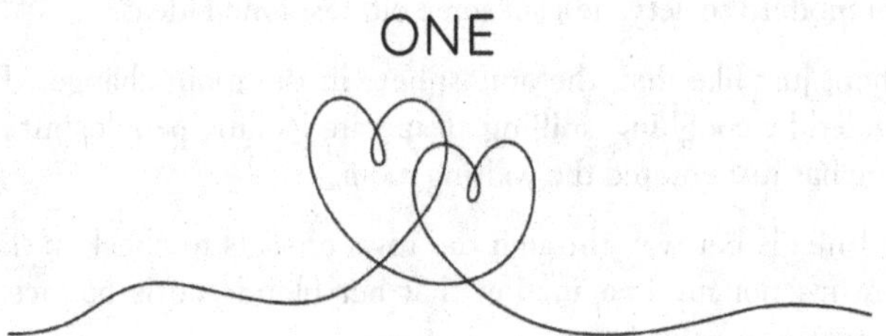

DAX

A doctor's waiting room is not where I'd choose to spend my time. Disease posters plaster the walls, and ancient magazines litter every flat surface.

And don't even get me started on the seats. You'd think, considering their reputation for running late, there'd be more padding.

The only reason I'm here is because my sister Charlotte works as a doctor at this practice. I haven't needed to see a doctor in over three years.

I'm not even looking forward to lunch with my big sis, knowing exactly how the conversation will go. It's always the same; that I should use my brain in pursuit of a serious career, not mucking around with fitness apps.

Never mind, I'm making more from my fitness apps than anyone else in the family does from a *proper* job. My father, in particular, frowns on my chosen profession, although that's not what he calls it.

A surgeon himself, he considers any career without an Ivy League degree attached to it as beneath contempt. He's never understood that being cooped up inside is as a slow death to me. Despite having the brains to be a doctor, helping people in that way doesn't appeal.

Being a personal trainer, I not only help people, I also get outside in the fresh air. I work as hard as everyone else in the family, just differently.

And it's still not enough for my father. Or even my sister, or mom, with all of them openly wondering when I'll stop 'fooling about' and get a proper job. Well, I've got news for them, and it's all bad.

Strange, but if I'd been born female, my father would have deemed my career acceptable. For someone who professes to have a finger on the pulse of modern society, he's got some old-fashioned ideas.

And then, just like that, the atmosphere in the room changes. I'm still surrounded by coughing, sniffing, desperate looking people, but a ray of sunshine has just entered the waiting room.

As she threads her way through the rows of seats to check in, I watch. I'm sure it's not my imagination that her blonde curls bounce as she walks, creating a halo of sorts.

This in concert with her dimples, bright blue eyes, and deliciously curvy body gives her an almost angelic air. For this reason alone, I shouldn't find her attractive, and yet I wouldn't mind helping this one get rid of her halo.

While she completes check in, I contemplate how I'd go about this, an exercise that leaves me sitting awkwardly.

She turns and acknowledges what I already know. The only free seat is the one next to me. Suddenly I'm hoping my sister is running later than usual.

As blondie makes her way across the room, I'm unable to keep my eyes off her, taking in every inch. Perhaps the sexiest thing about this woman is that she owns her curves.

The buttercup yellow dress is a snug fit; bringing attention to places I'd want her to hide if she was my girlfriend.

On her sitting next to me, I'm enveloped by a familiar scent. Perhaps it's that my sister or mom use the same fragrance? It's the sheer volume of dog hair on her dress that gives it away.

It's the doggy shampoo I use on Stella, my Staffordshire bull terrier, a sometimes misunderstood breed. And yet Stella is a complete love bug, without a mean bone in her body.

I clear my throat, causing the woman to turn slightly in my direction. It's enough of an opening for me. "Like dogs, do you?"

Rather than answer, she brushes furiously at her dress, for all the good it does. I know from personal experience how tenacious dog hair can be. Without a proper brush, she hasn't a hope of getting rid of it.

To help ease any embarrassment, I continue. "I've got a Staffy, myself. Stella sheds like a maniac around this time of the year."

This has her turning fully in her seat, and holding her hand out. When I take it in mine and stare into her baby blues, I'm lost.

BETTANY

After checking in, I turn and scan the waiting room for a spare seat.

There's only one, and it's next to a guy with go-to-bed eyes and a body to die for. I'd lean against a wall if it weren't for them being covered in posters and pins.

This has me wending my way through the rows of chairs and sitting next to the hot guy.

Never have I been so conscious of looking like I've been rolling around with a couple of Black Labs. I should've changed *after* I checked on today's clients, and not before.

With a packed schedule, I'm hoping Dr. Charlotte won't keep me long. Despite the waiting room being full, there are at least half-a-dozen doctors working out of the surgery.

But why would I want to rush away when I'm sitting next to a guy as gorgeous as this one? On him clearing his throat, there's nothing I can do to stop tilting my head in his direction.

When he asks if I like dogs, I know exactly what he's talking about. This has me desperately brushing my dress, trying to get rid of the dog hair.

It's a pointless task, and I don't know why I've bothered.

On him admitting to owning a Staffy, a challenging breed if not socialized early, I know I've met a kindred spirit. The love in his voice when he talks about his dog, Stella, and how badly she sheds, is lovely.

I turn in my seat, holding my hand out, as I would with a new client at Barkley Castle, the doggy day care I own. OMG if I thought his eyes screamed go to bed from across the waiting room, it pales compared to being this close.

The waiting room fades. My sole focus is now a pair of striking brown eyes, with more than a hint of a bad boy in their depths. There's also the promise of bad things. Bad things my imagination tells me would be sensationally good.

As transfixed as I am, it's only on the nurse calling my name for the second time that I take my hand back and stand. "Bye." I follow this up with a brief wave before rushing off.

I'm being shown into Dr. Charlotte's office when I realize that, despite shaking hands, I hadn't given him my name. Stunned as I'd been, saying more than my simple 'bye' had been impossible.

He must think me an idiot. If only I was as at ease with guys as I am around dogs. My life would be a lot fuller. I might even get asked out on the occasional date.

Despite Dr. Charlotte stating it clearly, I have to ask her to repeat herself. I'm unable to comprehend her refusal to give me cortisone injections.

At the end of a day spent running around after a dozen dogs, my knees are killing me. Of late, they've also been hurting at the start of the day. A couple of injections would have me keeping up as I once did.

"I'm sorry, Bettany. I can't, in good faith, prescribe those. They'd only be a stop-gap measure, if they worked at all."

This is news to me. I thought cortisone was the medical equivalent of the silver bullet. I have some injected into each knee, and they'd be good as new before I left the surgery. That's how I've heard it is for most.

"Well, what am I supposed to do? I can only afford a part-timer, and she's ancient. It's up to me to exercise the dogs." I wring my hands at thoughts of being incapacitated, and my business failing. Or even worse, the dogs going nuts because they haven't had the exercise their owners have paid for.

I decide to try again. "Are you sure we can't at least give cortisone injections a try?" Despite my best efforts, I can't keep an element of whining out of this request. But darn it, this is important. The future of my business is at stake.

All the while I've been pleading my case, I've been conscious of Dr. Charlotte assessing me. I spot the second she decides.

Unfortunately, it's not that she's buckled under the pressure and will give me the injections I'm after. Rather, the treatment she's got in mind will be far more painful.

On leaving Dr. Charlotte's office, rather than watching where I'm going, I focus on the business card she'd given me. Part of me is still in shock at her suggested treatment for my problem knees.

Not until I'm out front, do I kick myself for missing the opportunity to wave goodbye to the handsome doggy dad.

Then I laugh at my stupidity. As if that would make any difference to my attracting a man as stunning as that one. If not for me being covered in dog hair, he wouldn't have given me the time of day.

TWO

DAX

My seat is as uncomfortable as ever when Little Miss Sunshine leaves my sister's office. That she's in distress is obvious, leaving me longing to take her in my arms and comfort her.

I've even gotten to my feet and followed her outside when my sister joins me. Of interest is that she also appears upset. It can't be easy breaking bad news.

This has me pulling her in for a tight hug while watching the woman drive off in a silver van with BARKLEY CASTLE on the side in blue.

I pull back and check on my sister, pleased to see she's now more settled. "Martelle's?" The deli is a favorite of mine, with great coffee and a good view of the beach and I know Charlotte likes the place, too.

"That sounds lovely. It's been a... a morning."

I can only imagine, with this yet another reason, I've no interest in pursuing a career as she has. It's highly unlikely as a personal trainer that I'll have someone die on me.

I haven't even had a bite of my sandwich when my sister starts in on me.

Her "I wish you'd do something with your life" is first up. General chitchat about my high IQ and how well I'd done at school soon follows.

There's nothing I can do about my shoulders bunching up. Just once, it would be nice to catch up without getting a lecture. Much as I love my sis, her constant criticisms are a pain in the ass.

I'm waiting on her "Dax, you're wasting your talents" when she falls silent, although not for long.

After taking a deep breath, she blurts out. "I've given your number to someone."

Damn it, this is worse than I thought. "Hell's teeth, Charlotte, please tell me you didn't." I can only imagine the type of woman she thinks would be a suitable partner for me; boring being the dominant trait.

"Not like that! She needs a personal trainer, not a date."

What follows are the ground rules on how I'm to treat this woman. Decorum and professionalism are paramount according to Char.

"I haven't said I'll take her on as a client, have I? I'm up to my ears in getting my latest app over the line. The last thing I need is another of your special cases."

As a kid, Charlotte had a bad habit of dragging every waif and stray home. Her mission complete, she'd then leave me to deal with the practicalities. So many small crosses down the back of our property.

Of course, I'd told her they'd all made full recoveries and were off running free in the wild.

"It shouldn't be too much work for you. She just needs to build up her leg muscles so she can keep up with all those dogs of hers."

"Dogs?"

"Hmmm mmmm. She runs a doggy day care."

It can't be, and yet it has to be. What are the odds?

I hold off as long as I can before injecting as much reluctance as I can into my response. "I guess that doesn't sound so bad."

Her expression tells me I've failed. "Dax, don't you dare." She glares at me before adding softly, "I should never have given your number to her."

"Relax, would you? I promise I'll be good."

Again, she's not taken in for a second by my careful word choice.

Hoping to assuage her concerns, I hold my hands up, although I'm careful not to actually promise anything further.

I spend the afternoon at my desk with Stella snoozing next to me. Despite checking my phone regularly, I don't get any calls from Charlotte's patient.

I would have thought she'd have called by now. Most of my clients can't wait to get started on their transformations. Then I recall her distress when she'd left the surgery. Could it be she's not a fan of my sister's prescribed cure?

What happens if she doesn't call?

It's Stella drooling on my foot that gives me the solution. There can't be that many Barkley Castles in town, can there?

A quick Google search and I've got my answer, along with an address, and even a name.

Bettany Brooks. It suits her.

Right Bettany Brooks, you've got a couple of days to get in touch. And if you don't, Project Stella is a go.

BETTANY

Three days pass, during which the pain in my knees doesn't magically disappear, or even improve.

Three days in which the business card sitting on my desk taunts me.

No surname, no website. Just DAX and a phone number in light gray type on a dark gray background. It doesn't mention him being a personal trainer. If it weren't for Dr Charlotte recommending him, I'd have trashed his card by now.

I'm still tempted.

When Dr. Charlotte had suggested I join a gym, my expression must have said it all, because she'd backpedaled quick-smart. As a curvy woman herself, she should have known better.

It was the reason I'd chosen her as my doctor. With her also carrying a few extra pounds, there'd be less likelihood of her ramming diets down my throat.

Her next suggestion, while still unpalatable, had been an improvement. The personal trainer she'd recommended apparently prefers training out and about in nature.

While not ideal, it would be better than me huffing and puffing in distress while surrounded by beautiful people.

As if doubting I'd comply, Dr. Charlotte had stressed the importance of my being fit for the sake of my business. The final clincher had been her admitting Dax had helped her with her own fitness.

His card sits on my desk until I can take it no longer. An extra deep breath and I pick up my phone.

I haven't so much as opened the keypad when the buzzer on the outside door announces a visitor. Phew, saved by the bell, ah buzzer.

A quick check of the small inset screen on my computer shows there's a guy out there. Because of where he's standing, all I can see is the back of his head.

I only know he's got a dog with him because of the familiar clip of toenails on tiles sneaking under the ill-fitting door. Either that or the guy isn't wearing shoes and needs a pedicure.

I shake my head to free it from this ridiculous scenario. I don't know why my mind comes up with these things, but it does. Some call it quirky, others call it downright weird. I'm firmly in the second camp.

"Be with you in a moment."

After standing, I check my clothes. This morning's outfit is navy, utilitarian, and as with everything else I wear to work, covered in dog hair. It's an occupational hazard there's no avoiding.

Rather than keep the man waiting, I march across my office and open the door to the holding pen. I'd learned the hard way that it was best to have two, or even three, doors between any dogs and the outside world.

Less chance of escape that way, although on opening the door, I'd be happy for an escape route myself. What is HE doing here? And why did he have to see me looking like this?

As stunned as I am to be facing the hottie from the doctor's waiting room, I say nothing. He doesn't, either. Instead, he tips his head to the side in question. When I still don't respond, he looks down as if to remind me he's got a dog with him.

A quick peek over the counter that separates us has me looking into a pair of soulful brown eyes. "Hello cutie. Are you Stella?"

In answer, I get a brief yip and a broad doggy grin. The Staffy wears a red bandana and an air of high excitement, telling me I'll like this dog.

She's one for whom everything in life is a reward that has to be experienced to the fullest. With a man like that at my side, I'd be the same.

This has me looking back up and into another set of gorgeous brown eyes.

There's nothing soulful here. As they connect with parts of me, they shouldn't, at least not in a business environment.

Business? Oh, that's right. I should say something to this potential new client about the services on offer, but I'm darned if I can. Instead, I grab one of my brochures and hand it over, hoping this answers his questions.

And while he reads through it, I try to get a handle on the fizzing in my girly bits. Then I take in the length of his tapered fingers as he holds the brochure, and the fizzing only intensifies.

To distract myself, I curl my fingers and jam my nails into the palms of my hands. Unfortunately, because of how short I have them, this doesn't achieve much.

When the doggy dad looks up from the brochure and stares at me, he's smiling. It's a smile that has me both nervous and excited.

"You're exactly what I've been looking for."

My heart tumbles in my chest as I take his words at face value. Then reality reasserts itself. "Great, I offer concession rates, but only have availability in the afternoons at present. Would that suit?"

His smile broadens, and I hold my breath, my hackles already up.

"That depends. What are you like at break of day?"

I'm still wondering what on earth he means when he hands over a business card? The briefest glance down and I know I'm in trouble. Big, big trouble.

THREE

BETTANY

"Uh, uh, uh..." Nope, words are still failing me, never mind complete sentences. I only come to my senses when Stella licks my fingers. She's stretched up on her back legs, her face a picture of doggy concern.

If only life was as straightforward as it is for dogs from loving homes.

She does, however, center my thoughts, enabling me to answer Dax with a modicum of normalcy. "It's just that I'm so busy in the mornings."

I wave my hand vaguely toward my office. "That's when I'm getting everything ready for the day."

He nods slowly in response, although I doubt he's swallowed my small lie. His next words confirm this. "Five am. On the boardwalk."

It's not a question, it's an order. And while Dax is drop-dead gorgeous, I suspect exercising with him would be akin to basic training. There's only one problem with his plan. I haven't said yes.

"I'm sure it's lovely that early in the morning. Just a shame I won't be joining you." I pin him with a smile of my own, one my mother would recognize immediately. Stubborn as a mule was her summation when I was like this.

I then carry on as if he hadn't suggested us training together. "If Stella is up to date with her shots, I can book her in for a few afternoons."

His mouth twisted to the side, tells me he's not used to people—make that women—saying no to him. "Yeah, she's fully vaccinated."

He then reaches into the pocket of his jeans and retrieves her vaccination record book. "Can I schedule for every afternoon next week? I've got something I'm working on."

Happy to have something to do, I block time into the online schedule on the tablet I keep under the counter. He's made a note of the times in his phone, and even opened the outside door, when he stops.

"And do you exercise the dogs while they're in your care?"

"Absolutely! I take them for walks along the beach at ten and two, without fail."

With a wave from Dax and a grin from Stella, they depart, leaving me to get on with my day.

On walking back to my desk, I can't ignore the twinge in my right knee. My training with Dax being out of the question. I have to do something.

Maybe there's another doctor I can go to for cortisone injections?

Someone down the coast from Coogan's, if I'm to avoid Dr. Charlotte hearing about it.

I've come to no conclusions the following morning when I park my van down at the beach. The crash of the waves is enough to have the seven small dogs in the back barking in excitement.

I have to agree with them. My dodgy knees aside, it's a favorite part of my day, too. At least with us walking on the beach, it's low impact for me. Better than in the middle of winter when I'll stick to the boardwalk to avoid a soaking.

I've only just gotten them all hooked onto my special belt and locked the van when an eighth dog joins my pack. It's Stella, and she's not alone. And just like that, the ache in my knees is the least of my worries.

I have to concentrate on breathing, with me fighting to get air into my lungs. If I thought Dax was hot when dressed in jeans and a button-down shirt, it's nothing compared to now.

Shorts and running shoes topped off with a lot of bronzed skin and ink. It's more than enough. Even when fully clothed, there'd been hints of how amazing his physique would be. With him close to naked, there's no doubt.

And blast it. His filthy grin tells me he knows exactly what I'm thinking. He doubly confirms it when he reaches out and lifts my chin with a single finger.

Despite this small connection, I feel it deep inside my core. It's as if he'd actually touched me there. It's as if he's *still* touching me there.

My only saving grace is my doggy charges getting bored and pulling on their leashes. They're just as *excited* as I am. And because we're in a public place, Dax is quite within his rights to walk Stella on the beach.

I can't decide how I feel about having company this morning.

DAX

There'd been no missing Bettany's flash of arousal after I closed her mouth. If I can achieve that with one finger, think of the damage I could do with two or more.

It's enough to have me whistling as I walk down the beach with her and her mob of small yappy dogs. That she does so without tripping is an achievement.

They'd have taken me out, for sure. It's when I drop behind that I notice not only her peach of an ass, but that she over-pronates on both feet. It could explain why she stops and rubs her knees every so often.

While Charlotte hadn't gone into the specifics of why Bettany needed a personal trainer, I've now got an idea. It can't be easy keeping up with the sea of canines currently swirling around her ankles.

It would be even worse with bigger dogs, although I doubt she'd commit to seven of them at a time. Even a dog as well trained as Stella can be challenging if she spots something she wants a closer look at.

As if to show her good behavior, Stella trots at my side, with no tension on her leash. I'm sure it's the doggy equivalent of show-boating.

On seeing Bettany once again stopping to rub her knees, I go to ask if they're bothering her. That's when I recall her obstinate demeanor yesterday. Stubborn woman, I could have her body purring if she let me.

Instead, I decide to hit her with science. "Do you realize you over-pronate on both feet?"

Her response is immediate. She stops dead, causing a pile-up of small dogs. On her spinning to face me, a couple of leashes get wrapped tight around her ankles.

Seeing her falling, I don't think it through; I lunge, hoping to catch her. I do, for all the good it does, with us ending up in a heap on the beach.

Rather than scaring them when we land in their midst, the small dogs are thrilled. I'm kinda happy myself to find Bettany sprawled all over me. Perhaps the biggest surprise is that rather than being annoyed, she's laughing.

This has an incendiary effect on the ankle biters. One fluffy individual even decides Bettany and I make a great 'mountain'. He soon stands atop us, yapping his victory to any who'll listen.

Now I'm laughing, too. Right up to the point, I catch the glint in Bettany's eyes, and read it for what it is. I think briefly of Charlotte's warning to keep my hands off her patient, before placing my hand gently on the back of Bettany's head.

Again I search for permission, with the curve of Bettany's lips, answer enough. I'm not sure who makes the first move, but our lips soon touch.

What starts out as a quick peck soon deepens, our lips meshing perfectly. Her mouth, after she gives me access, is a delicious blend of cinnamon and coffee.

The small dog standing on her shoulders is having none of it. After growling his displeasure, he sinks needle-sharp teeth into the back of my hand.

I send him flying and wrench my lips away from Bettany's. "Ow, why you little b... Someone needs to teach you some manners."

Unaware of events, Bettany stares at me in shock.

"Not you, gorgeous." I hold my hand out to the side so she can see it. Sure enough, there's a small bite mark, although it's not as bad as it could have been.

To a background of Stella growling protectively, Bettany rolls off me slowly. This has her putting her hands in places that have me itching to pull her back and take her right there.

Then I rethink it. If I was to try, that little beast would probably sink his teeth into bits of me far more important than my hand.

While struggling to her feet, Bettany looks around the mob. "Which one was it?" Much to my surprise, she looks briefly at Stella and I sit up, ready to put her right. Stella would never bite me, no matter what the provocation.

However, Bettany's gaze soon centers on the little white powder puff.

"Pompom, was that you?"

The dog stares up at her as if butter wouldn't melt in its mouth. On my joining Bettany, it tries the same gambit with me.

"Seriously, you sad excuse for a dog? I saw you climbing up there." On rubbing the back of my hand, I'm surprised to see traces of blood. "It was you, I know it."

I'm still eyeballing Pompom when Bettany takes my hand, all the while admonishing the pile of fluff for being naughty. Next thing I know, Bettany has delved into her fanny pack and grabbed an antiseptic wipe.

When she follows this up with an industrial sized plaster, I have to wonder how often Pompom has drawn blood in the past. That dog trainer guy off TV would have a thing or two to say about its behavior.

Meanwhile, Stella waits patiently, her leash hanging loose. There's no missing the concern in her warm brown eyes as she gazes up at me. This prompts me to reach down and give her a reassuring pat.

Her worries assuaged, I go back to glaring at the powder puff. Even forgetting the bite on the back of my hand, the dog's timing had been rubbish, interrupting our kiss like it had.

Next time, I'll make damned sure it's not around to ruin things.

Next time?

Hell yes, there'd be a next time; I'd make sure of that.

On taking in the curvy beauty next to me, I resolve that there'll be a month of *next times*.

FOUR

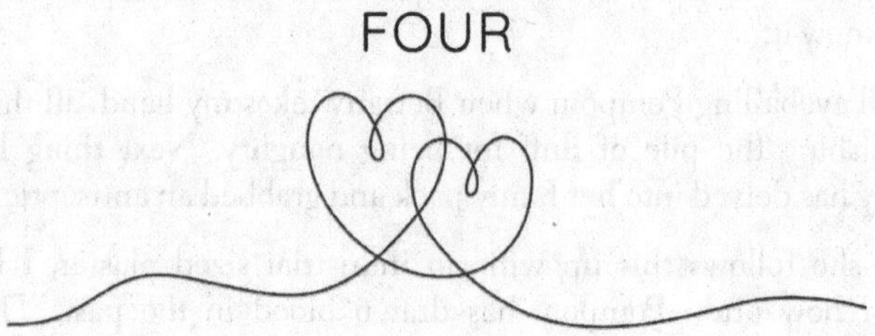

BETTANY

After treating Dax's hand, I focus on getting my charges and libido under control. Only then do I recall why it was I'd screeched to a stop.

Of course, this has my mind once again crowded with what happened when we tangled on the beach. Now, it's all I can do not to jump him. Luckily for my self-esteem, I refrain.

There was no reason for him to kiss me like he had, my lips still tingling at the remembered pressure. Why had he kissed me? I'm not his type.

His type would spend most of their time at the gym—on purpose—while wearing as little Lycra as possible.

We're walking back to my van, when I decide it will be quicker to ask him than wait until I get home and Google it. "What was that you said about me over-pro-something or other?"

Without slowing the pace, he answers. "Over-pronation. It's when your foot rolls to the side. It can lead to trouble with your knees."

I keep quiet, waiting for him to say more. Only he doesn't, leading me to think I'll need to Google it after all. Things like, can you fix the issue with cortisone injections?

With the pups safely secured in the van, I turn to Dax, my face flushing. I'm unsure of how to speak to a man I've just been rolling around on the beach with. It's never happened before. Eventually, I decide to stick to practicalities to cover my embarrassment.

"Your hand. No matter what people say, dog bites are anything but clean. Best you keep an eye on it."

He's looking at the plaster I'd applied when he says, "You could do that for me." He pauses, no doubt for effect, before adding, "When we're training."

I suck in enough air that I'm left coughing and spluttering. This has the dogs inside the van barking loudly enough that Dax and I both move away in unspoken agreement. Even Stella is pulling on her leash to escape the noise.

We're on the other side of the carpark next to a black Ford pickup, before Dax speaks again. "Bettany, you give me one month, and I can guarantee, your knees will be a lot better."

"A month!?" I focus on my feet rather than look him in the face. My mind is awhirl with images of how a month with this hunk of muscle would play out. Only then do I look at him again. "And you can guarantee they'll be better?"

It's then as if my hand belongs to someone else. I reach out and run my fingertips over the word *Trust* that's tattooed on his ribcage.

Now it's his turn to suck in air, with him placing his hand over the top of mine and slowly removing it. Why am I surprised? His kissing me had been a one-off. It had been a spur-of-the-moment thing, and nothing more.

His moving my hand speaks to the truth of this.

And I guess I'm okay with that. It's not as if it's a surprise or anything. It might also make training with him easier. While not as fast as cortisone, a month next to a half-naked guy definitely appeals.

So long as I don't lose sight of the fact that he and I will never be an item, I should be okay. I'm about to ask when our first session will be, when he again surprises me.

"Before we do anything, though, we need to set you up with some orthotics."

"Orthotics! I'm not ready for those. They're for old..." I clam up before I can say anything I'll regret.

But it's true, orthotics are worn by people in aged-care facilities. Ugly shoes with zips and Velcro that are best suited to sitting or shuffling. Not for someone my age.

Dax's eyes widen. The humor lurking in their depths soon rushes free in a burst of laughter. "Bettany, what are you talking about? I wear orthotics."

He lifts a foot and twists it around so I can see his running shoe. There's nothing aged-care about his neon orange shoes with their fancy soles.

"I'm talking about orthotic insoles that will help support your feet. You'll need some better shoes, though."

He looks down at the battered sneakers I save for beach walks. I've even punched extra holes in the sides to allow water to drain if I get caught by a rogue wave. So far as I'm concerned, they're perfect.

His expression says he isn't in agreement with me.

———

It's three days before our first official training session, during which I have impressions of my feet taken, with these sent away for custom insoles.

I'm having trouble accepting all this help from Dax. My Mom and dad had worked full time when I was growing up. This meant I was a latch-key kid, and self-sufficient to a fault. And even when they were home, they were more interested in catching up with each other than they were me.

These days, despite both being semi-retired, I still see little of them. They've never once asked to visit Barkley Castle, or seen the cozy home I've created out of the office space attached to the large warehouse.

I'd reach out to them, but there's no point when I already know what the response will be. There's a stark difference between them and Dax around my welfare, with this morning a case in point.

After I'd exercised the dogs and settled them with my part-timer, Dax arrived to take me shoe shopping. And for once, he's alone, with Stella having opted to stay at home.

"Last I saw, she was chewing on a bone the size of my femur!"

———

Ogling Dax while he's hunkered down on the floor next to me is a cardio workout all on its own. While helping me try on shoes, he seems to think it necessary to have one hand cradling my calf muscle.

It doesn't matter that his hand only strays as far as the back of my knee; my heart rate is through the roof. And that's not all.

The incendiary tingling set off by his touch burns straight up my leg before burying itself deep inside me.

Oh, if only.

DAX

Never could I have imagined shoe shopping to be an erotic experience, and yet I'm rock hard. All I had to do was run my hand up the back of one of Bettany's legs and I was a goner.

"How does that feel?"

While I'm asking her about the shoes, my mind responds as if I've asked about something else altogether.

Soft? Kissable? Best wrapped tight around my waist?

That's how I'd describe Bettany's legs. Her shifting in her seat in response to my touch tells me I'm not alone in being affected.

Damn it, maybe my sister had the right of it and I should back well away from Bettany Brooks. As she walks up and down the middle of the shoe store, my gaze follows her of its own volition.

I try closing my eyes, but all this does is show me the fun we could have if I were to ignore my sister. *Damn it, focus, will you?*

"What about the orthotics, Bettany? Are they okay?"

The custom insoles had arrived by courier this morning, prompting our shoe shopping trip. There had been little point in her buying shoes before their arrival.

Bettany continues walking, back and forth. She's no longer bouncing and hopping experimentally. Rather, she's concentrating, with each step measured.

"They were weird at the start, like I had something stuck in my shoe. Now, I can hardly tell they're there. Are you sure they'll help my knees?"

Her question has me looking at these dimpled delights, visible thanks to her denim shorts. Damn it, those shorts of hers mold to her luscious curves as if painted on.

I have to swallow before I can speak. "They sure will. A lot of what you're dealing with is down to how your feet naturally roll when you walk. We correct that. We help your knees."

Of course, there's more to it than this, but I don't want to frighten her off by mentioning corrective exercises. Despite being on the go from break of day to sunset; she's strangely averse to *formal* exercise.

In particular, she's got an abhorrence of gyms, with her mentioning this at every opportunity. Despite owning one, I'm not that big a fan myself, with this the rationale behind my fitness apps.

Given the choice, I'll always exercise outside, and the less equipment I have to use, the better I like it. While I have no issues with free weights, the idea of being hooked into a fancy-ass machine doesn't do it for me.

We're leaving the store when I turn to a grinning Bettany. "Do you fancy a coffee? We can go through our schedule for the next month."

I'm not sure if it's my use of the word *schedule*, but she loses all her bounce, her expression turning serious. To ease her fears, I press on. "We can work out what times best suit the both of us."

At no lessening in her dread, I hurriedly add, "We can even time our sessions for when you're walking the dogs, if that's easier."

Only then am I rewarded with another of her bright smiles. "We can do that?"

I nod in response, surprised at just how relieved I am to have talked her out of her exercise-induced panic. It's something I file for later, knowing that if she's like this about exercising, then others could well be the same.

"So, coffee?"

"That'd be lovely. Marcelle's?"

Now I'm smiling along with her. "Best coffee in town."

We both turn toward the beach, naturally falling into step. A quick glance down and I'm pleased to see there's already a marked improvement in her over-pronation.

If I was being truthful with myself, I could probably leave her to get on with her life, just as she is. Except there's something about Bettany that has me wanting to stick around. To see this thing through. Okay, the thought of seeing her hot and bothered also has a lot of appeal, especially if she's naked.

It's only once we've got our coffees and are sitting looking out at the beach that I carefully broach our 'schedule'. "It's best to commit to a month. They reckon that's what it takes to establish a habit."

She stares at me wide-eyed for a second or two, before asking, "They?"

Focused on her lips, I take almost as long to work out what she's getting at. "Oh right, *they*. Behavioral experts. Apparently, it doesn't matter what it is. If you give it a month, you establish a habit."

Not wanting to boggle her further with science, I continue. "Do you have a smart phone?" As a diversionary tactic, it works perfectly with her brow now wrinkled in confusion rather than worry.

It's a stupid question. I mean, who doesn't have a smart phone these days?

"Sure do. Why do you ask?"

When I drop Bettany back at Barkley Castle, I've got her number programmed into my phone, and she's got mine. She's also downloaded one of my fitness apps that she promises with a hand on heart she'll use, although I have my doubts.

On our way to the castle, I'd swung by and collected Stella with her spending the afternoon with Bettany. The last I see of my pup is her running around the exercise yard with a standard poodle in hot pursuit. Her doggy smile is wide, and her tail is high. Yep, she's one happy pup.

On the drive to my office, I find I'm in a good mood myself.

FIVE

BETTANY

My usual routine for getting ready to take the small dogs for their morning walk won't cut it this morning.

Whereas I'd usually throw on whichever clothes were to hand and head out the door, this morning sees me dithering. The only apparel that's a given are my new pink running shoes with their fancy orthotic insoles.

Other than those, I'm at a loss. I don't exercise; ergo I don't have exercise clothing. The thought of Dax seeing me in more of my usual dog-walking attire has me cringing. It had been bad enough when he'd caught me by surprise.

It wasn't something I'd want to happen on purpose. I also know he won't let me wriggle out of our session without a note from my doctor. And thanks to Dr. Charlotte recommending him, I know that's not happening.

Dressed in sensible underwear, I glare at the pile of clothing in the middle of my bed before blowing out in frustration. "Oh, what's the point?!"

There isn't a chance of my attracting the attention of someone as hot as Dax; I may as well be comfortable. With this in mind, I drag on my denim shorts from the day before, along with a hot pink crop top.

At the very least, this matches my new shoes.

On pulling into the carpark at the beach, I'm having second, and even third, thoughts.

Dax is already there, and as before, only wearing shorts, shoes, and sex appeal. The other thing I notice is that he's alone, with no sign of Stella.

As my gaze rakes Dax's chest, I have to wonder what I was thinking about wearing a crop top. And why did it have to be my only hot pink one? The black or the gray would have been less attention-grabbing.

As tempting as it is to put the van in gear and drive off, I know he'd only follow me. And it wouldn't be fair to the dogs in the back.

I'd never be so cruel as to drive them down to the beach and then leave without taking them for a walk. For this reason alone, I climb out of the van and race around to open the side door.

Surely if I'm fast enough, Dax won't be able to focus.

I wrench open the side door before I realize how nonsensical my strategy is.

The cacophony of barking has any further thoughts as to my outfit battered free. Thanks to the van's lack of acoustics, the din is deafening.

For this reason, I grab a leash out of the basket and collect the first small dog from its cage. With it safely clipped to my belt, I repeat the process with the next.

Despite only having five *clients* with me today, Pompom is still the last to be hooked up. I've learned the hard way what a trouble-maker he can be if he's first out the door.

There's something calming about following my usual routine, with it helping me to relax. Not enough that I can forget Dax is standing behind me, but it's better than being totally on-edge.

Only when I've got Pompom hooked onto my belt and locked the van door, do I fully acknowledge Dax. Despite my channeling my inner dog lady, there's no need to confirm it.

I'm about to move off when I realize I don't know what Dax has in mind for this morning. He was the one who'd suggested we combine my walking the dogs with whatever he's got planned.

"So, what happens now?" On asking, I realize I'll need to actually look at him to acknowledge his reply. I certainly can't keep staring at my troop of pups.

The briefest peep in his direction and the gentle sea breeze wafts away all other thoughts.

His eyes are dark, his gaze piercing as he looks down at me. Blast it; I should never have worn this top. Could this be why he'd wanted our training sessions to be at sunrise?

That early in the day, we'd have the beach to ourselves. It's certainly not the case now, with the carpark close to full. I'm about to tell him we can postpone or something. Anything is better than his current scrutiny.

"You look amazing."

As mired as I am in my thoughts about what an embarrassment I am, it takes longer than it should for his words to register.

I haven't managed a simple 'thank you,' when he adds, "Great color coordination with the shoes."

It's his smile, more than his words, that finally settles my anxieties.

"Where's Stella?"

He rubs the back of his neck before answering. "After she growled at the fluffy terror yesterday, I thought it better she hangs out in the truck. She was only being protective, but even so…"

He doesn't need to say more, although it doesn't sit well that the better behaved dog is being punished. We're about to move off when I think of a viable solution.

It's not something I've used before, but it could work. "Hang on a second." Without explaining things to Dax, I unlock the van door and reach inside. I've never used the backpack, but it will mean Stella can join us on our walk.

As soon as Dax sees what it is, he laughs, his rumbling mirth warming my solar plexus and other bits. "If the guys down the gym see this, I'll never hear the end of it."

DAX

There's no missing how Bettany takes my throwaway comment. Her face is an open book as to her feelings.

If she thinks I'm talking about being embarrassed to be seen with her, she is dead wrong. Being seen with a Pomeranian in a see-through backpack is nothing to me. I gave up worrying about what people thought of me a long time ago.

And I have my father to thank for that. If he'd cared less about what people thought, we'd be a lot closer.

Damn it, I don't want thoughts of him interrupting this morning's walk. This has me crouching down and lengthening the backpack's shoulder straps so they'll fit me.

Busy unclipping Pompom's leash from her belt, Bettany pauses. "Are you sure? I'm happy to wear it."

Rather than go into the complexities about why I don't give a damn what people think, I shrug. I can't stop a snort when zipping Pompom inside his plastic bubble. "At least this way, the little ankle biter can't bite mine."

In response, the dog bares his teeth at me, resulting in a little puff of condensation forming on the plastic in front of him. He's not a happy camper.

While doing my best not to laugh out loud, I carefully swing the backpack up and over my shoulders. "I'll just go grab Stella."

I've not taken two steps toward my truck when Bettany's laughter has me glancing over my shoulder.

She waves her hands wildly about in response to my questioning look. "No, not you, you look, ah em, great." When her voice breaks at the end of this simple compliment, she has to clear her throat before continuing. "It's Pompom. He keeps baring his teeth and then having to lick the condensation away so he can see."

<hr>

We're standing at the top of the wooden steps down to the beach before Bettany speaks again. "But my new shoes, I can't wear them on the beach. The salt water will ruin them."

Her expression leaves me in no doubt she's still annoyed I'd made her toss those hideous sneakers.

"Relax. Part of the reason I chose those shoes is that they can cope with the beach. A quick rinse and they'll be good as new."

On seeing her breathing in, ready to voice her next argument, I add, "Ditto your insoles, Bettany. Come on, let's move it."

Stella and I race down the steps and onto the beach, with me well aware of Pompom bouncing inside his bubble. It's something I'll need to be careful about. The last thing I want is for the dog to get motion sick.

Even Stella has trouble when we go off-roading.

Bettany follows at a more sedate pace; the other four dogs still proving they can be a trip hazard. Soon enough, we're all walking down the beach. Perhaps the biggest surprise is that, according to Bettany, Pompom now appears to be enjoying his new ride.

We're almost at the end of the main beach and I've avoided any talk of exercise. Instead, I've told Bettany all about my fitness apps and heard why it was she'd set up Barkley Castle.

All the while, I've slowly been increasing our pace. So long as she can carry on with our conversation, I know she's not pushing herself.

It's a sneaky, but effective strategy, and one that leaves Bettany perplexed.

In the end, she can stay quiet, no longer. "Ah, so what do you have in mind?"

As questions go, it would be so easy to respond with exactly what I've got in mind, and that's nothing to do with exercise. Then, my sister's words come back to haunt me.

Despite being vague in my response to her promise not to 'go there', it's proving harder than I thought to comply. Hell, I'm harder than I'd have thought possible on a simple beach walk.

And yet with Bettany in the mix, there's nothing simple about it, which surprises me. Was it down to the doctor/patient connection that Charlotte was so insistent I make no moves on Bettany?

Or was my big sister trying to protect me as she used to when we were little? Those were our roles. I took care of the critters she brought home, and she protected me from my father's criticisms.

Another glance at Bettany, and I decide she's worth the risk. Add in how kindly she speaks to her charges—even when they're being little monsters—and I know I'm in expert hands.

Hmmm, I shouldn't let my thoughts stray in that direction right now. Instead, I answer with a vague, "You're doing great," resulting in yet more puzzled looks from her.

Much as my pushing the pace is helping, she'll need more than this to build up those stabilizer muscles of hers. On spotting a tree that's washed up at the end of the beach, I make my move. "Are you okay with me showing you a couple of exercises?"

From her reaction, you'd think I'd suggested something truly awful, like dumping the dogs and doing a runner. "Nothing too strenuous. I was thinking we could tie the pups to that tree up there."

She's not convinced a break is a good idea until I draw attention to how tired the Dachshund appears to be.

"Oh Fritz, I'm so sorry. Are you okay, baby?"

Hell, if she was fussing over me like that, I'd be more than okay.

Soon enough, we reach the tree and Bettany unclips her belt and secures it around a branch. After doing the same with Stella's leash, I shrug out of the plastic bubble backpack and lean it against the log. There'll be no complaints from Pompom with him fast asleep in his little cocoon.

After walking down the beach to where the sand is firmer, by unspoken consent, we both turn to face the dogs. Despite Fritz needing to rest his legs, Bettany isn't comfortable being separated from her charges.

I'm standing behind her, using my feet to position hers a shoulder's width apart, ready for the squat, when all hell breaks loose. We should have been far enough up the beach to avoid getting wet. But transfixed as I'd been by Bettany's ass, I hadn't heard the rogue wave.

Next thing I know, we're rolling around in the surf, my hands all over her, and vice versa. None of it is intentional; rather, we're trying to hold on to each other to stop from rolling further.

All it does is see my knee jammed between her thighs, and her mons grinding into me harder than the beach.

And, just like that, all else ceases to exist. Instead, my worldview is of Bettany next to me, her clothes plastered to her gorgeous curves, and laughter in her eyes. It's a heady combination, and one I fully intend to make the most of.

Even better is that Pompom being locked away in his bubble, he won't be able to interrupt our kiss this time. It's something that has me savoring the moment; while my lips claim Bettany's laughter, my hands claim her body.

SIX

BETTANY

My teeth are chattering by the time we make it back to the carpark. Strange when you consider how hot I'd been only half an hour earlier.

Dax kissing me with the water lapping at us had been a sensory overload, and one I'd loved every second of. That man knew how to kiss, and more, if he could have me trembling without the need to remove my clothes.

My body is tingling with more than just the cold. And if it hadn't been for us being on a public beach, I'm sure things would have progressed.

Well, that and me needing to get the pups back to Barkley Castle for their owners to collect them.

Despite being cold, I'm still disappointed our walk is over. My charges safely loaded into the back of the van, I turn to Dax. "I can take Stella with me now, if that works for you?"

"That'd be great, thanks." Rather than put her in the back with the others, I open the passenger door. She doesn't jump in immediately, rather turning and looking at Dax for permission.

"It's okay, girl. You go with Bettany. Dad will see you later."

Permission granted, the dog jumps first into the footwell, and then onto the passenger seat. It would appear Stella enjoys riding shotgun, and even sits patiently while I hook the seatbelt through her harness.

Dax steps closer, and I automatically look up, my lips softening. However, there'll be no kiss, thanks to a group of tourists walking up to the car parked next to us.

I'm not confident enough to indulge in PDAs, even when I don't know the people witnessing them. I'm also unsure where I stand with Dax. He's kissed me twice now, but why? Is this something he does with every client? Am I just another number to him? It's these thoughts that shake the remnants of my arousal free for all the good it does.

As I pull out of the carpark, Stella and I both look at Dax with love in our eyes. This has me glad of the tinted windows as there isn't a chance I'd want him to catch me making puppy dog eyes.

In less than ten minutes, I'm back at Barkley Castle. There aren't many places in Coogan's Break that are farther away than this. I'd even had time to stop for a takeaway coffee, thanks to there being a park right out front of Skye High Pies.

After unloading all the dogs, I let them and Stella out into the exercise yard. It being neutral territory; I know Stella and Pompom won't start any fights. At least, I thought this would be how it was.

I've not taken more than a couple of steps when I hear growling from behind me. As always, Pompom is the instigator, with Stella doing her best to ignore the little brat.

"Okay Stella, you can come with me." I then pat the side of my leg and she trots over to join me. It's only on walking into the building and my office that I realize how much my legs are hurting.

That's weird; they rarely hurt after a beach walk. And we went no farther today than I do any other day. It has to be my new shoes. That's not good. They cost me a fortune!

Because of my various aches and pains, I opt for a quick bath rather than a shower. Despite adding bath salts designed to ease aches and pains, they make little difference.

***

With the morning pups collected by their *parents*, I'm looking forward to an afternoon at my desk. Stella is my only client this afternoon, and she's already had her walk.

As I sit, staring at my now-cold coffee, I have to admit my legs aren't the only part of me hurting. My heart aches, too.

It had been wonderful sharing my walk with Dax. In between sips of coffee, I bemoan the fact that the only way I can get a guy these days is by paying.

I check on Stella, who's made herself at home in the dog bed next to my desk. "I promise, when your dad comes to pick you up, I'll behave myself."

This has her quirking her head to the side, as if questioning my sanity, and I can't altogether blame her.

"I pinky promise there'll be no giggling and hair flicking. I'll treat him like any other parent on the school run."

In answer, she props her head on the padded edge of the bed and stares at me with pity in her somber brown eyes.

"And that'll be enough from you, madam." With this, I turn back to the mountain of paperwork on my desk. If nothing else, it will take my mind off Dax.

Before I know it, he's there to collect Stella. She'd already alerted me to this when her head popped up and she gave a small yip. Soon after, she's standing nose pressed against the door out to the holding pen.

I take a little longer, with my legs and ass really hurting now. It won't have helped that I haven't stirred for hours. As it is, I'm moving like an octogenarian when I stagger out into reception.

Stella bounces next to me, happy to see her dad hasn't forgotten her. It had been the same when he came to collect her yesterday. Is it sad that I'm jealous of a pup? Ah, that'd be yes.

Dax takes in my hobbling, his expression giving nothing away. "I wondered if this might happen."

"I don't understand it. We always walk to the end of the beach." I open the pen door to let Stella through, and follow in her wake. Every step has me wincing.

"They must have sent me the wrong insoles."

Dax briefly pats Stella, who's leaning against his leg, before turning his attention back to me.

"Bettany, forget your legs for a second. How are your knees?"

This has me walking back and forth, my concentration laser-like. "Oh, that's weird. They don't hurt as much."

Next thing I see is Dax shoving his hand in the pocket of his shorts. Soon enough, he holds up a bottle of Burn-Baby-Burn. On closer inspection, I can see that it's massage oil.

He grins, before saying, "I can help ease the pain, if you'll let me?"

This has me as hot as if he's just slathered me from head to toe in the stuff.

Does he realize even my ass hurts?

A peek tells he might just.

But will he stop there?

I sure hope not.

DAX

As luck would have it, the only place suitable for me to massage her legs is on her bed.

After throwing down a couple of large towels to protect the bedding, Bettany goes to lie down.

"Ah, um, it might be easier if you took your shorts off. I'll keep you covered with a towel. Chances are it won't just be your calf muscles that need attention. I'll no doubt need to work all your legs, and..."

Thoughts as to the other bits I'd like to give attention to have me struggling to see. This curvy bundle of joy pulls me in as no other woman to date. Despite my sister's admonishments ringing in my ears, I ignore them.

Bettany needs help, and I'm the guy to help her. That's it, nothing more. My tamping down my desire must show, with her nodding, even if she's unaware of it.

I put my bottle of oil down on the bedside table and step back. "I'll, ah, leave you to it. Just let me know when you're ready."

Hoping to walk off some of my excess tension, I pace up and down the hallway, and so it goes. It's to the point I think she's changed her mind when a strangled "Ready" makes its way out of her bedroom.

On seeing her spread out on the bed, I decide she's not the only one who's ready. Sure, she's covered herself with a towel, but only just with the curve of her cheeks on display.

It takes every ounce of my self-control to walk over to the bedside table and unclip the top of the massage oil.

I pool a small amount in one palm, before rubbing my hands together to warm them, and the oil. I then sit on the bed next to Bettany and stroke my hands up the back of one leg, and then the other.

Oh hell, I'm in trouble. It doesn't take me long to realize I'm not alone, with Bettany unable to stop her groan of pleasure. At least I think that's what it is. I've hardly touched her, so I doubt it's because she's in pain.

That said, the muscles running up the backs of her legs are tight as hell. No wonder she was hobbling like she was. This massage will be an interesting mix of pleasure and pain for both of us.

Ten minutes later, and I'm doubtless in more pain than Bettany with my cock now rock solid. As I run a thumb up her hamstring, she gasps, although when I continue onto her glute, the tone changes.

I'm unsure if this is to stifle moans of pain, or pleasure, thanks to what I'm doing. It's hard to tell with her face jammed into her pillow.

My thumb is now buried just under the lace of her panties. I press it hard into her glute, doing my best to ignore her keen of pain. I only ease off when I feel the muscle give under my fingers.

As the knot releases, so does Bettany, with her puddling under my hands. This has me running my thumb along the crease of her ass.

It would be all too easy to swipe right, to hit the spot we both want me to explore. Instead, I start work on her other leg with her groan, now one of disappointment.

"All in good time, baby. All in good time."

When I bury myself in her, I want her fully relaxed. I want nothing ruining her enjoyment of the moment. Although, by the time I'm finished doing to her what I want to, there won't be a muscle in her body not screaming for release.

I spend nowhere near as much time on her other leg. Instead, my thumb runs up the hamstring ever faster, getting me closer and closer.

I offer a silent thank you when I discover the glute on the other side is nowhere near as tight. Only when it's pliable under my hands, do I ease her panties down and off.

I think briefly about washing the remaining minty oil off my hands before giving into a dirty grin. I know from personal experience that it'll tingle, but not much more.

After spreading her wide, I run my still oily thumbs through her exposed cleft. I then zone in on her special little nubbin, running my fingers around and around it before giving it a gentle flick.

It takes a moment for the peppermint to make itself felt. There'll be no letup from me, though. This has me peeling her open to my gaze and blowing gently on her exposed skin.

She immediately squirms with need, angling herself in open invitation. It's exactly what I've been looking for, with me soon flipping her over. When I slide inside her, I want to see her eyes widen. I want to see her lips part on a sigh.

Hot and cold.

Hard and soft.

Fast and slow.

SEVEN

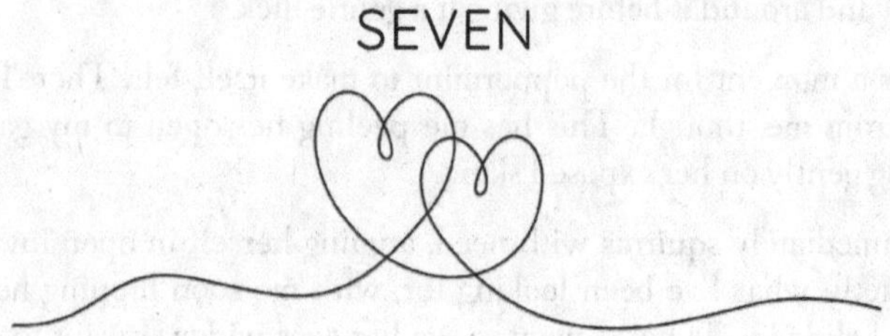

BETTANY

My senses are threatening to swallow me whole. The minty massage oil Dax had introduced to my most intimate parts was hot and cold at the same time.

While his cock filling me is hot, the air wafting between us thanks to our frantic coupling is cool when it kisses my skin. And I love it. My body loves it; with my muscles now as tight as they were before his massage.

The only difference now is there's no pain, only pleasure, inching me ever closer to the point my body will shatter. Even Dax looks to be enjoying our time together.

His gaze never leaves my face. Not once does he lose himself to the moment, leaving me nameless.

"Bettany, I can't hold out much longer." His words are slow, his lips tight as he fights to keep control.

All I can do to acknowledge his words is nod wildly; too busy giving into the sensation that's building deep inside of me. I don't have a hope of keeping quiet when it explodes in a shower of sparks that has me fizzing where we join.

"Oh, oh, oh, oh, Dax!"

Three even deeper thrusts and Dax shouts his release, before collapsing on my chest and hugging me tight. A scant second or two later, he kisses me first on the forehead, and then the lips.

Only when he lifts his head, am I capable of a complete sentence. "Are we going walking again tomorrow?"

He meets my question with a bark of laughter. "Are you sure you'll be up to that?" He kisses me deeply, before continuing, "Because I'm not finished with you yet, baby. Not by a long shot."

Sure enough, when I concentrate, I sense him coming to life deep inside me. It's something I automatically respond to by squeezing muscles I hadn't known existed before today. He meets this with delighted laughter, although it's soon followed by pathetic whining.

Dax stills, before turning and looking at the bedroom door. "Stella baby, your timing is way off." He drops his head in defeat, our foreheads barely touching. "Do you have any kibble to keep her happy?"

My snort of laughter has me even more aware of his length still filling me. However, Stella's pathetic grumbling pulls at my heartstrings.

"Ah yeah, three flavors, about fifty-pounds of each." I'm telling him exactly where he can find it, when I realize my instructions will be impossible to follow. "Never mind, I'll get some for her."

There's no missing the disappointment on Dax's face that our time together is effectively over. This has me wondering if there'll be a repeat performance.

Hah, not likely. My own thoughts on how unlikely are as a bucket of cold water to my arousal.

After Dax pulls free, I'm all business and pleased to be tasked with finding Stella something to eat. Luckily, I remember a sample pouch on my desk negating me having to raid the bulk supplies.

This at least will have Dax on his way sooner, allowing me to have a soak in the bath, a wine, and a good cry. It's because of this that I don't bother getting dressed, simply dragging on a robe and tying it snuggly at the waist.

Of interest is that Dax hasn't bothered to get dressed, either. Instead, he's grabbed a towel off the bed and wrapped it around his waist. Annoyingly, he's left his clothes in a pile on the bedroom floor.

It takes all my self-control not to pick them up and fold them; worried about what sort of impression it will give. It's seeing his bright orange shoes, next to mine, that is the wake-up call I need.

He's here now. I need to stop second-guessing myself and him, and make the most of it. Rather than waste more time in the kitchen watching Stella eating her kibble, I turn to Dax, ready to take action.

Only, I don't get the chance. His smart watch beeps twice, with him immediately checking it. Whatever it is, I know it's not good news, at least for me; the way he straightens, speaking volumes.

Unable to stop myself, I check the time on the microwave. Hah, it looks like I've just experienced my first quickie. Not even an hour has passed since he arrived to collect Stella.

This has me crossing my arms before saying, "You'd better get going, then." Far better I send him on his way than have to listen to his excuses about what the notification is for.

As I watch him walk down the hallway to the bedroom, my emotions are all over the place. Arousal is still there, especially when he drops the towel to get dressed.

Unfortunately, this comes with a healthy dose of melancholy in the knowledge this was a one-off. It had been too long since I'd been close to a man, finding it easier to communicate with canines than with guys.

I'm therefore surprised when, on returning to the kitchen, he pulls me into a tight embrace, his lips claiming mine. He doesn't hold back with that kiss, it curling my toes and other bits.

He's caressing my breasts through the thin silk of my robe when his watch beeps again. One last tug at my nipples, and he again looks at his watch, frowning. "She's persistent, I'll give her that."

She?

"Come on Stella, short of licking the pattern off the plate, you're done." Dax clicks his fingers, and she reluctantly abandons the empty plate and trots over to his side.

As I follow the pair out into my office and then the holding pen, I say nothing. The constriction of my throat, and keeping a hold of my tears, is making speech impossible.

If not for me having to lock the main door to the day care, I'd have left them to it, taking sanctuary in the bath. I'm therefore surprised when, after walking out, Dax steps back inside so he can give me another searing kiss.

"I'll see you down the beach tomorrow."

He's got Stella hooked into the passenger seat and has walked around to his side, before he adds, "Usual time?"

Still unable to speak, my nod is automatic. Also automatic, is my slowly closing the door and locking it. I've achieved all of this while avoiding much in the way of eye-contact. I'm strong, but not that strong.

DAX

I'm driving away from Barkley Castle when something occurs to me. Bettany had been awfully quiet when I was leaving.

Surely she's not having second thoughts about us? About hooking up with me? I hope not because I'm all for a repeat of this afternoon's action. There's something about her that appeals to me in ways other women haven't.

That aside, it's unusual for me to miss a woman going quiet on me. While I might look like a jock, I'm no-one's fool. However, having received TWO messages about dinner, my mind had been elsewhere.

Damn it, I'd wanted to spend more time with Bettany, and if not for Stella's Swiss Timepiece stomach, I would have. Her being hungry had interrupted some of the best sex of my life.

Of course, it also means I won't be late for dinner and the recriminations involved. I'd learned the hard way that it wasn't worth the grief.

A glance at the clock on the dash and I put my foot down. I don't want to subject Stella to being locked in the truck.

"Don't worry sweetheart, I'm dropping you home first." It's not unusual for me to converse with Stella, even if our chats are mostly one-sided.

When we stop briefly at an intersection, I turn and look at her. "Do you like Bettany?" Rather than stay staring straight ahead, Stella turns her baby browns on me. Her doggy grin says it all.

"Yeah, she's nice, isn't she?"

Although she hadn't been nice earlier, she'd been naughty and, if I was right about her, she had the potential to be naughtier still.

Sad thoughts. Sad thoughts. Sad thoughts.

Sheesh, the last thing I need is to be late for dinner AND sporting an erection.

On parking at the beach the following morning, I'm early enough that I've got time for a coffee. I'm therefore surprised to see the Barkley Castle van already there, although Bettany and her charges are nowhere to be seen.

Stella jumps out of the truck and waits while I hook a leash on her harness. That done, we wander over to Bettany's van to see what's up. On placing my hand on the hood, I'm surprised to find it cool to the touch.

Over at the top of the steps, I spot Bettany a long way down the beach. The flash of her bright pink shoes is as much a pointer as the small dogs swirling around her ankles.

"Feel like a run, girl?" Stella bouncing on the spot is all the answer I need. "Of course you do. What was I thinking?"

And with that, we're off, flying down the beach toward one of the most attractive women I've ever been with. I've settled into a steady jog when I wonder why she hadn't let me know she was arriving earlier today.

And with that, my jog slows to a walk, much to Stella's disappointment. This has me looking down at her as she trots at my side. "What if she doesn't like us? What if I moved things along too quickly yesterday?"

Rather than return my gaze, Stella examines the beach with laser precision. You just never knew when you'd spot the perfect stick, or even better, a forgotten ball. It happened once three years ago, it could happen again.

"Damn it, I've screwed up." Without warning, I break into a run. While Stella resists at first, she's soon belting along next to me. Her ears are back, tongue hanging out to the side, and tail positioned for the best aerodynamics.

I'm not quiet in my approach, and yet Bettany stares resolutely ahead. The same isn't true for her charges, who are glancing back nervously, with even Pompom on edge.

It's something that has me slowing down; worried I'll take her by surprise. However, on pulling up next to her I can see she hasn't got ear buds in, as I'd suspected. She's simply ignoring me.

"I'm so sorry Bettany. Yesterday should never have happened."

Rather than stop and acknowledge me, she speeds up, her movements stiff, her body rigid. Only then do I take time to analyze my apology.

You doofus!

This has me jogging ahead and blocking her way. When she goes to walk around me, I reach out and gently put my hand on her shoulder.

Finally, she looks me in the eye, and the hurt lurking there is like a sucker punch to the gut. Gone is the joie de vivre that would normally be in residence.

"Let me say that again. Sorry if I rushed things yesterday however, I'm NOT sorry we made love. I don't regret that for a second. I felt something I'd not…"

The unmistakable pain of a small dog sinking their teeth into my Achilles' stops me from saying anything further. It's the deep growl that follows that has me shouting, "Stella, down," and pulling hard on her leash.

Unlike Pompom, Stella is an obedient dog. She immediately stands tight against my leg, although she still growls at the nasty little powder puff. And I'll be damned if I'll reprimand her for that. She's just being protective of her dad.

I soon join her in glaring at the assailant. "You're just lucky I like dogs, or I'd be reporting you to animal control."

With the situation reasonably under control, I do my best to ignore the pain in my tendon when I look once more at Bettany. Has my second apology hit home? I'm not sure.

Bettany scans my face briefly, her gaze soon dropping to my ankle. "You really should get that looked at." She then glares at Pompom. "I'll tell his owner she needs to find someone else to look after him. He's a menace."

When she looks ready to resume her walk, I again step in her way.

She doesn't give me a chance to say anything, holding up her forefinger.

"Listen, you don't need to continue training me. I'm sure my legs are better this morning. If I keep wearing the shoes with my insoles, my knees should come right."

She then stares out at sea, while waiting for me to leave.

Like heck I will.

"Oh no, you don't. We agreed to a month. And a month it'll be."

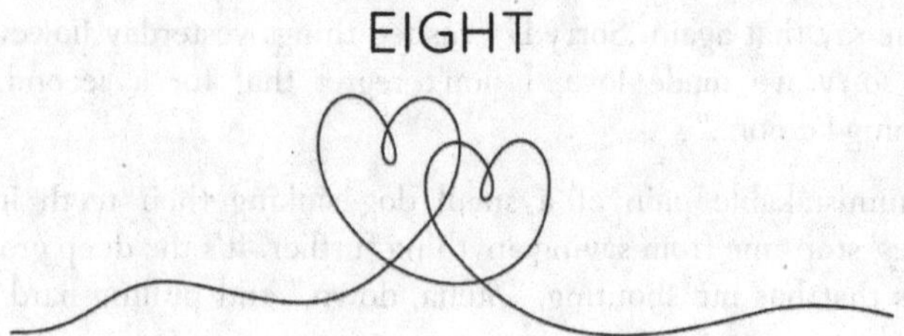

EIGHT

BETTANY

Back at Barkley Castle, I'm still thinking about Dax. Did he really mean it when he said he had no regrets about yesterday?

It seems hard to believe. He seems to be too good to be true.

I've come to no conclusions by the time I've let all the dogs, but one, out into The Keep.

Pompom, the nastiest dog in the kingdom, is in The Dungeon. Of course, it's nothing of the sort, it's just a crate in my office, but it's perfect for my brand.

"You, mister, are a disgrace. I'm calling your mom to come pick you up early." As if to reinforce my decision to expel him, he has the audacity to bare his teeth at me. "Hey you little jerk, remember I'm the one with opposable thumbs. You want treats, you behave yourself."

The hard call made, I settle down to my online learning. If I can offer dog grooming besides the day care, it'll surely broaden my client-base.

The major challenge I'm facing with my up-skilling is that the course isn't cheap. And I still have to organize to meet with a mentor in San Francisco for hands-on training. While I can learn a lot virtually, I'll need to groom a range of breeds in real life if I'm to graduate.

Failing isn't an option, because it could cause me to go out of business. The thought of working with people again is enough to have me shuddering. Dogs don't back-chat, nor do they complain to your supervisor.

My mind still on this, I log in to my account and start trawling through my next lesson. This is about animal behavior and how to go about grooming a nervous dog, or even a vicious one.

Before I can get started on the lesson, a flashing graphic pops up and fills the screen.

It's something that has me looking at Pompom in a new light. His aggressive nature is no doubt thanks to a lack of discipline at home, with his mom the one at fault.

If I signed on for the dog obedience course, it could give me tips on how to deal with naughty dogs like Pompom.

It's just a shame it wouldn't show me how to deal with bad boys like Dax.

I've been through the poodle cuts lesson twice before a disgruntled owner comes to collect Pompom. Rather than say the dog had bitten a member of the public, I said he was disruptive and aggressive. I also said he'd need to undertake dog obedience classes before he can return.

Okay, this might have been a direct quote from my recent online lesson, but the owner had agreed he could be a handful. I'd had to bite my lip to stop my comment in its tracks.

I've not long finished my lunch, when the buzzer sounds out front. Because I don't have any of my regulars booked in for the afternoon, it has to be Dax.

This has my heart momentarily on pause, although it's soon hammering away.

It had been weird enough this morning, when I'd done my best to avoid him by starting out early.

I'm still not sure how I feel about his insistence that we keep to the month of training we'd agreed on. His then leaving me to resume my walk on my own hadn't exactly reinforced this.

As I open the door to the holding pen, I have to wonder if the reason he's keeping me sweet is so I'll continue to look after Stella. Isn't he working on some enormous project? Because we'd finally agreed to trading services, rather than keep paying each other, it makes the most sense.

As always, Dax's good looks do a number on me. While my heart had already been rattling along, it's soon joined by my lady parts. Despite this being the last thing I need, they apparently didn't get the memo.

"You be a good girl this afternoon."

It's on the tip of my tongue to answer that I'm always good when I realize he's talking to Stella. He follows this up by stroking the top of her head, with her drooling in response.

Oh, I know that feeling all too well, Stella.

His fingers really are magic. It's when I realize he's watching me and not his pup that my face blooms. Sprung!

"Come on, Stella, it's just you and me this afternoon. You can keep me company in my office."

I reach out to take the leash, but Dax keeps hold of it, his hand tight against his side. We're at an impasse until he speaks.

"I meant what I said this morning, on the beach, about what happened yesterday. I've no regrets, anything but."

If I thought my face was red before, it's nothing compared to now. With fanning it out of the question, I instead ignore it. He can think of it what he will.

It takes all my nerve to say what's been bugging me since he left yesterday. He says he doesn't have any regrets, and that might well be true.

However, this doesn't mean there's anything special about me. "You say that, yet you left me yesterday because some other woman was texting you."

I'm expecting blustering and excuses. Instead, he's confused, his brows knotted as he looks around the room, as if for answers. I know to the second when he finds one he thinks will be acceptable to me.

Whether it's the truth is another thing entirely.

DAX

There's no stopping my laughter, although this is mostly down to relief. It sure explains why Bettany had been off when I left yesterday. I guess when I'd said, "She's persistent, I'll give her that," I hadn't exactly spelled out that it was my mom I was talking about.

"It's not funny. I'm not like that. I don't want to be part of some harem, not even yours."

Her comment stops my laughter in its tracks. As much as I'd like to tease her about joining my harem, I know now is not the time. I need to set her straight immediately.

"The other woman? Yeah, that would be my mom."

If I thought Bettany had stiffened in response to my laughter, now she's downright rigid with indignation. "Your mom? You really expect me to believe a guy your age is racing off because his mom texts him?"

All I want to do is shrug in response to her calling me a liar, but I need to put things right, and soon. I've got zoom calls coming up that I can't afford to miss.

"Yeah, sad isn't it? But it's the truth. My mom is beyond persistent. I've tried ignoring her in the past, but it only prolongs the agony."

Rather than keep going with our back and forth, I pull my phone out of my pocket and open the text conversation. I hand this over to Bettany so she can see for herself how innocuous the texts had been.

It's her scrolling through earlier texts from my mom that has me holding my hand out in silent request.

"Wow, she's one determined woman, isn't she?" Bettany looks up and I'm surprised to see the pity I've been expecting is missing. "But it's obvious she loves you so very much."

"That she does." It's funny, but until Bettany pointed it out, I hadn't really thought much of it. Sure my mom loves me, she has to. It's in the job description. And while her barrage of texts can be downright annoying, they're always about making sure I'm eating, healthy, and happy.

On Bettany handing my phone back to me, I give her Stella's leash in exchange. "I'll see you later this afternoon. We can talk more then."

Back at my office above the gym, the afternoon can't pass fast enough, and I rush through my zoom calls. There's none of the usual chitchat with the developers and designers working on my latest app. It's to the point I have to apologize, explaining I've got an urgent meeting I need to get to.

The speed of the calls is also thanks to the development finally progressing as I'd want. There'd been a few hiccups at the start that even had me taking my dad's criticisms to heart. If I believed in myself as much as he believes in himself, my life would be very different.

Despite all these misgivings, on driving over to pick up Stella, I sing along to the song on the radio. If things go as I want, this afternoon will go a lot like yesterday, perhaps even better.

This time, though, I'm making sure Stella has some doggy kibble to tide her over. No interruptions this time.

This has me thinking back to how Bettany had been moving when I dropped Stella off. Sure, she'd been stiff, but this was in response to my laughter, not because of sore muscles.

Her movement had been as much a thing of beauty as it always was. I wonder if she'll be keen on another massage, even if she's not in pain.

Bettany's not, but it doesn't take me long to see Stella is, although this is only because I know her as well as I do. That she stays put in the dog bed next to Bettany's desk is the first sign something is off.

The second is when I hunker down next to her and she doesn't so much as lift her head off the padded edge of the bed.

Bettany is soon crouched next to me, her voice tight with worry when she peppers me with a series of questions. "What's wrong with her? Isn't she just sleepy? Wouldn't she have been whining if something was wrong?"

"Usually she would, yes. I need to get her to a vet, and fast." With that, I scoop my none-too-light pup up into my arms and stand awkwardly.

Next to me, Bettany grabs her bag off the back of her office chair, and her phone off the desk. As she walks ahead of me to open the office door, she's busy scrolling through something on her phone.

"Bay Vets are the closest. I'll ring ahead."

While I get Stella settled on the back seat of the truck, I half-listen to Bettany's end of the conversation. After she's asked and answered a few questions, her side of the chat descends into a series of ah-has.

Eventually, she ends the call and turns to me. "They say it sounds like poisoning."

"It'll be something she's eaten." I shake my head in disbelieve that she still hasn't learned her lesson after the last time. "She's got a tendency to eat stuff you and I wouldn't want stuck to our shoe."

This concept has us both falling silent. I even turn the radio off, being in no mood for the upbeat chatter of the DJs. I'm glad of Bettany's company, with her monitoring Stella while I concentrate on driving.

On our arrival, there's been no change. Stella is even quieter, not so much as opening her eyes when I tell her to 'hang on'.

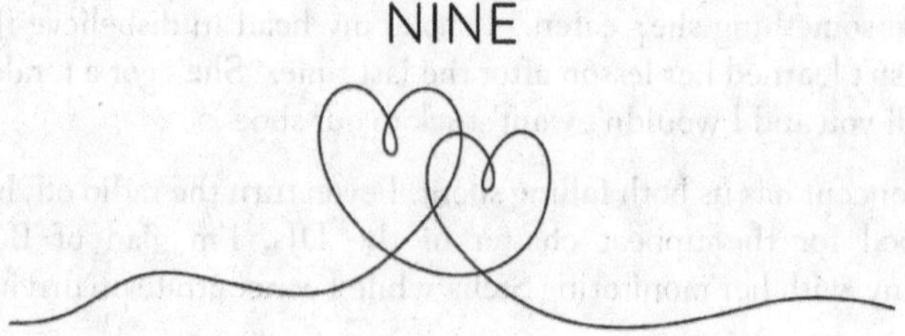

NINE

BETTANY

I'm wracked with guilt that I hadn't noticed how quiet Stella had been. Caught up in my online lesson and grandiose plans, I didn't notice she was sick. I should have remembered how hyperactive the dog was from her earlier visits.

For her to lie there for close to three hours was so out of character that I'm an idiot for not noticing. "I'm so sorry, Dax. I should have seen she wasn't right." A deep swallow and I continue, although my words are mostly for myself. "Let's hope we're not too late."

There's no time for anything further, with Dax turning into the carpark at the vets with little slowing. He slams to a stop alongside the main doors, kills the engine, and wrenches on the parking brake. He's out of the truck and around to grab Stella before I've got my door open.

By the time I make it inside, Stella is already out the back, with Dax slumped in a hard-backed chair in reception. On taking the equally unforgiving chair next to him, I wonder what it is about us sitting next to each other in waiting rooms.

Unsure of the response I'll get, I still reach out and lay my hand over the back of his, giving it a reassuring squeeze. "We got here quickly. That has to count for something."

I keep the crossed fingers on my other hand out of view. If anything were to happen to Stella, Dax would be devastated.

If it were me, I would be. I've loved dogs for as long as I can remember. My constant begging as a kid had finally seen my parents getting me my very own from the shelter.

I never knew what breed Rocky was. However, when I'd finally saved up enough to have her fixed, the vet said there were at least six breeds in the mix.

She was a purebred mongrel, and I loved her for it.

Thinking back on when I'd lost my special girl, I take comfort in Dax, laying his other hand atop mine and returning my squeeze. Even more comforting is when he leaves his hand there.

What feels like hours later, but probably isn't, a vet nurse walks out into the reception area. With Dax and I both having stood, and us being the only people out here, she looks at us.

The first thing I notice is that even in ugly green scrubs, she's stunning. The second thing I notice is her bright smile, every lumen directed at Dax.

On seeing him smiling in return, I drop back into my seat. Yet again, I find myself superfluous to requirements, my place taken by a woman who's a better match.

I'm curling in on myself just wanting this to be over, when Dax puts his hand on my shoulder. "Are you coming?"

I glance up, unsure if he actually wants me with him or not. There isn't a chance I'll accompany him through those swinging double doors if I'm not wanted.

"Come on, I know Stella would like to see you."

Only when I look closely do I see something in his expression that says more clearly than words, that he wants me by his side. It's when I stand next to the vet nurse that I notice my state.

~ Dog walking clothes? Check!

~ Shoes covered in sand? Check!

~ Curls windblown from the beach? Check!

I couldn't be in more disarray if I'd actually tried, and I truly hadn't. This is me. Yet it's me Dax wraps his arm around, not the gorgeous creature next to us. And if looks could kill, I'd be lying next to Stella.

Out the back, we meet the vet who's been working on Stella. The guy quickly explains they'd given Stella an emetic and also put her on a drip to flush any other toxins out of her system.

"She'll need to stay in overnight, but you can catch up with her now."

On being shown into a room that's lined with large cages, there comes a lackluster yip from one corner. Sure enough, it's Stella looking the epitome of sick as a dog.

After opening the front of the cage, the vet nurse leaves in disgust, leading to Dax smiling again. Still feeling somehow responsible for Stella's current state, I reach inside the cage and gently stroke the top of her head.

I'm holding it together until she moves her head to the side and licks my hand in gratitude. This could so very easily have turned out badly. I'm unaware I'm crying until Dax pulls me into a tight embrace and rubs my back.

Would he think I was weird if I reached out and licked him?

Yeah, he probably would, and he'd be right. There was a reason I felt so at home with dogs. Dax sniffing has me wondering if I'm not alone in shedding a tear or two of relief.

Eventually he pulls back, and after giving Stella some snuggles, turns to me. "Thanks for coming with me. I'll drop you back home."

And just like that, I'm back to being unsure of myself, and where I stand with Dax. This doesn't improve when we reach Barkley Castle. There's no mention of training when I walk the dogs in the morning, nothing.

There's also no denying I'm envious of Dax. People want him in their lives. While he might grumble about his mom and her flurry of texts, it shows she loves him. That his dad wants him to give up on the fitness apps and get what he calls a 'real job' also speaks of love, of caring, of being vaguely interested.

I'd love to have the chance to get annoyed with my folks because they were being overbearing and annoying.

The only time my folks are nice to me is when they want something, or have bad news to break.

Like the vacation to Mexico when I'd just turned 16. The vacation, I missed out on because I had to stay home to look after the house. "Make it look like someone is living here."

Maybe that was why Dax was being nice to me at the vets?

He had said nothing about keeping me up to date about Stella. Instead, he'd driven off without a backward glance. And I'll bet I know who it'll be who notifies him as to Stella's condition, and it won't be the vet.

It'll be the blasted Queen of Scrubs.

DAX

A personal training session wouldn't be my first choice this morning. However, it's better than moping around my office wondering how my crap-eating fur baby is faring.

It's this time crunch that has me knocking on the vet's door right on opening time. Stella's grumbling lets me know she's on the mend, and that she wants out of that cage.

"Sorry baby, I'll collect you as soon as I get the okay. Meantime, you be a good girl."

I'd muzzle her to stop any future episodes, but this'd give the impression she's dangerous, rather than just plain stupid. People give us a wide enough berth as it is, without that in the mix.

A quick check of the clock on the dash, and I can see I'm a little early. It hasn't even turned eight-thirty. She had better be on time and not keep me hanging around like usual.

If I hadn't been training her as long as I have, I'd tell her to find someone else. Of course, my sister would give me grief for this, with Chrystal yet another of her pet projects.

We're close to finishing our session when I spot a familiar sight. It must be later than I thought if Bettany is here already. However, a quick check of my watch says this isn't the case.

Damn it, she's gotta be here early on purpose.

I'm giving thought to running over when she spots me and my client. She immediately swings in the other direction and takes off down the beach.

This has the dogs she's leading taken by surprise. One Corgi is even dragged a little before he gets his feet under him.

Damn it, why is she always so quick to jump to conclusions where I'm concerned? She doubtless expects the worst of me, like everyone else. However, on watching Chrystal working on her lunges, I can see how the woman might intimidate Bettany.

And yet she has no right. I'd rather be spending the morning with the quirky, bubbly blonde thundering down the beach and not the fitness goddess next to me.

Sure, if I wanted pretty and vacuous, Chrystal would be perfect.

But that's not what I'm after at all. It's this simple thought that has me dwelling on exactly what I want.

Chrystal has completed her lunges and is looking at me for direction when I realize that it's Bettany I want in my life.

Not just as her trainer, and not just for a month, either

The question now is how the heck I'm supposed to convince her she's the one I want, and not someone like Chrystal.

The solution comes faster than I'd have thought.

"Okay, we're about done, Chrystal. I'll get you to jog to the end of the beach, and back to warm down. Make sure you concentrate on your foot placement." As she sets off down the beach, I follow up by yelling out, "And keep your head up!"

Rather than walk back to my truck, I stand and wait, my gaze swinging between my client and Bettany.

I'd like to yell at Bettany to hold her head up, too. While her stance could be because she's watching her clients, I suspect it's down to introspection.

It's only after Chrystal passes Bettany and her jog slows to a walk that I know my plan has some chance of success.

Soon the two women are busy chatting, with Chrystal pointing at each of the dogs. It had been remembering how much she gushes over Stella that was the catalyst for my rough-and-ready plan. Surely the fluffy handbag dogs in Bettany's care have to be a major draw card in comparison?

I know to the second when the conversation changes from canines to me, with both women staring in my direction. Bettany, however, is quick to look away when she catches me watching.

With nothing more for me to do, I wave briefly before walking up the beach and back to my truck. I won't know whether my plan has worked until later, with the time determined by Stella's recovery.

I'm sure the only reason I couldn't collect her this morning was because the vet nurse wanted another go at me. The woman's flirting had all the subtlety of a pit bull on meth.

There's nothing I can do to stop the shudder at thoughts of facing her again. Well, that, and being reminded of the scum behind dog fights. All things considered, Stella is a sweetheart, given what she went through before I rescued her.

She's also the pup who's about to be boosted from solitary confinement, and heaven help that vet nurse if she gets in my way.

TEN

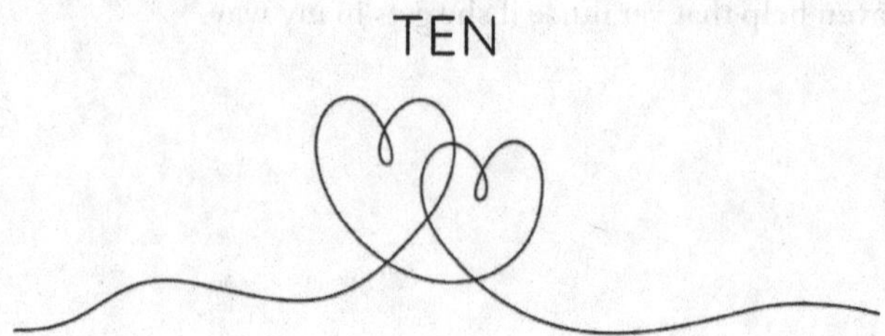

BETTANY

Blast it; I don't want to talk to the woman who'd been exercising with Dax. I'm depressed enough as it is without having more of the competition rubbed in my face.

If I thought she was stunning from a distance, it's nothing to when she's right next to me. Compared to her sculpted perfection, I'm all bumps and lumps, without even a tan to help camouflage my various faults.

Despite my monosyllabic answers, she chatters away, asking about the dogs' names and quirks. However, when she asks if she can pat them, I politely say, "No, you'd better not."

On the plus side, at least she'd asked. Not like some I encounter on the beach.

If not for me wearing a t-shirt with Barkley Castle branding on the back, I'd have done my best to shut her down by now. It gets to the point I can stand her chatter no longer.

Desperate to know what she is to Dax, my question lacks finesse. "You're dating, Dax?"

For the second time in two days, I have someone laughing at me, and as with yesterday, I don't like it. I'm about to storm off and leave her to it, when she says something that has me looking back down the beach.

Have I got it all wrong, again?

According to the woman, Chrystal, she's got a boyfriend, and one whose body is a heap nicer than Dax's. This has my gaze swinging back to her. What sort of person puts physical attributes ahead of things, like whether a person has an outstanding personality, is kind, or funny?

"Anyway, I'd better get going, or Dax will give me grief about stopping for too long."

It's watching her jogging away in all her physical glory that has me wondering who would value looks above all else.

And yet, this is exactly what I've been accusing Dax of, with him never showing this is how he thinks, ever. I've assumed it, without evidence, foisting my insecurities on him.

This has me realizing that even if he wasn't as hot as he is, I'd still like him. I'd like him a lot. Make that I do like him a lot.

I can't stop my grin when I finally admit that his being as hot as he is wouldn't have me kicking him out of bed, either.

It's after two and I've completed another online lesson. It has surprised me to find I know more about dog behavior than I've realized. None of this is down to book-learning, but to finding my way with Rocky, my special rescue pup.

Personality-wise, Rocky was a lot like Stella, which has me wondering how the pup is recovering.

Surely, if there'd been any major developments, Dax would have let me know? This leads to thoughts of him in a tight embrace with that vet nurse. Try as I might, I'm unable to clear my head of the distressing images.

It doesn't matter that he's given no sign he's interested in the woman. My mind still goes there.

It's only hearing movement out front that breaks through my thoughts. Hmmm, I must have forgotten to turn the buzzer back on after I unloaded those supplies from the van.

A second later, the door from the holding pen to my office opens, and Dax pops his head through the gap. Stella at his feet, is having none of it, squirming her way through the gap and over to my desk.

I swivel my chair to the side, allowing me to pat her with both hands. "Well, someone is looking happier than they were yesterday."

Actually, this is an understatement, with the dog wagging her tail hard enough that she's dancing under my hands. Add in her wide doggy grin, and I'm soon laughing at her antics.

It's glancing across my office and catching Dax's gaze that has my laughter dying. I'm not sure what to make of his expression.

There's nothing I can do to stop myself from licking my lips. He's just so gorgeous. His very presence overwhelms me.

And it must be obvious, with him sauntering over to my desk, his eyes never leaving mine. His gaze is as intense as it had been when he'd been filling me completely.

How can I want this man as much as I do after such a brief acquaintance? Whenever he's near, it's as if my heart wants to explode out of my chest and my body comes alive as with no-one before.

I want to stand, but my legs aren't up to the challenge. Instead, I sit there staring at Dax in quiet entreaty. And he hears me.

"Come on Stella, what say you go out and burn off some of that energy of yours in the exercise yard?"

A couple more bounces and the Staffy trots obediently over to the door that Dax has opened for her. With no other dogs out there, I know she'll be okay for a little while. How long Dax and I will be busy is something only he knows.

Soon he's back at my desk, where he helps me to my feet before leaning me against the edge of my desk. If it were any other man, I'd feel trapped. With Dax, I feel nothing of the sort, my body singing in response to his being near.

After a quick kiss, he again stands tall. "So, what have you got on this afternoon?"

My brow wrinkles before I list what's on the schedule. Rather than comment, he shakes his head before running a finger around the neckline of my top. "I'd say you've got too much on, by far."

Oh my, he's talking about what I'm wearing, not my schedule. This has my fizzy bits behaving like thirteen-year-old girls at their first concert. And if I can hear their screaming, then surely Dax can, too? The dirty grin I'm now the recipient of says that's a resounding YES.

"So, beautiful Bettany Brooks, do we make love here, or do we go next door?"

Until he'd said it, I'd never considered us making love in my office. And yet the devilish glint in his eyes says this is his preference. *Oh my.*

Unable to voice a preference thanks to my throat having closed up, I slip out of his embrace. After locking the door, I return to Dax's side.

Rather than slip back into his arms, I slide everything to one side on my, thankfully, large desk. Paperwork will never be the same following this afternoon's delight.

DAX

I couldn't have asked for a better desk, with it exactly the right height for me to get the angle just so. And Bettany holding tight to the side of the desk means she takes every inch of me, her eyes widening with each thrust.

Then, when I think it can't get any hotter, she arches in response to my raking of her nipples with a letter opener. Her core rippling along my length says she's close.

Without warning, I drop the letter opener, scoop her up, and drop back into her office chair. I've done so without pulling free, and am thankful the chair doesn't have arms that'll get in the way.

Instead, we spin away from the desk, giddy with desire and laughter.

There's no laughing when I slide Bettany back along my thighs, before dragging her forward on my length.

It's when Bettany accidentally hits the paddle that adjusts the chair's back that things get interesting. Now we're almost flat with Bettany riding me hard. She keeps this up, driving me deeper with every bounce.

Soon enough, we cross the finish line together, our cries filling the office. Only then do I sit up and wrap my arms around her, desperate to be closer still.

I've only got enough energy left to twist the chair first one way, and then the other, the motion soothing. And yet, tight in my arms, I can sense that Bettany is on edge.

Soon enough, she pulls back, putting some distance between us.

"Dax, there's something I need to tell you."

That she's nervous is obvious. It's the other emotion in the depths of her gorgeous baby blues that has me guessing.

Why do I get I won't like what she has to say? Have I read her wrong as no woman before? When she takes another deep breath, I steel myself by holding my own.

"Dax, I think I love you." Her color is high, and she's rushed through her declaration. Before I've responded, she races on. "It's not your problem. It's mine. I have to stop training with you. It's just too hard. I can't do casual like you can."

Out of words, she crosses her arms protectively. It's taken a lot of nerve for her to open herself up like this.

I nod briefly before uncrossing her arms and pulling her tight against me. "That's just too bad, because when I said we were training for a month, I meant it."

She stiffens, but when she goes to speak, I continue, not giving her the chance. "I also meant it when I said I had no regrets about our time together and..." I pause briefly for maximum effect, "I also think I love you."

As declarations go, there's nothing romantic about either. It's too early for us to know one-hundred percent that what we have is real.

That said, it sure as heck feels like it, with my heart pounding whenever she's near, and my desire to impress her. Yeah, all the signs point to it being the real deal.

If it was casual, it wouldn't have affected me as it did when we'd first made love. Despite it being our first time, I knew it was more than just sex—a lot more.

Even today, it hadn't all been 'wham bam'; there'd been moments of tenderness, of closeness, and, yes, of love.

With her too stunned to respond, I carry on. "Also, I don't run a harem, and I hate casual, too. So, what do you say, you and I start over?"

I'm expecting a lot of things in response to my declaration. Bettany bursting into tears isn't one of them, with me holding her even tighter until the tempest passes.

I'm pressing a kiss on her forehead when we both hear a scratching at the door to the exercise yard. It would appear Stella is over playing on her own and she's probably hungry.

On looking at Bettany, I have to admit, she's not the only one.

After Bettany spots my expression, there's no slowing either of us. While

I set Stella up with the bland food that the vet had given me, Bettany has a quick shower.

Stella has wolfed down her dinner and moved onto the vine leaves on the plate when Bettany calls out to me.

On walking into the bedroom, I find her only wearing a gentle smile. It's one that has something deep inside my chest unfurling. Could it be I've finally got myself a woman with a tendency to care about things as strongly as my mom?

But one who accepts me just as I am.

In the past, this would have had me desperate to escape, but not now, not with this woman. Despite working on a full-on seduction ever since the first time we connected, I want her squeezing my length. I want to bury myself deep and allow emotions to rule—mine, hers, and ours.

I'm getting close to coming when I deliberately slow the pace, keeping us on a precipice. There's something I need to say. "Bettany, I've changed my mind."

Beneath me, she freezes.

"I don't think I love you. I know I do. You complete me." My declaration made, I ramp the pace back up, soon driving us over the edge.

And while I call out her name, she gasps out that she loves me, too.

EPILOGUE

BETTANY

As Dax drives us up to the front entrance at Maddigan's Resort and Spa, I can't believe how nervous I am.

What surprises me more is that Dax also has the jitters.

Perhaps it's his first visit, too? Certainly, I've never been here before, with it out of whack with my financial and social standing. Ritzy is an understatement.

However, the images I'd seen on the website didn't prepare me for the sheer opulence of the foyer. It's enough to have me picking at my new dress, worried I'm tatty compared to the other women wandering around. They certainly appear more relaxed than I am. There isn't a chance I could laugh as they are.

I'd tried talking Dax out of having the launch here, but he'd been insistent. According to him, it has the best AV set-up in town, a necessity with the event being live-streamed.

Hah, no pressure then. I'm close to making a beeline for the ladies and hiding out for the rest of the night when Dax takes my hand. A gentle squeeze has me turning to him, doing my best to hide my sheer terror.

I need to remember that this is his night. I'm here to support him, not to make the night more challenging than it will already be.

"Come on, Bettany. There are some people I'd like you to meet."

We're halfway across the enormous foyer when I spot a familiar face. I don't understand why she's staring daggers at me, though. I took her advice. And yet her glare is as if I'd gone to another doctor for the cortisone injections I'd wanted.

It's when we come to a stop beside her I realize it's Dax she's glaring at, and not me. But why? Did she want Dax for herself? I knew he'd trained her, but didn't think there was any more to it than that.

"Well *brother*, is this why you've been keeping a low profile?"

Brother? But...

Her surname isn't Nichols. It's Proctor. However, with Dr. Proctor too much of a mouthful, I'd taken to calling her Dr. Charlotte.

My confusion must be clear when she answers, as if I've spoken.

"Divorced, but it was easier to continue with the name on my degree." She then leans closer so her words won't travel. "And it annoys the hell out of my ex." I'm confused until she adds. "He was so busy cheating on me he ended up failing med school."

The upside of her taking me into her confidence is that it diffuses the tension somewhat.

"Dr. Charlotte, I just wanted to say thank you for not giving me those cortisone injections. My knees are much better now thanks to the, ah, training." I smile to further lighten the mood.

Despite this, she doesn't immediately relent, with the speculation in her gaze enough to have me squirming. It takes longer than it should for her to return my smile.

When we're joined by a distinguished couple, there's no missing the family resemblance. *Oh, Dax, how could you, and without warning me?*

He squeezes my hand again, for all the good it does. It'd take a valium and a couple of hours under a weighted blanket for me to be okay with this.

"Mom, dad, I'd like you to meet Bettany Brooks, my fiancé."

His parents are as shocked as I am about the fiancé part of the introduction. Despite us seeing each other most nights and every day for the past three months, there's been no talk of anything official.

I don't even have a ring, something Dax hides from his parents by keeping a tight grip on my hand. I'm thinking things can't get any worse when I spot an older couple that look to be as out of place as I am.

It's bad enough that Dax's parents are here, and now I have to deal with mine? They confirm it's no coincidence they're here by making straight for us.

Apart from the free food, I don't have a clue why they'd want to attend an event like this. I find out soon enough, with Dax the only member of our little group not shocked by what happens next.

DAX

As I grip Bettany's hand like a lifeline, I'm conscious my palms are sweaty.

Never one to do things by half, my plan had made sense when I talked it through with Stella. Now I'm not so sure.

Will this stop me from going ahead with it? Heck no, it won't. I never back down from a challenge, and I'm not starting now. Rather, I turn toward Bettany's parents, specifically her dad.

"Mr. and Mrs. Brooks, I'd like to ask for Bettany's hand in marriage. Do I have your blessing?"

The response I get isn't the one I'm after. Rather than saying yes, as I've been expecting, they stall. If I was a betting man, I'd say they're calculating how they can win on the deal. This must be why Bettany avoids them.

Two things happen in rapid succession. First her dad nods, although I suspect this is more to acknowledge the opportunity than his assent. Then someone walks past with a tray that's laden with food.

"Oh, has the buffet started already?" Bettany rushes out, before staring at the back of the retreating waiter like an English Pointer. And it works, with her parents not even bothering to say goodbye before rushing off.

This isn't altogether a surprise. I'd had to confirm there'd be food at the event, before Bettany's parents would accept the invite.

Much as I now want to drop to one knee on the way to making things official, Bettany would kill me. Instead, I delve into the inside pocket of my suit jacket with my free hand and grab the ring I'd put there earlier.

All I need to do is look into her gorgeous blue eyes to see that she's more than okay with the informal nature of my proposal. Delirious would be my best guess, with her eyes wet with the sheen of tears when she whispers "Yes" and throws her arms around me.

With no fanfare, I then slide the solitaire onto her ring finger, all under the watchful gaze of my parents and sister. As engagements go, it's no-fuss, a lot like when we first declared our love for each other.

Of surprise, is hearing my mother and sister sniffling away. Without warning, my mom drags Bettany out of my arms, and in for a motherly hug of congratulations.

"Welcome to the family, dear. Thank you for making my boy so happy." She looks at me, before adding, "Happier than I've seen him in a long time."

Not to be left out, Charlotte also joins in the hug. "It'll be wonderful to have a sister." She then glances at me over Bettany's shoulder. "I knew when I told him to keep away from you, he wouldn't be able to resist." She follows this up with laughter loud enough to have everyone staring at us.

And true to form, I soon join her, and to heck with what anyone thinks. Actually, as I check on my dad, I'm aware this isn't true. Despite fighting it all my life, I want his approval as to my choice of bride.

I'm sick of fighting him over every little thing. He needs to know that if it comes down to me having to choose between them, Bettany will win every time.

And I can tell he knows. I can see it in his expression. The other thing that I can see is something I've seen very little of over the years, and that's pride.

Even more surprising is when he steps forward and pulls me in for an awkward hug. "Congratulations, son." Without loosening his hold, he looks at Bettany, still being squished by my mom and sister. "I can see you've made a wise choice."

After the excitement of our engagement, the launch of the latest app is a bit of a bust; for all it goes off without a hitch.

The AV plays ball, and I've impressed the technology journalists with the hands-on trials. We'll be starting strongly when it goes live tomorrow, that's for sure.

And yet, I can't wait for the evening to be over, to when Bettany and I are alone. Eventually, we are, and I turn to her and say, "Let's call it a night."

She smiles in response to my suggestion. "That sounds wonderful. My feet are killing me." On her starting toward the front doors, I tug on her hand.

"Not so fast." Then, in answer to her perplexed expression, I hold up a room key. And it's not just any room, but one of the hotel's penthouse suites.

"But what about the dogs booked in for the morning? Someone will need to walk them."

I peck her before putting my lips next to her ear to avoid anyone hearing. "Baby, by the time I've finished, you won't be walking anywhere."

It's only after I confirm I've arranged for someone to watch the dogs that she relents. Upstairs, the room is as spectacular now as it had been when I'd checked in earlier.

The rose petals on the king-sized bed are a pleasant touch, as is the bottle of champagne already on ice. "I know we've got the rest of our lives, Bettany, but I love you so very much and I wanted tonight to be special."

"With you in it, my life will always be special. Now come here so I can show you just how much I love you." She gives into her laughter, before adding, "and with what I've got in mind, it won't just be me who'll be having trouble walking tomorrow."

HEALTH

If you hate exercise, the latest life-style app from local trainer, Dax Nichols could be for you. With the help of wife Bettany—the owner of Barkley Castle—their GET-OUT app is taking the fitness industry by storm.

Rather than focus on diet or calories burned, it makes exercise part of your everyday life. As Dax says, there's more to life than being a gym rat.

Phoebe is a plus-size model who's in danger of having her career and life derailed. Wyatt is in the business of making sure people play nice, whether they want to, or not.

ONE

WYATT

I've been at my desk for all of ten minutes when Liam, the general manager at Maddigan's Resort and Spa, walks into my office. Despite my open-door policy, he'd tapped briefly as a courtesy before entering.

There's no need for him to speak. I can already sense something is off. It's enough to see me closing my laptop and giving him my full attention.

"What's up?"

Liam makes himself comfortable in my visitor's chair before he speaks, and even then his words are halting. "We've got a celebrity on the third floor."

I nod; knowing exactly who he's talking about. It's my job to know, despite them wanting to keep a low profile. It's an interesting approach for a woman as happy to flash skin as this one.

I don't even need to shut my eyes to see that cover of Sports Fan Magazine in all its glory. That was one smoking photograph. Look at it long enough and I'd need a bucket of cold water tossed over me before I could think straight.

"Phoebe Jackson?"

Liam tips his head before pressing on. "Yeah, well, she seems to think there's someone in the hotel out to get her." His expression says he doesn't share the woman's concerns.

Meanwhile, I sit taller in my seat, my scalp prickling. Unlike Liam, I've had first-hand experience of a woman sensing someone wanted to hurt her. There wasn't a chance I'd let it slide.

I also want to do the best job possible for Liam. He'd been the first person to see beyond my tattoos and my past, and to give me a chance to prove myself.

Unlike the old general manager, Liam is a born leader; loyalty earned, not demanded.

"I'll go check on her."

Liam gets slowly to his feet. "Just fit it in whenever you can. With our security set up, I'm sure she's imagining things. You know how these celebs can be."

"It's all good. I'll head up there now."

Soon after, I've used my keycard to access the service stairs and am on my way to check on her. It's unusual to find a celebrity on this floor. Their preference being the penthouse, as they believe, is their right.

And because our guest is in room 320 at the end of the hallway, the stairs will exit just across from it. It's thanks to the glass panel in the door that I see the guy loitering outside the room.

He isn't doing anything, just standing there. And yet it's enough to have my scalp prickling as it had when Liam briefed me on the job. Even back when I'd been a bouncer, I knew shady behavior when I saw it.

Unfortunately, on my opening the door, the guy doesn't wait to chat.

He immediately walks off, his pace neither too fast nor too slow, and his head angled down. Again, it's not enough to make it obvious, just enough to hide his features from me and any security cameras.

Out in the hallway, I'm ready to press the talk button on the radio attached to my belt. Rather than make the call immediately, I wait until the elevator doors close. On pressing a button on the radio, I'm connected to the main control room.

"Copy!" comes the response through my earpiece.

"Simon, can you get screen grabs from the security cameras in elevator 4B?"

There's no need to add it's urgent. Simon and I have worked together long enough that he knows that if I'm asking, it's important.

"On it."

"Great, send them to my phone."

Not a minute has passed when my phone pings in my pocket.

Human nature says the mystery guy will have looked up once the elevator doors closed. Most people do. And yet, the images Simon has fired through are from the camera at the bottom of the control panel rather than the one near the ceiling.

This confirms the guy was up to no good. No-one gets in an elevator and keeps their chin tucked into their chest like that, only the guilty. It was the reason I'd had the low-level cameras fitted when I took over security.

They're tiny and hidden within the wood trim, so unless you're looking for them, you'll never see them. This guy certainly hadn't.

"Simon, you copy?"

There's a brief crackle through my earpiece before he replies. "Did you get them?"

"Yeah. Something's off about that guy. Keep track of him."

It might be he was simply visiting someone he shouldn't, but my gut says otherwise. Better we monitor him, if only to get a clearer mugshot.

For now, though, I want to check if Phoebe Jackson is okay. I don't know whether the guy was on his way into, or out of, her room when I disturbed him.

This has me shoving my phone back in my pocket and knocking briskly on 320's door. A strangled cry comes from inside. It's one that twists my gut.

When there's no answer to my second knock, rather than shout through the door and disturb other guests, I grab my keycard.

Sometimes protocol has to go out of the window.

PHOEBE

After speaking to the hotel's manager to tell him of my concerns, I'm at a loss about what to do. Even though the door to my room is good and sturdy, I don't feel safe, anything but.

Instead, I feel trapped. I can't even climb out of my window. Funny—not really—when I'd booked a room on the third floor so no-one could climb IN.

I hate that a stranger—I call him Ralph, because he's wrecking my life—

has me scared of my shadow. I should be out celebrating making the cover of Sports Fan Magazine, not locked away.

There's no socializing for me these days, other than at work-related events I can't get out of. If not for another photo shoot tomorrow, I'd be back to the safety of my apartment in LA.

I'm always ready to leave at a moment's notice these days, my suitcase never fully unpacked. *He's close. I just know it.*

The manager said he'd send someone from security up to speak to me as soon as he could. *Did he not get that it was urgent?*

And just like that, my ability to pace flees, and I stand frozen, my breathing shallow. The room is silent, eerily so, with me having turned off the room's air conditioning on arrival.

It would be all too easy for someone to hide their movements under the hum of one of those things. Well, that's not happening today with me able to hear him moving around outside in the hallway.

I don't want to move, and yet I'm drawn to the peephole in the door. If it is him out there, much as I don't *want* to know, I *need* to know.

I inch my way over, grabbing my newly purchased can of mace off the console table next to the door. I'm about to put my eye to the peephole when there's a loud knocking right next to me.

There's nothing I can do to stop my cry of alarm, although I keep hold of the mace. When there's another knock, I step away from the door, ready to defend myself.

I'm sick of this man ruling my life.

My newfound bravado is out the door when I hear a keycard being inserted in the lock, and it releasing. I watch in horrified fascination as the handle turns, and the door opens, although not so wide that it reveals my stalker.

"Miss Jackson? Wyatt Cassidy, Hotel Security. Are you okay?" comes through the gap.

My relief it's not Ralph is enough to have tears running down my face and me hugging the can like it's a teddy bear.

What the heck was he doing hanging around out there? Why didn't he knock in the first place?

I've not moved when the door slowly opens. I'm not sure what I've been expecting, but this isn't it. Not by a long shot.

Despite him wearing a sharp suit, there's nothing civilized about Wyatt Cassidy. The tattoos visible at collar and cuffs speak to this. The brutal haircut gives the impression of someone who's on the wrong side of the law.

He's nothing like the men I'd dated before my self-imposed exile and yet he does it for me as none of them ever did.

It's then I see the concern in his dark blue eyes.

"Miss Jackson? Are you okay?"

I'm safe. It's not Ralph, and yet I'm unable to move. I hug the mace even tighter, leaving my tears to fall where they may.

As if sensing all this, Wyatt steps forward and gently takes the can from my fingers before putting it down on the console. He then does something completely unexpected. He hugs me as a mom would hug a distressed toddler.

This is the last thing I'd expect from a man like this. His comforting me to this degree is well beyond what his position calls for. It's as if he really cares. As if there's more to him than his tough exterior.

Whatever it is, it's enough to have the floodgates open and I sob at an embarrassing volume. Only when I've got it out of my system, ruining his suit, do I notice the guy, physically.

My first impression looks to have been spot on. He's all muscle, his subtle aftershave tickling my nose. *What the hell is wrong with you? How can I go from being scared senseless to aroused in a matter of minutes?*

Perhaps it's the adrenaline that had fueled my fear is now focused on something more attractive? It's enough to have me wriggling to be free of his hold, worried I'll give myself away.

By kissing him?

Or pushing him onto the bed and jumping him?

Or...

Oh, shut up brain, shut up!

He releases his hold, and I take a step back, all the while staring at the lush carpet. At least this is how it is until he speaks, with the deep timber of his voice hitting me in places that it has no right to.

"Did he hurt you?"

I glance up; mentally crossing my fingers that he won't read my recent thoughts, although these soon flee. There's something about Wyatt's countenance that says if Ralph had hurt me, this guy would repay him in kind.

And I'd be okay with that; it would be nice to have a man looking out for me for a change. No wonder the hotel manager speaks so highly of him.

Still not capable of speech, I shake my head in answer.

"I want you to check something." He follows this up by taking his phone out of the inside pocket of his suit jacket.

Soon enough, he's flicking through a series of images.

What starts out as trembling soon morphs into full-body shudders as Ralph stares back at me from Wyatt's phone. It's the first time I've gotten a proper look at him, with him doing his best to obscure his face.

Like when he'll slide up behind me at an event and whisper in my ear, only to be swallowed by the crowd before I get a good look at him.

That's no longer the case, with the crazed glint in his eyes cutting right through me. It doesn't matter that the photos are grainy, and the angle is weird, my reaction is studio quality.

TWO

WYATT

Phoebe doesn't need to say anything, which is just as well, because I doubt she's capable. Again, I throw protocol out of the window and drag her in for another tight hug. It worked when I was a kid and the foster dad I loved more than my own hugged me, and it works now.

She initially resists before melting against my chest. As I hold her tight, it strikes me there's something familiar about her and yet I know we've never met. It's something that has me wanting to protect her, to hold her and never let go.

To keep it vaguely professional, I override this innate magnetism, instead concentrating on calming her and letting her know she's safe.

It's difficult, with that cover photo of her in a bikini, not preparing me for reality. Sure, she'd looked hot on that cover, but it was nothing compared to being up close like this, to her fitting perfectly against my body.

The other thing that hadn't been on display on that cover was her tumble of dark locks. Instead, a thick braid had run down her back, drawing attention to her booty as she'd twisted to look at the camera over one shoulder.

It's the same booty my hands are itching to explore right now. Not fully trusting myself, I help Phoebe over to the couch, before sitting on the ottoman and facing her.

Much as I want to keep hold of her, I need background on this guy, because Liam hadn't given me anything.

It's after handing her a tissue and waiting while she dries her eyes that I see the lineup of small framed photos displayed on the console. Her family would be my guess, with the upscale silver frames telling me they're important to her.

For all that I don't really have one, family is important to me, too.

A closer look at the portrait gallery and I notice something I hadn't at first glance. The subjects appear very different to the woman across from me, at least outwardly. They seem practical, down-to-earth types. Could it be there's more to Phoebe Jackson than she's letting on?

Only once she's composed do I get down to finding out more about her man problem. "You want to start at the beginning? How long has it been going on?"

After a bit of sniffling, she starts slowly. "Six months. Six months of Ralph always being in the background." She shudders before adding, "Until recently."

"Ralph?"

She waves her hands around, explaining this is what she calls him for want of anything better. She also tells me that after a close call, she'd started delaying her social media posts. These days, her location only shows after she's moved on.

And yet none of it had helped, unless...

"Can I check something on your phone?"

After a moment's hesitation she grabs a large canvas tote from beside the couch, has a rummage through it, and eventually finds her phone.

I'm checking the location settings when she huffs out.

"Of course, I turned them off. That was one of the first things I did."

The tilt of her head, and her brow arching, let me know she doesn't appreciate my questioning her intelligence. Before I can apologize, there's a familiar crackle in my ear. I'm standing soon after.

"Ms. Jackson, I just need to speak to someone. I won't be long." While Simon's side of our conversation will be private, because I'm wearing an earpiece, I won't be able to speak freely in return.

On seeing alarm flare in her wide-set, amber eyes, I quickly add, "I'll be just outside the door."

When I hear what Simon has to report, I wish I was still sitting down. "He can't just have vanished. That's not possible."

And it shouldn't be. I've worked nowhere with as many cameras as there are at Maddigan's. Not to spy on people, but to ensure their safety, and never in sensitive areas, like bedrooms or bathrooms.

"Keep checking. Get help if you need it. Just find him."

Promises made, I re-entered Phoebe's room, ready to continue getting as much information as I can. Only she's not in sight, although clattering from the bathroom has me looking in that direction.

Apart from my mom, I've never seen a woman pack this fast. A wide sweep of her arm and Phoebe sends everything from the counter into her toiletry bag.

She's zipping it up a moment later.

"Hang on, hang on. If you run, he'll only follow you."

I haven't meant to speak this bluntly and my words slam home, leaving her using the vanity for support. Rather than tempt myself by hugging her again, I instead lift the receiver on the phone next to the bed. A brief call to Room Service and coffee, complete with sweet pastries, is on its way.

"Ms. Jackson. He can't get to you while I'm in here, and I need to know more if I'm to help you."

There's no amusement in her laughter at my suggestion.

"Help?! There isn't any help. Not until he hurts me. Don't you think I've reported him to the police?"

I know what she's talking about all too well. I grew up with this. It would be different if she knew who the guy was. Then she could take out a restraining order, although if he was determined or unstable enough, even that wouldn't help.

As we sit and wait for our coffee, she tells me as much as she can. It had mostly been notes and letters until a recent charity fashion parade. Then, despite security, the guy had made it as far as her dressing room, leaving flowers for her.

"After reading the note, I made confetti out of it and trashed it along with the flowers." As if to show, she's frantically destroying the tissue I'd so recently given her.

This has me shutting my eyes, overwhelmed by a scene from my childhood. A time when my dad had been trying to convince my mom, he hadn't meant to hurt her, and for her to give him another chance.

He'd sent flowers and a note, too. And like Phoebe, my mom had ripped the bouquet to pieces before stomping on it. He'd hurt her too many times for her to be taken in by sweet words and even sweeter blooms.

We're both deep in our thoughts when there's a knock at the door, although I'm not startled as Phoebe is. "Relax, it's just Room Service." I'm on my feet and opening the door soon after.

Sure enough, one of the staff stands next to a cart, and following a nod from me, wheels it into the room. Rather than get them to stay and pour the coffee, I send them on their way. I'm not so useless that I can't take care of this small task.

What I can't handle is Phoebe's reaction when she lifts the cloche covering the pastries. On spying the card and single rose sitting atop them, I'm as dumbstruck.

"How in the hell...?"

PHOEBE

I drop the stainless dome, not caring if I smash the plate. I don't want to read Ralph's note, to hear what he has planned for 'us'. Wyatt has other ideas, reaching out and removing the cover, but only as long as it takes to retrieve the note.

Despite my distress, I can't help but notice he's only holding the very corner of the embossed card. His reaction when he reads it has me curious.

Do I want to know what's in it, or not?

I don't get a chance, with him wrapping the note in a napkin off the tray. He then slides it into the pocket of his suit jacket.

Curiosity finally gets the better of me. "What... What did it say?"

Wyatt frowns briefly before answering, although not with what was on the note. "No specifics. Not enough to interest the cops, that's for damned sure."

He falls silent, staring at the ceiling just above my head, deep in thought. He can think all he likes, but I'm not hanging around to see what he comes up with.

"I'm out of here. At least in LA, the doormen at my building can stop him from getting to me." And it's true. There's even a standing order that all the flowers and candies he sends me are to be forwarded to a local hospice.

It's a head-in-the-sand approach for sure, but it's better for my peace of mind and ability to actually sleep at night.

"You're right. You're out of here. Finish packing!"

Coming from a man who only minutes earlier was offering to help me, this comes as a surprise, although not totally. Once I leave the hotel, I'll no longer be his problem and he can get on with his life.

It won't be that easy for me. I've just locked my suitcase when I have a moment's clarity. "Oh blast it, I can't leave."

Wyatt, busy checking something on his phone, looks up in confusion. "Why not?"

"I've got another shoot tomorrow, pool-side. It's actually the main reason I'm here."

And not just any shoot. My agent says if it goes well, it could see me breaking into mainstream modeling. And that's a BIG deal for a curvy girl.

Then reality comes crashing down and I sink onto the bed next to my suitcase. Much as tomorrow's shoot is the break I've been working toward, I can't stay. Not with Ralph nearby, and promising who knew what.

This has me thinking of other upcoming bookings. With Ralph able to track me no matter what precautions I take, I don't see an alternative.

I'll have to cancel everything.

Six months should be long enough for him to get bored and move on. Unfortunately, it will also be long enough to kill my career. Conversely, I won't have a career if he's got me locked away somewhere as he's promised of late.

"This is so unfair. Why the heck did he have to pick me?"

I'm not expecting answers from Wyatt, nor do I get any.

Instead, he crouches down in front of me, waiting until I look at him properly before speaking.

"Do you trust me?"

It's such a simple question, and yet complex all the same. I don't answer immediately, instead thinking back on the glowing reference the hotel manager had given him. There's also my gut instinct that I can indeed trust this guy, certainly more than I trust Ralph, a lot more.

Despite my nod being tentative, it's apparently good enough for Wyatt. After standing, he helps me to my feet, and then grabs my suitcase. That he lifts it as if it weighs nothing reinforces my earlier impression that he's strong.

"Come on, there's a place you can stay where you'll be safe from him, and still make the shoot tomorrow."

When he looks through the peephole before opening the door, it gives me reassurance that he's got my safety in mind.

After exiting my room, we cross the hallway, and he swipes us into a service stairwell. As I take in the unadorned concrete walls and stairs, and the no-nonsense steel balustrade, I balk.

"Where on earth are you taking me?"

Already on his way down the steps, Wyatt stops. "Just trust me, okay? The sooner we get you out of the main building, the safer you'll be."

Despite his assurances, I still dither. Caught between heading who knew where with this hottie, or retracing my steps and coming face-to-face with Ralph. It's a straightforward decision, really.

As I follow Wyatt down the stairs, our footfalls echo around us, loud to my ears, and easy to follow. Then I remember Wyatt having to use a swipe card to access the stairs.

As we descend, I can't stop from holding my breath every time we pass one of those doors with their skinny glass panels. This and being on edge —make that freaking out—sees me breathless when we eventually run out of stairs.

I'm also glad I was wearing sneakers when Wyatt suggested I move rooms. At least I think I'm staying in a room, because on entering a sub-level carpark, I'm having doubts.

Meanwhile, Wyatt is laser-focused. Alert to any movement in the cavernous space, although it appears we're alone. The one thing that is clear is his strength. Not once during our trip has he needed to change my suitcase from one hand to the other. I'd have been dragging it by now.

I've even relaxed somewhat when we reach the very back of the carpark. Faced with an unforgiving, gunmetal gray door, a close match to the concrete walls, my anxiety reasserts itself.

There's no lock, only an old-school alpha-numeric punch code. Without bothering to put my suitcase down, Wyatt punches in what proves to be a 12-digit code.

As someone who has trouble remembering the CSV code on their credit card, I'm impressed. I'm less impressed when he opens the door.

THREE

WYATT

So much for thinking I'd never bring a woman to this place. And yet it's the perfect spot to keep Phoebe safe from that creep. At least until I can have a *chat* with him.

While the police can't do anything until he actually hurts her, that won't hold me back. I'll do for Phoebe what I was too young to do for my mom.

On opening the metal door, as per my last visit, I'm assailed by scents of the past, of trysts and covert get-togethers.

"Come on in and don't let first impressions put you off. Once we're through the tunnel, the place itself is okay."

"Tunnel?" comes the squeaky response from behind me.

Rather than answer her immediately, I reach inside and flick on the lights. This goes a long way toward making the place less daunting.

To further lighten the mood, I turn and make a wide gesture. "It's not much, but it is safe." I follow this up with a wide grin, and one she automatically responds to.

Oh hell, if I thought she was stunning before, it's nothing to when a bright smile transforms her face. It's then I realize what it was about her that seemed familiar.

My mom often wore that haunted expression, despite her valiant attempts to act like everything was okay. There's not a chance I'll stand by and let that creep ruin Phoebe's life.

Once she steps through the gap, I reach out and grab the handle on the inside of the metal door. I'm pulling it shut when I see a flash of bright purple on the other side of the carpark. I pause only long enough to see that it's an old lady before I shut the door with a clang.

Strange that this simple act changes the atmosphere in the tunnel. It's no longer dark and foreboding, rather it's intimate, no doubt as the original architects intended.

Despite my calling it a tunnel, there's nothing subterranean about it. The carpet underfoot is opulent, with the walls and ceilings padded in dark red velvet. The place screams bordello, which is close to its original purpose.

Far from the prying eyes of the Hollywood paparazzi, the old hotel had been a favorite haunt of 1930s' movers and shakers. Along with people they shouldn't associate with. Mostly, it had been starlets desperate to give their careers a boost, although there were rumors of mobsters visiting.

As we start toward the villa, Phoebe's strangely quiet. This has me reaching out and taking her hand. On remembering what's up next, I give it a reassuring squeeze. Her hand tightening on mine tells she's seen the first piece of art.

Or should that be a piece of ass?

I don't blame her for reacting. The erotic prints that line one side of the tunnel had also robbed me of speech when I first saw them.

With males and females alike all wearing masks, their true identities would forever remain a mystery. The other thing the images had in common was the setting, being a heavily curtained four-poster bed

It was the bed I'd slept in only last night.

Soon enough, we reach the end of the tunnel, corridor, or whatever you'd call it, and face another metal door. Again, a 12-digit code is required to enter, and one that's different from the door from the carpark.

If not for me changing the codes to a combination of birthdays and anniversaries, I'd never have remembered them.

Only after I've unlocked the door, do I turn to Phoebe. Despite the dim lighting, it's easy enough to see she's freaking out, and rightly so. If I was in her position, I wouldn't be comfortable either.

"Hey, it's okay. It might not look the greatest, but it is safe." Then, despite the manners drummed into by my mom, rather than stand to the side, I enter first.

After walking into the main room of the villa and flicking on the lights, I take back my opinion that it's okay. This is mainly down to the brothel overtones than anything else.

It's a hell of a lot better than when I first discovered the place. Back then, a fine layer of dust covered every surface, with the bedding no better. It was just as well Liam had agreed to my using the place when I was on call.

This had allowed me to get fresh linens from the hotel's laundry and toss the original sheets. I'd also trashed the old mattress and bought a new one, because, yeah, I so wasn't going there.

After dropping her suitcase in the bedroom, I open the curtains covering the glass sliding doors and sidelights that frame one wall. Rather than facing the hotel, they open out onto a private courtyard.

A fresh look at the eight-foot walls that enclose the space, and I doubt anyone is getting in that way. Along with a profusion of dark pink flowers, the bougainvillea that tops the wall has thorns as effective as razor wire.

If not for finding a dusty folder at the bottom of an ancient filing cabinet, I'd never have known this place existed. Nothing shows on the floor plans of the new hotel, rebuilt after the old place burned to the ground from suspected arson. And on walking around the grounds, even though I'd been looking for it, I couldn't find it. There isn't a chance anyone would simply stumble across the place.

After unlocking, and opening the sliding doors as far as they'll go, I again turn to Phoebe, pleased to find she appears less on edge.

"You'll be safe here. Other than my boss, I'm the only one who knows about this place, and he doesn't even have the entry codes."

"You're leaving?!"

Her words are high-pitched rather than her usual mellow tones, telling me her nerves are back with a vengeance.

"Ms. Jackson, you'll be safer here than in the hotel." I don't bother telling her that Ralph has disappeared. "If you'd prefer, I can re-close the sliding doors. I just thought you'd like some fresh air."

"How long?"

I take a second to decipher her verbal shorthand. "I'll be back in a couple of hours with supplies." After thinking about it for a moment, I continue. "I'm not sure how long you'll be here, but it shouldn't be more than a day or two."

"But, but, but... but what about my shoot tomorrow? It's important. Like really, really important."

Yes, her shoot. While my preference is to keep her locked away until I lay my hands on her stalker—or even her—I can't. "I'll accompany you to the shoot. I'll make sure he can't get to you. You have my word."

PHOEBE

After watching Wyatt disappear down the Portal-O-Porn, I shut the metal door and triple-check it's locked. Wyatt is right; the place really is a fortress.

Re-entering the main room of the villa, I realize there's little point in 12-digit-codes if the sliding doors are wide open. Ralph has shown himself to be resourceful in getting to me in the past. It's not a risk I'm prepared to take.

My shutting the doors is nowhere near as easy as opening them had been for Wyatt. This shouldn't surprise me after seeing how effortlessly he'd carried my suitcase. That thing weighs a ton.

Thoughts of him running into Ralph have me grinning for the first time in months. It would serve that creep right to have his *ass handed to him on a plate*. Wasn't that how the saying went? It's strange enough that I give into an unladylike snort as I think about it.

"I'd pay to see that happen."

After closing the curtains, I turn and face my home for the next few days, or less if Wyatt is as efficient as he appears. The other thing he must be efficient about is cleaning, because the place is immaculate.

And it has to be him, because didn't he say he was the only one with the codes? A man who's not afraid to dirty his hands with housework? Now that's attractive.

I'd been expecting far worse after seeing the dust on the frames in the tunnel. What starts out as a quick check of the bedroom soon slows.

I'd recognize that bed anywhere. Sheesh, there isn't a chance I'm sleeping on it, let alone IN it, not with it having seen that much action.

And yep, my brain has to go there. My fear-based adrenaline happily diverting itself to memories of Wyatt when he'd hugged me. And from there onto what it would be like to share the four-poster with him.

As I walk about this monster piece of furniture, I'm torn between admiring the carving and being horrified by the hangings. They're of yet more dark red velvet, with enough gold tassels to outfit a strip club.

Designed by a man for men would be my guess, and definitely from a bygone era. Didn't Wyatt say something about the thirties? If he's right, then it's a wonder they haven't disintegrated.

This thought has me back out in the main room, and over to the curtains that cover the sliding doors. Again, they're in reasonable condition, given their vintage status.

If not for my being right next to the large doors, I'd never have heard the sounds from outside. Much as I want to run and hide, I can't. I need to see what's out there.

I put my eye up to the narrow gap in the curtains and am immediately blinded. The courtyard is so much brighter than the dimly lit interior of the villa. Eventually, my eyesight adjusts, and just as well. I'm in time to see a disembodied hand coming over the top of the wall.

I'm getting ready to flee when whoever it is—and it has to be Ralph—encounters the thorns of the bougainvillea. Even with the doors and curtains shut, I'm able to hear wild cussing and a subsequent crash.

I'm safe for now, but neither do I want to stay here on my own. I give thought to racing back along the tunnel, across the carpark and up to reception.

And I would, if not for knowing how quickly Ralph can move when he wants to. Fueled by pain and frustration, I suspect he'd be even faster.

I'd never make it. However, this isn't the only course open to me. Instead, I grab my phone and press my contacts list. Thank goodness Wyatt had programmed his number in for me. There wasn't a chance I'd be able to make the call with my hands trembling as they are.

True to his word, Wyatt is with me in under a minute, his rapid breathing telling me he'd run the entire way. He takes one look at me, drops the gym bag he'd been holding, and drags me in for a tight embrace.

I like this about him. Actually, I like a lot of things about him, especially how his muscled chest feels against my boobs. I also feel safe, safer than I have in months, and cared for by a man, as never.

He's an ocean of calm in my out-of-control life.

"I'm sorry. I didn't want to bother you, but..."

"You did exactly the right thing." He squeezes me even tighter for a second before continuing. "Did you shut the doors and curtains before or after he tried to get over the wall?"

"Before, thank goodness." Thoughts of what Ralph might have seen if I hadn't, and I'm back to trembling like a half-set jelly. "I still don't understand how he found me. You said this place..."

Before I say anything else, he loosens his hold on me and steps back. "Your suitcase?! It has to be your suitcase." Without explanation, he leaves me standing there, marching through into the bedroom.

After a moment's hesitation, I follow and am in time to see him heft my suitcase up onto the bed.

"Are you able to open it?"

This question has the cogs in my brain slowly catching up with him. "You think he's tracking me somehow?"

His nod is emphatic. "It's the only thing that makes sense. You said that no matter how quiet you were about your movements, he always turns up?"

Busy concentrating on the tumblers of my combination lock, I don't immediately answer. I wait until after I've released the lock, unzipped my bag, and flipped it open.

"I once got a note from him within fifteen minutes of check-in."

Only now that I'm standing in front of my suitcase do I realize I'll need to empty it, to rummage through everything. I'm not sure how I feel about riffling through my slinky underwear with a man this hot standing right next to me.

More to the point, how will he feel about me flashing my intimates?

I guess I'm about to find out.

FOUR

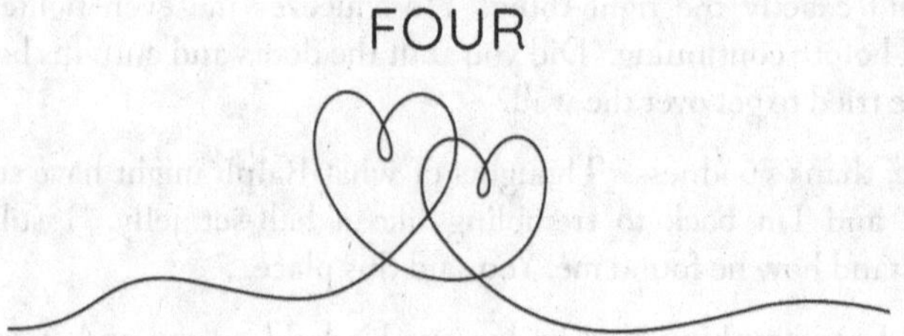

PHOEBE

There's nothing I can do about my face blooming. While I might be comfortable in underwear in front of a camera, this is different.

With my hair and make-up done professionally, it's akin to wearing armor. By comparison, after scooping everything out of my suitcase and into a pile on the bed, I feel raw and exposed. And there's no missing the hitch in Wyatt's breathing as he takes in my belongings.

It doesn't help that thanks to yesterday's shoot being for a lingerie company, there is a lot of silk and lace on hand. There's nothing *secret* about this range, with the designs featuring more cutouts than anything I'd buy for myself.

All I can say is thank goodness for breast petals or pasties, as some models call them, because without them, I'd have refused to pose. Without them, someone would have lost an eye.

It was a shame this nod to modesty made no difference to my parents' attitude toward my chosen career. In my last phone call home, they'd even gone so far as saying they wanted nothing more to do with me until I stopped flaunting myself in public.

I'm hoping they'll come around; in the meantime there are my fees to consider. My latest—albeit slightly dodgy—shoot would net me enough to extend the lease on my apartment in LA.

It's also enough to upgrade my sewing machine to the one I'd wanted since my obsession with Project Runway began all those years ago. One of my first sewing projects will be to close up the holes in the samples the X-rated lingerie company said I could keep.

All that aside, I'm still wondering if the shoot was a good idea with Ralph on the loose. Talk about adding gasoline to the fire. While the agency had assured me they'd obscure my face in any ads, there were no guarantees.

Obscured like those in the tunnel leading to the villa?

I've barely finished giving thought to the comparison when Wyatt shoves his hand into a pouch on the inside of my suitcase. Sure enough, when he pulls his hand free, he's got one of my nipple shields from yesterday's shoot stuck to the end of his finger.

Oh, let me die right now.

There's no missing the snort when he realizes what it is. After this, he doesn't even attempt to hide his laughter, and I soon join him.

It's been so long since I've laughed about anything, and especially something as silly as this. It only gets funnier when he flicks his hand to rid himself of the flower-shaped patch.

He does not know how sticky those things are if he thinks that'll work. It's something that has me grabbing his hand mid-flick and peeling the offending petal free. Experience tells me that other than folding it in half, it'll stick to anything and everything for days.

Only after I've done so, and slid it into the back pocket of my jeans, do I glance sideways at Wyatt. The flash of arousal in his eyes has me unable to look away. The difference now is I don't feel vulnerable, anything but.

It must be something that shows, with Wyatt immediately breaking eye contact. The moment, whatever it was, is gone, and my frustration is palpable. This leaves me struggling to get my emotions and body back under my control.

After clearing his throat, Wyatt continues searching the carcass of my suitcase. It's not until he unzips the liner to access the inner workings of the telescopic handle that he gets lucky.

"Got you, you bastard!" Soon enough, he's holding up two GPS trackers.

"The pink one's mine, but I'm not sure about—"

I don't bother saying anything else, when it's obvious whom it belongs to.

Blast it, all this time I've been sneaking around, keeping quiet about where I am, and where I'm going, and all for nothing.

I'm therefore surprised when Wyatt slides both trackers back into the lining of my suitcase.

"Aren't you going to destroy it?" There's nothing I can do to hide my glee at thoughts of smashing it with a hammer. It's what I want to do, to take out my frustrations at Ralph tracking me so easily.

Wyatt shakes his head before speaking. "Are you kidding? And let that low-life know we're onto him?"

If I could do so without looking like an idiot, I'd smack my forehead. The irony of catching Ralph using his own tracking device is perfect, and I want in on the action.

Next to me, Wyatt falls silent, although not for long. "Are you alright, Ms. Jackson? You keep kicking the bedside cabinet and muttering."

My head snaps up in response. "Sorry, I'm just thinking of what I'll do to him when we catch him."

"We?"

I nod emphatically. "He's made the past six months hell for me. If you think I'm standing back, you are so wrong."

Wyatt stares at me for longer than I'm comfortable with, his thoughts apparently taking him miles away.

He nods briefly before speaking. "Okay. I can understand that."

It's only when he gives into a broad grin that I know I'll get my wish. All the counseling in the world would pale compared to my getting even with Ralph by...

Actually, I'm not sure what I want to do to him, just that it needs to be painful. Am I capable of exacting bodily harm like that?

This has me looking at Wyatt again. Whereas I'm a wimp, I doubt Wyatt would be as squeamish. I'm now grinning as broadly as he is, maybe even more so with this appearing to cause him concern.

Not wanting to waste a second on exacting revenge, I toss all my belongings back into the suitcase and zip it shut.

I've yanked my case onto the floor and am attempting to drag it out the bedroom door when Wyatt stops me. "Hang on. Where do you think you're going?"

At my visceral reaction to him touching me, I'm momentarily lost for words, although thankfully not for long. "But you said, you said, I could be a part of it?"

"And you will. But before that can happen, we'll have to get a few things lined up. We'll only get one shot at this, so we need to be prepared."

"But, when? I want to get on with my life."

Wyatt looks at me and then at the bed. "It'll have to be after your shoot tomorrow." He then looks longingly at my suitcase before adding. "In the meantime, you may as well make yourself comfortable."

After this ambiguous aside, he turns and leaves me on my own.

I'm not sure how to take his suggestion. Part of me is all for slipping into some of that lingerie and to heck with wearing breast petals. I'm wildly fanning my face at the very thought when I realize Wyatt is watching me from out in the main living area.

As I take in how dark his eyes are, I know exactly what I'd like to do.

But do I dare? What if I've read the signals wrong? What if it's my being as aroused as I am that has me thinking he wants me?

WYATT

Damn it, I can't think straight. Not with images of Phoebe wearing some of the lingerie from her suitcase cluttering my mind. And without benefit of nipple covers, too.

I need to concentrate on trapping a man, not this woman. I definitely shouldn't be thinking about how her nipples would peek out of the slits in that bra.

Black silk always does it for me. Add in black lace and more holes than a Swiss cheese and my cock is raring to go. What I really need is a cold shower, but the only way to the bathroom is through the bedroom.

I can hardly breeze through there, telling her I've got a boner I need to deal with. That open invitation in her eyes would be too much. It's when looking through the gap in the curtains that the solution comes to me.

While Phoebe has to be careful about going outside, the same isn't true for me. The plunge pool in the courtyard will be cold. Experience tells me it'll be achingly so, and able to deal to my erection before I'm tempted further.

At least this way I can sort myself out without leaving her on her own.

That's not happening with Ralph on the loose and him knowing exactly where she is.

I speak while ensuring I keep my back to her. "I'm just stepping outside for a moment. Make sure you keep the curtains shut."

Without waiting for a response, I slide open one of the large doors, just enough for me to sneak outside. Once through the gap, the curtain falls back into place, concealing me from Phoebe.

I need to make this fast. After kicking off my shoes, I strip down to my boxers, the rest of my clothes folded and placed on one of the old-school wooden sun loungers.

I'm about to jump into the pool when I realize the only towels are in the bathroom. A brief glance at the still-closed curtains and I ditch my boxers.

After this, a simple step forward and I'm swallowed whole by the ground-level pool. Because it's over ten-feet-deep, I submerge fully, with every nerve ending screaming for release along with my cock.

It was the sort of setup that would usually go with a sauna, and yet there isn't one in the villa that I'm aware of.

One second I'm floating near the bottom, the next a vision in black lace drops into the water next to me. And damn if I wasn't right about those nipples.

But I can't go there. I'm tasked with taking care of Phoebe. And that doesn't include taking care of ALL her needs, but hell, I'm tempted. I know exactly how I'd go about it, too.

I'm even reaching out when she kicks urgently to the surface. This leaves me with a face-full of matching lace panties, slits and all. What the hell? Is she doing it on purpose?

As cold as it is, the water temperature just isn't up to dealing with my response. I'd need to chuck half-a-dozen bags of party ice in here for that to be the case.

Her proximity leaving me breathless, I also kick for the surface, banging into her. Sheesh, her nipples are every bit as hard as I'd hoped, and there's nothing I can do to stop from licking my lips. It's a movement she apes, and that has my cock leaping, desperate for some action.

"Ms. Jackson, I'm so sorry." I do my best to put some distance between us without my hands being all over her. "Please accept my apologies..." My thoughts distracted by her silk-clad breasts just below the surface. I can't manage anything further.

Instead, I haul myself out of the pool and grab my boxers, covering my arousal as best I can.

She looks disappointed, and I'm at a loss about what to do. I can't very well leave her out here on her own, and I need to get dressed. In the end, I turn my back on her and do just that, being as efficient as possible. It's difficult with my body still damp from the plunge pool.

Damp like she is?

This has me gritting my teeth as I struggle to button up my shirt. I'm making a hash of my tie when I hear splashing coming from behind me.

"A little help here?"

Damn it, I forgot the pool doesn't have a ladder. It had when I first discovered the place, but it'd been so badly rotted that I ripped it out.

Not bothering with my shoes and socks, I turn and help her. This has any residual effects of the chilly water wiped out in a flash; a flash of sun-kissed skin against jet-black silk.

Despite my best intentions, I pull her tight against me and my lips lower to hers. And damned if she doesn't taste every bit as good as I've imagined since that copy of Sports Fan Magazine first landed on my desk.

Soon enough, she's cradled in my arms and I'm working my way between the curtains and into the villa. I don't stop there, walking straight through to the bedroom and laying her still-damp form in the middle of the enormous bed.

A quick scan of her body and I'm smiling broadly. Thanks to all those slits and cut-outs, I won't even need to remove her lingerie to have her screaming my name.

FIVE

PHOEBE

When modeling the sheer lingerie only yesterday, I never could have imagined I'd be in my current state. Wyatt, or rather his tongue, is making use of the slits in my bra. My nipples pebbled and doing their best to escape.

He's teasing my curls through the slit in the front of the matching panties, when I hear a now-familiar crackle. On Wyatt taking his lips away from my nipple, I know he's heard it, too.

Noooooooooooo!!!!!!

While I don't voice my disappointment, it rings loud in my head. I've never wanted something—make that someone—this much in my life. Wyatt has me feeling safe for the first time in months.

Could this be why I feel safe enough to let my guard down sexually, to give myself over to him, to allow the pleasure to consume my body?

With him around, nothing bad can happen, unless he's the one doing the bad things. I'm not even naked and he's got me closer to coming than I have been in years.

His heavy sigh says it all, although he still puts his regret into words.

"I'm sorry. I'll have to take that. It'll be important."

What he doesn't say is that it might be news about Ralph. After my panicked call earlier, Wyatt has had people searching the grounds. They might even have caught up with him.

As I watch Wyatt straighten and leave the room, I'm torn. Do I stay spread out on the bed like this, or get up and get dressed? It's then I remember how much action this bed has seen, and I'm on my feet in seconds.

As consumed as I am by this, I don't give attention to Wyatt's side of the radio conversation.

I'm more interested in having a quick shower while he's still around to stand watch. Hmmmm, I really wouldn't mind him watching me. Nope, not at all.

Who are you, and what have you done with Phoebe Jackson?

My little voice has a point. Other than when I'm on a shoot, I don't flash myself around. I'm only confident in front of the camera. Other than that, I might as well be fifteen and without a date for the prom.

I've not moved when Wyatt returns. He doesn't need to say anything, his expression telling me Ralph is still on the loose.

"I'll need to leave you on your own for a little while." He softens the blow of his words by wrapping his arms around me and holding me tight.

He's wasting his time if he's trying to calm me. His shirt scraping my still-taut nipples has me more interested in sex than any potential attack by Ralph. As if sensing this, he pulls back while still holding my upper arms.

"Phoebe, listen to me."

Only when I'm looking at him properly does he continue.

"He's already failed to get over the wall, and I've locked the sliding doors. He can't get in through the tunnel, so you should be safe until my return."

"Should be?"

He then shows that he's thought things through more than I have. "I doubt he'll try scaling the wall again. If he does and smashes his way in, lock yourself in the bathroom. There's no way he can get in there."

I stare up at him open-mouthed for a second. "And no way that I can get out!"

"Take your phone with you and call me immediately. I won't be far away." He rubs his hands up and down my arms. "I'll grab us some lunch while I'm over at the main building."

And just like that, he's gone, leaving me with a sense of dread that it's only a matter of time before Ralph turns up. He always does.

This effectively kills off any remaining arousal and sees me dressed in a flash. If Ralph turns up, I don't want him to find me standing there in my X-rated lingerie.

Instead, I'm in my usual chain store underwear, jeans, and a t-shirt with MERMAIDS DON'T HAVE THIGH GAPS splashed across the front. After wrapping my hair in a towel, I pull on a pair of Chucks in case I need to kick someone. Finally, I tuck my phone in the back pocket of my jeans.

A couple of minutes of standing in the middle of the living room on high alert, and I'm a nervous wreck. I can't keep this up, but neither can I fully relax.

As I look around the living room, I'm struck by the lack of personal touches. Despite its bordello overtones, it's like hotel rooms the world over in that it's not one person's space.

Well, I can soon fix that, with this something I'd normally have done on first moving in. I guess it's no surprise that my libido being hijacked by Wyatt had me forgetting my usual ritual.

After arranging the framed photos of my parents, grandparents, and extended family atop the vintage sideboard, I step back to admire my handy work. Despite the rift over my career, they're still my family, and I take comfort in having them close by.

This done, it's time to explore the villa, because it can't simply be a living room, bedroom, and bathroom. Even in its heyday, they'd have needed the means of making a cup of coffee or cocktails, wouldn't they?

It's on my third sweep of the living room that I find the sliding panel. "Ah ha, I knew it." A fine layer of dust covers every surface in the small kitchenette, evidence I'm the first person to enter here in a long time.

I'm running my finger through the dust on the counter when I hear movement out in the courtyard. I'm sliding the panel shut when I hear someone—it has to be Ralph—attempting to open the patio doors.

The sound of smashing glass soon follows.

My heart thunders in my chest. I'm trapped in here, with no lock in evidence. I'm stepping from foot to foot, my flight, or fight in full flow, when my wild gaze spies a large chopping board on the counter.

If I can jam it between the end of the panel and the wall, it'll stop the panel from sliding open and Ralph won't realize it moves. Instead, he'll assume it's a panel like any other in the room.

Heaven knows, it had taken me pressing and prodding all the walls to find it. Meanwhile, I breathe through my mouth and move as quietly as possible.

There's no point barricading myself in if he knows I'm there. With the chopping board in place, I slide my phone out of the back pocket of my jeans. After killing any alerts, I send a text to Wyatt.

HE'S HERE. HE'S INSIDE!!!!!!!!!!!!!!!!!!!!!!!

With my phone on the counter so I can see any replies, I grab a dusty bottle from the wine rack. Thus armed, I stand at the ready because I am not going down without a fight.

Not this time.

Never.

WYATT

Simon and I wander around a standard room on the first floor. We're alert for something that will point to the guest's true identity.

But there's nothing, with the space as pristine as if room service had already prepared it for the next guest.

Apart from the large suitcase on the bed closest to the windows. Here, at least, I can see signs of habitation. "It has to be his."

The suitcase sitting wide open, I examine the contents, being careful not to touch anything. There's an interesting mix of clothing—both male and female—along with half-a-dozen wigs.

I instantly recognize the gray pin curls as being those of the old lady I'd seen in the carpark this morning. And if I was in any doubt, the bright purple dress next to it confirms this.

Simon uses his pen to move a brunette toupee to one side. There's a gray one underneath. "It's no wonder he's been able to hide from us."

I think about this for a moment. "Okay, I get that, but how did you work out which room he was in?"

It turns out no-one messes with our room service crew. They'd been furious to hear someone had slipped a note in with the coffee and pastries I'd ordered. This had them holding their own investigation, with the cleaning crew helping.

Because of Ralph's distinctive handwriting, it hadn't taken them long to narrow it down to this room.

Simon uses his pen to move a couple of other items before turning to me. "I'll bet when he scrawled that nasty note about his room not being clean enough, he couldn't foresee this."

I nod, mostly to myself, all the while wondering why Ralph's packed up. Does he know we're onto him, or was he simply ready to leave, taking Phoebe with him?

After easing a few things out of the way, I slide a GPS tracker inside the lining of the case, because two can play at that game. Thanks to my phone being as highly spec'd out as it is, I'll be able to track the tag to within a couple feet.

"What I want to know is where the hell he is now?"

I've come to no decision when I get a text that blasts my system with adrenaline.

"Crap, I know where the bastard is!"

I'm running soon after, and Simon's right behind me. Ralph's room being on the first floor, there's no need to take the elevator. Instead, we fly down the one flight of stairs to the basement carpark.

Behind me, Simon says nothing, saving his breath for keeping up. Soon enough, we're next to the metal door, and I'm punching in the entry code. I go as fast as I can without screwing up the numbers, but it's tricky.

I have to get to Phoebe before Ralph can hurt her.

There'd been no missing the threat hidden in the note delivered with our coffee. I'll be damned if I'll stand back and see a woman hurt. Not if I can help it. It was a pledge I'd made to nine-year-old me, and one I've stuck to.

Outwardly, his note had been innocuous, and if the guy got himself a talented lawyer, they'd convince the judge it was nothing.

"Nothing but a sexy game of hide-and-seek, Your Honor."

However, reading between the lines, he'd told her there was nowhere to hide, and the longer she kept him waiting, the angrier he'd get.

It was part of the reason I'd kept it from her. Well, that and any potential fingerprints. It might have been different with the old Chief of Police, but apparently the new guy is proficient. If I shove enough evidence in his direction, he'll run with it.

But before it got to that, I'd wanted to try a more direct approach, with a little *friendly* warning to back off. However, the number of exclamation marks in Phoebe's text told me we were way past so simple a solution.

If nothing else, we can get him for the break-in at the hotel villa.

But first we have to catch him.

When we reach the door at the other end of the tunnel, there's no missing Simon's surprise at the images we've raced by.

"I'll explain later." I've kept my voice deliberately low, and I'm as quiet when I punch the numbers into the keypad.

Before swinging the door wide, I put my finger to my lips as an insurance of sorts. His expression says Simon has no intention of making any sound. All this changes after I open the door.

If Ralph is still in the villa, then we have to move fast if we want to catch him. Despite the speed of our entrance, the living room is empty, but for the remains of one of the large glass side panels.

I also come up empty-handed in the bedroom and bathroom.

"Damn it to hell. He must have her."

I follow this up by bellowing my frustration. Guilt isn't strong enough to describe the emotion swamping me. I promised to keep her safe. I told her I'd stop that low-life from getting to her. And I've failed.

I drop boneless onto the ornate couch, head in hands. This is partly down to remorse, but mostly down to thinking about what the hell I do now.

"We need to get back to his room. He won't leave without that suitcase."

This commonsense from Simon has me back on my feet. Despite being able to follow the creep at my leisure thanks to that tracker, I don't want to waste time.

Phoebe wouldn't go willingly, meaning she's scared and possibly hurt. The sooner I can rescue her, the better.

I'm already on my way to the door leading to the tunnel when I hear movement on the far side of the room. Looking back, I watch in amazement as part of the wall slides to one side.

I'm across the room in a flash, pulling Phoebe into a tight embrace. "Shhhh, shhhh, shhhh. It's okay. You're safe with me. I've got you."

After pressing a kiss to her forehead, I add, "I won't leave you again."

SIX

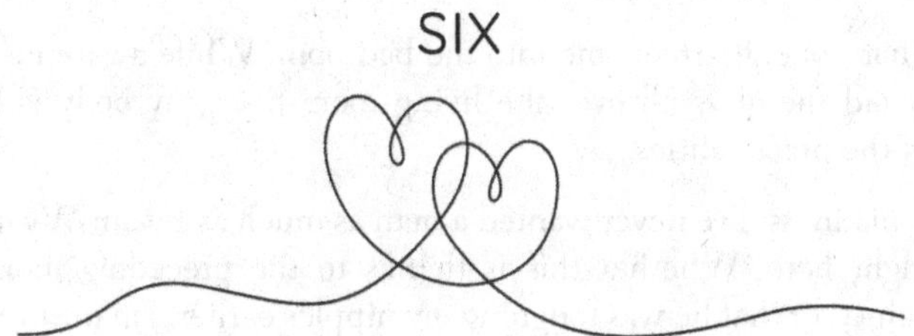

PHOEBE

Despite Wyatt's protestations that I'm safe, that's not what I'm feeling. From scared out of my mind minutes earlier, I'm now overcome with lust.

It seems with Wyatt in the mix, I've no control over my libido. If not for the man standing silently in the background, I'd already be acting on my arousal.

Without releasing his hold on me, Wyatt introduces the guy. "Ms. Jackson, this is Simon Phillips, my, ah, deputy, for want of a better word."

Perhaps it's that Wyatt's last name is Cassidy, but my scrambled mind has me picturing them in cowboy outfits complete with stars. Lucky for me, I'm able to hide my smile against his chest.

Who knew what they'd think if they caught me laughing?

What is wrong with you?

Someone threatened to hurt you.

You shouldn't be laughing.

Okay, so there might be a teensy hysterical edge, to my amusement.

"Simon, I'll stay here with Ms. Jackson to make sure she's safe. Do you want to speak to someone in maintenance and get them over here to board up that sidelight? I'll text you the key codes."

"On it!" A moment later, and he's gone.

After releasing his hold on me, Wyatt gives me a reassuring pat on the shoulder before he inspects the newly discovered kitchenette.

With that done, he steers me into the bedroom. While aware he's done so to avoid the glass all over the living room floor, my body is having none of the practicalities.

This is madness. I've never wanted a man as much as I want Wyatt right now, right here. Whether this is thanks to the preceding months of uncertainty, or that he was tonguing my nipples earlier, I'm unsure.

And yet my attraction to him is way beyond lust. He's shown himself to be kind and caring and a true gentleman. He's my knight in shining armor, or at least, a sharp suit.

The same knight who's just tucked me into bed.

The same knight who isn't joining me.

My frustration must show, because he immediately straightens and steps back. "I'm sorry, Phoebe. My earlier behavior was unacceptable. I should never have acted as I did."

His apology lands on my chest like lead.

He leaves, closing the bedroom door on his way out. The only light in the windowless room is now courtesy of the attached bath.

The dark is pressing in on me when I notice the smell wafting up from the bed. Rather than decades of illicit sexual trysts, it's of freshly laundered sheets, Wyatt's aftershave, and his own unique scent. This has me grabbing the spare pillow, wrapping myself tight around it and breathing in.

It's the next best thing to snuggling the man himself, something I suspect won't happen again. Disappointment aside, it calms me enough that despite the noise coming from the living room; I sleep deeply for the first time in months.

There's no way Ralph can get to me with Wyatt around.

I'm not sure how long has passed when I become aware the bedroom door has opened and Wyatt is next to the bed. On listening out, I'm met with quiet from the living room. I must have slept for hours.

"What time is it?"

A quick check of his watch and he says, "Just after seven. Come on, up you get. I've sorted out dinner for us."

"Dinner? But I thought I'd be moving back to the hotel." I wave toward the living room with its boarded-up sidelight. To me, it makes no sense to stay here when Ralph knows where I am.

Even with my having hid in the kitchenette, he'll have seen my things. He'll know this is where I'm staying.

Wyatt's shoulders drop, and I brace myself for the bad news.

"If you move back to the hotel, policy prohibits me from staying with you. The same doesn't apply here."

Sleep still clouding my mind; I don't immediately grasp the import of what he's said. Only after thoughts of us cohabitating have subsided do I come to my senses.

Had his shoulders dropping like that been a sign of resignation, or surrender, and am I brave enough to find out? As I'd been earlier today when I'd jumped in the pool in that skimpy underwear?

His response at the time told me he found me attractive, although I'm now second-guessing myself. Had he then come to his senses and vamoosed using that radio call as an excuse to escape?

It's something that's been bugging me ever since. Not that I've had a lot of time to dwell on it thanks to Ralph breaking in. We're out in the living room when I decide I need to know.

"Wyatt, when you left here earlier, why was that?"

I don't need to be a student of body language to see he doesn't want to answer. This has me torn between wanting to be kept in the dark and hearing the truth.

If he's only interested in me as a guest of the hotel and nothing more, I need to know. If he's not attracted to me, I've humiliated myself enough already.

With him yet to answer, I prompt him. "Please, Wyatt, I need to know. The not knowing is awful."

After hearing what he has to say, my heart falters. The good news is that Wyatt hadn't used the radio summons to escape.

The bad news is that it sounds like Ralph broke into the villa to kidnap me. To say this is an escalation from his earlier pestering is an understatement.

If I hadn't hidden in the kitchenette and he'd found me...

My legs fail, and as the dark claims me, I sink to the floor.

WYATT

I'm still half asleep the following morning when I notice two things. The first is my cock is hard up against Phoebe's ass and I've got a hand cradling one of her breasts.

I'm confused until I remember her telling me at some stage during the night not to be silly and to get under the covers. And I had, although I'd jammed a couple of pillows between us. Where they are now? Who knew?

None of this does anything to soften my morning wood. Rather, the opposite happens. And this when I'd promised to protect, not seduce.

After she'd fainted, I'd simply put her in bed and covered her up. I thought she'd come round, but she'd fallen into a deep sleep. If not for her steady breathing and relaxed features, I'd have called a doctor.

Dinner long-forgotten, I'd lain on top of the covers, more to provide reassurance if she woke, and because she smelled so damn good.

As I slowly take my hand away from her full breast, there's no missing the tightness of her nipple. There's also no missing her sigh of disappointment. It's something I share.

I roll onto my back to put some distance between us because if Liam found out I'd been helping myself to a guest like this, he'd be unimpressed. I'm here to take care of her Ralph problem, not her.

That creep got dangerously close yesterday. If I'm to avoid him getting even closer, I need to concentrate. If I give into temptation and bury myself in Phoebe's lush depths, I'll be no good to anyone.

You sure about that, buddy?

I've no sooner thought this, than Phoebe rolls over to face me, her eyes full of passion, her lips parted on another sigh. There's no missing the invitation.

It's at this point I think back on how her breast had felt in my hand.

Wonderful?

Yeah that, and naked! If not for my still wearing boxers and a t-shirt, I'd be worried we'd already made love. And if I stay here, that's exactly what'll happen.

A quick check of the ancient clock on the dresser next to the bed shows that it's still early. Much as I want to roll over and give into temptation, I can't.

And neither can Phoebe.

Hadn't she said she was due at hair and make-up at seven? And if the shoot is as big a deal as she's made out, shouldn't she be on time?

I turn my head on the pillow so I can look at her when I speak. "Your photo shoot?"

After a moment's confusion, her eyes widen. She then lifts her head off the pillow so she can check the clock on the other side of me.

"Oh, oh, oh."

A second later, she flings the covers to the side and jumps out of bed.

Now I'm the one whose eyes are widening as I take in her gorgeous curves. I've not seen nearly enough when she disappears into the bathroom, all the while wailing about how she'll be late.

Because I'll be accompanying her to the shoot, I'll also need to be ready. This sees me reaching into the bathroom, only far enough to grab a towel. Rather than join her, which would definitely see us late to set, I head for the courtyard.

A cold plunge will have me clean enough and hopefully take care of an erection that's showing no signs of abating.

Despite our departure being a blur, I'm still on high alert when we exit the tunnel into the carpark. There's no-one around, other than one of our casino guards. Whereas he'd usually be upstairs, this morning he's standing next to the elevator.

That he's on duty is obvious, with his stance pointing to him being ex-forces. There's something about those guys that says you can rely on them.

A brief nod to the guard, and we take the elevator to the second floor, where she's getting ready for the shoot. I leave only once Phoebe has entered the room, with her under strict instructions to phone me when she's ready to leave.

While she might be safe making her way downstairs with the stylists as they've offered, I veto this. With Ralph getting ever desperate, it's not a risk I'm prepared to take.

At this stage, all I know about the shoot is that it's for the Curvy Girl Resort Wear label, which is apparently a big deal.

What even is resort wear?

As I watch Phoebe shrug free of the toweling robe she'd worn from hair and make-up, down to the shoot, I couldn't even tell you my name.

I'd thought that bikini she'd worn for the Sports Fan cover was hot. It's got nothing on the silver bikini she's wearing now. Watching over her during the shoot will be both a blessing and a curse.

I'm keeping my composure until the photographer asks her to turn away from the camera.

It had to be a thong, didn't it? It's gonna take a couple of dozen bags of party ice in the plunge pool to take the edge off this erection. And the smile Phoebe gifts me over her shoulder says that she knows.

That's not all it says.

SEVEN

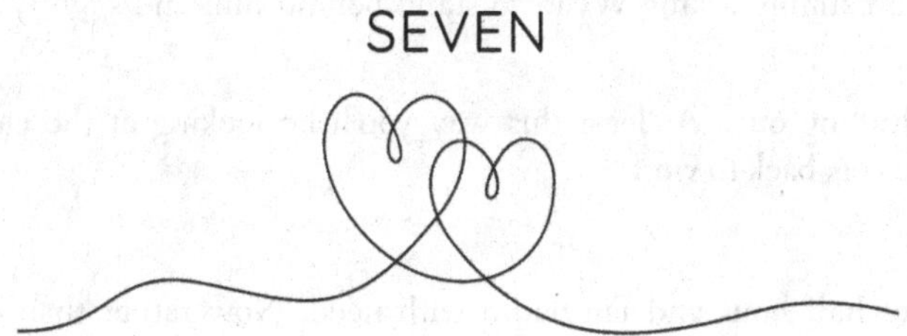

PHOEBE

As I recline on the sun lounger next to the pool at Maddigan's, I'm conscious of Wyatt in the background. He's doing his best to ignore me, but he's failing miserably.

"Darling, darling, look at me, look at ME!" Claude, the photographer, who I've worked with before, is fast losing patience. I need to concentrate if I'm to photograph at my best. But it's hard with such a distraction nearby.

"Imagine I am your lover!"

This instruction from Claude has me giggling, even if I know what he's trying for. Soon enough, he joins in. "Darling Phoebe, you know what I mean."

He takes a couple more photos before he straightens and turns away to see what I'm looking at. Soon enough, he's back facing me, where he mouths, *O-M-G, HE—IS—HOT!*

If I was in any doubt what he means, he follows this up by fanning his face with his free hand. Camera dangling at his side, he turns once more to face Wyatt.

"You there. Yes, you. Over here." His wild beckoning eventually has a reluctant Wyatt at his side.

This has me straightening in the sun lounger, at a loss to know what the flamboyant photographer is up to. It's anyone's guess whether he'll hit on Wyatt, or ask him to join me on the lounger.

It wouldn't be the first time Claude had a member of the public join a shoot, especially if he thought they were cute. I'm wrong on both counts, with him simply asking Wyatt to stand behind him and slightly to one side.

After huffing out, "At least this way you'll be looking at the camera," Claude gets back to work.

Another half hour and I'm damp with need. Now rather than calling out, "Imagine I am your lover!" Claude's calling out, "Imagine HE is your lover!"

It works. It works too well. So well that if Wyatt were to join me on the sun lounger, it'd be all on, and to hell with the camera.

My skin kissed by the sun, my hair, and make-up immaculate, and Wyatt looking at me as if he could eat me. It's a powerful combination.

"Now darling, I want you to lie flat. That's right. Now arch your back and twist your hips, just a little to the left. That's it. Lovely."

As awkward as the position is, I know it'll show my body off to advantage, with the tic in Wyatt's jaw speaking volumes. He's hanging on by a thread, would be my guess.

"Sharon, Julie. Water!"

Excellent, I am parched. However, rather than offering me a drink, the stylists unceremoniously upend small pails of water over me. I've not been expecting it, and the shock of the iced water has me arching up off the sun lounger.

"What on earth!?"

"Trust me darling, it will be magnificent! You are magnificent."

Only when I see him putting his camera away do I realize the shoot is over. It's probably just as well, with the bikini now soaking wet. A quick check of the top and I see what's behind Wyatt's mouth hanging open.

In a flash, he has me back in the toweling robe, tightly cinching it at the waist. Such is his haste to get me back to the villa that I worry Ralph must be around.

"Is he around? Have you seen him?"

Wyatt doesn't answer until we're locked together in the tunnel. And then it's not the answer to my question, but the answer to my dreams. His lips claim mine, the kiss taking my breath away.

And despite him having just tied my robe tightly shut, he's now undoing the belt. His hands are everywhere, and it's wonderful with me arching my hips and back in response. I'm exactly as I was in that last pose for Claude.

That crafty devil.

Perhaps it's that my hair and make-up are still fresh from the stylists, or a couple of hours of being told by Claude that I'm gorgeous. Either way, my confidence is such that rather than shying away, I'm fully into this.

"Not here. I want to open myself to you. I want you to see all of me."

On lifting his head from where he's been gently biting my nipples through the sheer bikini top, Wyatt's vision is glazed. I'm having trouble focusing, too.

"Oh hell, you're right. I'm so sorry."

I hold my hand up. "Please stop apologizing. You've nothing to be sorry about. I want this." I make sure I've got his full attention, before adding, "I want you."

There's no slowing him after this, with him marching along the tunnel, his hand wrapped around mine. Soon enough, we're in the living room of the villa. Rather than moving from there into the bedroom, Wyatt unlocks the sliding doors and leads me out to the courtyard.

Even better is him making quick work of getting rid of his clothes, dropping items one-by-one without care. This sees him standing in front of me, naked and magnificent.

I know why he's done it, and it warms my heart. His stunning body aside, he's deliberately levelled the playing field by stripping. When we meet, it'll be as equals with no male ego getting in the way.

His arms out to the side, he does nothing to hide his erection, and oh my, isn't there a lot of it? "You want it, Phoebe? Come and get it."

WYATT

I'm naked, but for the sun beating down on my skin. In response, she shrugs out of the toweling robe, my body reacting to the silver bikini as it had earlier.

Rather than drop the robe on the flagstones as I've done with my clothes, she instead spreads it out on one of the sun loungers.

This done, she makes a performance out of removing her barely there bikini. Her shimmy when she removes the thong is a thing of beauty.

As I think about how she'll soon be riding my length, I'm having more trouble standing than my cock is. Actually, it's having no trouble at all.

As Phoebe steps toward me, I step toward her.

We meet in the middle, skin to skin, with nothing between us but lust and heat.

My lips press hard against hers, opening them, and I explore her mouth as if I could swallow her whole, and I still might. A tight hold on her ass and I pleasure both of us by grinding her mound against my length.

Unable, or unwilling, to stand any longer, I shuffle back until the end of the sun lounger hits me behind the knees. On my sitting, she's straddling my lap, her heat close enough that she warms my cock. As if it needed it.

A bit of wriggling around from both of us and my length splits her curls. Close, but nowhere near as close as either of us wants.

"Hold me, Phoebe. Guide me."

She needs no more direction. She grabs my length as if her life depends on it. And after I scoop my hands under her ass and lift her, the rest is down to accuracy and gravity.

As I slide into her welcoming heat, I can tell she's every bit as aroused as I am. She's slippery, and, oh, so, ready for me. There's no friction, just mind-blowing pleasure as my cock gets rubbed up in all the right ways.

A jerk of my hips and I ram myself home. The widening of her eyes, and her joyous moan, tell me I'm not alone in loving the sensations flooding us.

But I'm not finished, not by a long shot. After boosting her almost free of my cock, I allow her to glide back down. Her breasts bouncing in my face are irresistible. I draw a taut nipple into my mouth and suck hard, her back arching in response.

Even better is when she flexes her muscles around my cock, bringing me closer than ever. "We fit so perfectly, Phoebe. We're made for each other."

It sounds corny, but it's true. I've never experienced this sense of sanctuary before. And much as I don't want to admit it to myself, I'm drawn to Phoebe by more than her stunning good looks.

Her energy melds with mine in such a way that I'm a better man for having her in my life. It doesn't matter that I've known her only days. She already means something to me. It's both frightening and exhilarating.

Phoebe lifts free of my length, with the sense of loss overwhelming me. Until she slams back down again, inching forward on my thighs, and crushing her clit against me.

"Holy hell. Do that again!"

This time I give her a boost, and then another, and another, until the tendons in my neck are like wire as I keep a tight rein on my control.

I want us coming together; something the rippling of her muscles tells me is close.

The second she tightens and her eyes flutter, I let go my hold, pumping out of control into her depths. She jerks uncontrollably atop me, her mouth open in a silent scream that I soon arch up and claim.

Unable to stay sitting upright any longer, I flop back on the sun lounger, taking Phoebe with me. I'm still deep inside her and happy to stay there while I can. Her flexing her muscles around me says she agrees.

It also tells me we'll be up for more fun sooner than I'd have thought possible. "Ride me, baby, take me with you."

She doesn't need to be asked twice, as she rears up, her legs now over the side of the lounger. And here I was thinking I couldn't go any deeper.

How wrong I am, and how wonderful it is, especially when I reach up to cradle her breasts.

"So responsive."

My calloused thumbs circle her buds.

"So tight."

I repeat the motion a little quicker, her chest rising and falling in response.

"And so perfect."

On my rolling her nipples between thumb and forefinger, her drawn-out, wanton moan lets me know she likes it. Boy, does she ever.

The edge taken off following our first coupling, we take our time with the second. Luxuriating in the sensations, exploring each other's bodies, getting to know what we like.

So far as I can see, that's everything, only reinforcing my earlier statement that we're made for each other. Certainly, I've never experienced this with a woman before. It's different with Phoebe.

Sure, there's lust and libido in abundance, but there are also gentler emotions. They're the sort that sees us in the four-poster for the afternoon, with no plans to go anywhere other than paradise.

EIGHT

PHOEBE

As I lay back on the sun lounger next to Wyatt's, I revel in the sun warming my skin. The courtyard being as private as it is, there's no risk of tan lines for either of us.

Unless you count Wyatt's body covering mine, as it so often does. Three days it's been, three glorious days during which Wyatt hasn't left my side. There's been no sign of Ralph. It's as if he's disappeared into the ether.

The biggest surprise in all of this is that even though Wyatt has seen me first thing in the morning, and without make-up, he's still keen.

Since becoming better-known as a model, I'm all too conscious of men wanting to date me, only to be seen WITH me. Some *influencers* will go to extraordinary lengths to garner more clicks.

If any of them had seen me bare-faced and with my hair all over the place, they'd have run a mile. With Wyatt, it doesn't seem to matter what state I'm in. He still looks at me with affection and desire. This has me able to relax around him, as no man before.

After sliding my sunglasses up on my forehead, I turn to Wyatt. "Has he been back in his room?" There's no need for me to reference who I'm talking about.

"No, he hasn't." Wyatt's brow wrinkles before he continues. "But he's paid through to the weekend, so we have to leave his stuff where it is."

He rolls onto his side and props his head up with one arm. "The license plate he gave us when he registered doesn't tie in with any of the cars on site, either."

This news has me flopping back on the sun lounger, my sunglasses automatically sliding into place. It makes no sense. He must have driven here, because what stalker catches a bus?

Ralph's location really is the one cloud in my otherwise clear blue sky. I know he's only leaving me alone because I'm with Wyatt. And much as I love spending time with this gorgeous, loving man, I have a life, too. One that's currently on hold.

The response to the poolside shoot with Claude has been encouraging. My agent even called the photos 'spectacular', which is saying something for someone as taciturn as Carol.

It's for this reason she wants to book me for another shoot, this time back in LA. And I'm torn. While it's another career-making opportunity, it will have me once again on my own; once again at the mercy of Ralph.

I've told her I'll get back to her tomorrow, but for now, I'm putting it out of my mind and enjoying the last of my halcyon days with Wyatt.

Following yet another dip in the plunge pool, Wyatt is about to drop back to his lounger when an alert sounds on his phone. This has him drying his hands so he can check it.

Unable to stop myself, I sit up, ready to hear the news I've been waiting for since Wyatt moved me from my room to the villa.

His rolling his eyes has disappointment flaring. Whatever it is, it's not about Ralph, but something mundane. Something he would have delegated to someone else if not for Ralph keeping such a low profile.

"Yeah, I'll be over as soon as I can." The look he gives me then warms me more than the sun. "Give me half-an-hour."

On my dropping back on the sun lounger, arching my back and rolling a hip in his direction, he adds. "Better make it an hour."

He leaves sixty-five glorious minutes later, but who's counting? He also leaves me languid and replete, my body soft and compliant. Of course, he'd also carried me inside and locked the patio doors.

I'm close to falling asleep when I hear noises coming from out in the living room. He must have hustled to be back here this soon. I'm not sure I'm up to a repeat performance just yet.

This sees me getting out of bed and pulling on the toweling robe I'd kept from the poolside shoot. I sashay out into the living room because, while I need a break before we continue our love fest, I don't want to look like a slob, either.

"Wow, you were..."

The room's empty. That's weird. This has me standing stock still in the middle of the room, my ears alert to the slightest sound. There it is, again.

It's coming from the kitchenette, and yet with the panel open I can see Wyatt isn't in there. Eeek, don't tell me we've got mice. Or worse, rats. This has me inching my way over to the opening in the panel work.

A quick check inside the kitchenette and I see nothing out of the ordinary, like little footprints on the counter.

I'm on my way back to bed when I'm grabbed from behind and a cloth stuffed over my mouth hard enough to mash my lips against my teeth.

My mind takes time catching up with my surroundings. I'm in the back of a van, I'm tied up tight, and there's a ball of cloth stuffed in my mouth.

Whatever Ralph had used to knock me out isn't helping my ability to process. I'm still at a loss to know how he sneaked up on me like he had. The villa wasn't exactly awash with hiding spaces.

Hoping to get rid of the gag, I roll onto my side. This has my face hard up against my suitcase, telling me that Ralph plans on keeping me with him. As thoughts of him forcing me to wear the skimpy underwear in my suitcase flare, my panic rises, and I'm left choking on the gag.

Hard as I try, I can't get rid of the thing, with my breathing panicky in response. It takes several slow, measured breaths through my nose to calm down enough that I don't risk passing out.

I'll need my wits about me if I'm to get through this. With that in mind, I lay there quietly, totting up what I know.

I'm in a van.

It's not moving.

I'm still in my toweling robe.

Best of all, I'm alone.

Unfortunately, hat soon changes.

WYATT

Back at the villa, the first thing I see is the note sitting on the coffee table. It's on hotel stationery, and the writing is appalling.

While trying to make sense of it, I check the bedroom, and sure enough, Phoebe's bag has gone. It's the same thing in the bathroom, with all her toiletries and make-up missing.

I can't believe she's left. I thought we had something together, even if my feelings were stronger than expected given our brief acquaintance. Sad doesn't describe my current mood. My world is lackluster, missing the spark that was Phoebe.

Back in the living room, I see something that has my blood freezing in my veins. No matter how much of a hurry Phoebe was in, she'd never have left her collection of family photos behind.

Her ability to settle in like she did was a major draw card for me. It had been the same with my mom. Every flea-pit motel and apartment we landed at, she'd unpack the knick-knacks she insisted turned a house into a home. The same knick-knacks she'd repack when dad worked out where we were.

This has me re-reading the note, the words easier to grasp a second time around.

> *Babe*
> *Landed big job in LA.*
> *Can't say no. Gotta rush.*
> *I had fun. Be good*

As a goodbye note, it sucks big time. And what's with the pet name? It was my name she screamed when she came, not Babe. And anyway, she always said it sounded like that pig from the movie.

The other thing re-reading the note brings home is that this is the first time I've seen her handwriting. And yet the scrawl looks vaguely familiar, perhaps too familiar.

After grabbing my phone, I scroll through the images until I find the one I'd taken of Ralph's note. Sure enough, his handwriting and that in Phoebe's goodbye note, while not identical, are damned close.

Close enough that I open the tracker app on my phone to see if Ralph's bag is where it's been for the last four days.

He's moved, and he's close. Like really close. The only thing I'm unsure of is whether he's got Phoebe with him. The very thought is enough to have my heart contracting and doing its best to reposition itself in my throat.

If he hurts the woman I love, I won't be responsible for my actions.

Another check of the app and I can see he has to be in the carpark. I'm out of the villa and sprinting down the tunnel soon after. Despite my flinging the metal door to one side, everything looks to be as it was when I crossed it not ten minutes earlier.

Yet something's missing, and I have to close my eyes to see what it was. The white van, the one parked right next to the elevator since I'd first escorted Phoebe to the villa.

This has me kicking myself for my decision to send the guard back up to the casino after three days of no action. There's no way Ralph could have bundled Phoebe into the van with him around.

That's if Ralph has taken her. And yet he must have, because in my heart of hearts, I can't accept she's left me. Either way, I need to follow the creep, because if she is with him, then it won't be by choice.

And if she has dumped me for that job in LA—a thought that has my eyes prickling—then there's still the matter of Ralph breaking into the villa.

As I sprint across the carpark and up the exit ramp, my emotions are in turmoil. Either Ralph's kidnapped her while she was under my care, or the past week was just a laugh for her. I wish I could say the same, but I care for her.

Yeah, the sex is great, but Phoebe's more than that to me. As corny as it sounds, it's as if I've found my other half. I can be myself with her and not have to play the hard-man twenty-four-seven.

She accepts me as I am, and after a lifetime of people taking me at face value, this is a big deal.

Soon enough I reach my Wrangler in the staff carpark. It's seen better days, but the motor is in mint condition, as is the upholstery.

After jamming my phone in the holder on the dash, I radio Simon in the control room and tell him what I'll need. Confirmation received, I start the engine and am soon roaring down the road into town. A glance at the map on the screen, and I turn south, toward LA.

There's nothing polite about my driving, with me screaming past anything slowing me down. I have a couple of near misses before I settle down and concentrate on catching Ralph without killing myself.

We're only five miles out of town when I notice a white van up ahead. Rather than pull in right behind it, I keep a couple of cars between us. I'm sure it's him thanks to a combination of what's showing on my phone, and that distinctive decal on the back door.

The only thing I don't know is whether Phoebe is with him. If I knew for sure she was on her way to LA and excited about that big job, I'd run the bastard off the road. In the end there's no need, with him pulling into a country store with a couple of gas pumps out front.

Rather than stop next to the pumps, he keeps rolling through and into a gravel parking lot off to one side.

Of course, he'd have a full tank of gas. The neatness of everything in his case spoke of his being buttoned down in all things. It had also spoken of a disordered mind. What was that saying about people with neat desks being unhinged?

Unable to pull in without Ralph spotting me, I drive slowly by. Slowly enough that I can see there's no passenger sitting up front. After a death-defying U-turn involving a cliff and a truck, I'm soon on the way back.

I'm in time to see an old lady jump out of the van, the gray pin curls and purple dress marking her as Ralph in disguise. Rather than engage an alarm as I've expected, he simply shuts the door and totters over to the store, all while staying in character.

While the style of dress says he's not carrying, the handbag that completes the disguise is large enough to conceal a weapon.

Another U-turn and I pull up behind the van, parking in such a way there isn't a chance he can leave. After radioing Simon again, I climb out of the Jeep. My chief priority is to see if Phoebe is in the back. It's something that sees me trying the handle on the back door, surprised to find it's open.

After looking inside, rage blinds me. There's no missing the terror in her eyes. But if she's ever to have a normal life, she needs to hang tight.

After putting my finger to my lips, I reach in and take the gag from her mouth. "Trust me, you just need to keep quiet for a little longer. This will soon be over. Whatever happens, don't forget, I love you."

While saying those three little words to her is one of the easiest things I've had to do in my life, shutting the door is the hardest.

NINE

PHOEBE

The van was still in the hotel carpark when Ralph opened the back doors and shoved his case in next to me. This had given me my first proper look at him, although it had taken a second to realize it was actually him.

If not for the surveillance photos Wyatt had shown me, I wouldn't have recognized him, but there was no missing the mania in those eyes. Without that, I'd have thought I was being kidnapped by an old girl out to play the slots.

As thoughts of him locking me up—sorry, protecting and caring for me—crowd my mind, I'd much rather this was the case.

It doesn't help that he's driving like a myopic old lady, appearing to hit every pothole on offer and bouncing me around. With my hands tied behind my back and my feet tied to something else, there's nothing I can do to brace myself.

"Dearest Phoebe," he calls out over the easy listening track on the radio, "it really didn't need to be this hard."

Unable to speak, I scream my frustration against the gag in my mouth with this having me fighting to get enough air in through my nose.

"I know you've been testing our love with your resistance, but you'll see, we'll have a wonderful life together."

If he'd said this to me at an upscale cocktail party, I might have viewed it as sweet, if slightly delusional. With me tied up in the back while he drives us who knows where, it's enough to qualify him for a jacket that buckles up at the back.

"You'll love your new home. I've got all your favorite things."

He then falls silent, something I'm thankful for as it makes it easier to blot out my current reality. It's just a shame he doesn't remain this way. "You're lucky I'm a patient man, but I tell myself our first time together must be special."

Terror messing with my head, I don't immediately grasp the import of what he's said. I'm slow to realize that all he'd had time for when I was out cold was manhandling me into the van.

"I really don't know what you saw in that brute? Although that blonde he was cozying up to at the pool bar earlier seemed enamored."

While his words are offhand, there's nothing casual about the way my heart crumples like a soda can stomped on for the recycling.

It doesn't matter that I've known Wyatt for less than a week. It's as if I've known him my whole life. As if I've been waiting for him my whole life. Much as I'd never say the words 'soul-mate' within his hearing, this is exactly how I think of him.

As Ralph whips around another corner, I'm slammed into the side of the van. My tears aren't down to the pain of the impact, but thanks to the knowledge Wyatt was never serious about me. How could I have gotten it so wrong?

I feel... I feel... I'm not sure what it is, but it's like nothing before. While the initial attraction had been physical, I now see the man behind the mask. The hard shell created to protect the little boy still hiding inside.

"Sorry, I had to avoid a slow car."

Ralph's apology is as insincere as everything else about him. I ignore him, doing my best to wedge myself between our suitcases and the side of the van. With the way he's driving, I'll be a study in bruises by the time we get to wherever we're going.

The realization then hits me that the bruises won't matter because my modeling days are over. Life as I know it is over and I'll never see my family again. It hurts even more to know I'll never see Wyatt again. It doesn't matter that he wasn't serious about me, I was serious about him.

As my new reality makes itself felt, tears run unbidden down my face.

How long before the psycho up front wearies of me? How long before I'm as nuts as he is? How long before he gets rid of me?

My mind is awhirl with images of me dressed like something out of the Stepford Wives, when he slows down and pulls off the road. Surely we're not already at the 'love nest'?

I'm not sure why, but I'd thought it would be in LA, although this could have been down to my optimistic nature. If it's out in the country somewhere, I'm truly lost forever.

Unable to face so bleak a future, I shut my eyes tight and take some comfort in squishing my face up against my suitcase. However, there's nothing wrong with my ears and I know to the second he exits the van.

I'm on high alert, waiting for the back doors to open. Only they don't.

Never have I been so pleased to be left alone. It tells me we might not have reached our destination, so if I can make enough noise, perhaps someone will hear me?

Unfortunately, because of how I'm hog-tied, the only thing free to smack against the side of the van is the back of my head. My hopes of a quick release dashed, I once again close my eyes and sag to the van floor.

On the back door opening, they soon flash open and I'm momentarily blinded by the light streaming in. However, it's not Ralph. It's Wyatt, and he looks as relieved to see me as I am to see him.

I don't care that I was only light relief; he's here to save me.

My tears fall fast, although it's now down to relief rather than resignation at my fate. When he reaches inside to pull the gag from my mouth, I'm ready to tell him everything. However, him putting a finger to his lips says we're not in the clear yet.

That's not all he has to say, with his next words flooring me as much, if not more, than Ralph's ramblings.

I'm still grappling with the fact he's said he loves me when he shuts the door. This leaves me staring at the unadorned metal doors, unable to grasp how he could tell me he loves me in one breath, and then leave me to my fate.

He'd also said to trust him, and I do, although it's difficult given the circumstances. What if Ralph has a gun? What if he kills Wyatt?

A hiccup of tears, and I slump, giving into them again. Now I'm more worried about the man I love than I am about myself. It's saying this inside my head that has me acknowledging it as fact.

I love him.

I love him more than life.

What if I don't get to tell him?

WYATT

On staring at the back doors of the van, I want nothing more than to reopen them, untie Phoebe, and get the hell out of here.

But with Ralph soon to reappear, and likely armed, it's not a risk I'm willing to take. And, anyway, if we simply take off, we'll always worry Ralph will try again.

He's gotten too close to give up now.

That's no way to live, meaning this has to end here and now. I want no shadows cast over our relationship, and for that, Ralph needs to be locked up, preferably with no one dying.

This has me sprinting down the side of the store and around the back. Ralph will pay for what he's done to Phoebe. He's frightened her and that bruise on her forehead has me wanting to hit something. Ralph is at the top of my list.

The security door around the back is wide open, as it had been last time I called in, the owner liking the through-breeze. A quick check inside is enough to see Ralph chatting to the cashier as though everything is normal.

There's nothing about his behavior to say he's in the middle of an active kidnapping, nothing to alert the cashier to anything out of the ordinary. Any eyewitness report would reference a little old lady, not a psychopath.

After watching Ralph gather his purchases, I ready myself to move.

Seconds after he's left, I'm walking purposefully through the store. A brief nod to the cashier and I exit through the front doors. If I'm taking Ralph down without getting shot or knifed, then I need to take him by surprise.

Fueled by rage, I move quickly and quietly, determined he won't get anywhere near Phoebe.

So often when I was a kid, I'd had to listen to dad 'teaching mom a lesson'. And while I'd been too little to do anything back then, the same is no longer true.

It's this determination that has me right behind Ralph before he knows what's happening. Much as I want to flatten the guy, I instead grab him by the upper arm, sending his snacks and handbag flying.

My arm snakes around his neck, and I tighten my hold. This creep isn't going anywhere, let alone near Phoebe. I'm wondering how long I'll need to keep him in the headlock when a police cruiser pulls alongside.

The new chief of police doesn't immediately get out, his focus on his radio call. Soon enough, though, he stands in front of me and Ralph, his stance shrieking of outrage and authority.

"Officer, officer, arrest this man!"

Ralph's words have a high-pitched, old lady quality to them, as if he's hoping to get away with his disguise. Even the Chief of police appears shocked by my manhandling a sweet little old lady. He soon changes his mind when I rip Ralph's wig off and dump it on the ground next to the handbag.

"This is the bastard. Ms. Jackson is in the back of the van. You want to take care of this trash while I get her out?"

There's no need to go into specifics thanks to my earlier instructions to Simon. The chief, being a man of few words, answers by pulling a set of handcuffs out of the pocket of his vest.

To an accompaniment of the Chief reading Ralph his rights, I wrench open the back door of the van and climb inside. After untying Phoebe, I drag her into my arms, wrapping the toweling robe tight around her, protecting her modesty.

"It's okay. You're okay. The Chief of Police is here. He's got him. He won't be bothering us again."

Dropping back onto the floor of the van, I simply sit with her in my lap, unaware of how tightly I'm holding her. Only after she squeaks in protest, do I loosen my grip. However, I don't let go.

I never want to let go of her again. If I'd lost her, my life would never have been the same. The mere thought of that awful powerlessness has it threating to engulf me.

"I'm so sorry. I said I'd take care of you, and I failed."

Her response to my apology is incoherent. I need to get her back to the villa so she can rest. She'll also need to be checked over by a doctor because she's not looking good, although in my eyes she'll always be beautiful.

We still haven't moved when the Chief pops up, his gaze taking in the lengths of rope in the back of the van. His stern gaze then catches mine.

"I'll head back to town now, but I'll need a formal statement from you and your lady."

My lady? Yeah, I like that. I like that just fine.

"Can we catch up with you tomorrow? I'm worried she's going into shock."

A curt nod is the only response to my request before he's on his way.

I press my lips to the bruise on Phoebe's forehead before putting my finger under her chin and lifting her face so I can brush her lips with mine. Her eyes flutter open, tears clinging to her lower lashes.

"I thought that was it. And when he said..."

She bites hard on her bottom lip, keeping the rest of her words where they are.

I lower my head until our foreheads touch. "Phoebe, what did he say? You can tell me. You can tell me anything, you know that, right?"

She takes a couple of tries, but eventually gets the words out.

"A blonde? But I haven't been near another woman since I met you."

I'm thinking about the reason I'd left Phoebe alone when the realization hits. I'm unable to stop myself from a brief chuckle with this also one of relief.

Because of the hotel's strict **NO DOGS** policy and the owner going full 'Karen', I'd been called on to kick her out. Given the choice, I'd have been happier dealing with the pooch, because it was better behaved.

"Yeah, that blonde Ralph said I was with. She was a Golden Retriever and her name was Butterscotch." To further make light of the accusation laid at my feet, I scratch my arm. "I think she gave me fleas."

Finally, I'm rewarded with Phoebe's gentle laughter. It's not much, but it's enough to let me know she's accepted my explanation. It also says the terror that had been close to overwhelming her was lifting.

"Come on, let's get out of here. I want to get you home and check for myself that he didn't hurt you."

TEN

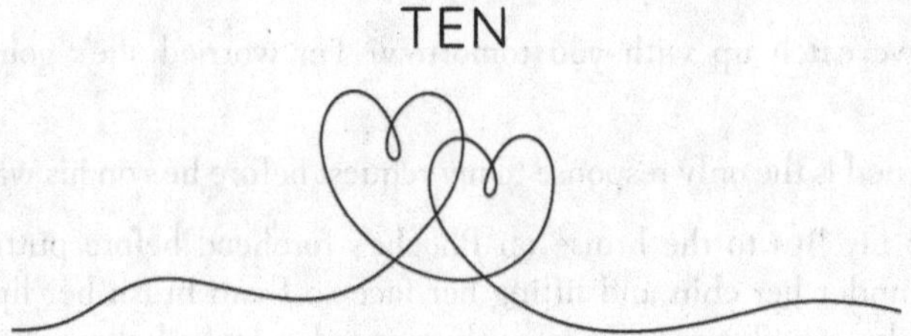

PHOEBE

Wyatt's helping me out the back of the van when I notice my state of undress. That Ralph had seen me like this has the shivers I'd just mastered back with a vengeance. I feel unclean, somehow soiled.

Wyatt tightens his hold on me. "Hey, hey, you're okay, Phoebe. You're safe."

A hiccup of tears and I bury my face in Wyatt's chest, unable to face him when I speak. "He put a rag soaked in something over my face. I blacked out..."

Wyatt stiffens, but instead of loosening his grip in revulsion, he keeps a tight hold on me. "Phoebe, I don't care." He kisses the top of my head. "Well, other than how much I want to beat the crap out of him."

After buckling me into the passenger seat, he returns to the van and grabs my suitcase. Rather than head straight back to the villa, Wyatt swings by the emergency room. There I'm prodded and poked and declared relatively unhurt, apart from a multitude of bruises thanks to Ralph's driving skills.

Soon enough we're back at the villa, but rather than allow me to get dressed, Wyatt slowly removes the toweling robe and tucks me into bed. Even better is when he strips down to his boxers and climbs in next to me.

Despite the ordeal I'd just been through, my body responds, although he's having none of it. "Phoebe, let's just cuddle. We've got our whole lives ahead of us. For now, I just want to hold you."

He then spoons me, his arm wrapped protectively around my waist, his breath warming my shoulder. I'm not sure why, but I get that he's taking as much comfort from our closeness as I am.

He holds me tighter for a moment, before pushing my hair to one side and kissing me softly on the back of the neck. "When I got back and found the note saying you'd left for a big job in LA, it destroyed me."

Immediately, love, peace, and longing flood my body. "You know it wasn't from me, right?"

"I do. I did. You'd never start a note by calling me Babe because..."

"... that's a pig's name," I finish for him. There's no missing his smile when he presses his lips to the nape of my neck.

This has me wriggling around in his arms until I face him, our bodies tight enough we share a heartbeat, our legs tangled. I want to gauge his response to what I've got to say.

"You know what you said in the van," I pause briefly, before continuing, "about loving me." My asking, "Is that true?" is one of the hardest things I've ever had to do.

Other than family, it's the first time anyone's ever said it to me, and so I'm finding it hard to believe. Could it be I've finally found my true north, and that I'm his?

Even before he speaks, I know it's the truth.

There are some who say a man crying is a sign of weakness. Faced with Wyatt's tears, his strength is clear.

"After I opened the van and saw you, leaving you there was torture. But I knew I didn't have time to get you out. I didn't want to risk you being hurt if he was armed."

He gathers me up for a searing kiss before briefly pulling back. "I knew if I didn't take him down, we'd never be free of him. And Phoebe, I don't share."

If Ralph had said that, I would have been screaming for help. When Wyatt says it, I feel protected and cosseted, and above all else, loved.

This time, it's me who pulls back. My words, while simple, are heartfelt. "Wyatt, I love you, too."

I leave it there because if I was to tell him exactly how much I love him, he'd be worried I was a bunny boiler. Part of me already thinks this, because I've never felt this deeply about a guy ever, and certainly not so soon after meeting them. Despite the wait for a man who loves me just as I am has been long, it's been so worthwhile.

WYATT

Eventually Phoebe falls asleep in my arms, her full lips parted, her face relaxed. She's beautiful, even in her sleep, leaving me unable to believe I've finally found the perfect woman for me.

It had gotten to the point I'd given up on a steady relationship, and the chance to be a husband and father, nothing like my own.

Gently pulling free of Phoebe's arms, I slide out of bed and through to the bathroom, pulling the door quietly shut. I fill the bath and add salts that, along with the heat, should soothe her aches and pains.

With the room full of steam, I light a multitude of candles and kill the lights, leaving the room in soft-focus. It's time to pamper my lady.

Only she's having none of it, refusing to get in the bath, unless I join her. I've not seen this stubborn side of her before and decide I like it. Better this than the fragile woman I'd comforted in the back of that van.

I like it even more when, after stripping, the heat in her eyes tells me there'll be nothing soothing about this bath, nothing at all.

We last all of ten minutes before overheating and having to climb out. I might have made the water too hot, especially in combination with the heat we were generating.

As always, the plunge pool takes our breath away, cooling us instantly.

After helping Phoebe out of the pool, I throw towels down on the sun loungers. I needn't have bothered with Phoebe eschewing hers in favor of sitting in my lap.

The only difference between now and when we were back in the van is that there's now nothing between us but love.

"Are you sure, Phoebe?"

Much as my body is ready as ever, I don't want to push things in that department, especially not after such a traumatic event.

"I want you to make love to me. I want you to wipe away all memories of the trouble Ralph caused."

"Well, I can definitely help with that."

From holding her as if she's fragile, I explore her body, my hands skimming her breasts, and her tummy. Her gasp when I bury my fingers in her curls is not one of distress, but of love and lust.

Following some rearrangement on both our parts, she soon straddles me, taking the upper hand and calling the shots. Meanwhile, I continue running my fingers through her curls, circling that little bundle of nerves and pinching it now and then.

I know Phoebe is enjoying herself, with her hand on my cock gripping harder every time I squeeze her clit. As tempted as I am to push her over the edge, when she comes, I want to be buried deep inside her.

This happens when Phoebe stands and takes a step forward on shaky legs. When she sinks back down, I'm as ready for her as she is for me; my cock is now heated by her core as the sun heats my skin.

"Damn, but I love you, Phoebe Jackson. I love you more than life itself."

Busy rocking back and forth, her eyes are shut tight. She doesn't immediately acknowledge my declaration. I have to buck my hips and bury myself deeper still to get her attention.

Her eyes flutter open, although her movements don't slow, the response she's causing getting harder to control. "And I love you just as much, Wyatt Cassidy. Now hurry and make me yours."

While I know she's talking about our lovemaking, my mind is on something far more permanent. When you have someone like Phoebe in your life, you worship them so they'll never want to leave.

EPILOGUE

SIX MONTHS LATER

PHOEBE

On Wyatt and me entering the tunnel to the villa, the changes are drastic. His reaction says the removal of the salacious images is not of his doing. The other thing that's missing is that weird velvet padding on the ceilings and walls.

This is nothing compared to the changes we encounter when we enter the villa itself. Gone is the ornate—and supremely uncomfortable—couch, replaced by a Scandinavian-inspired sectional in a dark gray.

Wyatt's as surprised by the upgrades as I am, looking around in wonder. "It has to have been Liam. He's the only one with the funds and okay to make changes like these."

He's right, with Liam Maddigan, the manager of the hotel, also son of the owner. It doesn't hurt that he's a millionaire in his own right.

Despite all this, we've only been gone for two weeks, with Wyatt taking time off to accompany me on a couple of shoots down in LA.

Actually, Claude, the photographer, had insisted Wyatt be there for one of them. Whether this was because Claude fancied Wyatt for himself, or that he liked the carnal glow in my eyes whenever Wyatt was around, who knew?

Either way, the photos he'd taken of me next to the pool at Maddigan's all those months ago have curvy brands clamoring to book me. I'm even getting the occasional booking from mainstream brands.

My life has changed beyond recognition. Six months ago, I was single and being stalked by a madman. Now I'm in a relationship, and Ralph is in prison.

Turns out when they searched the 'love nest' he'd prepared for me, there was already a woman in 'residence'. Thankfully, Ralph had left her with enough to live on while he pursued me.

This had meant our testimony was a formality, with Ralph being sent away for a very long time. Of course, we'd still had our say, with this adding to his sentence.

Whenever memories of Ralph crowd my brain, I automatically search for Wyatt, feeling safe in his orbit. The counseling is also helping, but I've still got a way to go.

I still have trouble believing someone as outwardly tough as Wyatt would be the one to suggest I engage a therapist. Yet he had, telling me he'd benefited from it after his mom passed away.

My first thought on hearing she'd died when Wyatt was a kid was that his violent father had been responsible. Instead, his mom died of a heart attack in her sleep. The only plus in what had been an awful experience for him was that his last words to her were, "I love you, Mom."

Doing my best to clear my head of these gloomy images, I look through to the bedroom. Even from out here, I can see the fringed hangings on the four-poster are missing, although the bed itself remains.

A check of the courtyard and I see there's now a slim line stainless ladder in the plunge pool. While Wyatt was always happy to help me out, this means I'll be able to use the pool when he's not around.

"Does this mean he's opening the villa up to hotel guests?" This saddens me, as I think of it as being our special place. When Wyatt doesn't respond, I turn to find he's no longer there.

I'm back to taking in the other changes outside when he wraps his arms around me from behind and stands with his chin atop my head.

"Phoebe, there's something you need to see."

Never one to miss an opportunity, I squirm around in his arms until we face each other. "Do I have to? I can think of better things to do. Have you seen the new double sun lounger?"

There's nothing I can do to stop the giggle that follows. Some of my most memorable times with Wyatt have taken place out there.

My reaching up on tiptoes is all the invitation Wyatt needs, and as always, the impact of our kiss is spectacular. My soul unfurls in response, my heart thumps in my chest, and blood pulses through my most sensitive parts in readiness.

I'm therefore surprised when Wyatt lifts his lips from mine, reluctance clear in every muscle. "Soon enough, darling, soon enough. In the meantime, you really need to check this out."

WYATT

As tempting as it is to surrender to Phoebe's teasing and christen the double sun lounger, I resist. After her voicing concerns that Liam is opening the villa to paying guests, she needs to see this.

"Come on, it won't take long." There's nothing I can do to hide my smile. "Trust me. You *really* want to see this."

With her finally compliant, I lead her over to the sliding panel that conceals the small kitchenette. I then stand to one side and gesture at it like some game show hostess. "If you'd like to do the honors?"

Her brow wrinkles in confusion. However, she still steps forward, and after putting her fingers in the small gap, slides the panel to the side.

This changes everything, because rather than reveal the small kitchenette, we enter a large open area. What had been a mirror image of our villa was now a great-room.

It's so very different to how it was when we'd first discovered it. Back then, it was a dark and foreboding place, with the glass doors and sidelights boarded up, except for where Ralph had broken in. Any connection between this villa and the carpark long-ago sealed.

Because Ralph had been hiding out through there, he'd known to the second when I left Phoebe alone. It was because of a concealed doorway between the boarded-up villa and the kitchenette that he'd been able to take her unawares.

The place now couldn't be more different, being bright and welcoming, with a kitchen twice the size of the former kitchenette. There's also a dining area and more seating, complete with an ethanol fireplace mounted on the back wall.

However, that's not where I direct Phoebe's attention. That would be to the enormous bouquet in a vase on the kitchen island. I've already read the note, but rather than spoil the surprise, I lead her over, so she can read it for herself.

Soon enough, I see my mistake, having forgotten how many unwanted bouquets and notes she'd received from Ralph before I caught him.

"It isn't from him. It's from Liam, my boss."

As she opens the card with trembling fingers, I put my arm around her shoulders and give her a reassuring squeeze. I then re-read the note along with her, still having trouble believing how generous my boss has been.

"He's giving us the villa as an engagement present?"

Her words, halting as they are, tell me she's as surprised as I am by Liam's generosity. I'm also at a loss to know how my boss knew we were engaged. Phoebe had only said yes two days earlier, with not even her family aware. As spontaneous as it'd been, we haven't given thought to anything beyond me asking and her saying yes.

After taking her hand, I lift it and kiss her knuckles. "Would you be okay living here? In Coogan's Break I mean?"

Besides being bored stupid when I first moved here, I'll admit the place has grown on me. But not so much it's a deal-breaker where Phoebe is concerned.

"If you don't want to, I can put in for a transfer to one of the LA properties."

Phoebe turns to face me. "Are you kidding? I love this place. It's where I fell in love with you." She then throws her arms around me, before adding, "Wyatt Cassidy, my home is wherever you are."

Now I'm smiling as broadly as she is. "In that case, I say we go try out that new sun lounger."

A second later, my arms are empty, with my happily squealing fiancé well on her way to the courtyard. Even if I didn't already know the way, I'd have no trouble following the trail of discarded clothing.

Rather than hurry, I follow in her stead, stripping as I go before finally ditching my jeans and boxers, and joining her on the double lounger.

Home at last.

FASHION

If you're in the market for the latest beachwear, then make sure you're poolside at Maddigan's this Saturday.

Ex-supermodel, Phoebe Cassidy nee Jackson, will be showcasing her latest beachwear collection, with styles to suit all body shapes and sizes.

Phoebe says, "This year's collection is all about looking back to a time when women embraced their curves."

Natasha loves everything about Christmas. Lucian is more bah humbug about the season. Will sparks fly when the elf in charge of illuminations and the electrician connect?

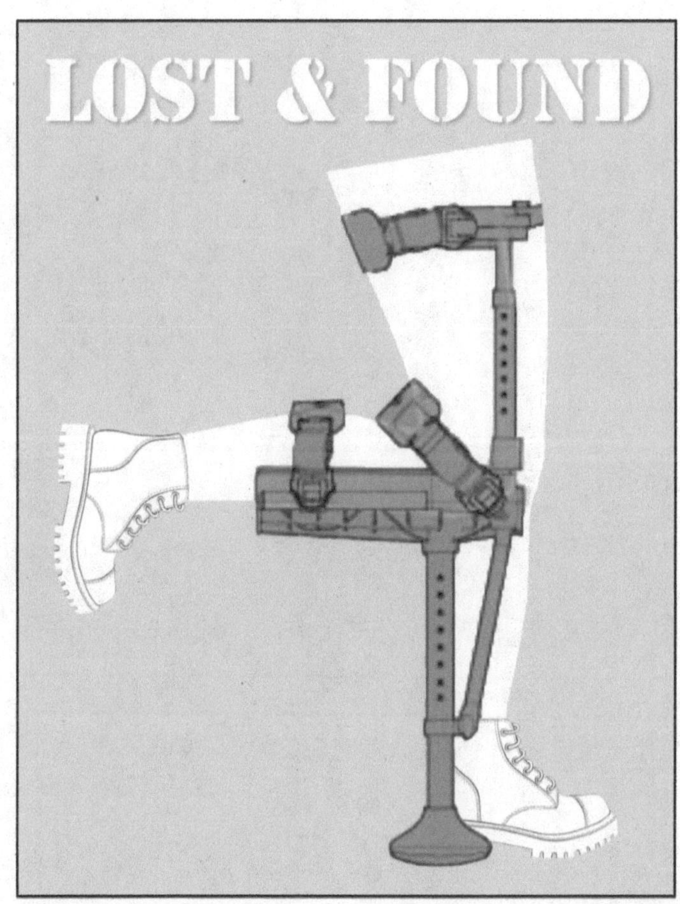

HANDS-FREE CRUTCH, BRIGHT PINK, SIZE XXXL

If this is yours, it can be claimed at the Coogan's Break Welcome Center.
If not claimed within 90 days, it will be donated to Veterans Services.

ONE

At first I think I'm imagining things. But, nope, there it is again. The shop's lights definitely flickered and I know I'm not responsible.

I also know, having worked as an electrician for ten years, that whatever's causing it, it's nothing to do with the shop's wiring system.

How do I know? Because I was the one who installed it, and I know it's up to code, and possibly beyond. As suddenly as the flickering had started, it stops.

After making a mental note to follow up on it, I get back to work. It's the end of the day, and I'd rather finish up now than return in the morning.

And then the lights flicker again, something that has me grabbing my phone to see if there are any alerts from the utility company. There's nothing.

I haven't had time to put my phone away when the lights flicker again. This has me opening the Main Street Facebook page, and sure enough, the feed is full of shop owners moaning about the problem.

Damn it, I can't just ignore this. That's not how I roll. As I stow my tools, the enamel on my teeth is in danger of being cracked, with the tic in my jaw off the charts.

There are a lot of things that annoy me this time of year. Number one is people overloading their electrical panels with Christmas lights, although I doubt that's what is causing an issue this wide spread.

What is it about some folks that they need their illuminations to be spectacular enough we could see them from space? I don't get it. Actually, I don't understand the fascination with Christmas at all. To me, it's just another day of the year.

I'm shutting my toolbox when Callum, the owner of the store, joins me in the storeroom. "Is that you messing with the lights?" As if to back-up his accusation, they flicker again.

"It's not. I'm off to check and see if I can find out what's causing it. I'll have to finish installing these outlets in the morning."

His annoyance is now more than a match to my own, and I don't blame him. "Sorry, but if it's something major, then I don't want to risk frying your wiring." As tempting as it is to add "Or myself", I remain close lipped.

After a moment's hesitation, when I expect him to tell me to carry on, he backs down. It's just as well, because once I've made my mind up, I rarely change it.

Out on the sidewalk, I amble along, trying to discern if there's a rhythm to the flickering, but there isn't. It's random, with the gaps never the same. Sometimes short, sometimes long. The same is true of the length the flickering lasts. Whatever it is, it's arbitrary.

Five minutes later and I spot something—make that someone—that might be responsible. As arresting as the sight is, my steps slow of their own volition, to the point I stop dead in the middle of the sidewalk.

It's as well there wasn't anyone behind me, because I'm not going anywhere. I couldn't move if I tried. The same isn't true of the gorgeous elf currently skating around on the roof of the Coogan's Break Welcome Center.

What the hell is Natasha Frank doing up there, and in conditions like these? When the fog is heavy like it is today, it leaves everything slightly damp, especially roof tiles, like those she's currently slipping and sliding across.

It's when I see where she's heading that I move. And I don't just move, I run. If she touches the lights wrapped around that reindeer, she'll likely kill herself.

While string lights are usually safe, when they're wrapped around a metal reindeer that's touching overhead lines, it's a different matter. A potentially lethal one.

As I run, I yell her name, eventually getting her attention. After giving me a cheery wave, she continues slipping and sliding across the roof, her eyes locked on her target.

"Natasha, stop!" I bellow this last at such a volume that she freezes. She's dangerously close to a reindeer with enough volts running through it that, if it wanted to, it could pull a sleigh.

She still hasn't moved when I arrive in front of the welcome center. "Do not touch that reindeer, it's live!"

Rather than show concern, she laughs, with the bright cheerful notes warming me as always. "Don't be silly, it's not alive, it's made of metal. See..."

She slip-slides forward and reaches out as if to give the monster decoration a pat on the rump. The only thing that saves her from being electrocuted is her feet flying out from under her.

She's not safe yet though, sliding down the angled roof in my direction and gaining speed with every second. A couple of steps forward and I brace myself, ready to catch her.

It doesn't matter that she's around five-foot-eight and blessed with curves that I'd be all over if I was brave enough. At six-foot-six, and built like a tank, I'm more than capable of catching the bubbly redhead, and having fun while I'm about it.

As she shoots over the edge of the roof, her screams fill the air, coming to an abrupt stop when she lands safely in my arms. My relief that she's unhurt is enough to have me squeezing her tight before kissing her like my life depends on it.

A moment's hesitation and she returns the kiss, my cock twitching in approval. The only thing I'm unsure of is whether her enthusiasm is down to me having saved her life or something else entirely.

My cock seems to think it's more than gratitude.

NATASHA

Lucian's lips move over mine with a mastery that has my toes curling as much as those of the bright red boots that complete my elf costume. It's as if I'm still in freefall. My entire world focused on how amazing his lips feel against mine.

Roof? What roof?

It doesn't matter that he's only kissing me because he's relieved he stopped me from being hurt. I obviously need reminding we're on friendly terms and nothing more. Yet he electrifies me, with it this way from the first time he called at the welcome center to change a bulb in the foyer chandelier.

It was by chance I discovered if I turned the lighting feature on and off rapidly, I could blow at least two bulbs on cue. It was also amazing how often that happened.

As he cradles me in his arms while continuing to kiss me, I marvel at how easily he'd caught me. I've never been one of those girls that guys pick up and swing around. And to be honest, none of the guys in my life to date have been capable. But Lucian is capable, and then some, with him showing no signs of needing to set me down.

I've just decided I can live with that, when I hear a discrete cough from nearby. It must be something Lucian hears, too. But, rather than end our kiss as I'm expecting, he instead takes a step back to get us out of the middle of the sidewalk.

Unfortunately, it's one that also sees us sprawled in a heap between two parked cars. I'm lucky when Lucian again breaks my fall. He's not so lucky in that he's somehow hurt himself.

And how do I know this? That would be because he looks even grumpier than usual. "You're hurt?"

I extricate myself from his arms as carefully as I can, unsure of exactly what he's done. If he's hurt his back, we shouldn't move him. Neither should he have me spread all over his chest like ham-on-rye.

Once on my feet, I examine him, as if a glorified marketing assistant can complete a diagnosis by simply ogling the patient. Despite my lack of medical training, there's no missing the pain in his dark brown eyes as he stares back at me.

"Is it your back? Should I call an ambulance?"

"Not my back, I just rolled my ankle, is all." As if to show the truth of this, he struggles into a sitting position and, after briefly rubbing the back of his head, hastily unlaces his right boot. While there's no outward sign of damage after he removes it, I know from personal experience it'll show up soon enough.

"I'm calling for help!"

I'm halfway across the sidewalk when a couple of guys cut me off. The logo on their bright orange shirts identifies them as being from the utility company. Their good-natured ribbing at Lucian's expense confirms that they know him.

What is it about men that they can find humor in any situation? Lucian certainly doesn't appear happy to be the subject of their jokes. A quick look at their lanyards and I let them have it. "Marc, Nigel, don't just stand there. Help him up and get him inside!"

When they don't move fast enough, I stand with hands on hips, eyes narrowed, toe tapping. Despite my being dressed as an elf, I don't need to say anything else with my unspoken orders loud and clear. There are pluses to having managed male staff over the years.

This sees them on either side of Lucian, hands stuffed in his armpits, and him soon on his feet. Make that foot because when he'd tried putting weight on the damaged one, he'd yelped in pain before he could stop himself.

After grabbing his abandoned boot, I lead the way, showing the trio into the staff break-room and the small cot that sits against one wall.

This will be the first time I've seen anyone actually use it in the six months I've been working here. That it creaks when it takes Lucian's full weight is worrying.

The utility company workers then get their own back by telling me off about the reindeer on the roof being in contact with the overhead lines. Only after they've left to rectify this, does it dawn on me why Lucian had been yelling at me.

Sure, the reindeer I'd ordered online was bigger than I'd expected, but there's nothing an elf can't achieve when they're determined. And I was the Elf in Charge of Illuminations. It's a hokey title, but it's one I take seriously, wanting my first Christmas in my new hometown to be extra special.

While the beast's antlers were close to the overhead lines after I'd installed it, they weren't touching, so I figured that was okay. Who'd have thought the wind getting up like it had would have things going pear-shaped?

Or was that deer-shaped?

After all this has finished running through my already over-crowded brain, I look at Lucian and simply say, "Thank you." It's nowhere near enough, but it's all I can manage right now. If I'd patted that reindeer's patootie, I'd have hurt myself, or worse.

The mere thought is enough to have me shivering and dropping into the seat next to the small cot. "I didn't think. All I wanted was for the center's illuminations to be amazing."

I'm still mired in self-recriminations when Lucian's words cut through my internal clutter. According to him, I've ruined Christmas, although not in the way I'd have thought. I mean, who deliberately plans to be on call over the holidays? Apparently Lucian does, and I'm responsible for him not being able to work.

I'm wondering how I can put things right, when I remember seeing something in lost-property that will at least have him back on his feet. The center staff had laughed about how it was even possible for someone to leave the item behind.

Now I'm glad about it.

Lucian doesn't share my enthusiasm when I show it to him.

"It's bright pink! There are butterfly stickers! I am NOT using that."

As I look at the hands-free crutch, I'll admit it is rather childish, which is surprising given the sheer size of the thing. Whoever left it behind was no toddler.

"You'll have to, at least until you can get something better. Monique, my boss, has already locked up. We have to leave."

He glares at me before asking, "We?"

He's being deliberately obtuse, and I'm sure it's on purpose. I'll admit it, I messed up big time. But I'm trying to make it right, and he's being an ass about it.

"Yes, *we*, because I'll doubt you can drive with that ankle."

TWO

Back out on the sidewalk, Lucian stands as tall as possible, which is pretty tall in his case, his pose rigid with indignation. While some of this is down to what he deems is the unmanly color of the hands-free crutch, mostly it's thanks to my demanding his car keys.

"Do you really want to leave your truck in town, with all your tools in there?"

Busy panicking over thoughts of me driving his precious truck, this apparently hadn't occurred to him, which is odd because he's usually so sharp. This has me inspecting him, noticing for the first time his apparent confusion.

Could it be he clipped the back of his head when we fell? He had rubbed it briefly after he sat up, although he hasn't mentioned it since, too busy grumbling about my having ruined Christmas.

Eventually, his posture softens to the point I think he's about to relent. Then I take in the flat line of his eyebrows as he glares at me. It's time to put the pressure on, because it's getting late and I've still got to get him to the emergency room.

Not something I'm sharing with him, just yet, because you don't get eyebrows like that by being agreeable.

"Do you really want to go to the hassle of putting in an insurance claim if your truck gets broken into and your gear stolen?" I pause for a moment before pressing on. "That's if they don't steal the truck, too."

"My insurance won't cover you driving my truck!"

His smug grin, after delivering what he doubtless thinks, is the crowning argument, has me wanting to give up. Then I remember I'm the reason he's hurt, thanks to my refusal to back down when that moose-sized reindeer arrived.

As the street empties of vehicles, with people off home for their dinner, he still won't budge. The only good thing about his delaying our departure is that I can now see his truck parked down the road.

The humongous lightbulb on top helps a lot. Certainly Lucian is staring at his beloved vehicle, indecision rife in his gaze. It's enough of a distraction for me to take action.

Sometimes a girl just has to take matters into her own hands, or in this case, hand. I stuff mine in the front pocket of Lucian's work pants and help myself to his, ah, keys.

Oh my. It would appear the tackle fit the tool box, something that has me gasping almost as much as Lucian.

"What the hell, woman? Give me back those keys!"

He lunges at me, but still not used to the hand-free crutch, comes close to toppling, and if not for my steadying him, he would have.

Unfortunately—or not—it gives him the opportunity to hold me tight as he attempts to get his keys back. This has me holding them hard up against my spine, because the one thing my elf costume doesn't have is pockets.

It's a maneuver that also has me tight against his chest, exactly as I'd been when he'd kissed me earlier. As memories of that kiss sweep through my body, my gaze locks on his mouth. His bottom lip is just begging to be nibbled on. It's a thought that has me biting my own.

The Main Street shops shut for the night; we're alone on the sidewalk. There's no chance of anyone interrupting our kiss this time.

When Lucian gives up trying to get his keys and instead crisscrosses his arms behind me, I know he agrees. And for the second time in the past hour, his lips claim mine. It's even better this time.

Oh, who am I kidding? It's incredible and the stuff of dreams. Make that *my* dreams, because there's rarely a night passes that Lucian doesn't invade them. More often lately, I've been waking with an aching need.

On his tongue sweeping across my lips, I open my mouth on a sigh and he comes a calling. I'm only vaguely aware of the keys slipping from my nerveless fingers, but I'm in control enough to kick them across the sidewalk and into the gutter.

If it comes down to a race, I know I can reach them quicker than he can. That worry dealt to, I'm able to surrender to our second kiss with it better than anything I could dream up. Despite how grumpy Lucian is, the man sure knows how to kiss.

And because of how he towers over me, I feel petite and protected in the circle of his arms. This is a rarity for me, given my five-foot-eight. If I went on a date with him, I could even wear those hot-pink heels I'd bought on a whim.

It's this very thought that brings me to my senses. What am I thinking? I see him regularly at work. What if things went wrong? The embarrassment of him visiting the welcome center after would be cringeworthy.

Despite my not having said anything, Lucian must pick up on my reticence, because his lips leave mine and he straightens. The way he then looks at me has me squirming. I hadn't meant to lead him on, the very idea making me uncomfortable.

It's as if he can see every thought in my head, every emotion in my heart. And for that reason, I need to put a stop to this right now. His hold on me, having loosened, makes it easy enough for me to slip free.

I then waste no time retrieving his keys and taking off for his truck.

His, "Natasha, stop! You don't know how to drive a truck like that," follows me down the street.

Oh boy, how wrong he is. I've been driving trucks like his, and even bigger, since I was tall enough to reach the pedals. He's about to get his second shock of the day, although maybe I shouldn't use shock, given his profession?

When I'd dressed in my elf outfit this morning, the last thing on my mind was getting up close and personal with Lucian Davis. It truly is the stuff of dreams, with my having drooled over him for all these months.

Yet I can't risk taking it any further, because while we're not exactly friends, we are on friendly terms, and I don't want to ruin that.

By the time I arrive at his truck, excitement at driving the beast has overtaken my other emotions. I haven't driven a vehicle like this since I was living at home back on the east coast.

Actually, that truck was even larger, much to my mother's dismay and my father's anger. Hey if he didn't want me driving it, he shouldn't have left the keys in the ignition. It's a thought that has me realizing my own keys are in my handbag in the bottom drawer of my desk, along with my phone and wallet.

Not knowing the center manager's phone number by heart, there's no way I can get them back until the following morning. Thank goodness I've got a spare house key under the concrete frog in the garden. Even better was that I'd shoved my credit card in my bra when I went out for a coffee earlier.

After climbing into the truck and adjusting the seat, I start the engine with a roar. The vibrations rip right through me, causing bits and pieces to buzz as much as they had when Lucian kissed me.

The very thought of driving with him next to me is one that has me come close to putting the truck in the wrong gear. After a steadying breath, I find the right one and ease forward.

I'm off to collect the man I want, but cannot have.

LUCIAN

As I watch Natasha marching off down the road toward my truck, I'm furious for so many reasons.

First, that I've badly damaged my ankle, the pain telling me it won't be a five-minute fix.

Second, that she has no right looking that good dressed as an elf, of all things.

Finally, that she'll doubtless disembowel the gearbox on my truck before admitting she can't drive it.

This last is something that has me hobbling slowly after her. While I can't drive myself, I can at least grab all my expensive tools and have an Uber take me back to my place.

I'll also remove the battery, so I know the truck will be there come morning when I can arrange for one of my buddies to collect it. It's too late to bother any of them now, with them already sitting down to dinner with their families.

I'm going through all of this in my head when I hear my truck roar into life. I then hold my breath, waiting for the sound of metal-on-metal as Natasha does her best to dismantle my gearbox.

Only it doesn't happen. Rather, she gets the truck into gear and pulls away from the curb like a pro. No bunny-hops, no stalling of the engine, just a smooth acceleration in my direction.

This surprises me. Isn't she a professional party organizer, or something? And if so, how is it she knows how to drive a truck like mine? This has me thinking back on what I have heard about her, with all of it vague.

Apparently she's from a small town in upstate New York, and has lived in Coogan's Break for a little over six months. Other than this, I'm drawing a blank. Now if you were to ask me what she looks like, then I could go into fine detail.

Like, really fine. She's tall, with a cloud of red curls and curves I'd describe as just right. Perhaps the most arresting thing about her is that her eyes are different colors.

When I first saw it, I thought I was imaging things, but I wasn't, with one eye green, while the other is blue. On my remarking on it, she'd merely snorted, saying she'd dated one guy for nine months before he noticed.

I hadn't asked, but hoped she'd dumped him on the spot, because a guy that stupid didn't deserve a woman as gorgeous as Natasha. The very woman who is driving my truck as smoothly as I could myself.

There's also no missing her wide grin when she brings the truck to a stop next to me. Instead of keeping the truck idling, she shuts the engine off and climbs down, the bells on her hat jingling a merry tune.

Damn it, as much as I want to be angry, I just can't. There's something so endearing about this woman, something that has me smiling despite myself. This doesn't last long after I hear what she's planning next.

"I don't need to go to the emergency room. Just need to go home and ice it. I'll be fine come morning."

In a heartbeat, gone is my jingling happy elf, replaced by a woman who'll brook no argument. I'm off to the emergency room if she has to throw me over one shoulder and carry me there. Her words, not mine, although I'd like to see her try.

"Lucian Davis, you get your butt up in that passenger seat. You are going to the emergency room, because for all we know, you've broken your ankle, not just sprained it."

As when she'd faced off to the guys from the utility company, she's fierce, passionately so. I love a feisty woman, and Natasha is definitely that when fired up as she is now.

"Fine! Fine, I'll go get it checked if it'll get you off my back."

With her help, I then undo the hands-free crutch. Because short of being strapped across the hood, I can't travel with it in place. My then hauling myself up into the passenger seat is easy enough, with this mostly down to arm strength.

She soon hands the crutch up to me and slams the door before I've had a chance. After skipping around in front of the truck, she climbs in next to me. It's not until she starts the engine that I remember how other women have responded to the vibrations the engine produces.

With Natasha next to me in the cab, they're also doing it for me. How am I supposed to walk into the emergency room sporting a cock hard enough I could use it instead of that stupid crutch?

I'm in no better state when Natasha helps me out of the truck on arrival at the emergency room. The only thing that takes the edge off my erection is the thought of walking into a crowded room with an elf and a pink crutch.

Actually, the elf I can handle and I would, if not for her, subtly distancing herself during our second kiss. While many a woman has called me a big lump, I'm not stupid. I can read body language just as well as the next guy.

And I know a NO when I see it.

There were pluses and minuses to living in a smaller place. The plus in this case was one nurse having gone to school with my older sister. This saw Natasha and me in a cubicle off to one side instead of in the main waiting area.

When a doozy of a headache kicked in, I was relieved I could lie down. I guess I must have smacked the back of my head harder than I'd thought when we fell.

I'd been more interested in Natasha spread all over me, like she belonged there. One of her strong thighs nudging my groin and her luscious breasts filling my field of vision had it finally feeling like Christmas.

Perched on the seat next to the gurney I'm stretched out on, Natasha picks at her red and green striped leggings. It's as if she's suddenly self-conscious of being in fancy-dress, and yet there's no need.

Hell, if I was Santa, I'd be happy to have her on my knee. I then have to stop my thoughts in their tracks to keep a handle on my body's responses.

"It'll probably be ages before I see a doctor. There's no need for you to wait around."

She peers at me briefly before shaking her head. "No, that's okay. I'm happy to wait. I can get us some coffee, if you'd like?"

It's when she offers I realize I don't have my wallet on me, with even rubbish coffee not free.

It's also then I notice she's not carrying a bag of any sort. As if to answer my unspoken question, she delves inside her top and comes back with a credit card. This has me wondering what else she's got down there.

Of course, I already have a good idea thanks to our being hard up against each other earlier. It's dwelling on what her breasts would feel like without that brightly colored top getting in my way that has me relieved when she disappears in search of coffee.

THREE

On the drive out to Lucian's place on the edge of town, I'm exhausted. Despite him apparently knowing one nurse, it hadn't sped things along any.

There wasn't a chance I was abandoning him there, not when it was ultimately my fault he'd hurt himself. By the time he'd been X-rayed, seen by a doctor and had his ankle strapped, it was past midnight and I was having trouble focusing.

And I wasn't the only one not seeing straight. Lucian, against Doctor's orders, took one of the prescribed painkillers the moment he got them. There'd be no going home and taking it once he was in bed, as recommended.

To make matters worse, he'd then decided it "wasn't working" and had swallowed another before we'd even left the emergency room carpark. Whatever they were, they were strong enough to have the patient singing and happier than I'd ever seen him.

His base notes fill the cab, with the rumble of his voice a perfect accompaniment to the deep throb of the engine. It isn't the only thing that's throbbing. While the rest of my body is dead on its feet, my fizzy bits are living up to my name for them, and then some.

As if to focus his thoughts, Lucian blows hard and helps himself to more air before speaking. "I didn't like the way those guys were looking at you."

Despite the soft edge to his words, I've understood them just fine. Does this mean I understand what he's getting at? Ah, that'd be heck no.

"Even the doctor had his eyes all over you."

The temptation to turn and look at Lucian is overwhelming, but I resist. If I was to lose myself in those dark brown eyes, we'd end up in the ditch running alongside the road.

Even without my looking at him, his tone tells me all the attention I'd received had annoyed him. Hah, he's a fine one to talk. The nurse charged with strapping his ankle was so busy flirting with him she'd dropped the bandage and had to start over.

It's not something I'll point out, because the less he knows of my infatuation, the better. If I'm lucky, he'll think he's imagined everything that happened tonight. That it's all down to a painkiller-induced high. I won't forget our kiss—kisses—though, not for a very long time.

On seeing Lucian's lightbulb-shaped mailbox up ahead, I slow the truck. When I stop out front, I'm horrified to see how narrow his driveway is. The trees crowding in both sides, I'll be lucky not to damage the paint, something I'd never hear the end of.

It takes all my concentration to navigate the driveway safely, and after parking the truck next to the house, I slump over the steering wheel in relief.

"You did good," slurs Lucian, before adding. "You're a great driver." Even with the cab only dimly lit thanks to the security lights having gone on, there's no missing that this surprises him.

"Yeah, well, it helps when you've been driving since you were twelve."

As I engage the park brake and turn the engine off, he splutters out, "Twelve? Isn't that illegal?"

"Not if you're on private roads, it isn't." Unwilling to go into more detail, I grab the keys out of the ignition and climb down from the cab, putting a close to the subject.

After walking around the front of the truck, I steel myself for what a mission it'll be to get Lucian out of the cab and into the house. He hadn't been easy to deal with before the painkillers. With him all floppy and singing, it'll be a nightmare.

And so it proves true when the foot of his good leg slips on the bottom step of the truck and he comes close to flattening me. His yowls of pain tell me he's knocked his bad ankle, but when I look at him, it's the back of his head he's rubbing.

Blast it. As tired as I'd been when the doctor finally saw Lucian, I'd completely forgotten to mention it.

Once he's safely propped against the side of the truck, I grab the hands-free crutch. With Lucian incapable of strapping it on himself, there's nothing but for me to do so.

This has me jamming my hands between his legs so I can wrap the Velcro strap around his upper thigh. His resultant hiss when I cinch it tight has nothing to do with pain.

"Careful darling, don't damage the goods."

Doing my best to dampen thoughts of 'the goods', I get on with wrapping the Velcro strap around his calf muscle and securing it. Now comes the hard part, getting the pair of us over to the front door without taking a tumble.

It's close, but we make it. I've already got the key in the lock when something occurs to me. "Is there an alarm?"

Lucian shakes his head, doing a good impression of a dashboard bobble toy while he's about it. He is so close to passing out that it's not funny, especially with me in charge of getting him upright again.

Inside the house, I flick the lights on, surprised at how stylish the place is. Just goes to show, you shouldn't judge a book by its cover. I'd know, with plenty of folks judging me in the past.

Because I'm tired, I don't immediately notice what's missing, although once I do, I can't ignore it. There are no decorations, not even a card or two on the mantelpiece, leaving Lucian's home like the place Christmas forgot.

"Your bedroom?! Where is it?!" I usually wouldn't yell like this, but with every passing second, Lucian was becoming less aware of his surroundings. I need to get him into bed where he can't fall and hurt himself.

Rather than answer, he wobbles off to our right, and I follow along, my hands gripping his upper arms from behind to help steady him. Strangely, he seems to cope better with the pink crutch when legally stoned, than he had when sober.

Sure enough, we enter a hallway, and from there, a bedroom. The size of the bed alone says this is Lucian's domain, confirmed when he totters over to the end of the bed and promptly face-plants it.

I'm met with loud snoring soon after. Blast it; I can't leave him with his foot sticking up in the air like it is. This has me struggling to remove the crutch from his dead-weight, before rolling him into the recovery position.

After removing his other boot, and unable to move him further up the bed, I pull the covers over him as best I can. I then leave him to sleep it off.

My phone is in my desk drawer and there is no landline that I can see. This means I can't even call an Uber, nor can I leave Lucian alone in his current state.

Thank goodness the large sectional in the living room looks comfortable.

When woken by loud cussing the following morning, I take a while to work out where I am, having slept later than I'd meant to. My plan had been to walk into town before Lucian woke up.

I've definitely failed on that count with him not only awake, but like a bear with a sore head by the sound of things.

I'm lying there wondering how to announce my presence when he stumbles into the living room. When he stops at the end of the sectional, I'm pleased to see he's wearing the hands-free crutch.

However, that's all he's wearing.

LUCIAN

On coming to an abrupt halt at the end of the sectional, the searing pain in my ankle fades to a background buzzing. "Huh, what the?"

I'm not capable of anything more intelligent, my mind a muddle, and Natasha in that elf costume as tantalizing this morning as she had been yesterday.

While she's a welcome sight, why is she out here? If I'd had my way, she wouldn't be on the couch; she'd be in my bed. Damn it, the only thing I can remember about last night is catching her when she fell off the roof.

I wouldn't have a clue how the hell I hurt my ankle, and yet I've apparently done a real number on it.

A hazy image of us sharing a passionate kiss flickers briefly to life before being extinguished. It's so fleeting that I put it down to a dream and not a memory.

Other than these incoherent images, everything else is a blank, and yet a lot must have happened, because I've hurt my ankle big time.

And how is it I can see my truck parked outside, because I don't remember driving home? For my memory to be as full of holes as it is, I must have been over the legal limit.

My fuzzy brain having taken its own sweet time to trawl through the known facts, only now do I give thought to my being naked.

And right there I discover yet another benefit of the hands-free crutch when I'm able to cross mine in front of my standard morning wood. I'm struggling with my first question of many when I see her lips twitching. Soon enough, she's rolling around on the couch, holding her tummy as she laughs joyously.

My being naked is one thing. Add in that I'm strapped into the heinously pink knee crutch I'd found next to my bed, and I'll have to admit I must look farcical.

The device wouldn't have been my first choice. However, after attempting to put weight on my damaged ankle, and an experimental hop, I'd realized it was the least painful option.

Only after she's got her laughter under control does she speak, although she's careful to keep her gaze averted. "Ah, do you think you could put some clothes on?"

Back in my bedroom, I make quick work of unstrapping the crutch and dragging on whatever is to hand. It's what I'd worn to work yesterday, and while crinkled and musty, it'll do for now.

Back in the living room, I'm met by the aroma of freshly brewed coffee, which is good because I've a desperate need for caffeine. It might help center my thoughts and even knock a few memories loose.

On hobbling into the kitchen, I find Natasha sitting at the island with mug in hand. Opposite her, another waits for me, the barstool next to it already pulled out.

This is good because I suspect I'll need to be sitting down when I hear what the hell happened last night. The Velcro closings on the crutch are quick enough to release, and I'm seated soon after.

I grab my coffee ready to enjoy that first sip of the day, but soon put it back down.

"Before you start, can you tell me who drove my truck?"

This has her taking her lips away from her coffee, her mouth a perfect O.

It's only once she's put her mug down carefully on the marble counter that she answers me for all the good it does.

"You don't remember?"

"Not a damned thing after catching you when you fell off the roof."

"Oh."

I'm expecting her to carry on; instead she picks up her coffee and gulps a couple of mouthfuls, the planning in her dual-colored eyes on full show. This has me sitting up straighter on my barstool, interested to see what she comes out with, and whether I believe it.

I'm on my second coffee before I'm fully up to date. Or so she says, because there are as many blanks as there'd been before she started. She says she drove me home in my truck and if I close my eyes, I have a vague recollection of her next to me in the cab.

The other hazy memory I have is of us kissing, although she's omitted that in her run-through of events. She's also been very careful to avoid eye contact during her recounting of the night.

At least now I know why I'm stuck with that stupid pink crutch, with it apparently better than anything the emergency room had on hand.

This has me glaring at my bad leg propped up on the barstool next to mine.

"Damn it, this is going to cost me a truck-load of work."

"I'm so, so, sorry. I didn't realize the roof would be so slippery."

There's no missing her remorse, and that she holds herself responsible for my accident, for all the good it does. She can say she's sorry as much as she likes. It won't help me get through the next week.

"What the hell were you doing out there, anyway? If you'd touched that stupid reindeer, we'd have been scraping you off the sidewalk."

She doesn't apologize again, instead falling quiet and staring into her empty coffee cup as though to forecast the future. She must see something, because she's soon back looking at me, the cogs in her brain again visibly whirring.

"If you could somehow get from job to job, would that help?" She taps the top of the pink crutch that I'd propped against the end of the kitchen island. "You can walk okay with this, can't you?"

Despite my being all kinds of wobbly on the pink monstrosity, practice should make perfect, meaning she's got a point. If I can get to the jobs, then I should be able to complete most of them.

The problem is, I can't drive, and I don't want to blow a stack of cash on Ubers. According to Natasha, the doctor had said I wasn't to drive for a week, the busiest week of the holiday period, for me and Uber drivers.

I'm mentally sifting through the current jobs I'll have to cancel, when Natasha says something that gets my attention, my head snapping up.

"You'll drive me?!! Aren't you working at the welcome center?"

"I'm off for the next ten days. Fixing the Christmas lights was the last thing I had to take care of until just before New Year's Eve."

As mad as it is, I kinda like the idea of being chauffeur driven by an elf for the next week. As unlikely as her continuing to wear the costume, is me finding anyone else who can drop everything to help, with most of my mates being family men.

It'll also give me the chance to find out if Natasha and I had shared a kiss, as I seem to think. Because damn it, if I shut my eyes, I can still taste her on my lips.

FOUR

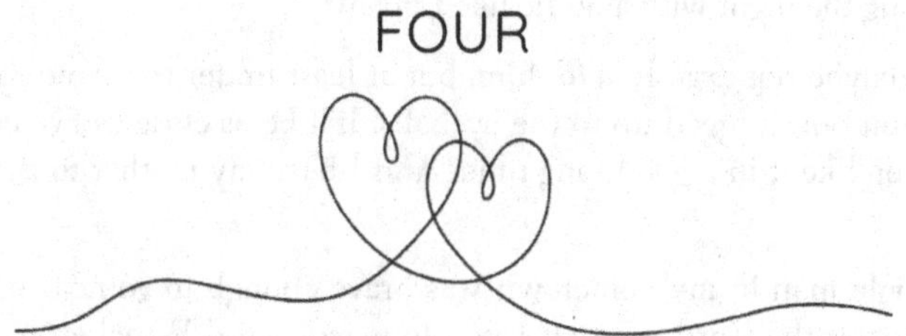

NATASHA

Yesterday, when parking Lucian's truck at my rental after collecting my things from work, I'd been beyond annoyed with the infuriating man. And why was that?

That'd be because he'd insisted I show him I could safely drive his precious vehicle to the point it had been akin to completing my road test all over again.

Despite my telling him I'd been driving since I was old enough to reach the pedals, he wasn't buying it. Infuriating he might be, but he was still gorgeous, even when grumpy like he'd been yesterday.

If I didn't know better, I'd think he was doing it deliberately, and I'd know. Grandpa Bob, my dad's dad, had also been an ornery so-and-so used to getting his own way. I'm still tucked up in bed working through all this when I get a text.

Those who know this number are few, with my family definitely not in the know. It will either be work, or Lucian. This last has me grabbing my phone off the bedside table and unlocking it. Sure enough, it's from him, and he needs me at his place pronto.

It's the last line that has me wondering. An overnight bag? What does that mean? It means I'll be spending the night at his place, and I won't be sleeping on the couch in my clothes. It's enough to have my heart thundering in my chest and me flinging the covers to one side.

I'm on my feet before I'm ready for it, the spins having me close to collapsing. This much excitement first thing in the morning isn't good for me.

The dancing around my bedroom stops soon enough when I give thought to packing. What on earth am I supposed to take when I'll be spending the night with a hottie like Lucian?

Well, maybe not exactly *with* him, but at least under the same roof and with him not drugged up to the eyeballs. It'll be as close as I've come to anything like it in a good long time. And I have my mother to thank for that.

No single man in my hometown was brave enough to go near me after mother put the word out that I was to marry Jarod Winchester. Never mind, I'd told her, and even him, that I wasn't interested.

While cultured and rich, a lack of firing synapses and a missing chin spoke of his parents being related long before their marriage. He's the sort of man my mother would have married if her parents had given her the choice.

However, with my dad's family filthy rich thanks to the success of Frank Logging, my maternal grandparents had stood firm on their choice for her. There isn't a chance my parents are forcing me into a loveless marriage like theirs.

It was why I'd left no forwarding address when I disappeared.

After shucking memories of the man my parents had wanted me to settle for, I rush around the house, selecting and rejecting outfits. The last thing I stuff in my overnight bag is my elf outfit.

I doubt I'll need it, but the memories of how Lucian had looked at me when I was wearing it are enough for it to make the cut. For all I know, I could run full-tilt into a Christmas miracle and have need of it.

It's just a shame I can't wear it today, finally deciding on my three-quarters white jeans and newest Christmas sweater. Red and white stripes with a reindeer head on the front make it perfect for the festive season.

Unfortunately, Lucian doesn't agree with me on this.

On answering the front door at his place, he doesn't bother with a hello and how are you, instead spitting out. "You can't wear that!" His staring pointedly at my chest leaves me in no doubt what he's referring to.

"What's wrong with it? It's perfect for Christmas."

There's a certain resignation when he slowly shakes his head. "Because I need to look professional. If I turn up with the Ghost of Christmas past, people will think I've helped myself to too much eggnog."

Lucian channeling grandpa tells me that with picking fights, this wasn't one of them, at least not right now. "Fine, I'll change into something else." Only once I've agreed, does he open the door wide, allowing me to enter.

Of course, then I don't know where to go because I won't be sleeping in Lucian's room, that's for sure

"You can put your stuff in the guest room." He turns on his heel and disappears inside, leaving me to follow as best I can.

I'm not sure what I've been expecting, but this isn't it. The guest room is... Actually, I'm unsure how to describe it. Plain? Utilitarian? Monk-like. The room lacks personality of any type. It's as if Jarod Winchester—my mother's choice of son-in-law—has been ground into spackle and spread over the walls.

Boring, so very boring.

Perhaps more surprising than the lackluster nature of the room, is how freely Lucian is moving courtesy of the pink crutch. His natural athleticism doubtless has him making it look easier than I'll suspect it is.

I'm dropping my bag next to the twin bed when Lucian coughs behind me.

"As soon as you've changed, we can get going."

This has me spinning to face him, conscious he's looking at where my ass had been when I do so. Conscious enough, I yank on the bottom of my sweater to make it longer.

"You were serious about that? But I'll just be staying in the truck, won't I?"

His gaze finally meets mine, and he sucks on his bottom lip in a manner that has me wanting to do the same, only to his lip, not mine. "Yeah, well, I'll need you to help carry my gear inside and hand me stuff as I need it."

"Oh."

"Oh?"

"It's just that the only other clothes I have with me are like this."

And it's true, I'd packed with looking attractive and festive in mind, not being a glorified electrician's assistant.

"We can swing by your place on the way to the job so you can change." Without giving me another option, he swings deftly on the crutch and leaves me to follow.

I'm not sure how I feel about this. There's nothing flash about the glorified beach shack I'm renting, but after the ostentatious nature of the home I'd grown up in, I love it.

It was what my Grandpa Bob would have called down-to-earth. A lot like him and me, with us both standing out like sore thumbs at any family gathering.

LUCIAN

On Natasha turning into the driveway of the old Garcia place, I'm surprised, not having given it much thought about where she lived.

When I think of her, it's in connection to the welcome center, and yet she had to sleep somewhere. Not where I'd like, but somewhere all the same.

On her turning off the engine and engaging the park brake, I disrupt the silence that'd settled on the drive over. "Make it something simple, and the darker, the better." I slap my leg to highlight the color of my gear.

She's standing next to the truck and about to shut the cab door, when I add, "Grab a couple of outfits. We're on call for the next two days."

Given her surprise at this news, I hurry to explain I'm covering for a mate of mine. "It's his first Christmas as a dad. He needs to be there."

Rather than gush over this as I've been expecting, Natasha stares at me briefly before closing the door. She's not far down the path at the side of the shack when she turns and gazes at me again.

I'm not sure why, but I feel as though I've been *seen* for the first time in years, like truly *seen*. Not just as a great lumbering fool and an electrician, but as me. It's something that strikes at my core, leaving me glad she's disappeared inside.

She's not gone for long, but when she reappears, she couldn't look more different if she tried. Gone is the Christmas outfit, with her now dressed head-to-toe in unforgiving black. Skin-tight-black that is, and enough to have my mouth watering. She's also carrying a plastic bag, presumably stuffed with more of the same.

Sheesh, the next couple of days will be hell with Natasha tempting me at every turn, and I've only got myself to blame.

And I'm right. One-and-a-half days of sporting a semi and all down to my gorgeous new assistant in her figure hugging clothes.

Damn it, the t-shirt she's wearing today is tight enough I can see the outline of her nipples if I look hard enough. And I have, and I am.

It's therefore a relief when I get a call from the Rose Haven Rest Home at lunchtime on Christmas Eve. If anything can take my mind off Natasha's ah em assets, it's the old people who are unlucky enough to call that place home.

Previous call-outs have me knowing exactly what I'll find, with today being no exception. Honestly, on walking into the place, you'd never know it was Christmas Eve, with it lacking cheer of any kind, although I've no right to judge.

There's also no ignoring the pseudo whisper from the old girl slouched off to my right. "The cutie's back again!" It's something that has me turning and winking broadly, my response being met with delighted laughter, as always.

The old man next to her is as quick to comment on Natasha's presence. "And look, he brought company. Hope my pacemaker's up to it."

Beside me, Natasha's sharp intake of breath has her coughing and spluttering out, "This is... awful."

For a moment I think she's talking about the residents' cheeky comments, but I couldn't be more wrong. While there's no avoiding their summation of us, there's also no missing the other residents sunk deep in their beaten-up recliners. Eyes focused on something only they can see as they patiently wait for death.

Natasha has moved off, and I'm still taking everything in when the older couple next to me have a whispered conversation. As is often the case with older people, it's one where their every word carries clearly.

"They make a lovely couple, don't they, Fletch?" The old girl follows this up by patting the back of her companion's discolored hand.

"That they do, Alice. That they do."

I'm about to refute our status as a couple when the old man gently turns his hand over and squeezes the woman's reassuringly. After this, I don't have it in me to burst their little bubble of humanity.

Natasha's right, this place is awful, but what can you do?

According to Natasha, there's plenty, and after firing up the truck on departure, rather than turn left out of Rose Haven, she turns right.

"Ah, where are we going?"

She looks briefly in my direction, the fire in her eyes enough to burn a man. "Everyone deserves to have a fun time at Christmas, especially old people."

Outwardly, she's simply made an observation, and yet I get there's a lot more to it than this. I therefore don't argue when she turns into the carpark at a nearby strip mall.

When she pulls the truck to a stop outside the dollar store at the end, I understand some of what's about to happen. And yet after only ten minutes in the store, I'm still surprised by the mounting pile in the trolley she's charged me with pushing.

The final aisle is where she slows; the white string lights overhead, having turned it into a magical place. However, this isn't what captures her attention.

Instead of snapping up the simple white lights, she stacks box after box of the multi-color variety atop the already full trolley.

"Are you sure about all those colored lights? White might be, uh, easier to, um, coordinate."

Her glare when she looks up has me stepping back and straight into a teetering pile of yet more lights. The noise of the boxes hitting the floor is enough to have an employee with us in a heartbeat.

"You'll have to buy those." His tone is resolute, so is the manner in which he taps a note taped to the front of the shelf.

YOU BREAK IT, YOU BUY IT.

A good look at the boxes and boxes of hideous snowmen novelty lights I'm being forced to buy, and my shoulders drop. If not for us being in a dollar store, I'd be parting with a serious chunk of change.

After paying for everything else, Natasha asks if I can take it all out to the truck while she picks up a few more things. She follows this up by shoving the keys in the pocket of my cargo shorts.

Damn it, do you have any idea how hard it is to control a trolley with a wonky wheel when you're also dealing with a crutch and an erection?

It's hard. Actually, it's on its way to being damned hard.

FIVE

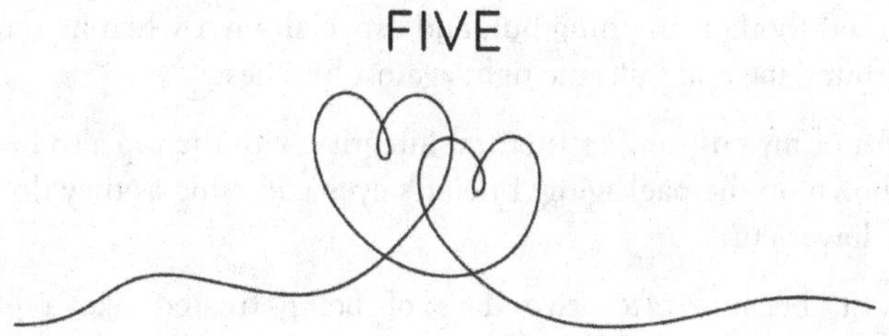

NATASHA

I suspect the atmosphere in the truck would be chilly even without the boxes of snowmen lights the shop had forced Lucian to purchase. I hate to think about how he'll react when I show him what he's wearing tomorrow.

That's if he even agrees to accompany me to the retirement home. Thankfully, I've got twelve hours to convince him, and just the outfit for the task. The misery of those old people, coupled with my overwhelming desire for Lucian, has me willing to risk our friendship.

I'm still haunted by memories of Grandpa Bob being shipped off to the country just before Christmas, only to return three days later. It was all part of mother's determination to pretend that side of the family didn't exist. It was also the start of many an argument between us.

With Lucian busy grilling something for dinner; I leave him to it while I go change. With no mirror in the guest room, I have to use the one in the hall bathroom to check myself out.

The costume is both shorter and tighter than I've been expecting. Thank goodness it's Lycra, or I'd be stuck with wearing my elf costume again. And while I love it, my new outfit definitely has the edge.

I find out just how much of an edge when I join Lucian outside, and he drops the sausage he'd been checking for doneness.

"What in the hell?!!"

"You don't like it?" I spin to give him a better look, and he loses his grip on the tongs, with them clattering to the deck.

"Oh, I like it just fine."

He takes a step toward me, coming close to squashing the sausage. He then takes another and another until he looms over me. I don't feel threatened though, anything but, and especially not when he wraps his arms around me and pulls me tight against his chest.

It's a test of my costume's structural integrity with the top also lower-cut than shown on the packaging. Lucian's eyes widening as they do, say it's a LOT lower-cut.

Excellent, because after two days of being treated like a glorified apprentice, I'm over it. While he can't remember our kiss, I sure as heck can with the memories keeping me awake at night, especially since moving into the guest room at his place.

A moment later, Lucian's lips touch mine, with my body coming alive in response. The kiss is every bit as good as I remember, perhaps even better. Oh, who am I kidding? With my body jammed tight against his, and my boobs doing their best to escape the Mrs. Claus outfit, this is my idea of stupendous.

When he takes his lips away from mine, I'm having as much trouble staying upright as he is. When he staggers off to one side, I think he's lost his balance. Instead, it's so he can turn the gas off on the grill.

Just because we're about to go up in flames doesn't mean the same should be true of our dinner. When Lucian step/clomps back to my side and scoops me up, I know the only thing on the menu tonight is each other.

Yet again he shows me how well he's managing the crutch, negotiating the hallway to his bedroom with ease, and not once banging me into the walls. My focus purely on him, he probably could have, and I wouldn't have noticed in the slightest.

It's the first time I've been in his bedroom since the night I brought him home from the emergency room. It's as I remember, but rather than be dark, the room is lit by the setting sun.

After he lays me gently down on the bed, Lucian races to unstrap the crutch, letting it fall where it may. He removes his t-shirt as haphazardly, tossing it across the room to land in a corner.

When he kneels next to me, waves of longing flood my body. Never have I wanted anyone—or anything—as much as I want this gorgeous man, right here, right now. His torso bathed in golden light from the setting sun, there's nothing I can do to stop from reaching out and raking my nails down his chest.

His response is encouraging enough for me to arch off the bed in order to remove what little there is of the top half of my costume. My tummy muscles aren't up to holding the position, and I sink back into the mattress.

My bra is the perfect accessory for the Mrs. Claus outfit, being red and white stripes with embroidered cherries and a heart clasp at the front. The panties are a perfect match, although this is something Lucian will only discover if…

The rest of this thought flees when he unclasps my bra, freeing my breasts to his gaze. After taking his fill, he copies my earlier move, raking his nails across my nipples, my back arching in search of more pleasure, so much more.

I couldn't lie still if my life depended on it, my body rippling in response to his touch. More than this, it responds in places his hands are nowhere near, although I suspect they soon will be.

The mere thought of opening myself to his gaze has me juicy and overcome with need. I want Lucian so badly I can feel it at a cellular level. I revel in the knowledge he'll fill me completely, stretching me as I've always longed for.

LUCIAN

As I draw on Natasha's nipples, I'm wondering if this is indeed a Christmas miracle, or whether I'm dreaming as I have for the last three nights. Dreams of burying myself in this gorgeous woman as I've wanted to since I first saw her at the welcome center.

It must be a dream she shares, with her doing her best to wriggle out of the scandalously short skirt of her outfit. The length being what it is, we could probably work around it. However, that wouldn't have her as naked as she is in my dreams. The very thought has me rushing to help her remove first the skirt and then her matching festive panties.

There's been no need for me to be seductive about it, with her apparently every bit as aroused as I am. A discovery I make when I run my hand down her tummy and cup her pleasure dome.

The heat she's generating promises good things to come.

I confirm just how good when I bury my fingers in her curls and she opens to my touch. The merest press of her clit and she quivers in response, a guttural moan forming in the back of her throat.

It's encouragement enough for me to slide my fingers lower to open her even more. Wide enough I can slide first one and then two fingers deep inside her warm depths, spreading them in preparation.

There's nothing striptease about how I ditch the rest of my clothes. With Natasha lying there as she had in my dreams, I don't want to waste the time. Instead, wrenching free of everything and tossing it across the room. There's a sense of relief when I join her on the bed, flesh-to-flesh.

She fills my arms completely, with her height, delicious curves, and firm body a perfect foil for my own. Certainly, I've no worries about accidentally hurting her. No matter the task at hand over the preceding three days, Natasha has been up for it.

She's carried tools, and even my ladder, never once complaining, and never once looking as though it's too much of a challenge for her. She's the perfect helpmate for a man like me, perhaps too perfect. What if I'm setting myself up for heartache?

I've no sooner thought this than Natasha's hand closes tight around my cock. On her hand moving, I couldn't tell you my name. I'm a fool if I don't make the most of this, to take it for what it is.

And because it is the season for giving, what sort of man would I be if I didn't give a present in return? It's one I can even gift wrap, thanks to the stainless cock ring in the top drawer of my bedside table.

I'm not sure why, but I get the idea Natasha will be up for it. Anyone brave enough to climb out onto the roof of the welcome center, as she did, is more than a little daring.

"What is that!?"

Her eyes are wide as she watches me slide it into place, her earlier stroking of my length making this harder than it would usually be.

"Just something that'll have me lasting longer." On her reaching out and tapping the ring experimentally, my cock twitches in response, making me glad the hardware is in place. After months of dreaming of this very night, the last thing I want is to blow before we've enjoyed ourselves.

Whatever we get up to tonight, it'll need to work around the limitations of my damaged ankle. If I had my way, I'd take her against the wall, allowing gravity to connect us fully.

The next best thing will be for her to be on top, something that soon has me flat on my back, my cock bouncing around, and ready for action. All it takes is the merest jerk of my hips for her to catch on.

"Ride me, baby. Let me fill you completely."

Again, she shows her daring side by straddling me and opening herself up. After spreading her even wider with my thumbs, I guide myself in, finding her slick with want and able to take every inch of me. Looks like I'm not alone in being ready to blow.

While she's whimpering as other partners have before her, it's not from discomfort. Her back arched in ecstasy, her nipples puckering in response to my pinching them is evidence of this.

Her euphoric moan is encouragement enough for me to buck my hips and fully seat myself in her fiery core. It also has me digging my sore ankle into the mattress, with nothing I can do about my yelp of pain.

"Oh, oh, I'm sorry. Did I hurt you?"

"No, you're good, just my ankle."

In response, she tries to lift herself free, but I'm not having it. I want this so badly she could break my ankle and I'd still want to keep going. A couple more bucks and I take us far enough down the bed that my damaged foot hangs over the end. No chance of jostling it now, but every chance I get some other jostling in.

As she grinds away on my length, I'm glad of the cock ring. Without it in place, I'd have blown by now. Instead, the pressure builds as I continue to fill her with sharp jerks of my hips, her breath coming in gasps.

Soon, it's not the only thing coming, with the cock ring, no match for the glorious creature writhing and moaning on top of me.

Her cries of release are a match for my own, when she collapses on my chest and holds on tight as if to stop us from shattering completely.

It's a fruitless task with my heart no longer my own. Rather, it belongs to Natasha, a concept that scares the crap out of me. Even scarier is that she doesn't know how I feel, and I'm not sure I'm brave enough to tell her.

SIX

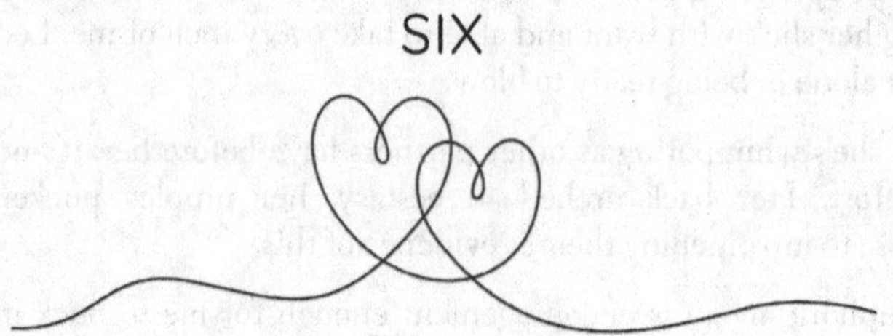

NATASHA

My body is languid the following morning when the alarm on my phone sounds. I have to slam my hand down on the bedside table several before I find it and hold it up. Five o'clock? I never get up this early. It's still dark outside.

My brain is slow to catch up with the alarm and realize Christmas Day has finally arrived and it'll be so different to last year! The next thing I remember is what happened last night with Lucian, the deep ache between my legs enough to have me smiling.

On the alarm on my phone ringing out again, I know I don't have time to dwell on it. I've got an important task, and if I'm to pull it off, I'll need Lucian's help.

On quietly opening the guest bedroom door, I'm met with gentle snoring from Lucian's room. Good, it sounds as if he finally fell asleep despite the pain in his ankle.

After grabbing some clean underwear and my reasonably modest elf outfit, I scuttle down the hallway to the guest bathroom. There isn't a chance I can wear the Mrs. Claus outfit today.

Things will go smoother if my boobs and ass aren't on display when it comes time to set everything up at Rose Haven. I'd be as likely to cause heart attacks as spread Christmas cheer if I wore that scandalous costume.

As I rush through my shower, even I'll admit there's a slightly manic edge to my deciding Christmas has to be joyous for the old folks. Too often I'd stood at the window and watched Grandpa Bob ceremoniously driven away, as though it was a treat for him to leave.

Rather, it was that my mother thought his old man clothes would clash with her upmarket Christmas decorations. To my young mind, he'd have made the perfect Santa, but my mother wouldn't hear of it, instead holding yearly auditions for the role.

She'd prefer a fake beard and tummy to Grandpa Bob's real-deal. Only after police checks and sound checks—the 'HO-HO-HO' requiring gravitas—was the role awarded.

And I'd hated every curated second of it. One year, I'd even asked if I could go to the country with Grandpa Bob, much to my mother's horror. Such was her reaction. I hadn't asked again.

It's all of this that has me bound and determined to make today the best Christmas those old folks have ever had.

If it works as I've planned, it might even be the best Christmas I've ever had. And it's this last that propels me into Lucian's bedroom after my shower, flicking the lights on while I'm about it. On seeing the state of him, I want to flick them straight back off again in case I'm tempted.

He's not happy about being woken, although he looks to be happy about something. Parts of him appear particularly 'happy'.

"Come on, up you get. We need to be at Rose Haven sooner rather than later."

I follow this up by throwing the costume I'd bought for him at the dollar store over his lap to further hide his growing tent in the sheets. I then skedaddle into the hallway.

This isn't to avoid seeing his glorious body when he gets out of bed, but to avoid the fallout when he realizes what I want him to wear. When it comes, I could already have been at Rose Haven and still heard his bellowed, "I'm not wearing this stupid get-up."

If it was my mom, or even Grandpa Bob carrying on like this, I'd know exactly how to play it. With Lucian, I'm at a loss. Do I yell back, or hit him with a guilt trip epic enough he'll need a passport?

In the end, I go for the later, not wanting to resort to yelling and screaming this early in the day. On stepping into the doorway of his bedroom, my, "I guess I can take care of it on my own," is as woebegone as I can make it.

I might overreach when I throw in the trembling bottom lip.

And sure enough, he sees right through me.

However, rather than berate me for my theatrics, he snorts. "Honey, you are a lot of things, but pathetic isn't one of them."

To reinforce this, he grabs the Santa costume off the bed and hop limps into the master en-suite, although not without giving me the once over first.

"Just hurry, will you? Those residents aren't getting any younger."

There's no missing when he gets out of the shower and struggles into the Santa costume, with his whining and moaning audible even from out in the hallway. To speed things along, I open the door of the en-suite and pass the hands-free crutch through to him.

As much as he dislikes the color and stickers, the device makes it a lot easier for him to get about. It's also faster and we'll need to hurry if we're to have everything set up in time for breakfast.

We're on our way to Rose Haven quicker than I'd have thought. This is mostly down to us not bothering to unpack the truck after the trip to the dollar store.

Neither do we run into any traffic on the way over. No one else is nuts enough to be up this early, especially not on Christmas Day.

We therefore have to ring the front bell twice to rouse anyone enough that they can let us in. Even then, it takes Lucian pulling down his fake beard to reveal himself for the orderly to unlock the front doors.

The guy redeems himself by helping unload the truck, taking the decorations through to the dining room, although he doesn't stick around after that. This room makes the most sense because then the residents can open their gifts after enjoying their breakfast.

I only hope they like the gag gifts I got them, with the deciding factors being what would have amused my Grandpa Bob and absolutely horrified my mom. Never having had the creative freedom to fashion Christmas as I'd like, I'm making the most of it.

The other plus about being so busy is that it hasn't given me time to get embarrassed about how I'd thrown myself at Lucian. While he could apparently forget a couple of kisses, I doubt he can forget what we got up to last night.

I know I never will.

LUCIAN

As I watch Natasha flitting around the dining room, setting the tables with centerpieces of baubles and balloons, it's as if last night never happened. She'd fallen asleep in my arms, but when I'd woken in the middle of the night for more painkillers, I'd been alone.

Could it be I'd forced her out of bed by hogging the mattress as I usually did? Or did she leave of her own volition?

As I continue to struggle with the boxes and boxes of string lights, I decide to park it for now. If we're to have the dining room as brightly decorated as Natasha obviously wants, then we'll need to hustle. Or at least I will, because she looks to be completely under control.

Her innate calm doesn't last long after she disappears through the swinging door into what I know to be the kitchen. Her shrieking, "No, no, no, no, no, no, no!" soon rents the air, before she adds, "They cannot eat this disgusting slop, not on Christmas Day!"

The 'chef' reacts badly to her feedback, with the sound of a heavy metal pan hitting the floor heard even out in the dining room. Rose Haven's own Gordon Ramsay slams out of the kitchen shortly after.

Interestingly, Natasha doesn't follow, instead staying in the kitchen. From what I've seen of her so far, this is no doubt to rustle up a tasty breakfast for the twenty-odd residents.

This has me rushing to check the strings of brightly colored lights are working, before I zip-tie them to the low rafters of the dining room. Well, they're low enough I can reach them without a ladder.

This done, I join Natasha in the kitchen. My first task was to clean up the large pot of creamed oats the chef had dumped on the floor in response to her criticisms.

Thanks to the consistency of the goop, this is easier than I'd have imagined, especially when Natasha hands me a spatula the size of your average shovel.

Breakfast is a riot, with me pitching in to help Natasha. The news that scrambled eggs were on the menu soon spread, with the dining room filled with the squeals of cranked up hearing aids. No one can believe they've heard right.

This coupled with the novelty string lights and centerpieces, and the room takes on a celebratory air. This is doubly so after the residents snap Christmas crackers open, and brightly colored party hats hide gray hair.

All this pales to the gift giving part of the morning, when the establishment's menfolk wheel a recliner in to act as Santa's throne. And in this case, that'd be me, with Natasha handing me badly wrapped gifts as the oldies stepped forward.

It was when an old girl demanded a photo of her sitting on my lap that things truly got out of hand. Add in the gifts Natasha had selected like wind-up false teeth, giant sunglasses, and plastic dog poop, and I doubt the place had heard this much laughter, ever.

Things were finally calming down when Alice, the old lady from the day before, said it was only right that there was a photo of Natasha sitting on my knee. It was something soon backed up by the other residents, with their croaky, "Sit on him, sit on him," soon ringing out loud.

If it hadn't been that she'd done so recently, I wouldn't have reacted as I did, with me now glad my fake stomach hides my burgeoning cock. I don't want anyone to expire on my watch, even if Natasha looks ready to die of embarrassment.

Could it be I read the signals wrong last night? No, that can't be right. She was as into it as I was into her. Damn it, I don't need to think about things like that. If I do, even my fake gut won't be enough to hide the resultant erection.

Of course, none of this will matter, because as soon as Natasha sits on my lap, there'll be no hiding it. That's if she sits down, because right now, it doesn't look like a given.

The old girls are having none of it. The one dressed in a tutu, of all things, hooks her arm through Natasha's and corrals her over to my side. For an old lady, she appears incredibly strong, moving Natasha as easily as she would a toddler.

Soon enough, Natasha is in my lap, with my arms automatically closing around her to stop her from slipping. There's no missing her reaction to my current state, with her turning to look at me in horror.

It takes a second before I see how she's taken it, with me wasting no time in whispering, "I wanted to be ready when you sat on me." I follow this up with a cheeky wink, leaving her in no doubt that she's the one who has me as hard as rock candy.

We duly grin while the old folks take our photo with some confusion about how the camera on Natasha's phone works. However, the old girl in the tutu hasn't finished with us yet. She skips forward and holds a piece of plastic mistletoe over our heads, her wide smile splitting her face.

I think momentarily about ignoring it, instead splaying one hand across the back of Natasha's head, our lips mashing together soon after. The resulting cheer from those assembled is one of pure joy.

I take my lips away to whisper, "That's the most fun I've had on Christmas Day since I was a little kid."

I'm as surprised by this as she appears to be, although she soon responds with a declaration of her own. "This is the most fun I've had on Christmas Day, EVER!"

SEVEN

NATASHA

As the morning progresses, I'm aware of Lucian watching my every move, leaving me both aroused and self-conscious. The heat generated by his dark brown gaze skimming my body has me damp with longing.

Not what I'd have expected when spending the morning at a retirement home. It's also obvious enough for the most myopic of residents to notice, with us both receiving good-natured teasing.

That Lucian, even after last night, still finds me attractive, is uncharted territory so far as I'm concerned. I've always been the funny girl, not the sexy one, getting by on laughs and good humor, not good looks and confidence.

My mother has to take some of the blame for this.

Rather than look on me with favor, she'd loudly pronounce me a changeling when comparing my solid build to her waif-like figure. After ruefully shaking her head, she'd follow with, "A moment on the lips, a lifetime on the hips."

The woman is delusional. I could give up eating for a year and not come close to being recognized as my mother's daughter. She's skin and bones, with a heart to match, while I have dad to thank for my height and fiery locks. It's a pity he doesn't have the matching temper, letting my mother walk all over him.

As I look around the festive dining room, I have to smile, make that grin. Mom would hate my decoration choices with a passion, declaring them garish and an abomination.

I'm not aware I've said anything until Alice, who's next to me, chirps out, "Just as well she's dead then, isn't it?"

Her blunt observation snaps me out of my introspection, although I don't bother correcting her assumption regarding my mother. To further bury my past, I clap my hands to get everyone's attention.

"Who's for charades?"

Apparently everyone is, even Lucian, with this surprising me most of all. He doesn't strike me as a charades type of guy, and yet, he's a natural.

It's mid-morning before everyone tires of the game and we break for coffee and hard-tack cookies. It's at this stage I realize that with the glorified kitchen hand having left in a huff, it'll be up to me to sort out lunch.

I'm scouting around in the kitchen when Alice joins me.

"If you're looking for lunch, it'll be in a fridge."

As neutral as her words have been, I'm unsure if this is a good thing, or bad. Then I remember the lumpy oats Lucian scraped off the floor earlier and suspect it'll be the latter. It also tells me none of the residents are expecting family to visit, and on Christmas Day of all days. That's just so sad.

Even sadder is the pile of ham sandwiches I find in the fridge. Tragic might be a better descriptor. Polystyrene white bread that's curling at the corners and ham thin enough you could see through it if you held it up to the light.

I've got the plates of them lined up atop one of the stainless prep tables when Lucian joins me. "Sheesh, what the hell is that lot?"

"Lunch apparently." I lift the top slice of the nearest sandwich and discover there isn't any butter, never mind mustard. "I can't serve these. Not on Christmas Day."

He obviously agrees, because he grabs the nearest plate and dumps the sandwiches into the trash next to him. He repeats the process with the others, stacking the empty plates as he goes.

"While I don't blame you, what are we supposed to serve them for lunch? Everything else is just as basic, or frozen solid."

"Jump in the truck and head back to my place. There's a family-sized ham in the fridge." On my raising my eyebrows, he adds. "It was a holiday gift from one of my regulars." He strokes his nose in contemplation before adding. "You'll find heaps of bread in the freezer."

It's strange being in Lucian's home without him there. However, I push this to one side as I raid first the fridge, then the cupboards, and finally the freezer.

As I gather everything together, I have to wonder at the Spartan fare on offer at Rose Haven. Those places aren't cheap, with Grandpa Bob sharing what my mother was prepared to pay to keep him out of our lives.

The only plus was that the rest home mother shoved him in was nearby, allowing me to visit him every afternoon on my way home from the office.

Once he'd passed away, there was nothing keeping me in the town I'd grown up in. Without fanfare, I'd packed up a few things and departed the evening of the funeral. I'd even left the Mercedes my parents gave me for my twenty-fifth birthday, sitting in the garage.

There were to be no reminders of my old life.

I'm surprised on my return to Rose Haven to see the orderly who'd helped unload the decorations earlier, is back again. Even more surprising is when he helps me unload all the food and carry it into the kitchen.

"Thanks for getting some decent food for them. It doesn't get more miserable than Christmas Day around this joint."

There's nothing miserable about lunch at Rose Haven today, with animated conversations interrupted by the delighted hooting of party favors. While it's still ham sandwiches on the menu, they're nothing like those provided by management.

After seeing the first few slabs of ham Lucian carved, I'd asked him to tone them down, telling him to use thin but not transparent as a guideline. Ill-fitting dentures had their limitations.

Even packing everything away had taken on a festive air, with the residents helping where they could. According to the C.A.N. on duty, the place had to be back to how we'd found it to avoid complaints from the manager.

. . .

Back at Lucian's having restored the beige of the dining room, I'm exhausted. While it was fun, it was also hard work with Lucian and me responsible for all the heavy lifting.

It's also the first time we've been alone since this morning. While he'd flirted with me throughout the day, it had mostly been light-hearted and PG. He'd been friendly, but not a lot more.

There'd been nothing of the man who'd reduced me to a quivering wreck last night. Even the kiss under the plastic mistletoe had been tame by comparison. Perhaps it was a one-off thing? That the moment his ankle is better, we'll both go our separate ways and that'll be it.

I'm then struck by something even more depressing. What if he no longer wants to work with the welcome center and someone else takes over? At this discouraging thought, the smile that's kept me company throughout the day slips away.

LUCIAN

As I watch Natasha stacking the decorations in the utility room, I'm having trouble seeing straight. I'm also having trouble relating this model of efficiency to the tigress I'd spent the night with. After connecting like we had, why had she returned to her own room? Had I messed up, or worse, disappointed her?

It made no sense and I've no recollection of why. It's for this reason I decide to play it smooth, to act as if we're just friends, and nothing more.

Damn it though, with her still prancing about in that elf outfit, it's difficult. Perhaps we could be friends with benefits? I've no sooner thought this than I discard it. My emotions around Natasha are anything but casual, and after last night, they're way beyond *friendly*.

Our sexual connection to one side, she's shown me today what a wonderful, caring woman she is. She'd made a lot of old people—and me —happy thanks to her infectious Christmas spirit.

I'd laughed harder than I had in years, and it felt good, somehow liberating. The pink crutch no longer hindered me, with my movements also freer than they'd been in a long time. It's as if something deep inside has been unlocked, and I have the gorgeous creature shoving the unused bread back in the chest freezer to thank for this.

The padded foot of the crutch is stealthy enough that I'm able to sneak up and run my thumbs along the creases of her ass before she knows what's what. Her squawk of surprise echoes in the icy depths of the freezer before she straightens and turns.

There's nothing cold about her response to my kiss, or my sliding my good leg between hers and pressing it to the juncture of her thighs. My lips hard against hers, I shove my hand deep inside the freezer, my fingers soon finding what I'm after.

After standing tall, I break our kiss, shove the ice cube in my mouth, and suck on it. "When I tongue your clit, I want you to know about it, to experience fire and ice, and everything in between."

Her eyes widening, has me thinking I've got the upper hand, but then she twists and grabs a couple of ice cubes of her own. After sliding them into her mouth, she resembles a cute and sexy chipmunk, one who's eyeing up my nuts.

And I'm okay with this. I'm more than okay, sweeping her off her feet and stalking through to the bedroom before our ice melts.

After setting her down on her feet, I get rid of the crutch in record time, before starting in on the weirdest one-legged striptease, ever. Next to me, Natasha is as quick to shuck her clothes, neither of us wanting to waste a minute, or our ice.

Once naked, she lands in the middle of the bed with a bounce and laughter that nearly sees her lose her ice cubes. With her now splayed before me, I rush to introduce my icy mouth to her fiery core.

Not to be outdone, she spins around and takes the tip of my cock into the icy cave of her mouth. After the initial shock, my body decides it likes it. She must also like the cold because when I run my icy tongue through her swollen cleft, she trembles in a silent plea for more.

I'm about to put the ice cube back in my mouth when I decide there's somewhere better I can put it. Her keening fills the bedroom, while her muscles spasm around my fingers as I hold the rapidly melting ice cube in place.

Likewise, the remnants of the ice cubes in her mouth bump the head of my cock, leaving me cold and slick and burning with need.

I need to warm up and soon, and I know the best place for that. This has me spinning Natasha around and under me before her orgasm dies away. I last mere seconds after my icy cock slides deep inside her, her muscles milking my release.

As it consumes me, I wrap her tight in my arms, my lips soon finding hers, our mouths still cold. There's nothing cold about how I feel where

Natasha is concerned, with her warming my heart as no woman before her.

But what if she doesn't feel the same way? What if it's just sex for her?

It's a question of the ages. It's also one that has me deepening our kiss, desperate to show her how much she means to me. And without having to put it into words, something I'm not great with.

On waking in the morning, I've still said nothing, although I'm pleased to find Natasha snuggled at my side, my arm draped along the sweep of her hip. Asleep, there's none of the happiness she spreads like confetti.

Rather, her expression is grim, with this so at odds with her usually cheerful countenance that I rock her slowly to wake her. While it doesn't appear to be a full-on nightmare, neither does she look to be having fun.

Confusion clouds her unique eyes when she opens them, although she relaxes when she sees me. "I dreamed, I dreamed, my mother..." She clamps her mouth shut, leaving me in no doubt she doesn't want to share what it was about.

To distract me, she instead blurts out, "You didn't kick me out. That must mean your ankle's getting better."

"What do you mean, kick you out? I'd never do that."

"No, no, not consciously, but you were thrashing about so badly the night before last I thought it safer to move."

After stroking her hair back from her forehead, a drop a kiss there. "I'm sure I can make it up to you somehow."

Her laughter is infectious, the curve of her lips as she giggles, only adding to our kiss. Soon enough, our laughter fades as we concentrate on exploring each other's bodies in the filtered morning light.

Early morning loving with a new partner is always a true voyage of discovery and one that begs to be savored. I want to explore every inch of Natasha's body. To have her screaming my name as I overwhelm her senses, to have her begging for release as she had last night.

Only then will I be happy to lie back while she returns the favor.

EIGHT

NATASHA

Much as I'm loath to do so, it's time to pack my things and return to the little home I rent near the beach. Lucian is moving more freely every day, and once again able to drive his truck without hurting his ankle.

Sadly, our little idyll is over with me due back to work this morning. Just as the Christmas lights had been a big deal, so was setting up the stage for the New Year's Eve celebrations.

It'll be there they'll announce Miss Coogan's Break, with the town's young women already fizzing with excitement about who'll take this year's crown. And of course I'm running late thanks to Lucian insisting we start the day with an orgasm powerful enough to throw the earth off its axis.

I'm sure the time we've spent in bed over the past few days has had something to do with the rapid healing of his ankle. The doctor *had* said for him to keep off his feet and he'd definitely done that.

As if to show his return to good health, he walks into the kitchen unaided. If I wasn't on the lookout for it, I doubt I'd have seen his slight limp.

Lucian's kiss when he drops me off at my place has me wanting to call in sick to spend the day in bed with my gorgeous man. And yes, I'm claiming him as mine, at least for now. Deep down I know it's unlikely to last, something that has me making the most of it, and of him.

My overnight bag abandoned in the utility room until I can wash everything later; I skip into my bedroom and change out of my leggings and t-shirt. There'll be no elf costume today with Christmas well and truly over.

Today sees me dressed in my usual uniform of navy pencil skirt, white blouse, and navy pumps. The last thing I add is my name badge. This often leads to people calling me by name on the street and confusing the heck out of me.

To further distance myself from my old life, I'd even given thought to going by Ash, my Grandpa Bob's pet name for me. He said it was because of my fiery red hair, with this apparently making sense to him.

However, when it came time to fill in the paperwork, I decided this was one part of my old life that I didn't want to share. It had been special between my grandpa and me. I didn't want just anyone using.

The shortening of names had been something mother objected to strongly, and the reason Grandpa Bob insisted on calling her Ginny at every opportunity. When I was little, I thought it was a term of endearment. It wasn't until adulthood I'd realized its true intent.

It's only a five-minute walk from my little shack to the welcome center, during which I fantasize about spending New Year's Eve with Lucian. On walking into the welcome center, the unwelcome sight of my mother shatters my daydreams.

She's leaning menacingly over the front counter, the young woman I take to be our new intern, leaning back as far as her chair will allow.

"I demand you show me through to Natasha Frank's office this minute!"

With the intern having started while I was away, chances are she won't know who I am. This has me doing my best to retreat before mother spies me. I'm almost out the door when I bump into something solid. A glance over my shoulder shows me it's Lucian, and he's holding an iced coffee that bears my name.

It's then I hear the intern splutter, "I'm sorry, but Miss Frank isn't due in until later, I think."

"You think?! You think?!"

My mother's voice has all the finesse of chalk on a blackboard, with the intern now looking around wildly as though for salvation.

Eventually, she spots me and my uniform. Unable to get any further words out, she instead points repeatedly, doubtless hoping to pass her problem onto someone higher up the food chain.

There'll be no escape now.

Mother turns on me, as incandescent with rage as she'd been the last time I saw her. As usual, my dad slinks away, fading into the background like he always does when my mother is one of her moods.

As she stalks in my direction, her words are venomous. The one thing missing is any worry over my disappearance all those months ago. Rather, it's all about her, and how my running off has affected Virginia Frank.

"You're coming home with us. How dare you embarrass me in front of the whole town by running off like that?"

Behind me, Lucian leans over and whispers in my ear. "You want me to hog tie and gag her for you?"

It's exactly the levity I need to stop my Pavlovian response to my mother's bullying. It also reinforces my decision to get as far away from the woman as I could without leaving the country. I've no regrets about leaving Frankton, the town that got its name from my family.

I've never looked back, having been happier in Coogan's Break than I ever was living back home, and that was before Lucian. With him in my life, there isn't a chance I'll accompany my parents back east.

"You're lucky Jarod forgives you. That he understands it was just cold feet and nothing else."

Damn, I was hoping he'd have given up by now.

"Anyway, now we've found you, the wedding can go ahead exactly as I've planned."

There's no missing the sharp intake of breath from behind me, with Lucian following this up by placing his hand gently on my shoulder and squeezing it. It's something my mother immediately notices.

"Natasha, who is this, this, ah, person?"

The chilly edge and lack of tact at how she's voiced her question has me reaching up and placing my hand protectively over Lucian's. I don't bother answering my mother, instead talking to him over my shoulder. "The marriage was her idea, not mine, and I never once said yes."

I then turn and address my mother, for all the good it'll do. She doesn't listen at the best of times. "I said NO on seven different occasions. Damn it mother, if you want Jarod Winchester to be part of the family as badly as you so obviously do, I suggest you adopt him!"

There's some pearl clutching in response to my plain talking, before she replies in deliberately cultured tones, "There's no need for language like that. I only want what's best for you."

A stranger would take her words at face value. However, I'm no stranger and well aware there's only one person she wants the best for, and that's herself. To her mind, my marrying a Winchester will somehow boost her social standing.

It'll see her invited to more society events, allowing her to rub shoulders with those she considers her equals. My mother makes no secret of the fact that she believes she married beneath her station.

"Sorry mother, I won't be accompanying you back east. I've made a new life for myself here, and it's not one I'll abandon to further your societal aspirations."

My never having spoken to her like this, she's now right up in my face, rigid with indignation, fire in her eyes and her lips an unbecoming slit. Her fingers, when she drags my hand away from Lucian's, are as talon-like as I remember from childhood.

The big difference now is that with Lucian backing me up, I won't let her get her claws into me again.

LUCIAN

I'm having trouble associating my gorgeous, loving Natasha with the bitter little woman confronting us. A quick look at the man I have to assume is Natasha's father, and there, at least, I can see a family resemblance.

However, it stops there, with Natasha's dad having none of her fighting spirit. It's something that has him putting as much distance between himself and the argument between mother and daughter as he can.

Meanwhile, Natasha is refusing to back down and comply with her mother's wishes. And damn it if it doesn't turn me on.

I love Natasha's feistiness in bed, and am even re-running last night in my head, when it's as if a skeleton has wrapped itself around my hand. However, when Mrs. Frank tries removing my hand from Natasha's shoulder, she comes unstuck.

There isn't a chance this glorified mannequin is shifting me unless I allow it. If I want to leave my hand on her daughter's shoulder, then damn it, I will.

"Unhand my daughter, you brute!"

"Natasha, are you okay with me manhandling you?"

Natasha's response to my question is to step back and lean against my chest. To help reinforce her unspoken response, I wrap my arm—with coffee still in hand—in front of my woman and pull her closer still.

It's my kissing Natasha's neck right next to her mother's hand that proves too much for the woman. Her screeches of frustration at being ignored for perhaps the first time in her life echo around the welcome center.

It's still not enough for the woman, with her grabbing at my other hand and attempting to move it away from just under her daughter's breasts. It's a move that sees the toxic piece wearing Natasha's iced coffee from head-to-toe.

"You, you, big oaf, you threw that at me. This is, this is, Vintage Versace." She follows this up with threats of dry-cleaning bills and the cost of a replacement, for all the notice I take.

"No, I didn't throw it at you. You grabbed the takeaway cup, and it exploded. You've only yourself to blame." I follow this up by shoving the now empty cup in her direction, her natural reaction being to take hold of it.

"Come on Virginia," says Natasha's father, taking the cup off his wife and dropping it in the nearest trash can, "you've had a nasty shock. Let's head back to the hotel and get you cleaned up."

Honestly, Natasha's father is spineless or a saint. I've come to no conclusions when he steers his wife around us. They're on their way to the nearest exit when he pauses only long enough to address his daughter.

"When you change your mind, you'll find us at Maddigan's. We'll be there for the next five days. That should be long enough for you to come to your senses."

They leave to a soundtrack of Mrs. Frank voicing the affronts inflicted upon her person, with the center then falling mercifully quiet but for canned music.

Rather than be upset as I've expected, no sooner have the doors shut on her parents than Natasha laughs delightedly. A happy dance soon follows.

Eventually, she spins in my direction, throwing her arms around me and squeezing me tight. "Lucian, you were wonderful!" She kisses me soundly, following this up with more dancing. I even join in, with her joy infectious.

It's not until we've finished spinning around that I ask if she'd like me to get her another coffee.

"Are you kidding? It'll take me the rest of today to get over that one. That's the most I've enjoyed a coffee, ever!" As suddenly as her laughter had appeared, it stops. "Oh, you must think me terrible to speak to my mother like that."

I shake my head before speaking. "Ah, that'd be a hell no. If her behavior today is anything to go by, I totally get it. If you don't need another coffee, I'll be on my way."

"Go, go. I'll see you after work." I've only taken a couple of steps when she runs up and helps herself to another kiss. A man could get used to this.

What I'll never get used to is receiving yet another emergency callout. This time to Rose Haven because the industrial range hood in the kitchen has shorted out, again.

It makes no sense that a place charging as much as they do should have such rubbish equipment. Still, it'll be nice to see the old folks and check how they're doing.

On arrival, the clouds of smoke that fill the kitchen and dining room have me lucky to see anything, let alone the residents. As it is, the place is a veritable ghost ship, with nobody around.

It's the lack of visibility that allows residents Alice and Fletch to pop up out of nowhere and scare the crap out of me.

"Shhhh!" Alice's stage whisper is of such a volume that her putting her finger to her lips to signal for quiet is a complete waste of time.

Next to her, Fletch taps the side of his nose, telling me that whatever it is they're about to tell me, it's top secret. At least in the minds of these two.

"Smoke bombs? Seriously?" I shake my head before continuing. "Couldn't you have just phoned me?"

It turns out Rose Haven doesn't like residents to have phones of their own after too many prank calls.

"And we couldn't tell you what we've discovered if we used the phone in the manager's office."

This comment from Fletch has me putting the notion of smoke bombs to the side. One plus in all of this is that there's actually nothing wrong with the range hood, although I'm not switching it on just yet.

"That man listens in on all our calls," adds Alice, helpfully, although I take a second to realize she's referring to the rest home's manager.

By the time they've told me why the place is as bad as it is, I'm staring at them open-mouthed. What the hell am I supposed to do with the information? I don't even know what sort of regulatory body would cover a place like this.

Of course, there has to be one. I'm just not sure what it is. It's something I'll discuss with Natasha when I catch up with her later. I'm not sure why, but I suspect if she puts her mind to it, she can solve anything.

She's beautiful, practical and, all-in-all, the perfect package.

After swearing on my mother's grave to help the residents—even though mom's not dead, just living out of state—I turn the range hood on. That whirring away, I open all the doors and windows to further clear the smoke from the two rooms.

Despite there being no need to fix anything, after what I've just heard about the crooks running the place, I'm still charging them for my time.

The last thing I do is to take possession of what the old couple assures me are the remaining smoke bombs, because, "Management searches our rooms, looking for contraband."

A half-a-dozen of the devices now hidden in my toolbox and I'd say it's for good reason.

NINE

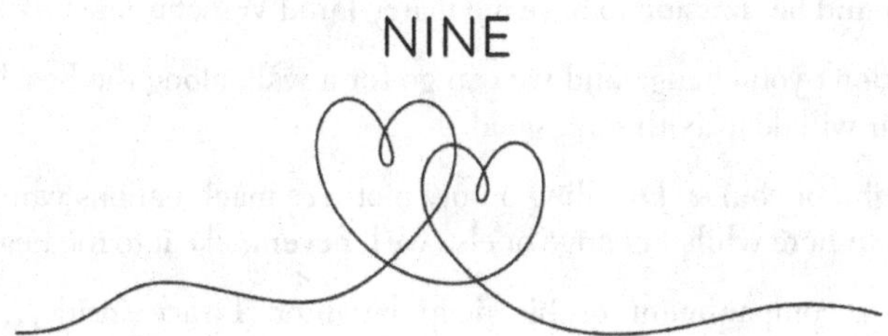

NATASHA

When I get home from work, I find Lucian parked out front. It's a welcome relief after spending the day worrying about my mother's unwanted arrival, her timing, as always, dreadful.

It doesn't matter that I stood up for myself for once. The woman is tenacious, and I know from harsh experience that she'll pick away at me until I give in.

My father gave up fighting years ago, with him a virtual shell of the man I remember from childhood. The only one to continue standing up to her had been Grandpa Bob, and even he'd succumbed in the end, although not without a fight.

My worries disappear the moment Lucian climbs out of his truck and pulls me in for a tight embrace. He doesn't kiss me as I've been expecting, he simply holds me. My head pressed against his chest, I fully relax for the first time since the run-in with my mother, my heartbeat eventually matching his slow and steady one.

When he speaks I feel his bass tones as well as hear them.

"I'd ask how your day was, but don't need to. It can't have been easy standing up to her."

There's no need to say who he's talking about, with him also a target of my mother this morning. Perhaps more so now that she knew there was something between us.

Ensconced at the best hotel in town, she'll be scheming on how to break us up, a distressing thought this early in our relationship. Despite only being together for a little over a week, I've known and admired him since our first meeting.

But will our bond be strong enough to survive the onslaught of my mother and her mission to have me marry Jarod Winchester?

"Why don't you change and we can go for a walk along the beach? The fresh air will do us both some good."

He's right, of course. Dwelling on my mother's machinations won't help. "Wait out here while I change or else we'll never make it to the beach."

To an accompaniment of his deep laughter, I race inside, already undoing the buttons on my blouse when walking up the path at the side of the small house.

It's when I'm dragging on a pair of cut-off jeans my mother most definitely wouldn't approve of, that something occurs to me. Focused as I am, my tank top goes on backwards. After swapping it around, I grab my keys and run back outside, determined to find out what's bothering Lucian.

After cutting through a couple of walkways, we step down onto the sand soon after. Lucian's right, the wind whipping around us does more to clear my thoughts than all that worrying throughout the day.

After threading my fingers through his, I give his hand a squeeze. "You want to tell me what's bothering you? Was it what my mother said about you being a big oaf?" When he doesn't respond, I press on. "She's wrong, you know. You're no oaf, and while you're big, it's in all the right places."

Before he can decipher my meaning, I pull my fingers free and walk backwards along the beach in front of him. While watching him process my words, I slowly gather speed, putting some distance between us, my smile wide.

"Why, you cheeky minx!"

His laughter is a match for my own when he hobbles after me. There's no need for me to run to avoid him, and anyway, why would I?

I want him to catch me and never let go.

"Please don't let her cruel words hurt you. It's how she operates." Back in his embrace, my words muted by the hard planes of his chest, I continue. "Just because she says it doesn't make it true."

This last had been what Grandpa Bob said when I'd eventually break down and tell him why I was upset. I think without his constant presence in my life, my mother would truly have messed me up. Six months living in Coogan's Break away from her constant carping has done me a world of good.

"I know. I've met her kind before." He falls silent for a couple of beats. "I had a job at Rose Haven today."

There's something in the way he says this that immediately has me asking what was wrong and how everyone was.

After he finishes telling me, I'm furious. I'd watched my grandpa suffer under a similar regime; I'll not stand by and watch it happen again. Price gouging, profit skimming and over-dosing of sedatives, it truly was the trifecta of retirement home nightmares.

As we plod our way down the beach, both deep in thought, Lucian drapes his arm across my shoulders, our steps perfectly matched.

"I'm just not sure what we can do about it. They said their kids—when they bother to visit—think they're making it up and that it's down to dementia."

I stop in my tracks, forcing him to do the same. "Dementia?! There was nothing slow about the old people we met on Christmas Day." I walk on again, dragging Lucian along with me. "There's a controlling body of sorts. I know because I got my grandpa's lawyer to report the conditions at the place my mother dumped him in. I'll call him first thing tomorrow."

After another night of showing Lucian how much I love him, I phone grandpa's lawyer, and am put through immediately. This is unusual. It's more likely he'd have to call me back.

"Miss Frank, thank goodness you've rung. We've been trying to track you down for months."

"You have?"

"Did you not get the message I left with your mother that your grandfather's will was to be read straight after the funeral? It would have been so much easier if you'd been there."

"Straight after the funeral, are you sure? My mother said they had a meeting at the bank."

There's a moment's silence before the lawyer confirms my parent's being at the reading of the will as requested by my grandpa. "I contacted them the moment I heard of your grandfather's passing."

However, it was hearing I was his sole heir that explained why mother had been incandescent with rage when she got home from 'the bank'.

Even beyond the grave, my grandpa had riled her. Her covering the cost of his rest home when he could probably afford it himself would have cut deep, exactly as intended.

"Your mother said you were too distressed to attend."

While I'd been sad Grandpa Bob had finally gone to be with his 'Darling Maisie', I wasn't so cut up that I'd disrespect him by not attending.

He'd been ninety-eight, so it wasn't as if his passing was unexpected. It had still come as a shock though, with him such a permanent fixture in my life. He'd been a calming influence in the sea of chaos that was my mother.

Only then do I tell Mr. Langley what I've actually called him for, rattling through everything Lucian and I know, and theorizing what we don't. The call ends with him promising to follow up on those behind Rose Haven and a copy of the will on its way to me by urgent courier.

LUCIAN

After ending the call, Natasha is optimistic about Rose Haven, and furious at her mother for not telling her something.

"The funeral was three days after he passed away. She had plenty of time to say something, and she didn't. She said they had an appointment at the bank they couldn't cancel."

It's what she says next that gives me pause.

"Darn it. I refuse to let it slide, not this time." She punctuates this by flinging the covers to one side and jumping out of bed, her actions fueled by anger. "Can you drop me off at Maddigan's?"

"Of course I will, but not this early, and not with you as dirty as you are right now." When I follow this up with a broad grin, she soon responds in kind.

After a hot sudsy shower that has us no cleaner than when we'd started, I'm none the wiser about what it is her mom is up to. Out in front of the most expensive hotel in town, I offer to wait, but Natasha says she'll grab the hotel shuttle into town. "I'm not due at work until lunchtime."

On driving away, my mind is all over the place. What was it she had to speak to her mother about? I worry she'll leave herself open to manipulation by Mrs. Frank.

According to the woman I care about, her mother is a master of the art; with it bad enough, she'd moved to the west coast to avoid it.

What if her mother wins out?

Thoughts of Natasha marrying the aristocrat she's told me about are enough to have me gripping the steering wheel to the point my knuckles turn white. There isn't a chance I can give her the sort of life she's apparently used to.

Hell, I'm off to fix a pump at a poultry farm, something that'll see me liberally coated in chicken poop and feathers by the end of the day.

And so it proves true when I finally finish the job late that afternoon. Because of the state of me, I haven't been able to check my phone, instead leaving it in the cab of my truck. Thank goodness I'd packed a portable shower, because I can't go near my truck in my current state.

After cleaning up as best I can, I climb into my cab, dressed only in my boxers. A quick check of my phone shows I've missed ten calls from Natasha and that there are also a couple of texts.

The first text is also from her, telling me she needs to talk to me, which would have my heart in my boots if I was actually wearing any. It's the second from her mother that gives me hope, with the amount the woman is offering me to disappear, eye-watering.

Either way, I need to speak to Natasha, and a phone call won't cut it for what I've got to say. Unfortunately, when I arrive at her place, she's not home and my phone call goes straight to voicemail.

Not wanting to wait any longer, I back it up with a text, telling her to call me as soon as she gets it. Having done everything I can, I head home, my earlier euphoria now missing.

Despite more phone calls and texts, on waking the following morning, I've still not heard from her. Could it be she's up and left for home in NY, the planning for the society wedding of the year already underway?

Mid-afternoon and the beers in the fridge are looking mighty good.

What a way to end the year.

I'm about to open a cold one when a text pings on my phone. After waiting anxiously for her to get in touch since yesterday, I'm now reluctant to read it.

MEET ME AT STAGE - 7PM. SORRY IT HAS TO BE THIS WAY.

The little sad face at the end says she's dumping me on New Year's Eve, and in front of the whole damned town. More to the point, am I man enough to front up and take my medicine?

No, but I'm sure as hell man enough to turn up and fight for the woman I love. And for that, I need the counsel of those older and wiser than myself.

Fortunately, I know exactly where to find them.

On arrival at Founders Park, I'm surprised to see Natasha up on stage wearing a hot-pink dress that clashes wonderfully with her fiery locks. That's not all it does for her, with my cock signaling its eagerness to bring the New Year in with a bang.

Soon enough she looks out and sees me, a simple task with my standing head-and-shoulders above everyone else. This is especially true of Alice and Fletch from Rose Haven, who crowd next to me.

They're not supposed to be out, and we all know it. However, when I'd called in to get their advice, they'd said they wouldn't miss it for the world.

After she finishes emceeing the Miss Coogan's Break Pageant, Natasha hands the microphone over to last year's winner to give thanks and crown her successor. Then, instead of leaving the stage, Natasha stands off to one side, obviously nervous.

Soon enough, I see the reason for her anxious glances to the right. Her mother and father stand at the bottom of the stairs as if ready to join their daughter on stage.

Ever so slowly, I inch my way over until I'm standing one row back from the older couple. I'm in time to hear her mother bemoaning Natasha's choice of dress, deeming it inappropriate and too flashy by far.

The freshly minted Miss Coogan's Break helped off the stage in happy tears. Natasha again steps up to the microphone, calling for everyone's attention. Of interest is her voice breaking when she looks at her parents.

Damn it, as I watch her hanging onto the microphone stand in order to stay upright, the need to comfort her is overwhelming.

"Mother, father, if you'd like to join me on stage?"

Despite the chatter of the crowd, there's no missing Mrs. Frank's, "I told you she'd knuckle under. She always does," with this backed up by a triumphant smile before the woman steps forward, her hapless husband at her side.

Not until they're standing next to their daughter does Natasha start up again. "I'd like to thank my mother and father for teaching me right from wrong and truth from lies."

There's a smattering of applause from the crowd, with them doubtless wondering what's going on, with nothing in the program about this.

Natasha's mother looks to be just as confused.

"I'd especially like to thank my mother for trying to force me to wed a man I don't love, and who's more interested in my money than me." Natasha shakes her head with disappointment before continuing. "Tell me, mother, is the reason he's still keen on marrying me after I've repeatedly said no, down to the full extent of my inheritance?"

The gasps from the audience are enough to have her mother squirming and her father examining his shoes.

"And if you're selling me off, what's your cut on the deal? Enough to pay for that place in the Hamptons you've a hankering for?"

Her mother's gaze darting nervously about as if seeking an escape route, says Natasha is onto something. How cold-hearted do you have to be to sell your daughter off and take a commission?

Unlike the crowd, I've been stunned into silence. No wonder Natasha was so angry after that call to the lawyer. She'd had every right. It might also explain the radio silence overnight. It sounds as if she'd had a lot to deal with.

Only once the audience has settled does Natasha take a deep breath and continue. Despite her staring straight ahead, I know her next words are for me.

"The man I love isn't one my parents would choose. And yet he's the perfect man for me."

I'm still processing this when a small withered hand wraps around a few of my fingers and gives them a squeeze. I'd squeeze back, but would be likely to break the bones in Alice's hand. Instead, I bend over and kiss her snow-white hair, being met with a glowing smile and a few tears in response.

The crowd, having erupted in cheers and whistles following Natasha's declaration, means it takes time for things to calm. There's no calming where my heart is concerned. My whole body buzzes in response to the woman I love, stating she feels the same way about me.

After acknowledging the support of the crowd, Natasha presses on. "Mother, father, I'd like you off the stage and out of my life!"

After a moment's silence, the crowd erupts in an enormous cheer. However, before things settle completely, a chant of, "Off the stage! Out of town!" starts up. A glance down at Alice and Fletch and there's no missing who's kicked it off.

Rather than join in, I inch my way ever closer to the stage, with Alice and Fletch right behind me, safe in my shadow.

It's show time.

TEN

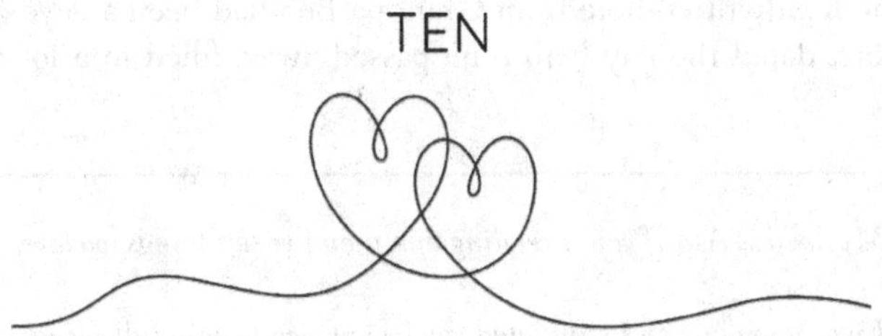

NATASHA

As my parents scuttle off the stage, I'm filled with happiness and relief, along with more than a few nerves. I can't believe I just declared my love for Lucian while up on stage in front of the whole town.

I still haven't looked in his direction to check his reaction to my big announcement. As much as anything, it was to highlight my mother's conniving behavior. It also told my parents they had no say in whom I wed, let alone turning a profit on it.

They—my mother—needed to know this once and for all.

Of course, it's too early for Lucian and me to be discussing anything as serious as marriage, but he's definitely the frontrunner at this stage.

Six months of getting to know him thanks to blown bulbs, coupled with ten days getting closer, and in my heart of hearts, I know he's the one.

Sure, he's a grumpy devil. I doubt that'll change. But he's my grumpy devil, perfectly balancing my exuberant approach to life.

He reminds me of my Grandpa Bob in a lot of ways. It's sad the old coot won't get to meet Lucian, because I suspect they'd have gotten along like the proverbial house on fire.

My parents have barely made it off the bottom step when Lucian towers over them. His booming, "Ginny, Max, or should I call you mom and dad?" is loud enough for me to hear up on stage.

There's no missing my mother's outrage, with Lucian hitting a nerve by inadvertently using the nickname Grandpa Bob gave his daughter-in-law. The one he'd used at every opportunity because he knew she hated it.

While the will had been straightforward enough, with me as the sole heir, the handwritten note from Grandpa Bob had been an eye-opener. The note, dated the day before he passed away, filled in a lot of gaps for me.

My dearest Ash, if you're reading this, then I've left things too late.

I was wrong when I stipulated you be married to gain full access to your inheritance and for your husband to manage the funds. But you have to understand, you were much younger back then.

When I overheard your mother boasting of your upcoming marriage to Jarod Winchester, I knew I had to change it.

The Winchesters are not to be trusted, something I know from my business dealings with Ronald Winchester. The man was a liar and a thief, his progeny doubtless cut from the same cloth.

I also know if you had plans to marry, you'd have told me. Rather, I suspect Ginny is busy empire building again. Either way, I've made an appointment to see Mr. Langley tomorrow to update my will.

I want you free to make your own decisions about whom you'll marry and how you spend your money. As always, choose wisely.

With much love, Grandpa B

The moment Lucian arrives on stage, all thoughts as to the intrigues of my mother and her choice of son-in-law scatter to the wind.

His expression neutral, I'm unsure if he's here to make a declaration of his own, or put things right where we're concerned. When he leans forward and taps the microphone. I know I'm about to find out, and at volume, too.

My nerves are through the roof when he turns and gazes at me.

And right then, I know.

LUCIAN

I'm not good with words at the best of times, allowing my grumpiness to have people backing away and leaving me the hell alone. Tonight, in front of more people than ever before, I know exactly what I want to say. Even better is that the words come easily.

However, before I speak, I have a quick check where Natasha's parents are. From the little I know of her mother, she's given up too easily. Sure enough, when I see them at the edge of the park, Natasha's mom is on the phone, her agitation conveying what her unheard words can't.

She's up to something, her narrowed eyes as she stares back at me, not boding well. Not wanting to waste any more time, I clear my throat in readiness.

"Excuse me. Can I have everyone's attention?"

I get this far quicker than I've been expecting, with every man, woman, and child in the crowd stopping whatever they're doing and staring up at me.

To them, this has been like watching a live-action soap opera of sorts. They want to miss nothing.

"Natasha, there's no one I'd rather share my life with than you. I've loved you since the second time you deliberately blew all the bulbs in the welcome center chandelier."

At her shocked expression, I'm unable to stop my explosion of laughter, with her sheepishly joining it. We're both still chuckling when I sweep her off her feet and into my arms, holding her exactly as I had the night I caught her when she fell.

The crowd shows their support by whistling and hooting.

The only members of the crowd not joining in are Natasha's parents, their expressions grim. This is especially so when a limo pulls up behind them and a couple of goons climb out.

Sheesh, they'd seriously try to take their daughter back to NY by force?

Just how much did Natasha inherit?

Enough to warrant her being kidnapped and forced to marry? Well, not on my watch, they won't. The rest of my plans are out the window. I nod farewell to Alice and Fletch before I clamber off the other side of the stage, still holding Natasha tight against my chest.

There's no point setting her down, as the killer heels she's wearing would only sink into the grass. Instead, I stride through the crowd, being clapped on the back on my way. Only after we're safely on the other side of the park from Natasha's parents do I slow and with good cause.

Behind us, all hell has broken loose and on turning, I know just who's behind it. It also explains away the size of the handbag Alice insisted she bring with her.

Meanwhile, Natasha stares open-mouthed at the mayhem being caused by the old couple with their smoke bombs. I'm shocked myself, with Alice and Fletch swearing with hands on hearts that they'd given me everything.

Of course, Fletch could have made more, with the recipe apparently available on the 'interweb'. Even more surprising had been hearing Alice helped with the manufacture, declaring it to be, "Just like whipping up a batch of cookies."

Whatever their rough-and-ready origins, the devices are working a treat, the park filled with smoke thanks to there being little to no breeze.

It's enough to mask our retreat and for me to put a goodly distance between us and Natasha's parents' hired muscle. Enough of a distraction to see us in my truck and out of there before there's any chance of capture.

We're soon on our way south, with no headlights showing in the rear-view mirror. There isn't a chance we go can go back to my place, or hers. Not with her parents prepared to stoop that low.

"I love you Natasha Frank." Reaching out, I cover her hand protectively. "I swear on your Grandpa Bob's grave that so long as I draw breath, nobody is taking advantage of you."

It's only when the headlights of an oncoming car light up the cab that I see her reaction to my words. Not once since I've known her have I seen her cry, and yet there's nothing sad about her tears.

"Is there any way you can get your mother off your back, once and for all?"

Another glance finds her chewing on her bottom lip, as if searching for the right words, which she does soon enough. "There is one way, but..."

She then stumbles through the basics of the will, and in particular her grandfather's stipulation that she only inherits once married. Something he'd have updated but for him passing sooner than he'd expected.

Sure, it's a sticking point, but I've got one hell of a solution. Luckily, the widening of the road makes it possible for me to pull off.

This has her turning to face me, although I can't see her face enough to gauge her reaction. All that changes when a line of cars comes from the other direction, their headlights illuminating the cab in bursts.

"Natasha?" Soon enough, her gaze locks on mine. "Vegas?" I raise my eyebrows for emphasis, but I know to the second when she understands.

She grins broadly before responding. "Vegas!"

"Okay, an Elvis wedding it is. But we are not getting hitched until I sign a pre-nup, because I don't want anyone saying I married you for your money."

EPILOGUE

ONE YEAR LATER

NATASHA

On climbing out onto the roof of the welcome center, I'm greeted by the sight of Lucian in his new Santa Claus costume.

Gone is the perpetually grumpy man of last Christmas, replaced by one who laughs almost as much as I do. And with him in my life, I'm laughing more than ever and happy beyond belief.

I'm also now able to understand why it was Grandpa Bob lit up whenever he spoke of his dearest Maisie. It didn't matter that she'd long left this world. In his heart, she lived on.

Lucian's been up here most of the day after promising me, "The light show to end all light shows." And stuck on the front desk thanks to this year's intern imbibing too much in the way of Christmas spirits, I haven't been able to help him.

There's no chance of my slipping today, with Lucian insisting I wear proper shoes with my elf outfit. However, the gleam in his eyes says I'll be changing into my Mrs. Claus costume as soon as we get home. Despite its seasonal design, it's amazing how often I've worn it throughout the year.

Mid-summer Christmas anyone?

The very thought has me unsteady on my feet, with Lucian pulling me tight against his side to steady me. It does nothing of the sort.

"Stop it! We'll never finish the lights at this rate." I smack at his hands until he lets go, my laughter telling him I'm anything but angry.

As we settle down to installing the Christmas lights, my mind is full of how complete my life is now. The last year has been a whirlwind that started with our elopement. While it was a spur-of-the-moment decision, nothing had ever felt as right and I've no regrets.

To avoid my parents' goons catching up before we were married, we'd taken turns driving, reaching Las Vegas in the early hours of the following morning.

While it's fun to be part of a crowd counting down to midnight, rumbling down the highway next to the man you love, wins hands-down.

As I watch Lucian securing the reindeer that brought us together, I marvel at how easily he moves around on the roof. Sure-footed, confident, and all mine.

"I've been thinking..." I wait until I've got his full attention before pressing on. "Have you given any thought to our first anniversary?"

Despite the hasty nature of our wedding, there's no need to rush celebrating our first year together. There's also no chance of him forgetting it, with it being the first day of the year.

He looks up from where he's cable-tying lights to the reindeer's antlers, something his impressive height makes look easy. "I have. I was thinking we could go into it in depth this evening."

The crinkle of his eyes leaves me in no doubt as to his double entendre. "Lucian Davis! You keep that up, and we'll be going into it in depth up here!"

In an instant, he's dropped what he's doing and is stalking across the roof.

"You wouldn't dare!?"

Apparently he would, with me squealing and clambering back through the window. There's only so much excitement Coogan's Break can take in one year. Besides, those tiles don't look comfortable.

"You finish up here and I'll see you at home." I pause briefly as I remember something. "Better give me an hour. I need to call into Rose Haven and see how everything is."

"Take your time, Ash. I've got a couple more hours to finish up here."

On his using my grandpa's pet name for me, my smile is wobbly, the endearment, making me both happy and sad.

. . .

The Rose Haven I enter on the way home is unrecognizable as the miserable place we'd encountered last Christmas. After I'd tasked Grandpa Bob's lawyer with digging up the dirt on management, he'd delivered big time, although only after employing a private investigator.

It had been enough to have the manager fired, and a new team taken on. It was also the catalyst for me putting my grandpa's fortune to good use and buying the place. Because of how run-down it had been, it was a steal, with me using the money saved for some long-overdue upgrades.

Despite mother saying grandpa owned nothing more than a pocket watch and some vintage postcards, this had been a lie, a multi-million dollar lie. It was apparently something she'd only learned at the reading of the will.

I'd have loved to have seen her face when she heard that, especially with her footing the rest home bill for all those years. She'd said it was money well spent to not have him cluttering up the estate, although I doubt she thinks that now.

After a quick catch up with the new manager of Rose Haven, a lovely woman, I enter the residents' break-out room. The sound is deafening. Gone are the zombies of old, replaced by feisty, joyous old people who crowd around in greeting.

"We're about to give strip poker a go. Are you in?"

Fletch, Alice's partner in crime, backs her outrageous invitation up.

Only when I've stopped laughing do I answer. "Thanks, I'm all good. Already got a game booked in at home."

There's no need for me to ask how things are for the residents, with this clearly on show. After a cheerful goodbye and promises to see them on Christmas Day, I head for home with its distinctive lightbulb mailbox.

As easy as it would have been for me to buy us a new place, Lucian had insisted I move in with him. He'd even gone so far as declaring, "No woman is going to support me," with us leaving it at that.

And anyway, in my mind, home will always be wherever he is.

LUCIAN

Much as I want to get on with installing the lights, I pause long enough to watch Natasha cross the road to her car.

When she'd moved in with me, it became a necessity, with me not always able to drop her off. Her choice of vehicle had surprised me, with it not fitting the image of a millionaire at all. According to her, there were better things to spend her money on, like Rose Haven.

Despite this taking a good chunk of her inheritance, she'd gone into it with eyes wide open. Even with the cost of the upgrades, she's getting a good return on her investment. It helps that her girlfriends Angie and Josie are a lawyer and accountant respectively, with their advice invaluable.

Perhaps more surprising was Natasha had opted to stay working at the welcome center, declaring she'd go out of her mind if she was stuck at home. Nope, there's nothing pretentious about my wife.

Thinking this has me smiling broadly and whistling when I get back to finishing up the lights. As promised, it'll be the biggest and best lighting display that Coogan's Break has ever seen. Epic had been Natasha's brief to me.

True to my word, I turn into our driveway exactly two hours later. Inching the truck between the trees, I'm still in wonder at how different my life is these days and how damned happy I am.

Of course, there were a few challenges along the way, not least of which was the disappointment of my family at missing our wedding. However, when I'd explained the situation, they'd understood, if saddened at not being there on our big day.

Regret still hovers when I open the front door, although this soon dissipates. And why is that? Well, that would be my gorgeous wife standing waiting for me with a cold beer.

However, it's not the drink that captures my attention. That'd be her being sensationally naked, but for a large red gift bow stuck to her tummy just above her bellybutton.

After grabbing the beer off her and taking a welcome swig, I nod toward the bow. "Don't you think that's a little high for my Christmas present?" On my deliberately lowering my gaze, I'm met with delighted laughter.

"It all depends what you're after?"

I'm not sure what she's getting at until I notice something else. Usually when she greets me with a cold beer at the end of a long day, she's also got one for herself. Hang on a second; didn't she say something about having a check-up at the medical center this morning?

"Are you...?"

"Two months." There's no missing her nerves as she waits for my reaction. Never one to keep her on edge—unless we're both into it—I slam my beer down on the console and sweep her off her feet with a whoop.

I've only got one destination in mind, and that's the bedroom, but not for what you'd think. Instead, I set her down on the bed before making a beeline for the walk-in closet and specifically for the light fixture.

I had to hide it somewhere she'd never find it, with it even a reach for me.

Back in front of her, being a man of few words, I don't bother with any preamble, simply dropping to one knee.

"Natasha Davis, would you do me the honor of becoming my wife?"

I follow this up by opening the small velvet box and presenting the solitaire nestled inside. After removing it, I take her left hand. "Well, what do you say?"

Her brow crinkles in confusion. "But we're already married."

I tip my head to the side to acknowledge the fact. "We are, but I don't think a quickie wedding courtesy of an Elvis impersonator is the best we can do."

The moment I see the merest hint of acceptance, I slide the solitaire onto her ring finger next to the plain gold band we'd bought in Vegas. I then seal the deal by leaning forward and kissing her knuckles reverently. "I want my family to witness my commitment to you. Hell, you can even invite your mother."

"My mother!?" she splutters out. "That'd be a hard pass for me." She falls silent for a beat, before adding, "But I do like the idea of friends and maybe my dad being there, just not her."

Her gentle smile soon morphs into a dirty grin when she flops back on the bed. If there was any confusion about what it is she's after, her peeling the bow off her tummy and repositioning it lower—a lot lower—leaves me in no doubt.

It's as if all my Christmases have come at once.

Macie spends her days designing and making jewelry. Brad also makes things, although he's happier with wood. Are they destined to build a life together, or will his past get in their way?

ONE

BRAD

As I look around the kitchen at Eagle's Nest, I can't believe how much my life has changed. While the large Victorian on the cliffs north of Coogan's Break is like something out of a magazine, it's also homely and welcoming.

Only six weeks ago, I'd have been in the prison kitchen back in Florida. Stuck preparing meals for the prison's governor and whichever mover and shaker he was trying to impress.

My promotion to cooking for the top guy came about when someone saw I actually knew my way around food. That and I were the con least likely to poison the asshole, but mainly because he wasn't worth risking the extra time inside.

My skills in the kitchen weren't down to formal training, but to a mom who saw cooking as a punishment, mainly because she hated it herself. Add in that I was always in trouble because of my parents' strict regime, and I'd spent a lot of time getting dinner on the table. Only it wasn't a punishment, it was a joy.

It was overhearing what the governor and one of his cronies were planning next that led to my sudden and unexpected expulsion from the prison system. I'd also make sure the right people heard about it before the governor knew I'd caught on. His bad for thinking all of us were dumb asses.

There'd been no warning the day of my release. I hadn't even started cooking breakfast when I'd been called into the governor's office. It was there I was told I was being released early for good behavior.

Only it wasn't the governor, it was some guy I'd never seen before and I knew it was BS. Even the stranger knew it was BS, but either way, I soon found myself out front of the prison, a free man.

Perhaps the biggest tell was they didn't get me to sign anything promising I'd keep on the straight and narrow, with a list of crimes to avoid. They never wanted to see me ever again, something I was fully in agreement with.

Three years inside had been a small price to pay to ensure my parents' continued good health. It could have been longer, but all the cops could pin on me was receiving stolen goods. It was more a case of wrong place, wrong time, than wrongdoing, at least on that occasion.

Instead, here I am on the other side of the country cooking Eggs Benedict for Ethan Hunter and his wife, Lindsey. Of course, when we'd shared a cell, he'd gone by another name, only sharing his birth name after his release.

He'd dropped this on the back of a Coogan's Break postcard and sent it to me in prison. And if not for my recognizing his atrocious handwriting, I'd never have worked it out. It was thanks to that little card that I could head in the right direction after I got out.

As I take in the couple sitting at the large kitchen table, it's easy to see I'm not the only one whose life has changed beyond recognition.

The only thing left of my old cellmate is him still having that 'don't mess with me' attitude he'd had down to a fine art when we were inside. It was something that'd saved my ass more than once in the early days.

However, it was my bulking up courtesy of hours in the exercise yard, and hefting laden pots, that saw an end to the random beatings. These days, I'm more than capable of giving Ethan a run for his money in the 'you really want to go there, buddy' department.

On pulling up behind Ethan at the job site, I come close to driving into the back of his truck. I'm not concentrating, and who can blame me? All I can see of the woman is her ass as she loads something into the back of a Ford Woodie straight out of the 1960s.

What can I say? It's a fine ass, and one that could see me giving the station wagon some competition in the Woodie department. It's been too long, three and-a-half-years too long, and it has to stay that way. I don't dare start a relationship with my past still hanging over me.

And then she straightens, and all thoughts of leaving her the hell alone, flee. She's stunning, even in faded jeans and a yellow top. Curves where curves should be, and even where they shouldn't, but that I like just fine. A startling white pixie cut tops off this luscious gem of a body, in a combination the woman owns.

It's also one that draws attention to her eyes, and oh man, those bright red lips. What I wouldn't give to see those wrapped tight around my...

Ethan smacking the window right next to my head scares the crap out of me. Damn it, it doesn't matter that I'm no longer inside. I still need to keep my wits about me. While I'd escaped the east coast before my old gang knew about it, they wouldn't give up easily.

I need to keep my head down for six months at least, just long enough that they'll move on to easier targets. It'd helped that my folks moved out of state while I was inside, removing them from my life for good.

That they'd done so without bothering to provide me with a forwarding address said it was intentional. Perhaps they'd thought it would be a new start for all of us?

It's as well Ethan interrupted my thoughts, because if I'm making a go of my new life, I have to concentrate on the job at hand. With no formal qualifications, the only job I could get in a kitchen now would be one washing dishes.

Meanwhile, my goal is to learn everything Ethan has to teach. His new company, being this busy, says he's as good at woodwork as he ever was. All that aside, there's nothing I can do to stop watching the woman as she gets behind the wheel and closes the door with a solid thunk.

Not once during all of this does she take her phone away from her ear, laser-focused on the call. It's as if Ethan and I don't exist, which is probably for the best. I'm locking my truck when Ethan joins me in watching the station wagon as it disappears around the corner at the end of the street.

"Brad, mate, you are not to go there."

What he's talking about only becomes clear when we walk into the house and I see a photo of the mystery woman on the mantelpiece. There's no missing that spiky silver hair, even from across the room.

Does his warning stop me from walking over to have a closer look? Hell no, it doesn't.

If I thought she looked hot in runaround clothes, it's nothing compared to the photo of her in a fitted red evening dress. I'm unaware Ethan is right behind me until he speaks, again taking me by surprise. What the hell is it about this woman that has the world falling away?

"Macie Hart, jewelry designer." He pauses before adding, "And yeah, she's single. But she's also the client, and a friend of Lindsey's."

A friend of Ethan's wife? That has her firmly marked as a keeper and not someone to be treated casually. It's as well she's not around while we're working at her place, because despite all his warnings, I doubt I'd be able to ignore her.

Not for long enough, anyway.

Still not confident of my agreement, he stares at me until I eventually hold my hands up in surrender. A brief nod in acknowledgement, and he walks through the plastic sheeting put up to protect the main house from the building work.

On following him through the frosted barrier, I'm surprised at the size of the addition, with it almost as big as the living room. Designing jewelry must pay really well.

After completing a circle to take it all in, I turn back to Ethan. "If she's single, why does she need all this space?"

MACIE

On pulling up outside my house, I'm dismayed to see a new dumpster out front. Even in the dark, I can see it's bigger than the one here when I stopped by a couple of days back.

While I'm having fun staying with my friend Cara; it's not the same as sleeping in my bed. And the size of that metal beast says it isn't happening as soon as I'd like.

The only plus to dropping by after Lindsey's book launch at Maddigan's is that I've got the place to myself. No danger of running into one of the Lucky Break Construction crew this late at night.

With Lindsey having told me every guy on the team was as good-looking as Ethan, her husband, I know they'll all be out of my league. It's therefore something of a relief to be here when they're not.

And I wouldn't be here now if not for worrying about the box of semi-precious stones sitting on a shelf in my walk-in closet. The back of the house partially open to the elements—coupled with the spate of burglaries I'd heard about at the launch—and I can't leave them where they are.

Better I collect them so I can lock them in the big safe at the artists' co-op as I'd meant to before moving out while the renovations took place. The hassle of replacing the gems aside, I'm on deadline for a Valentine's Day collection that I'm showcasing at a gift fair in San Francisco. While the special day is months off, the gift fair is only a matter of weeks away.

It's there I'll take orders, giving me the time I need to have stock produced and in-store by mid-January. So far, the feedback to my designs has been positive, telling me the new line will be as successful as any of my others. If this is true, it'll see my income set for the next year and possibly beyond.

It's a shame I'm not as successful at attracting an actual Valentine myself. Sadly, the chances of me spending the special day alone are as great as they ever were.

Being on my own and having no-one to support me if things go belly up, I need to attend the gift fair with a full complement of pieces. Any drop off in sales could see me forced to do something awful, like sell my house.

Given how much money I've invested in making the mid-century home my own, I'll do anything to avoid that. The addition at the back is the final project, and one that will see me able to work from home.

Much as I love the buzz of the artists' co-op, the old brick building owned by the city has seen better, safer days. Every time there's a quake, I end up covered in dust from the rafters above, although it could be worse.

A lot worse, and that's why I'm investing in a home studio, one where I won't be in danger of being killed by a falling rafter.

I've grabbed the gems and am back out in the hallway when I hear movement downstairs. I know I locked the front door after me, and yet it sounds as if there's someone down there.

If I was in any doubt, the loud creaking of the open staircase confirms it. Unless you know to keep to the edges, the noise the heavy boards kick up is like something out of a horror movie.

My heart hammering in my chest, I inch slowly back into my bedroom, being extra careful about where I put my feet. Unlike the intruder, I know where all the squeaky boards are and avoid them, thus keeping my presence a secret.

Meanwhile, my brain is running a million-miles-an-hour, working through the various scenarios. While the house is dark, the streetlight out front takes the edge off this.

It was because of this I hadn't bothered turning on the lights in the hallway. Familiar with my home, I'm more than happy to traverse it without them on. While a lot of women are afraid of the dark, I find it comforting, although I'm rapidly reconsidering.

The change in the creaking tells me to the second when the intruder reaches the upstairs hallway. A sneaky peek around the corner of the door frame is enough to tell me it's a man. The height and shape of the shadow on the wall opposite the top of the stairs confirms it.

I'm giving thought to trying to climb out my bedroom window onto the roof of the addition, when something occurs to me. What if it's not the gems he's after?

Another glance across my bedroom also confirms I don't have a hope of climbing out that window. It's too high and too narrow, by far. This has me quietly placing the box of gems on the dressing table and easing out of my jet black heels.

I then give thanks to my late aunt Kirstie's wooden tennis racket, complete with guard, hanging up on the wall as decorative art. After lifting it free of the hooks, I grip the leather-wrapped handle, ready to defend myself.

My breathing is now as it was during childhood games of hide-and-seek. Mouth wide open, I draw in much-needed air, slowly and quietly, although it's not a simple task. A bead of sweat works its way down my forehead, then another. Much as I want to wipe them away, I daren't for fear my evening dress will rustle.

A board just outside the bedroom door creaks and my brain shuts down on how I'll defend myself. He's close enough I could reach out and touch him. That he could touch me. Tears now stream unbidden down my face, merging seamlessly with the sweat.

Another creak, and my dark and silent world crashes around me and I lash out with no clear idea of what I'm doing. This is about preservation, and nothing more. There isn't a plan, just a primal need to defend myself.

I know I've hit something with the tennis racket, but in the dark, I don't know what that is. It could just as easily have been the door frame as the intruder.

There's then no missing the grunt from out in the hallway, with this immediately followed by a loud crash. The sort created by a guy north of six-foot, hitting a polished hardwood floor.

But I'd be an idiot to try running by him in the dark, and he's between me and the only other way out of the house. This has me reaching around the corner of my bedroom door and flicking on the lights in the hallway.

I need to see what's what, so I'm fully prepared.

The light doesn't help. Nothing could have prepared me for what, make that who, I see, nothing.

TWO

MACIE

I know I'm suffering from shock, when my first thought on regarding the man spread-eagled in my hallway is how freaking hot he is. It's easy enough to see with him completely naked.

I've examined every inch—and I mean every inch—of him when I become aware I'm also under scrutiny. His eyes are the color of the mid-Atlantic, although nowhere near as cold.

Despite my having just laid him out with a vintage Slazenger, his gaze is strangely devoid of anger. It's heated, with the temperature enough to burn me to my core.

"I'm calling the police." I've no sooner said this than I remember my phone isn't in the pocket of my dress, but charging in the car. Too many Instagram posts of the sumptuous meal had left the battery teetering on the edge of oblivion.

I'm inching past him when he grabs my ankle, causing me to squeak and drop the racket. However, it's the electricity shooting up my leg and making a beeline for my hoohah that has me wondering what's wrong with me.

He's just broken into my house. I shouldn't be reacting to him like this. I've never reacted to a man like this. It's as though my body isn't my own, as though I'm possessed by someone a lot hotter than I am.

"Macie, there's no need. I'm from Lucky Break Construction. Brad McKenna."

My world slows. Not because he's identified himself. Rather, it's because the gravel in his voice has sent an arrow straight through my heart.

"I'm sorry I scared you." He follows this up by squeezing my ankle gently.

I'm processing my response and that he's just apologized even though I was the one who'd done the damage when I realize something else. He's no longer simply gripping my ankle, he's caressing it. I'd put his actions down to a potential concussion, but there's nothing hazy about his regard as he stares up at me.

Again, the rumble of his voice has cut through me, although this time, his target was lower, with it then taking all my willpower to break eye contact. Of course, this has my gaze once again settling on his crotch, with it hard to ignore, even if it's technically not 'hard'.

To rein my rampant thoughts in, I reach inside the hall bathroom and grab the nearest towel. As disappointing as it is to cover even part of him, I can't concentrate with him lying there like that.

After dropping the towel over his, ah, fun bits, I'm back, staring at his gorgeous face. "Why are you even here this late?" Despite longing to ask him why he's also naked, the less attention I give that, the better my equilibrium.

While he struggles to his feet, I take the time to wipe my eyes and face, horrified to see mascara on the back of my hand. Just typical. I'm with the hottest guy I've seen outside of a magazine or book cover, and I look like a panda.

Thoughts about what he'll think of my messy face disappear as I watch him wrap the towel tight around his waist. It's pointless, with the outline of his manhood still as plain as day. It also reveals how tall he is with me having to look up to avoid staring at his chest, not that I'd mind. No, not at all.

"There've been a heap of break-ins of late. We didn't want to risk any of our gear being stolen, so I chucked a bedroll in the addition. I'm sorry we didn't think to let you know."

Until he's said it, I didn't even consider burglars targeting building equipment, but I guess everything has a street value these days.

"You really need to think about getting an alarm."

Mesmerized as I am by the color of his eyes and that dark russet hair, I take little notice of his recommendation. Built like he is, I doubt there would be many brave enough to call him a ginger.

It isn't a color I'd usually find attractive, but on him it looks good. Forget that. On him, it looks spectacular. And anyway, his hair is closer to a piece of dark red beach glass than the Prince Harry end of the ginger spectrum.

I've hardly done categorizing the guy when he rubs his forehead, bringing my attention to the angry red mark there. I must have cracked him hard to knock him down like I had. He strikes me as being no easy target.

"Oh, oh, I'm so, so sorry I hurt you. I wasn't thinking straight."

As he slowly makes his way over to the top of the stairs, there's no missing that he's unsteady on his feet, dangerously so. He's wobbly enough that I don't want him taking the stairs, not with me the only one on hand to catch him.

"Why don't you settle in the guest room?" I follow this up by opening a door off to the right and turning on the light. "There are fresh sheets on the bed."

Rather than accept my invitation, he balks in the middle of the hallway. "I can't... I mean, it wouldn't be right."

I have to breathe out slowly and steadily through my nose before I can answer him. "Hey, my knocking you out with my aunt's tennis racket wasn't right, either, yet here we are."

I follow this up by tipping my head toward the open door. "Better you lay there for a while than risk a tumble down the stairs."

He still doesn't move, to the point I think I'll have to get handsy with him. I'm disappointed when he eventually totters into the guest room, confirming he was in no condition to navigate the stairs.

There isn't a chance he'd have made it to the first floor without risking personal injury. Part of me is already worried he'll press charges, with him having a legitimate reason to be here.

It's when he stands staring down at the bed without moving that I realize he's in worse shape than he's letting on. This has me stepping forward and pulling the covers back to reveal crisp white sheets. I then reach up and put my hands gently on his shoulders so I can turn him around.

I'm trying to make him sit when his arms wrap tight around me. At first I think he needs to steady himself, but when his lips claim mine, I know it's nothing of the sort.

Now I'm unsteady on my feet. At least I am until we land in a tumble of arms and legs in the middle of the bed. As he rolls me onto my back and presses me into the mattress, part of my brain analyzes his actions and my response.

Thankfully, it's only a teensy part, and I soon shut it down. All that's between me and this god of a man is a couple of yards of black taffeta and a thin towel. It would appear I'm not alone in wanting more than a kiss, so much more.

I've surrendered to the moment, when he groans, following this up by once again rubbing his forehead. It's enough to have me untangle myself and stagger to my feet. The poor guy needs painkillers and sleep, not me doing my best to seduce him, more's the pity.

BRAD

Even without opening my eyes, I know the lights must still be on, and that she's next to the bed. The woman smells of fresh-cut flowers and a summer morning. Just two of the many scents I'd missed when locked away in that steel and concrete box.

Then I pick up the scent of coffee, my brain pinging in the knowledge it won't be the powdered variety that's coffee in name only. It's this very firing of synapses that draws attention to the killer headache that's doubtless been waiting in the wings.

My eyes snap open and I'm not sure what grabs my attention most? That she's wearing a black tank top and distressed jeans that lovingly skim her curves? Or that as well as the coffee, she's also holding a bottle of painkillers?

She puts these on the bedside table and steps back. If I didn't know better, I'd think she was trying to keep her distance, specifically from me. And honestly, who can blame her after the way I manhandled her last night?

So much for my promises to Ethan about keeping my hands to myself. After tasting those delectable lips and getting up close and personal with that magnificent body, I'll be hard-pressed to keep to my word.

"I'm so very sorry I hit you last night. How's your head this morning?"

"Morning?" With the drapes open, it's easy enough to see it's still dark outside. This means it has to be well before dawn, and if so, why is she up and about, and why am I still in the guest bed?

I don't remember a lot after she'd disentangled herself from my arms and fled. I'm not sure why she had, because until that point, she'd been a more than willing participant.

Even thinking about biting that plump bottom lip of hers has me rolling onto my side to face her. It's not just my forehead that's experiencing swelling, although it's my big head that needs help the most.

Much as my cock WANTS her body, my head NEEDS those painkillers. This has me dragging myself in a sitting position, my knees drawn up. My lack of concentration when I do so has me accidentally smacking my head against the headboard. And damn if it doesn't feel like someone's just parted my hair with an ax.

The pain is blinding enough that there's nothing I can do about a hiss of pain that has Macie hurrying to help me.

After opening the bottle, she takes hold of my hand and tips two painkillers into my palm. No sooner have I jammed these in my mouth than she's handing me an untouched glass of water that had apparently been on the bedside cabinet overnight.

As I swallow the pills and then continue to chug the whole glass, I regard her over the rim. Even without make-up and her hair sticking up in all directions, she's gorgeous. She might even be more gorgeous than she had been last night when obviously dressed for an evening out.

She's more approachable somehow, maybe more in my league, even if she gets points taken off for being such as early riser.

After putting the empty glass down, I grab the mug of coffee. "You've no need to be sorry. I shouldn't have been sneaking around in the dark like I was."

Of course, when I'd heard movement upstairs late at night with no lights on, I hadn't thought it would be the owner. I'd thought it was someone out to take something that wasn't theirs, in which case I wanted the element of surprise.

Sadly, the creaking of the stairs ruined any stealth, even with my moving as slowly and carefully as I could. Unfortunately, there was no avoiding that a jewelry designer armed with nothing but an old-school tennis racket had taken me out.

Okay, that frame gizmo had definitely added to the heft, but even so. I'd be the laughingstock of C-Block if any of them ever heard about it.

It was my dodgy past that had me keen on stopping any crimes on site. It wouldn't matter that Ethan knew he could trust me. If word got out that I was on site when a break-in occurred, people would jump to conclusions, because once a criminal, always a criminal.

I'm about to ask Macie what time it is, when I hear a bird chirping, with this surprising given how early I suspect it is. There's nothing avian about the bright pink phone Macie drags out of the back pocket of her jeans.

A quick look at the screen and her eyes widen. "Blast! I need to hustle. I have to get my equipment out of the artists' co-op before the city locks the place down." Her gaze then settles on me, followed by the nightstand. "Have you got everything you need?"

Her imminent departure in concert with the panic in her eyes overrides my physical desire for her. Instead, I want to help her in whatever way I can, and to hell with my headache. The drugs should kick in soon enough.

This desire to help another without being asked is a revelation. I've only looked out for myself, and occasionally Ethan, in recent years. It also lets me see I've viewed her as nothing more than a body, and not a person.

It takes longer than it should for me to recognize the emotion I'm experiencing is one of shame.

Macie could have kicked me out last night, and yet she'd welcomed me into her home and taken care of me. It wasn't something I was used to. Even my parents had wanted nothing to do with me after my arrest.

Memories of my mom telling me I'd made my bed and must lie in it before hanging up on me momentarily fill my head. I'm therefore not thinking straight when I fling the covers to one side and stand ready to help Macie however I can.

I only come to my senses when the cool morning air wraps itself around my semi-hard cock. Macie splutters out while desperately fanning her face, although I can't help but notice she doesn't look away.

"Oh, sh... I mean, I'm sorry. Just let me get dressed and I'll come help you."

After grabbing the towel off the floor next to the bed, I make quick work of wrapping it tight. I then walk out into the hall and make my way slowly down the stairs. It's a shame I'm not in the market for a 'keeper', because Macie is all that, and more. The sooner I'm safely dressed, the better.

I daren't get close to any woman meaningfully, not with my past having the potential to intrude at any second. Even after my parents rejected me, I'd still done time to keep them safe.

What would it be like if it was a woman I cared for that my old crew was threatening in order to keep me in line? The mere thought has me shivering, as if someone's just walked across my grave.

All that aside, there's no reason I can't help Macie retrieve her things. Once that's done, I'll do my best to keep away from her. It won't be easy, with my attraction to her making the buttoning up of my jeans all kinds of hairy as I race to be ready to help her.

After meeting up with her in the kitchen, I know I'll need to keep reminding myself of this. Even without the years of abstinence, I'd still want her every which way I can think of, with no shortage of positions coming to mind.

THREE

MACIE

I'm tight on Brad's heels as he makes his way down the stairs, his steps measured. This lack of speed is telling with him not striking me as a guy who takes his time with anything.

When the words "Wham Bam, Thank You Mam" drift across my prefrontal cortex, it's all I can do not to misstep and crash into the back of him.

A double check of the guy's ass and I know this'd be no hardship. The last time I saw cheeks that firm was at Fiona's bachelorette party. Brad's might be even tighter than any of the dancers that night.

Even at this hour of the day, I'm as attracted to him as I had been last night. I don't even care that he has the faint beginnings of two black eyes, other than my being the cause, that is.

These give him a dangerous air that appeals, with me always a sucker for the bad boys in the dark romances I favor. Having an actual bad boy in my house is hotter than simply reading about it. This has my brain sending out warnings that my body has no intention of heeding.

As I watch him slip behind the plastic sheeting into the addition to get dressed, I marvel at how well this simple barrier is working. On turning the lights on in my bedroom last night, I'd expected to see more dust. And yet it was no worse than if I'd been on vacation for a couple of weeks.

Clean enough that there's nothing to stop me from moving back home, especially now that Brad is on site to provide security. At least this is the reason I tell myself, when deep down I know it's not the reason at all.

While I wait for him to get dressed, I pour coffee into two go-cups. It's too early for any of the bakeries or cafes in town to be open, and the task ahead will require caffeine, lots of it. The other thing I do is slide the bottle of painkillers into my backpack in case caffeine isn't up to the challenge.

I'd hoped to take my time transferring everything from the artists' co-op to the new home studio. Instead, I now have to bundle everything out of there in a rush to beat the city when they padlock the building.

A quick look at my watch says we've got a couple of hours before anyone from the city's engineering department is even awake. The other certainty is that without Brad's help, I'd not have stood a chance of getting everything out.

I'd even been compiling lists of what to collect first, treating it like a supermarket grab where you go for the big-ticket items first. While the artists at the co-op would usually pitch in and help each other, this morning it will be a case of everyone out for themselves.

So much for the city officials giving us plenty of warning, as they'd promised. I guess the recent uptick in quakes has them wanting to avoid any potential damages. That's not damages to the members of the artists' co-op, but to the city's bank-balance when they got sued for negligence.

Any further thoughts crackle and pop when Brad flips the plastic sheeting to one side and rejoins me in the main part of the house. How is it he's even sexier when dressed than he had been when naked?

Oft-washed jeans ride low on his hips, clinging to strong thighs, and drawing attention to his junk. His black t-shirt, complete with the Lucky Break Construction logo, is tight enough I can still see his six-pack and pecs. He's holding a pair of beaten up work boots that have definitely seen better days.

There's no need to shut my eyes and fantasize as I had last night when I was trying to fall asleep. Everything is right there for me to drool over. There's no missing that my hand is trembling when I pass him a coffee and I'm relieved when he takes it.

Better if he doesn't know the effect he has on me, with what happened last night, an aberration, and nothing more. He'd been delusional after I'd come close to knocking him out. That's why he'd kissed me, and run his hands over my body, and jammed one of his strong thighs between mine.

Courtesy of these thoughts, my next mouthful of coffee is more of a gulp, one that sees the scalding hot drink burning my throat. It takes every ounce of my self-control to swallow the pain and not to let on what's happened.

Thankfully, Brad announces that before we go anywhere, he needs to visit the half-bath off the entryway. While he does that, I can get myself back under control.

This morning will be challenging enough, without me constantly on the verge of a spontaneous orgasm. No guy has ever drawn me like he does, to the point of overriding my usual reserve. While confident of my design abilities, my confidence stops there.

And yet here I am, ready to throw myself at him with the least provocation, or simply to reach out and touch him. Even that would be enough.

He's sitting on the bench in the entryway, pulling on his boots when I join him, his head bent as he concentrates on the task. There's something about how slowly he ties his laces that has me asking, "Are you sure you're okay to help me? I really didn't mean to hit you so hard last night."

My reason for asking is two-fold. Much as I need his help, I don't want him to do so if he's suffering from a concussion. It might also make it more difficult for me to concentrate. I'm just as likely to forget to pack something if I'm constantly checking him out.

It's only once we're outside that I see what I'd missed last night. There's a truck that I have to assume is his, parked just along from my place. Doubtless the dark color had it merging with the night.

On unlocking my station wagon, I'm surprised to see he isn't waiting by the passenger door, and is instead walking toward his truck. "I thought..."

My half sentence is enough to have him stopping to face me. "It makes more sense to take both vehicles. The fewer return trips we have to make, the better. I'll follow you." He then hesitates before retracing his steps.

I'm wondering what he's forgotten when he stops in front of me.

"Don't think for a second that I regret last night."

I'm unsure if he's talking about me flattening him with a tennis racket, or our kiss. Right until I see the glint in his eyes, with mine widening in response.

He steps even closer, my head tilting back automatically. After putting his coffee on the roof of my wagon, he takes mine and sets it next to his.

With both of us now unencumbered, he slowly wraps his arms around me before waiting, his eyes locked with mine. Whatever he sees, it's enough to have him pulling me even closer, before lowering his lips to mine.

His lips move confidently, his tongue teasing the crease of mine until they open on a sigh. As his tongue crowds my mouth, it's as if he's filling me in other ways, blood pumping through my core as surely as if it was his cock.

On him pressing me against my station wagon, I'm pleased it's as early as it is, because my neighbors would never let me live down this wanton behavior.

And yet I've never felt more alive in my life, my body singing with want.

BRAD

After she'd rushed off last night and closed her bedroom door with a definitive thump, I honestly thought I'd blown it. And then she'd undressed me with her eyes while handing me a coffee this morning.

Even after all that time in prison, there was no missing the arousal in a woman's eyes. No missing that unspoken message, although it was one I'd ignored until I was halfway to my truck.

It's only looking in the rear-view mirror as I follow her into town that I get a good look at my face. Strangely, there hadn't been a mirror in the half-bath, not that it bothered me.

What bothers me is the large lump in the middle of my forehead and, if I look closer, the start of two black eyes. Damn it, I look like I've been in a fight for dominance in the exercise yard, and come out the loser. No wonder she'd looked at me like she had when she'd brought me the coffee and painkillers.

And yet her response to my kiss told me I'd read the signs right, and that she didn't find the damage off-putting. If not for us needing to collect her all her stuff, I'd now be tonguing her to fulfillment and loving every second.

This thought is enough to have me close to mounting the curb when we arrive at a ramshackle brick building just behind Main Street. Despite only being in the construction industry for less than a week, even I can tell the place is close to collapse.

One good shake and it'd be a pile of bricks. The other thing that's evident is that Macie isn't the only artist collecting their things this morning. Despite the early hour, the place is a hive of activity.

Which is a shame, as the desire to kiss her again is overwhelming, the thoughts about other trouble we could get up to, tantalizing. But none of that can happen with this many people about.

It's when we step through the large double doors at the front, and Macie starts up the broad staircase, that I realize this will be no simple task. Why the hell couldn't her studio have been on the first floor?

I question this over and over, between trips to her wagon, and then my truck. In hindsight, I think we should have started with the heavy stuff, but Macie was adamant about what we should collect first.

It's only when the studio is nearly empty that I realize what her rationale had been, and it makes sense, at least fiscally. The same isn't true of my back and head, the complaints from my body having me gobbling painkillers like candy.

We're sliding her workbench down the stairs on a large blanket when the creaks and groans that have shadowed our every move increase. As tempting as it is to abandon the workbench, it'll impede others trying to get the hell out of this death-trap.

This has both Macie and me tugging and shoving the workbench, eventually sliding it down the rest of the stairs and out through the front doors. We're loading it into the back of my truck when a loud crashing comes from inside the building.

Half-a-dozen people rush out the front doors, followed by an even louder boom from inside. Only after a hurried headcount do we relax somewhat. On the plus-side, no-one is inside. On the down-side, a few of the assembled artists are about to have their gear swallowed up by the building.

Macie and I are just pulling away when a vast cloud of dust shoots out the front doors, engulfing both our cars. The middle of the building has finally collapsed.

On arrival at Macie's place, both of us get out of our vehicles, meet halfway and hug each other as if our lives depend on it. That was close, too bloody close, but it had taken the drive back to her place for both of us to realize how badly this morning could have ended.

Would the building have collapsed without everyone moving out at the same time? We'd never know. All I know is the thought of this wonderful creature dying or being hurt hits me hard.

We're still in a snug embrace when Ethan drives up, and man, he is not happy with me. I think on it for only a second before my hold on Macie tightens. It wouldn't be the first time I'd fought for something I wanted.

And it won't be the last.

The question I'm now facing is that in taking on the fight, I risk losing everything, including Macie. It's a thought that has me squeezing her until she squeaks.

FOUR

MACIE

Thanks to Brad's hold on me, I'm having trouble breathing, something that doesn't become any easier with Ethan standing glowering at us. On second thoughts, he's not glaring at us, just Brad.

The air between the two men is electric, and not in a good way. Lindsey told me Brad was an old friend of Ethan's. However, there's nothing friendly about the current atmosphere.

I pull myself free of Brad's death grip, and turn to face Ethan head-on. "I was just saying thank you to Brad for helping grab my stuff from the artists' co-op."

His "Right?" complete with arched eyebrow, says he doesn't believe me for a second. It's backed up by him turning to Brad and saying, "Second warning, mate," with a hard edge to his words.

I'm not sure what he's talking about, having not heard the first warning. My best guess is that it's work-related. "Ethan, it's my fault. If he hadn't helped me, I'd have lost most of my equipment."

It's this comment that has Ethan finally taking a proper look at my station wagon, and then Brad's truck, both of them jammed full. Until it came time to empty everything out, I'd no idea just how much equipment I'd accumulated.

It's so easy to lose track when you move things in piecemeal. I can only hope the new studio will be big enough to hold everything.

Another problem I face is where I'll store everything until they complete the addition. "Ah hem, Ethan. How much longer will it be until you finish up?"

My reason for asking is two-fold. First, I want to diffuse the current atmosphere. Second, my knowledge of construction is zip, and the size of the new dumpster had thrown me last night. For all I know, it could be another month until it's ready for me to set up there.

And how on earth am I supposed to keep working in the meantime? I'm only on track to make the gift fair deadline by a hairs-breath as it is. Any delays will be catastrophic.

Unless I plan on selling everything in DIY kits, then I can only delay a day, at most. I'm still mulling this over when a bright red truck pulls up on the other side of the road, and two guys climb out.

They're both dressed the same as Ethan and Brad, pointing to them being part of Lucky Break Construction. The driver is enormous, with his beard and full arm of tattoos only adding to his menacing appearance.

Next to him, the other guy looks small by comparison, and yet when the pair crosses the road to join us, I see he's well over six-feet.

Ethan tips his head toward the bigger guy. "Macie, I don't think you've met Tyler Pierce."

This has me looking up, and even up some more. Tyler has to be six-foot-four if he's an inch, and if not for the width of his shoulders, he'd be out of proportion. Seen from a distance, he could easily be mistaken for a much smaller man.

This isn't all that draws my attention. The wolfish grin when he finally smiles softens his face almost as much as the laugh lines that frame his dark green eyes.

I'm still busy assessing him, when Ethan turns to the other man, adding, "And this is Zac Thomas."

Zac couldn't be more different from Tyler if he tried. There's nothing menacing about this man, with him exuding warmth, charm, and good humor in equal parts. It's a combination that could see a girl under him before she knew what was happening and with no complaints.

Tyler Pierce and Zac Thomas? Even their names are sexy; with both men easily able to moonlight as entertainment at bachelorette parties.

Cute they might be, but they're also strong, making light work of emptying my wagon and Brad's truck, of all my equipment.

. . .

Three hours later and we've trashed my open-plan living area, but in a good way. All my mid-century furniture sits along one wall, covered in plastic, while my workbench sits against the wall under the clearstory windows.

Stacked on either side are vintage apple crates, all full of supplies and equipment whose value far outweighs that of the pieces themselves.

This tableau sits resplendent on large sheets of cardboard and battered plywood. The hope is that these will protect my polished floorboards from the worst I can throw at them. The same is true of the wall behind my workbench, with it never ceasing to amaze me how far metal filings and sparks can travel.

I'd been concerned when I saw the team screwing the large plywood sheets in place. However, Ethan has promised to put everything right after I move into the studio. Even Brad had backed this up, although only in passing.

The atmosphere between him and Ethan is strained, with Brad only coming near me when his boss is out of sight. So much for my thinking the reprimand this morning was work-related. The more I think about it, the more I suspect this is to do with me. But why?

I'm a big girl with no need for Ethan Hunter to involve himself in my personal life. Not wanting to be distracted, I park it for later, eager to get to work, and back on track for the gift fair in San Francisco.

This sees me grabbing my leather apron and headband jeweler's loupe out of one of the apple crates, ready to get started. The last thing I retrieve is my noise-canceling headphones, which I plug into my phone. Rather than listen to tunes, I select a soundtrack of binaural beat music with theta waves to help me focus. The better my focus, the faster I work. It also means I'm less likely to mess up, because I don't have the time for that.

They also help block the banging and crashing from on the other side of the plastic sheeting. However, it isn't only the noise that could distract me.

While the barrier is opaque enough that I can't make out the individuals, Brad is through there somewhere, the knowledge warming me.

Before I know it, I've finished the piece I've been working on and my back is killing me. When I slide the headphones down to sit around my neck, I'm greeted by silence.

It's only when I turn off the light on my jeweler's loupe that I notice how dark it is. Not so much outside, but that there's no light coming from the addition. A quick peek behind the plastic sheeting is enough to show me why this is.

Rather than more plastic covering the window openings, as had been the case, these are now closed in with yet more plywood. I suspect this is for added security after I told Ethan I was moving back in tonight.

The only thing I'm not completely sure of is whether I'll be alone. Everyone, including Brad, having left without saying goodbye, tells me this is a big fat yes. However, this being my first day on site, for all I know, the team leaving like this could be normal.

Or had Brad taken advantage of me being lost in my work, to slink away with the others? Even though we'd only shared a couple of kisses, I truly thought we had a connection. Especially so after he'd made a point of saying he didn't regret kissing me last night.

I guess I was wrong.

It wouldn't be the first time.

I'm still trying to make sense of this when there's a loud knock at the front door. Like really loud. Loud enough, that on looking through the peephole, I expect to see police in full riot gear, or a bail bonds officer.

Instead, it's Brad, and even better, he's got pizza, something that has me aware of just how hungry I am. Did I stop for lunch? As focused as I'd been on my work, I honestly can't remember.

A quick sniff of his aftershave has me realizing it's not only the pizza I'm hungry for. Fresh from the shower, and dressed from head to toe in unforgiving black, he's easily as mouth-watering as the large pepperoni.

BRAD

On stopping outside Macie's, I'm surprised by how nervous I am.

I'd tried getting her attention to say goodbye earlier, but her focus on whatever she was working on had been all-encompassing.

Then I'd started second-guessing myself. What if she'd reconsidered and was deliberately ignoring me? It was this that had me giving up and leaving with the others.

It might even be Ethan had told her of my background, although he had no reason to take the moral high ground, having done time himself. That sure hadn't stopped him from being really pissed when he'd found me hugging Macie on his arrival at the house this morning.

I know I'm staying at his place and he's given me a job and all, but that doesn't give him full control of my life. I've done my time, my sentence is over.

None of this stopped me from being mired with thoughts of my not being Macie's equal. It was these that had me telling him and Lindsey I'd grab dinner in town and catch them later. I just needed some time alone to think things through, an impossibility back at Eagle's Nest.

It was while parked down at the beach watching the waves roll in that I had time to recall how Macie had responded to my kisses. She sure as hell hadn't been ignoring me then.

Her lips opening and her tongue sparring with mine weren't the actions of a woman who didn't find you attractive, who didn't think you were good enough. They were the actions of a woman who'd happily devour you. The actions of a woman who thought you were her equal.

It was these recollections that had me ordering pizza and then playing the part of the delivery boy. I know for a fact Macie hadn't stopped for lunch. She'll be hungry, for sure.

Eventually, I'd grabbed two pizzas, one a meat-lovers and the other vegetarian. On looking at the boxes stacked on the passenger seat, I have to hope she's not a vegan. If she is, I'm screwed, because they'd smothered both pizzas in an unhealthy amount of cheese.

Even walking up the front path, I'm on edge. I guess if everything goes to hell, I can give her the pizzas and leave. Only when she opens the door, do I think everything will be okay.

After eyeing the two pizza boxes, her gaze wanders slowly over me, with my heart and my cock both deciding they like the attention.

I'm not sure if she knows she's smiling as brightly as she is, but I take it as an unspoken yes. This is especially so when she steps to the side in silent invitation. My knowing the layout of the house, there's no need to ask where the kitchen is, and I'm soon strolling down the hallway and into the open space.

With the dining table piled high with stuff and protected by plastic, I put the boxes down on the kitchen island before turning to face her. She's still wearing her leather apron and there's a mark across her forehead where her jeweler's loupe had sat, signs she hasn't long stopped work.

Or had she still been hard at work?

"I hope I didn't interrupt you, but I thought you might like something to eat." I follow this up by flipping both the lids open. There's no missing the hunger in her eyes when she looks first at me, and then the pizza, in particular the meat-lovers.

"They look delicious!" Her stomach then growls in support, with both of us laughing after mine joins in.

A second later, and she's a flurry of activity, grabbing plates, napkins and even bottles of beer. It's either that Macie is ravenous, or she's doing her best to ignore the sparks between us.

If I had my way, the pizza would be on the floor, and it'd be Macie on the counter waiting to be eaten. It's something that has me busy with my phone, looking for just the right playlist to set the tone.

While I know the songs are old-school, they're still good. What little music there'd been in prison was all too often drowned out by the soundtrack of men fighting, crying, and even dying.

Since getting out, I've used music to suppress those memories, to lift my spirit and have me feeling human again. The playlist takes me back to a time before my life of crime, with Macie, the first person I've shared it with.

We've clicked our bottles together, and each taken a swig of beer before I get up the nerve to speak again. Even if Ethan has said nothing about my past, I want to come clean. Better she hear about my past from me. Also, better that she hears about it sooner rather than later.

And once I start, I'm incapable of stopping. I've sure as hell told her more than I ever did my parents or the prison's chaplain. Perhaps it was down to all of them being sanctimonious do-gooders that kept me quiet?

Eventually, I run out of words, my stomach now in enough knots that the idea of eating the untouched pizzas has me close to throwing up. Not a good look.

Opposite me, Macie is quiet, eerily so. In the end, I can't stand it any longer. I've laid myself bare, and she's not said a thing. "So, should I leave?"

After a deep swallow, she opens her mouth to speak, before changing her mind. Unlike me, it would appear she's having trouble finding her words.

It doesn't matter; I've heard her loud and clear and am on my feet in a flash. It's probably not a bad thing. A woman as together as Macie doesn't need a no-hoper like me potentially screwing up her life. While I'd escaped my old life on the east coast, I'm not yet free, not by a long shot.

I'm walking past her on my way to drown my sorrows when she reaches out, her hand resting on my arm. "Please, stay."

When I don't immediately move, she adds, "I want you to stay. I don't care about your past." She laughs nervously, before adding, "Unless you plan on stealing from me, that is."

Only your heart, Macie. Only your heart.

FIVE

My mind is still reeling after Brad's confession; meanwhile, my heart hammers away in my chest. I don't know why it is, but I get that he's shared things with me he hasn't shared with anyone else. Not even Ethan, his old cellmate.

That snippet had come as a surprise because despite knowing Ethan had been in trouble in the past, I hadn't realized he'd actually done time. From the way the local paper had spun it, Ethan being in trouble was just a silly mix up. A mix up that saw quite a few police officers losing their jobs.

It's only after inspecting the cheese atop the pizzas that I realize how long Brad must have talked for. "I can reheat some slices for you if you like? I know it's weird, but personally, I prefer mine cold."

This has Brad laughing in what looks to be a mix of relief and genuine good humor. "That's too funny, because so do I." He even backs this up by lifting a slice from the box and taking a big bite. "Hmmm, still tastes great."

I copy his actions and have to agree with him. To my mind, the sign of a truly good pizza is one that tastes good, even when cold. Actually, make that, especially when cold. The flavors are richer when not masked by cheese hot enough to incinerate your taste buds.

We've had three slices apiece and finished our beers before we slow. I hadn't realized just how ravenous I was until I'd taken that first bite. "Thank you, I needed that. Would you like another beer?"

Brad shakes his head. "Not yet." He then confuses me by sliding off the barstool and getting to his feet. "Dance with me, Macie."

If he'd asked me this before his confession, I'd have thought he was nuts. My knowing what he's been through in the last few years, I completely understand. If they had locked me away like an animal, I'd want to experience everything anew, too.

A moment later, I'm in his arms and we're swaying slowly to the song playing on his phone. While the music has a tinny quality to it courtesy of the small speaker, it does nothing to kill the atmosphere.

Tight in Brad's arms, in my imagination I'm dancing to a full orchestra. And so it goes on. Three tracks later, and he hasn't so much as tried to caress my ass, much less kiss me.

Then it hits me. He wants us to start over, to start again with me fully aware of his past. I don't know whether to indulge in a heartfelt sigh as to the romanticism of it all, or grit my teeth in frustration.

I've never wanted a guy as much as I want Brad right now. And I know he feels the same way. The evidence pokes me in the stomach each time I press back up against him after yet another flamboyant turn.

It's only after we've been through his playlist three times that we stop and simply stand holding each other. My head pressed against his chest, I can hear that his heartbeat is easily a match for mine, and still he makes no move.

When he does, it's not the one I've been expecting.

"I'd better get going. I've got an early start in the morning. Plan is to get the windows installed." He pauses before adding. "That's if the blasted things turn up."

This has me lifting my head so I can speak to him directly. "They're late?" This comes as a surprise, with Ethan saying nothing to me about the timeline running over.

Brad nods. "Yep, they're a week late, according to Ethan, although he doesn't appear fazed."

With nothing else forthcoming, I return to my position against his chest, enjoying our closeness. Despite this, it still takes me a moment to get up my nerve to speak again.

"Brad, would you be okay staying here again tonight?" There's no missing the hiccup in his heartbeat, with me hurrying to add. "I mean in the guest room or even the addition, if you prefer."

I then hurry through my reasons for wanting him around, although I leave out anything to do with my wanting to help myself to his delectable body.

Baby steps.

"You'd be doing me a big favor if you stayed."

It'd be one thing if I had an alarm, or even a safe like the one I'd been able to use at the artists' co-op. Without either of those, my supplies will be at the mercy of any budding criminals.

"We weren't exactly quiet at the co-op this morning. It'll be all over town by now that I've moved all my things back here."

This has Brad leaning back, although he keeps ahold of me. "That might not be a bad idea. If it wasn't so late, I'd pass it by Ethan."

I stare up at him, my brow wrinkled in response to his words. "What does your staying here have to do with him?" While I know they have a past, and Brad works for his old cellmate, that doesn't give the guy the right to rule Brad's life.

Unable to stay still any longer, I pull free of Brad's embrace before completing a couple of return trips to my workbench. "This is none of his concern." I bristle in defense of Brad's independence before continuing. "I'll take it up with him in the morning."

Brad stills for a moment before acquiescing to my suggestion. "We'd better call it a night, then. If I'm up early enough, we might not need to bother explaining everything to him."

He's right, only I'm not having it. "No, there's no need for you to hide. You've nothing to be ashamed of. I'll explain everything to him in the morning and he'll like it, or I'll get someone else to finish the studio."

I'm unaware of my stance, until Brad laughs, although I get that he's not laughing at me. Rather, it's at my readiness to stand up for him, a novelty according to him.

If what he'd said earlier is true, and I believe it is, his parents weren't there for him, even when he needed them most. Reading between the lines, they'd been more interested in what others thought of them than in their own flesh and blood.

BRAD

I'm in bed in the guest room when something occurs to me. Damn it, I'd been so transfixed by Macie, I hadn't given it any thought. I'll have to be up super early if I'm to make it back to Eagle's Nest so I can change into my work gear. And for that, I need to be there before Ethan and Lindsey are up and about.

It's a thought that immediately takes me back to my teenage years. It's also one that has me getting out of bed and inching my way across the room in the dark.

A second later and the drapes I'd just closed are open again. The plan is that the sunrise will re-boot my circadian rhythm, allowing me to wake on time.

Well, that, and setting the alarm on my phone. As much as Macie wants to stand up to Ethan on my behalf, my preference is to avoid confrontation. It was a lesson I'd learned the hard way when I was in prison, and one I intend on sticking to.

I'm still trying to settle when I hear movement outside my door. Now I'm torn. As much as I want to take things slowly, if that's Macie after a nightcap, I don't know if I'll be able to resist.

It had been hard enough giving her a peck on the cheek out in the hallway before closing the guest room door in her face. And yet I know my pulling back is the right decision, at least for now.

Not only is she worth the effort, part of me is still nervous about starting something serious. It's tempting fate, with fate having bitten me on the ass more than once in the past.

As I lay without moving, all my energy is devoted to listening out for what's happening on the other side of the bedroom door. I'm at the point I think she's changed her mind and gone back to bed when I hear the lightest tapping.

Only a fool would turn her down when this is clearly what she wants. It's what I want, too. This is enough to have me out of bed and easing the door open soon after.

What I'm not expecting is to see Macie out in the hallway, her finger already pressed against her lips in an unspoken plea for silence.

If not for the hallway being illuminated by the streetlight out front, I'd have missed this. I'd also have missed the fear in her eyes, something that has me once again listening out.

The sound from the first floor is faint enough that if I'd been asleep, it wouldn't have woken me. Out in the hallway and now wide awake, there's no missing that someone is moving around downstairs.

A quick check and I know I don't want to be ambushed naked tonight. This has me grabbing my boxers from the chair next to the door and dragging them on. My dark jeans and t-shirt soon follow, helping me merge with the night.

I think briefly of my boots sitting next to the front door, before deciding I'll be quieter without them, anyway.

It's only when I join her out in the hallway that I remember how blasted noisy that staircase is. I don't have a chance in hell of taking the intruder by surprise if I use them.

This has me leaning in tight against Macie to mask my words. "I can't go down the staircase. What about the window in your room?"

I know from working on the roof of the studio that it'll be easier climbing out that way than using the window in the guest room. My keeping quiet enough that I don't alert our unwanted visitor will be the hard part.

She nods in response, the movement having a pantomime aspect to it. She then points repeatedly at her feet and then the floor with me soon catching on. There was a reason I hadn't heard her walking from her room to mine, and that was an owner's familiarity with every squeaky board.

I'd used the same knowledge when I was a teenager and coming home later than I'd ever admit to my parents. The only difference between now and then is I'm following in the footsteps of a gorgeous woman.

And one who's wearing a teddy that shows off her every curve and does funny things to my body. If not for the intruder, tonight would end differently. Give me five minutes and the teddy would be gone, and I'd have my mouth full.

Progress down the hallway is slow, with me careful to put my feet exactly where she does. The same is true when we cross her bedroom. To keep as quiet as possible, I'll need to climb onto the bed so I can more easily reach the window. This has me leaning down and whispering in her ear.

"Get into the closet and hide amongst your clothes. They probably think the place is empty, so let's keep it that way." After indulging in a quick kiss, I'm on the bed and easing open the window latch. The last thing I see before sliding out of the window is her disappearing inside the closet.

My knowing she's as safe as she can be allows me to focus on getting down off the addition and finding out where the thief got in. And having spent most of the week working on the house, I know of only one or two places.

This has me dropping silently to the ground, before I walk around the side of the house and in through the wide-open front door. I then waste no time sneaking across the entryway and into the living room, thankful there aren't any squeaky boards on this floor.

Seconds later and I'm right behind whoever it is rummaging through the apple crates next to Macie's workbench. As tempting as it is to ask them what the hell they're up to, I go for the element of surprise.

There's nothing gentle about how I wrap my arm around the guy's neck, jerking it even tighter to show I mean business.

"So, punk, you've got to ask yourself one question. Do I feel lucky?"

When he doesn't answer me quickly enough, I spike the pressure on his throat.

"B-Mac, is that you!?" He squeaks out. "You wanna to ease up? I can hardly breathe?"

Talk about dropping him like he's hot. As shocking as the guy having used that name, is my knowing exactly whose throat I've got my arm wrapped around. Damn it, I always knew my past would catch up with me; I just didn't expect it to be so soon.

There was only one of the old crew who called me B-Mac, and that was Jeremy Walker. But how? I'd been so careful when I left the east coast.

After discovering myself a free man, I'd gone straight to the bus station, purchased a ticket on the next bus out, and left. I was in and out in less than ten minutes, not nearly enough time for anyone to have followed me.

Driven by desperation, my thoughts soon turn to how I'm supposed to keep Macie's presence a secret. "Sorry, mate. I've been casing this place for weeks. I thought you were someone moving in on my job."

It's the first of many lies I tell him, all designed to have him leaving empty-handed and without knowing Macie is upstairs. I also want to keep him in the dark about how much she means to me, with my desire to protect her primal in its intensity.

SIX

MACIE

As I hide out amongst my belongings in the walk-in closet, my heart beats erratically. Despite listening out, I haven't heard so much as a pin drop downstairs.

On the plus side, this surely has to mean Brad is okay. On the negative, it could mean the burglar got away with the box of gems I'd been stupid enough to leave sitting on my workbench.

When Brad arrived with pizza, all rational thoughts had fled, replaced by something else entirely. Twenty minutes later, and I can't wait any longer, the suspense is killing me. My plan is to sneak to the top of the stairs and listen out.

And of course I'll be taking Aunt Kirstie's tennis racket with me.

This sees me easing the pocket door silently to the side, although I'm soon shrieking like a banshee in response to the shadowy figure right in front of me.

Meanwhile, my hand plasters my chest in a vain hope of stopping my heart from exploding through my rib cage. Only once I realize that it's Brad and not the intruder do I promptly burst into tears.

"Hey, hey, it's okay. You're safe." He follows this up by pulling me in for a tight hug, one hand rubbing circles on my back, the other snug around my waist. "Shhhh, shhhh, you're okay, they got away."

Eventually, desire overrides the crippling fear. Perhaps it was that I'd been so scared that my level of desire was now as wild as it is? Either way, it's enough to have me reaching up on tiptoes while wrapping my hand around the back of his head.

Our lips touch, and my body is aflame in an instant. While he's dressed for the street, I may as well be naked. Such is my desire to touch him that my hand soon strays first to the waistband of his jeans and then inside.

While not exactly unfamiliar with his body, I'd like to get to know it better. A lot better. I'm cherry-picking through what I'd like to do first when something occurs to me.

It's enough to have me wrenching my lips away from his. "Oh, oh no, my gems! They were in a box on my workbench!"

I do my best to struggle free so I can fly downstairs to see for myself, but Brad is having none of it. "Relax Macie, they got nothing. I got there in time."

As if to further distract me, he claims my lips in another kiss. It's one that has me forgetting the intruder, even forgetting to breathe.

"Come on, let's you and I get some sleep. We can deal with the front door in the morning."

Even preoccupied as I am by him absently rolling my nipples through the sheer fabric of my slinky sleepwear, there isn't a chance I can ignore this. "The front door?"

It turns out this is how the intruder had gotten in, ruining the lock while they were about it. "Yeah, but I've jammed a piece of wood in place to secure it. No-one's getting in that way tonight."

As much as I want to go downstairs and see for myself, Brad has other ideas. Ideas I interpret correctly after turning on the bedside light. If the gleam in his eyes wasn't evidence enough, the bulge in his jeans seals the deal.

In the past, the thought of getting naked with a guy as hot as Brad would have had me rushing to turn the lights back off. Not tonight, though.

Whether it's down to him saving me from whoever was downstairs, or how he's looking at me, I'm not sure. Either way, rather than be self-conscious, my confidence is such that I'd happily pose for the front cover of Curvy Magazine.

I'm even giving thought to falling back onto the bed and striking a pose when I pause. It'd all be very well my laying akimbo on the bed a la model. However, when I lay next to Brad, I don't want even a thin layer of silk between us.

This has me changing tack and staying on my feet next to him. I slide first one strap of the teddy and then the other down in silent invitation.

It is one Brad both accepts and then acts on with enthusiasm when he steps forward and pulls the top of the teddy tight across my chest. I'm wondering what he's up to when he slides the top first to the right, and then the left. The raspy lace edging does wonderful things to my nipples.

"Ohhhhh, take your time." To reinforce my request, I stick my chest out, increasing the pressure. Brad proves to be a quick study, rubbing the fabric back and forth across my nipples ever faster, with them tightening in response.

And still it's not enough. As corny as it sounds, I want to be so close to him it's as if we're welded together, unable to tell where I finish and he starts.

It's this that has me resting my hands atop his and pushing down on them. And, sure enough, my breasts pop free and he breaks into a wide smile. It's when he runs his tongue across his lips that I know I'm in for a fun time.

My teddy is soon history, kicked across the bedroom by Brad after I step free of it. Next to go are his clothes, with him soon as gloriously naked as he'd been after I'd knocked him out with the tennis racket.

The difference tonight is that he's alert and ready for action, with him stepping forward to kiss me again. Not stopping there, his large calloused hands cradle my breasts, the nipples getting more attention than they know what to do with.

We're soon in a wonderfully naked tangle of arms and legs on the bed, his strong thigh nudging my mons, my body effervescent in its response. As if gauging my need, the next thing I know, he's shoved a pillow under my hips, angling my core toward his willing mouth.

And still he wants more, peeling me to the sides, sucking and licking my pearl. I'm now way beyond being effervescent. My body thrums with passion and some other nameless emotion.

It doesn't remain nameless for long, with Brad's name wrenched from my soul as a climax, the likes of which I've not experienced, claims my body. This marks me as his, even if he doesn't know it.

I don't fight it, letting it consume me, and while my gut instinct is to yell that I love him, I stop myself. Instead, I content myself with screaming it inside my head, having made the mistake of declaring my feelings too soon in the past.

A moment later and I have to ruin it by bursting into tears again.

BRAD

When Macie shattered beneath my mouth, I'd come close to losing it myself. I'd never had a woman respond like this. It was as if she'd handed herself over to me, body-and-soul, believing me capable of caring for her.

This leaves me both humbled and nervous. I haven't always been the most reliable person, so for someone to trust me, as she so obviously does, is nerve-wracking.

This has me promising to myself that I won't let her down, that I'll be there for her. I've barely finished repeating it when I remember the promise I'd made to Jeremy downstairs not half-an-hour back.

The only difference is that I have no intention of keeping that one. And I won't just break it; I'll smash it to smithereens. Only by doing so can I get on with my life. Only by doing so will I know Macie will be safe, even when I'm not around.

All thoughts about how I'll do so scatter to the winds when she bursts into heart-rending sobs. They're enough to have me forgetting for a moment my growing need to bury myself in her swollen core.

That's not what she needs right now.

After crawling up the bed, I drop next to her, dragging her in for a tight, full-body embrace. I want to absorb her pain, even if I don't understand why she's upset. Then I worry I might be the cause.

Communication was never my strong point, even after all those anger management sessions inside. Not that I needed them, being one of the least angry people I knew. No, it was that I wanted to better understand all those bastards with murder in their eyes.

It was Ethan who got me onto the counseling, although he only went because it got him out of earning yet more money for the prison's governor. Whatever our reasons for attending, we'd both benefited.

"Hey, hey, it's okay." I bury my face in her messed up hair before softly kissing the top of her head. Only once her sobs have subsided somewhat do I clear my throat. "You want to tell me about it?"

That's what the counselor always asked, and if it worked for the bearded guy in the rumpled linen suit, it might work now. I'd sure as hell seen some hard-asses spilling their guts after being prompted like that.

It's getting to the point I don't think it's worked, when she stutters out,

"It's just that... I've never... Not once..."

My stomach is in knots before she finally whispers,

"It was wonderful."

And just like that, all is right with my world. First, I kiss her forehead, then her nose, and finally her lips. What starts as a chaste peck soon deepens, with both of us obviously keen to keep exploring.

Our lips melded. I run my hand up and down her voluptuous body, taking delight in every curve, dimple and especially those puckered nipples. While the first thing I'd noticed about Macie had been her ass, her breasts were just as stunning. This is especially so with the buds tight in answer to my touch.

While my rolling of her nipples is casual, there's nothing casual about the way her hips lift off the bed, accompanied by a growl from deep in her throat. Looks as if I've got a tiger to tame, something I'm definitely up for. Anymore 'up' and I'd explode.

This time, when I run my hand down her body, I keep going to bury my fingers in her curls, her thighs splaying in response. With the invitation implicit, I play briefly with the little nubbin nestled there, before sliding first one finger, and then two, deep inside her lush heat. Again, her hips arch, causing me to wriggle my fingers as a reward of sorts.

However, she's having none of it. "I need you. All of you." If I was in any doubt, her wrapping her fingers tight around my distended cock, clears that up.

A moment later, and I'm poised between her thighs, ready to make love for the first time since my release. Sure, I've had sex, but experience tells me there'll be nothing casual about being intimate with Macie.

If I'd thought it was wonderful when her heat branded my fingers, this is nothing compared to that same heat engulfing my cock.

And it doesn't just warm my member.

It warms all of me, from skin and bones, through to heart and mind. Damn it, I'll be lucky if I don't end up in tears after this. And then I decide I don't care. I want Macie's purity of spirit to wash away all the terrible times, the stupid mistakes, my past. I want to start over, specifically with her.

When Macie hooks her ankles behind my back and I slide deeper still, my ability to think dissolves in a blaze of desire. Every ounce of my concentration is now on plunging into her fiery core again, and again, driving us ever closer to oblivion.

It arrives sooner than I'd like, and yet it's still perfect, with her muscles fluttering along my length drawing me in, loving me as no other. Much as my plan had been to pull out, I can't, nor do I want to. With Macie, I don't care about the consequences. Rather, I welcome them.

Hours later, and I know I need to leave. After slipping out of bed, I scoop my clothes up off the floor and tiptoe through to the guest room. I then make quick work of getting dressed, ready to go secure my future.

However, before leaving, I retrace my steps to her bedroom, marveling that even in sleep, she's beautiful.

A quick kiss goodbye and I'm on my way back to Eagle's Nest. Not to cover having been away for the night, but to talk to Ethan about last night's break-in.

He, better than anyone, will know the best way forward. Whatever we come up with, it'll need to stick if I'm ever to move on in my life. And for the first time in a long time, I've got good reason to leave my past behind.

SEVEN

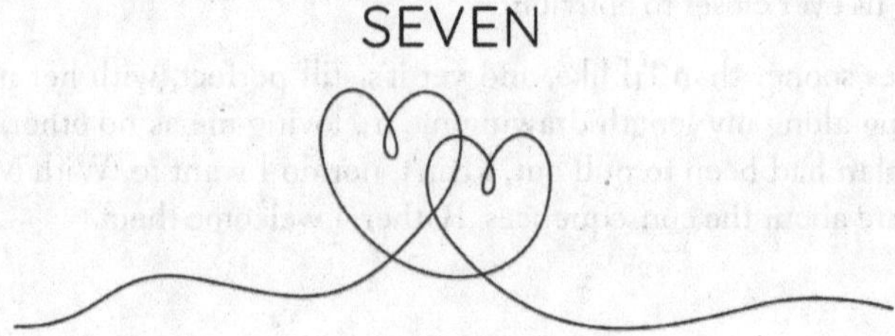

MACIE

The following morning, I'm slow to wake, only doing so when I hear banging and crashing downstairs. My immediate thoughts are that the burglars have returned, although happier memories soon replace these worries.

Delicious memories of Brad driving into me, with my entire world centered on where his hard length filled me almost to the point of pain. And yet, I wouldn't have changed a thing, apart from him not being in bed next to me right this minute.

I'm not sure exactly when he left, only that he'd kissed me briefly before departing. Exhausted after our intimacies, I'd been unable to rouse myself enough to ask, before sleep claimed me as effectively as he had.

Even thinking back on how wonderful our lovemaking had been is enough to have me bubbling with need. Damn it, if not for Ethan and the others, I'd be on my way downstairs for another go around.

It takes longer than it should for me to remember that there are other reasons I need to be downstairs. Work reasons. A glance at the clock on the bedside table and I'm out of bed in a flash and racing into the main bathroom.

Those Valentine Day pieces for the gift fair won't make themselves. And knowing Brad is on the other side of the plastic sheeting will shatter my concentration as effectively as he'd shattered my reserve last night.

Even now the flashbacks of how fantastic sex with him had been are clouding my judgment. Then I pause.

No, last night had been about so much more than sex, at least for me. How Brad feels about it, who knows, and I have no way of finding out, at least until this evening.

The only thing I can take comfort in was him kissing me before he left. That surely has to be a good sign? It's one I cling to while lathering up in the shower, my movements efficient.

Thank goodness today is Friday and the Lucky Break crew doesn't work on weekends. It's a shame I can't say the same, not with that looming deadline hanging over me.

With this in mind, I dress as I usually would for any other workday, skipping downstairs as is my want. I soon come to a halt halfway down the stairs when I see Zac fixing the lock on my front door.

As focused as I'd been on last night, and the hours spent making love to Brad, I'd completely forgotten about the front door being damaged.

It's enough to have the memories of last night's break-in back with a vengeance. I'm soon flying down the rest of the stairs desperate to check my gems were as safe as Brad assured me. I come to a standstill next to my workbench, relieved to see the small box sitting there, ostensibly untouched.

This doesn't stop me from lifting the lid and emptying the contents. A quick sift and I'm relieved to find all twenty semi-precious stones are snug in their little envelopes.

It had taken me ages to decide on just the right cut and color for the prototypes. For me to replace them at this late stage wouldn't just hurt financially, it'd also hurt artistically.

I'm putting them carefully back in the box when I sense movement behind me. The merest sniff and I know that it's Brad, his aftershave as unique as the man himself.

"I told you I got down here in time."

There's no criticism in his tone, it being a simple statement of fact. There's also no censure visible when I turn and face him. Rather, his eyes are alight with a carnal longing that I respond to in kind.

Unfortunately, it's something neither of us can act on, with it taking all my willpower to squelch my body's response and speak sensibly.

"I know you stopped them, but now I'm worried they'll come back."

And it was true. How many of my friends had had their homes broken into, only for them to replace everything through insurance, and then have the replacements stolen?

"They'll definitely be back. That's a given," says Brad, doing nothing to ease my concerns.

I'm about to question him on it when Ethan appears from behind the plastic sheeting. "And when they do, we'll be waiting for them."

I'm wondering who the 'they' are that he's talking about when Tyler and Zac join us.

That evening, I'm still coming to terms with Ethan and Brad's plan as regards last night's break-in. Perhaps the hardest part is the bit where I need to complete a dummy set of jewelry to be used as bait.

While I understand the logic, it's a lot of extra work for me. I'm muttering about this as I finish up another genuine piece. As focused as I've been on this and the ideas for the dummy jewels, it's only when Brad waves in my periphery that I remember he's staying on.

While Ethan had evidently been unhappy about this, there'd been no option but for Brad to stay over, with no-one else available to babysit.

On turning to look at him, I see why he wants my attention, with it enough to have me removing my headset, loupe, and apron in response.

I can't decide what I like the most about Brad staying with me. That he'll share my bed again tonight or that he's been busy rustling up our dinner. Whatever is on the menu, it smells wonderful.

That he can cook comes as no surprise, with him mentioning this when he'd told me about his murky past. What does come as a surprise is that there's nothing prison food about the meal he sets before me on the kitchen island.

There'll be no compartmentalized trays for us tonight. Rather, the meal looks every bit as good as anything served at Lindsey's book launch a couple of nights back. And the taste doesn't disappoint, either.

"Oh, good lord, this is wonderful." I take another mouthful and savor it, before blurting out, "If you can cook like this, why on earth are you working for Ethan?"

It turns out that despite his on-the-job training while incarcerated, it's not the sort of thing you make a big deal of in a resume. To me, this is such a shame, and yet I can also understand employers being cagey.

While some felons are prepared to turn their lives around, for others, it's the only way of life they've ever known. Sadly, it's also one they're destined to return to on release.

"I'm worried I won't be able to make enough pieces." It takes Brad a second to work out I'm back to talking about jewelry rather than food. "Those fakes will double my workload."

I then swallow my doubts as to my abilities to do so with an overly large mouthful of wine, not bothering to give it the appreciation it so deserves.

"Macie, they don't need to be quality. This guy isn't a jeweler. In fact, the flashier you make them, the better they'll work as bait. Have some fun with it."

I stare agape at Brad before I take yet another large mouthful of wine. It's as if he's flipped a switch, giving me permission to create without worrying if I can sell them or not. This has a certain appeal. An appeal that has me smiling.

"This could be fun."

BRAD

Another night of lovemaking and breakfast-in-bed on Saturday morning, and I'm sunk deep in a beanbag I'd found in the garage. With all Macie's furniture safely off to one side, it had been a relief when she'd told me about this beaten up relic from the seventies.

I hadn't been looking forward to a day spent perched on a barstool or sitting on the floor. Neither did I want to leave her on her own. While I'd told Jeremy to chill until there was something worth stealing, I didn't trust the guy not to try again in the meantime.

Actually, it was close to one-hundred percent that he'd try again, with him not averse to doing so in broad daylight.

His surprise at running into me last night said his being in town had nothing to do with me, which was a relief. However, I still don't trust him not to say something to the guys back on the east coast.

It didn't matter that he'd tapped his nose and told me it'd be our little secret. It'll be a little secret that will cost me big time, with my sudden disappearance apparently not sitting well with the old crew.

According to Jeremy, the boss hadn't found it easy to replace me, and the calculations I saw in his eyes didn't bode well. With Jeremy, it was all about the deal, and that was one hell of a deal I'd made with him last night.

After making a second round of coffees, I decide I can't sit there all day and stare at Macie while she works, although it'd be no hardship. It's then I remember seeing a small bookcase in her bedroom.

"I'll just grab a book, if that's okay." When she doesn't respond, I see soon enough that she's got her headphones back on.

Rather than interrupt her flow, I race upstairs to have a look at the books in her mini library. I'm crouched down, running my finger along the spines, when a name jumps out at me.

It's a name I recognize from the bookshelf in the guest room at Eagle's Nest. While Ethan's wife goes by Lindsey Hunter in her private life, she still publishes using the penname Lindsey Abbott.

It's only after taking the paperback down from the shelf that another connection slots into place. I've seen this book before, and it wasn't back at Eagle's Nest.

I last saw it years ago, when Jeremy's wife, Holly, had been reading it. Back before my lifestyle and the cops caught up with me and I ended up in prison.

I normally wouldn't have remembered, but for the ragging I'd received about how much I looked like the bare chested guy on the front cover of HEART OF GLASS.

"Of all the crappy luck." After surging to my feet, I slap the paperback against my thigh in frustration. Jeremy had said he was in town because of some event Holly nagged him to take her to.

It had to have been the launch of Lindsey's latest book. Sure enough, when I close my eyes, I can see Holly Walker holding up her battered copy of Heart of Glass and professing, "It's by Lindsey Abbott. She's my favorite author of all time."

This tells me how it was Jeremy had latched onto Macie as a potential target. While I'd been lying naked and dazed on the floor in her hallway, there was no missing the necklace she'd been wearing.

It was quite the statement piece, and would have appealed both to Jeremy's magpie tendencies and how much he could sell it for. Of course, that all depended on whether he'd been at the book launch at Maddigan's.

Then I mentally berate myself. Of course, he would have been there. Jealous bastard that he is, he doesn't like Holly out in public on her own.

If she'd attended, then so had he. This preference of his was the key to a problem we'd faced with our plan. It's also one that has me unplugging my phone from the charger next to the bed. I need to let Ethan know I've just worked out how to force Jeremy into a second attempt, and at a time that suits us, and not him.

And it was something we needed to be careful about, because while Jeremy was a thieving asshole, he wasn't a complete fool.

Back down in the living room after my call to Ethan, I sink low into the beanbag. After I finally settle, the paperback in my lap falls open. Not to the first page, but to chapter six. Interested to see why that is, I read.

By the time I finish the chapter, I'm getting uncomfortable. It isn't the words themselves that have me well on the way to packing wood. That's all down to thoughts of how aroused Macie would be after reading that sex scene.

I'll be the first to admit that I might have picked up some handy seduction tips, too. Certainly, there were a few I'd love to try now if not for Macie being as busy as she is.

A quick flick through the rest of the paperback and there's no missing how well-thumbed the pages in chapter ten are. A glance up at Macie perched on her tall work stool is enough to see she's still fully lost in her work.

I open the book again, with chapter ten not disappointing. The heroine of the piece is without question happy with the ending she receives from the bad boy hero. If I was any harder myself, I'd be in danger of my own happy ending.

When Macie answers me, I'm not aware of what it is I've said.

She repeats herself. "I didn't think you had to work this weekend?"

On looking at her in confusion, I'm quick to see her headphones are sitting on her workbench. She's obviously replied to something I've said, but what? "Sorry, what was that?"

Now she's looking as confused as I no doubt am. "You said something about wood."

While continuing to look at me for clarification, she stretches her arms above her head and wiggles them about. If only it was that easy for me to take care of my stiffness in the same way.

After removing her jeweler's loupe and placing it carefully on her workbench, she adds, "I didn't think you worked weekends?"

Unsure how to explain the wood in question isn't pine, but all Brad; I clamber to my feet and saunter over to join her at the workbench. When

I casually drop the paperback next to the jeweler's loupe and she spots the cover, her cheeks bloom. Add in her pupils dilating and I know she wants this as much as I do.

This has me swiveling her work stool around and, after pushing her knees to the sides, I step into the gap. The only impediment is her long leather apron, although there'd be no complaints from me if that was all she was wearing.

Now, there's a thought... In the end, it's one I discount.

I want nothing between us.

EIGHT

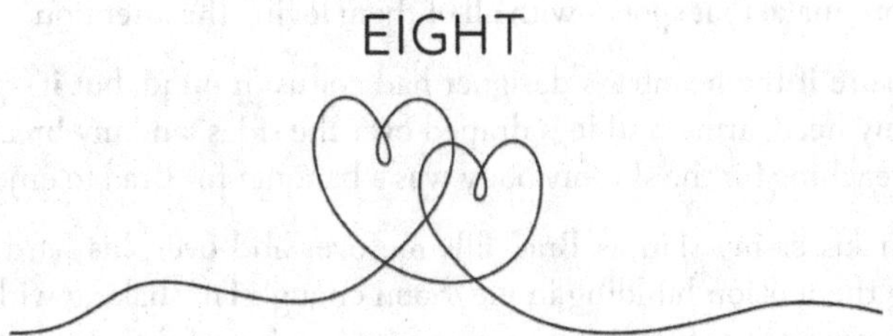

MACIE

I'm still trying to deal with the lust and longing that threatens to consume me when Brad deepens our kiss. His lips scorch mine, leaving me glad the boys had put down plywood to protect the floorboards, because I'm about to go up in flames.

If not for my leather apron forming a barrier between us, Brad would be in danger of third-degree burns. When he breaks the kiss and steps back, I'm momentarily bereft.

"We'll need to make it fast."

For a moment, I think his need for speed is to accommodate my workload, but on dropping my gaze to just below his belt, I see the truth of it. Thoughts of what my first quickie will be like are enough to have me wildly fanning my face, for all the good it does.

Brad puts his hands on my shoulders and helps me slide down from my work stool. I've barely touched the ground than he swings me up into his arms, but rather than make for my bedroom, he stops in front of the beanbag.

Surely not?

How wrong I am, when less than two minutes later, I find myself naked. Brad has also stripped, revealing how ready he is for our coupling.

Next thing I know, he's lowered me to the beanbag, leaving me wide open to his gaze. A wantonness I've not experienced before has me arching over the side of the beanbag, opening myself fully to his gaze and in other ways.

Ways that have Brad burying himself in a heartbeat. And OMG he hits the spot—make that spots—with all of them loving the attention.

I'm unsure if the beanbag's designer had coitus in mind, but it's perfect. With my head, arms, and legs draped over the sides, and my breasts and mons reaching for the sky, my body was a banquet for Brad to enjoy.

The air kisses my skin as Brad fills me over and over, his hard length fueling the tension building in me. Soon enough I'm shaking with need, on the very edge of handing myself over to him for safekeeping yet again.

And oh, he takes such good care of me. After hooking my feet over his shoulders, he drives into me, with each thrust pushing me deeper into the beanbag's embrace. He keeps it up, until I can go no further, nor wait any longer, every nerve ending screaming its release before coalescing to where we join.

I come hard, and after a final few thrusts, Brad follows me over the precipice, destroying us both and, unfortunately, the beanbag.

It takes longer than it should for us to come back to earth after that shattering climax. It takes even longer to get rid of all those polystyrene balls.

Eventually, we resort to using the dust buster with Brad, taking extra care of my breasts and anywhere else those little balls were stuck to.

He's thorough to the point I come twice more, and end up three hours behind on my work. But as I watch him tidying up the remains of the beanbag while still laughing occasionally, I wouldn't change a thing.

I enjoy seeing his countenance lightened like that. Only then do I realize I haven't laughed that hard in a long time, either. Too busy working myself into the ground to establish my jewelry line.

This makes the idea of someone taking it away from me even more devastating. I don't care how hard I need to work on the fake collection, so long as it'll protect my Hart of Gold pieces.

It's only when I spot the Heart of Glass paperback that had kicked off this afternoon's activities that I know exactly what I'll call the fake collection. And if I close my eyes, I can even see the completed pieces in my head.

I'd loved collecting beach glass when I was a kid. I still do if I ever get the time. It's because of this that I have a lot of the burnished glass on hand. All I need to do is use beach glass in place of gems and refer to the fakes as my Hart of Glass collection. That way, the new offering will all make sense.

It was during one of our post-coital chats that Brad told me some of what he and Ethan were planning. It's something that will need Lindsey Hunter to be wearing a piece from the fake collection and that's completely over-the-top.

I need to come up with something that'll catch the attention of both Jeremy and Holly. So long as Lindsey can 'sell' the piece's provenance to the wife, we'll be home free.

The potential designs crowding my mind tell me there'll be no missing the piece Lindsey wears at her impromptu signing at a local bookshop.

If the boys want the jewelry to be extravagant, I'll give them extravagant, and then some. The finished choker will, without a doubt, be the boldest and most theatrical I've ever produced.

As if sensing I need help to finish the current Hart of Gold piece I'm working on, Brad hustles in the kitchen, getting our lunch ready. After raiding the large freezer in the garage, he even talks about what we'll be having for dinner.

I could get used to this, and let's not forget the mind-blowing sex. I then berate myself for thinking of it in such simple terms. While not exactly sure what Brad and I have, I know we've got something. It's definitely more than I've felt for a guy in a long time, and never this soon in a relationship.

Can I even call it a relationship? This is something I dwell on as I force myself to finish up the beautiful bracelet I'm working on. I'm eager to get started on Lindsey's choker.

Actually, I can't believe how excited I am about the piece. It's been ages since I fizzed in anticipation about starting something from scratch. Is it because I'll be working on something without commercial viability playing a part?

Or is it thanks to the gorgeous man in my kitchen?

BRAD

As I busy myself getting lunch underway and preparing for dinner later, I marvel at how at peace I am. Even with the sting operation hanging over my head, there's nothing I can do to stop from whistling as I work.

At first I'd worried this would bust Macie's concentration. Then I'd spotted she had her headphones back in place. Because she's listening to some special track and the headphones are noise-canceling, I can whistle without bothering her.

I'm content playing happy families until I'm not. It's while straightening the contents of the fridge that I come up short. Until I get the monkey that is my old life off my back, I've no right taking things further with Macie.

I've got baggage aplenty, with a lot yet to be unpacked. Despite spilling my guts to her only yesterday, I hadn't told her all of it, not by a long shot. It wouldn't matter that they'd locked me up for being in the wrong place at the wrong time. That hadn't always been the case.

There'd been other times when I'd been in exactly the right place at the right time. The Parkour skills I'd picked up as a teenager allowing me to get in and out of buildings without making a sound.

While I might come down hard on Jeremy for his criminal ways, until I went inside, our 'career' paths had had a lot in common. It was only seeing what I'd become if I stuck to that way of life that brought me up short and made me see sense.

I honestly thought I'd left that all behind. And yet here's my old life, once again knocking on my door. I hope to hell Ethan's plan works, because as I look at Macie, intent on finishing up one of the legit pieces, I know I don't want to go back.

If I work hard, I can have a new life here in Coogan's Break, one I'll be proud to share with Macie. There was a reason Ethan had called his fledgling construction company Lucky Break.

Because that's exactly what it was for guys like me, Tyler, and Zac.

Dinner is long over when I help Macie climb the stairs to her bedroom. She really was dead on her feet, having worked into the night to finish the bangle she'd been working on.

And yet she appears happy. She's even happier when she sees the candlelit bubble bath I'd run for her.

After the day she's put in, tonight has to be all about her. Much as I want to continue exploring her body, I can't, not least because she needs the sleep, and I'm camping out in the entryway.

And I've taken the coward's way out on that front, waiting until Macie was safely asleep before retrieving my bedroll from the addition. Sure, it was a crappy move, but it was better than having to explain why I needed to cool things. Of course, that's not the only reason I'm out here.

The other reason I'm playing guard dog is the risk of Jeremy breaking in again, even if I'm hoping he doesn't.

While I'd convinced him I was only casing the joint when he broke in the other night, I won't get away with that twice. Not if he trips over me stretched out just inside the front door.

Even he'd catch on that I wasn't here by chance, and that there was something between me and Macie.

All that aside, if he comes back tonight, he'll have to go through me, because I'll be damned if all Macie's hard work is being stolen out from under her. Not while I'm around. This concern has me wired until after two a.m. when the alarm on my phone sounds briefly.

There are pluses to knowing the MO of the guy targeting the house, the best one being the knowledge that Jeremy hates early mornings. And in his book that's anything after two o'clock. If he was going to try again tonight, he'd already have been in and out.

Macie couldn't be more different if she tried, with her apparently doing her best work early in the day. It's with this in mind that I force myself to close my eyes, willing my body to relax, hoping to get some sleep.

Come morning and I'm wrung out, with what sleep I'd gotten anything but peaceful. Plagued by a recurring nightmare, when the alarm on my phone eventually sounded that it was time to get up, it was as if I hadn't slept at all.

Much as I want to wake Macie by sucking hard on the little gem that hides at the entrance to her core, I can't, not while Jeremy is in town. If he gets so much as a hint that there's something between us, he'll use it against me.

I've come to no conclusions on how to proceed when Macie pads down the stairs, not bothering to avoid any of the creaky boards. That she's dressed for the day makes things easier for me, with there being no need to avoid further intimacies.

"Why on earth are you sleeping down here? I thought..."

There's no missing the hurt in her eyes and guilt assails me, affecting my ability to respond. Also, there's no simple answer, although I have to say something, anything.

"We need to talk," is out of my mouth before I think it through. If I thought she looked hurt earlier, it's nothing to how distraught she appears now.

Macie is furious, her artistic temperament on full show as she glares at me across the kitchen island.

"So, let me see if I've got this straight? The guy who broke in is a friend of yours." She ticks it off on a finger before continuing.

"He got away without you catching him." She ticks off another finger.

"Tell me Brad, was sleeping with me all part of the plan? Was your job to distract me?" She doesn't bother ticking off this accusation, the censure in her gaze cloaking me in shame.

Still not finished, she presses on. "I cannot believe you've used me like this. I thought we had..."

She's unable to continue, with tears streaming down her face, and a loud hiccup stopping her words from forming. It's as though I've done something awful, like kicking a dog. Damn it, despite my best efforts, my past is here in full force, ruining my current life, just as it had my old.

"Just, just go!"

She reinforces her request for me to leave by pointing repeatedly toward the front door.

"I would, Macie, but I can't. With Jeremy targeting your place, you're not safe. You either move back out, or I stay with you. Those are your options."

While my ultimatum is harsh, I've made it with her safety in mind.

A sharp intake of breath is enough to rid her of the hiccups, and she fires her next words at me like bullets.

"So, let me get this straight. I'm in danger because of you? Is that right? And why is he targeting me, Brad?"

There's no letup in her attack as she marches back and forth across the living room. "Did you set it up after you helped me move out of the artists' co-op and saw all my things? Hmmm. Is that right?"

Despite her accusations being wide of the mark, I don't dare interrupt her.

After all, it wouldn't be the first time someone accused me of things I hadn't done, and I doubt it'll be the last. There are some things that stick when you've led a life of crime. And yet, this time, it hurts as never.

I'm wondering how I can put things right when it's as if the prison counselor is whispering in my ear. *"Speak your truth."*

It was a strategy that hadn't done me a lot of good in the past, but I care for Macie. I can't leave it like this.

She needs to hear that the first I knew of Jeremy being in town was when I caught him breaking in. Damn it, I'd hoped to deal with it on the sly and look at the trouble that's caused me.

Only when she finishes pointing the finger at me do I speak, although I only say as much as she needs to hear. There are some things best left unsaid for her peace of mind.

NINE

MACIE

The silence in the living room after Brad stops talking is deafening.

Furious doesn't come close to describing my current demeanor. I'm way beyond that, although I'm no longer angry at Brad. Instead, I'm angry at myself for being taken in by a handsome face and a hot body.

I should have known better.

If only he hadn't apologized for sleeping with me, even if he'd been quick to add that it was never to distract me. How can I take him at his word about that, or any of it? There was such a thing as lying by omission, and he'd left plenty out.

It's then I realize my current angst will affect my ability to work on the fake designs, making me angrier still.

The only reason I'm stuck making a second collection is because of Brad's dodgy friend. If not for that Jeremy character gate-crashing my life, I'd still be working on my Valentine's Day pieces as part of my Hart and Art brand.

My life would be as normal as it could be after having to move out of the artists' co-op early. Then I begrudgingly acknowledge that without Brad's help, I'd never have retrieved all my equipment and supplies.

And while he'd sworn his seducing me wasn't so he could check out my place after hours, I can't help but wonder. It was far easier to believe he'd sleep with me as a distraction than because he found me attractive.

And just like that, my anger pops, replaced instead by heartache and a feeling of foolishness.

As I comb through my collection of beach glass, searching for inspiration, a red, heart-shaped piece jumps out at me. As I hold it up to examine it, the frosted surface shines where my fingers have touched it after wiping my tears.

How could I have been so gullible? Guys as hot as Brad weren't interested in curvy girls. For that to happen, something else had to be at stake. I grip the piece of glass to anchor my emotions, my tears falling freely and smudging the design I'm working on.

Make that scrawling, with my pen strokes angry enough that I've made holes in the paper. And yet, I can't seem to stop crying or scribbling, the design taking on a life of its own. I rip the page free, and start over, ignoring as best I can the holes in the second sheet of paper.

I'm unsure of how long I've been feverishly working away when Brad places a cup of coffee carefully on the workbench. Next is a plate of what looks to be homemade cookies.

I didn't realize I even had the ingredients for something like that. More surprising is that as focused as I'd been, I hadn't even noticed the delicious aroma of the baking. There's no missing it now, with the spicy, sugary scent tickling my nose.

"Thank you." I'm unable to utter anything else, my underlying hurt making speech almost impossible. Likewise, I keep my gaze locked on my sketch pad, not trusting myself to cave if I look at him.

"As soon as Jeremy leaves town, I'll be out of your hair. I'll tell Ethan he has to find someone else to help finish the addition."

After having said his piece, he retreats behind the plastic sheeting, leaving me feeling more alone than I have in a long time. "Meanwhile, I'll stay out of your way, but I'm not leaving, not with Jeremy around."

Wait, what? What is it he's not telling me? I don't want to be left in the dark. There's been enough of that already. This sees me on my feet and ripping the plastic to one side before it's settled.

"You need to tell me everything. And leave nothing out this time."

What was that saying about forewarned being forearmed? Whatever it was, I wanted to know everything, be it good or bad, and especially about Brad. While my gut tells me he's a good guy, my brain has other ideas.

However, without hearing every detail, no matter how small, there was no way of telling which part of me was on the money.

By the time he's finished fully unburdening himself, I'm wracked with guilt. I'd accused him of everything but first-degree murder when at the height of my rage.

Sure, he's no angel, but neither is he the monster, as I've portrayed, with that role already taken by Jeremy. Apparently, that creep isn't averse to a spot of home-invasion if it'll get the job done. It was something that often led to him leaving in possession of both the stolen goods and the homeowner's peace of mind.

Was that what would have happened if Brad hadn't intervened the other night? That thought alone is enough to have my body wracked with chills. No wonder Brad is insisting he stay on, despite my repeatedly asking him to leave.

"I can only say I'm sorry so many times, Macie. I'd give anything for things to be different, for me to be a good man as you deserve. But I'm not, and I have to live with my screw-ups."

He stills for a moment before continuing. "If things were different, I'd... we'd..." He shakes his head as if to clear his thoughts, but it doesn't lead to him saying anything further.

When he turns his back on me and drops in a heap on his Spartan bedroll, I know our conversation, such as it was, is over. There's also no getting around my being stuck making that fake collection.

If Jeremy is as tenacious as Brad says, there isn't a chance he'll leave town empty-handed. It's far better he leaves with a handful of beach glass and recycled metals than gold and semi-precious stones.

And I'm of this opinion until I settle back at my workbench.

Next to my untouched coffee and the plate of cookies, there's no denying the designs I'd spent the morning on are some of my best to date.

While I'm as modest as the next artist, even I know that if a design leaps off the page, the finished piece will stop hearts.

Maybe I need to get angry more often?

Eager to get on with actually producing the designs, I chug my now-tepid coffee, then gobble the cookies, unable to believe how freaking good they are. I've got everything lined up to start when I hear a phone ringing on the other side of the plastic.

My head is now cocked to the side. I'm listening intently when Brad appears from behind the plastic. Without pause, he makes for the front door, closing it after himself with a bang. Short of jamming my ear against it, I can't continue to eavesdrop.

There's no denying, though, that when he returns, his expression says it wasn't good news. This is something he confirms when he stands at my side after having promised to leave me on my own.

After scanning the designs laid out on my workbench, he tips his head toward one in particular, even reaching out and tapping it. "What are the chances you can complete this one by ten tomorrow morning?"

I'm gulping for a reply, when he adds, "It doesn't need to be perfect, just flashy enough to appeal to the wife of a low-level thief."

BRAD

It had been the one unknown when Ethan and I discussed a sting that would see Jeremy leave town without me at his side.

Lindsey had tried delaying her author signing event until later in the week, but the largest bookshop in town had been adamant. It was to take place at ten on Monday morning, or not at all, doubtless so they could sell books at what would usually be a quiet time.

To have as many people attend as possible, Lindsey has been blitzing her social media. She'd even sent a newsletter out to her subscribers on the off-chance Holly was one of them.

With luck on our side—something sadly lacking to date—Jeremy's wife will hear about the event and, even better, attend.

With the signing earlier than planned, the chances are the sting itself will have to be moved forward, too. This barely gives Ethan and me enough time to get everything set up. It would be one thing if we were career criminals on a working holiday, like Jeremy, but we're not.

With Ethan's company picking up more jobs every day, we can't afford to stop work on Macie's addition while we deal with Jeremy. Not if Ethan wants to avoid people canceling on him because of delays to start dates.

And, I'll be the first to admit I have a vested interest in the company succeeding. If I'm to make a go of my life in Coogan's Break, I need this job.

Despite Sunday traditionally being a day of rest, there's none of that for Macie today, and all I can do to support her is keep her fed and watered.

However, as time passes, I also make sure she takes regular breaks. This has her standing and stretching out her back, neck, and shoulders.

Initially, she'd resisted my interfering. However, she'd soon seen that to last the distance, she'd have to pace herself. She's jamming into twenty-four-hours, a design that would usually take two or three days to complete.

Even though I'm as much a victim as she is, remorse assails me every time I see her hunched over her workbench. Despite my saying that all she had to do was bang something together, she'd balked. She looks to be investing as much effort into creating the fake as the high-end piece she'd been working on.

I've just handed her another coffee when Ethan calls. It's not the first call I've received from him today, and I know it won't be the last. Even with the book signing set in stone, we've still got work to do on the actual take down.

Until I've spoken with Jeremy, we don't even know when it will take place. Because he hadn't given me his number when I interrupted him the other night, the only way I can speak to him, is by running into him again.

No matter which day, the sting has to take place at night, because some things are better completed under cover of darkness. Fewer witnesses and more drama are never a bad thing when you're faking it as much as we will be.

It wouldn't be my first choice to have as many people involved as there are, but there'd been no stopping Tyler and Zac when they heard about it. Rather than be reticent, Zac appears eager, even talking about bringing his Uncle Cole along for the ride.

On hearing his uncle was in his late forties, I'd said no. That was until Ethan gave me a rundown of just what Zac's uncle was capable of. If what he says is true, the old guy will probably leave me in the dust.

Come dinner time, Macie insists she'll eat at her workbench, but I'm having none of it. "And ingest a stack of metal filings and glass dust while you're about it? Hell no, you won't."

After glaring at me, she climbs down off her work stool and stretch-walks to the kitchen island. Much as I want to push the point, I instead grab my dinner and leave her to it. I'd rather eat alone on the front porch than ruin her meal.

What I'm not expecting is for her to join me, sitting quietly on the bench opposite. The only sounds she makes after this are inarticulate and in appreciation of the meal.

I'm unsure what her joining me means, and neither do I want to ask, preferring to enjoy our unspoken truce. This continues once dinner is over and she goes back to work.

The next time I speak, it's just before midnight, and I'm telling her to go to bed. I then follow this up with, "I'll set the alarm on my phone for seven."

As she trudges up the stairs, leaving to me to bed down in the entryway, she throws, "Better make it five," over her shoulder. She then adds, "I've still got a lot to do to finish the piece."

While we don't exactly go to bed angry, neither are things as they were before I'd put her off this morning. In hindsight, it wasn't my best decision.

I guess I hadn't expected her to take my retreat as hard as she had. We've only known each other for what amounts to days, and yet there's a closeness that's new to me.

Her reaction to my telling her I couldn't commit to anything had been intense enough as to give me hope when I have no right.

The pain of not taking things forward, I can cope with. However, the pain of Macie being hurt because of me would destroy my peace of mind for the rest of my miserable life.

As I settle down in the entryway, my mom's words about me making my bed and having to lie in it come back with a vengeance. Am I destined never to be worthy of a woman like the beauty sleeping upstairs?

Not with my past constantly hanging over me. And just like that, I go from maudlin to mad in a heartbeat. There isn't a chance I'm letting my old life ruin my chance for a new one, not now, never.

Jeremy better look out if he tries anything, because I won't slip quietly into the night, not this time. For the first time, I've got something worth fighting for, and fight I will.

TEN

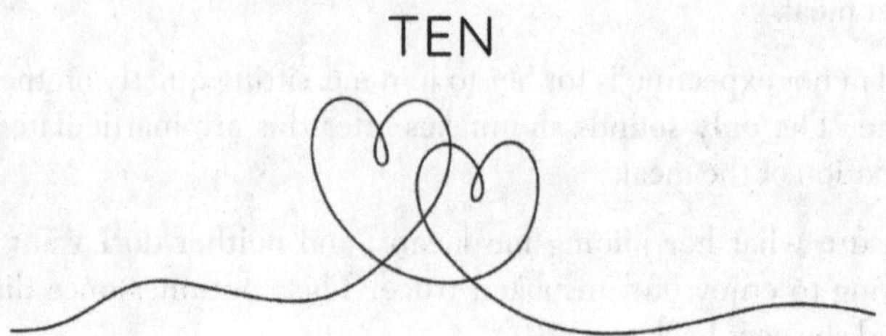

MACIE

Five on Monday morning and I'm already at my workbench, determined to make the choker Lindsey is to wear the best I can. Not to tempt our visiting thief, but because my professional pride won't allow for anything less.

While I get on with the final assembly, Brad putters about in the kitchen sorting out coffee. He's even toasting bagels he'd found in the freezer, with his ability to uncover things I didn't know I possessed, borderline mystical.

I wouldn't usually have started work quite this early, but there was never a chance I could bang something together as Brad had instructed.

There's also part of me that is proud of the design, every angry sweep of the sketch jumping off the page. And just as I'd hoped, that has translated into a statement piece, there'll be no missing.

Not because of sloppy craftsmanship, but because it has a life of its own rarely seen in jewelry. Even sitting in bits on my workbench, I know it's good, maybe even better than good.

As I solder and polish the last few links, I know the only way to tell for sure is to try it on. To truly shine, jewelry needs the human body as a backdrop.

The complexity of the closure being what it is, I'm not doing that on my own. While I could ask any of others who are now banging away in the addition, having them close enough I could feel their breath on my neck would be unnerving.

It's therefore Brad's attention that I catch before showing him how the choker fastens up at the back. Despite him doing so in a business-like way, my body reacts to his feather light touch as it always has.

I should be excited about finishing a piece that has the potential to change my career forever. Instead, I'm overcome with melancholy at what might have been with Brad.

"There you go, all done." Brad punctuates this by resting his hands lightly on my shoulders and squeezing gently. I'm surprised when he then kisses the nape of my neck through the choker, as if to seal the deal.

He straightens and immediately backs away, a ready apology on his lips, but it's one that I wave away. I don't need his sympathy, nor do I want it. This week will be hard enough to navigate without his pity in the mix.

Rather than stay next to him, I march through to the entryway and into the half-bath. Only then do I remember the mirror in there had fallen off the wall and smashed into a thousand pieces.

It's a shame it's not still strewn across the floor, because it'd be a perfect foil to my heart. However, needing to have a look at the choker to check everything is as it should be, I race up the stairs to my bedroom.

On standing before the full-length mirror in the corner, I reach up and touch the choker, surprised to see my reflection also move. Was it possible for a piece of jewelry to be so beautiful that wearing it led to an out-of-body experience?

Or was that simply a dream on my part?

"It looks stunning. You look stunning."

I whirl around to find Brad standing in my bedroom doorway, a strange cast in his eyes. Unfortunately, it's not one I can decipher, nor do I have the time with it already gone nine-fifteen.

"Can you please undo it for me? I need to meet Lindsey at the bookshop so I can fasten it up for her. Can you get Ethan to call her and tell her she'll need to have her hair up on top?"

Brad is as careful in his removal of the choker as he had been putting it on, although on feeling the final clasp loosen, I back away. There'll be no more kisses; my heart couldn't cope with it.

I leave him to follow, racing down the stairs to grab a gift box from a crate next to my workbench. After wrapping the choker in a couple of sheets of tissue paper, I place it carefully in the box.

Purse and keys are next, although I'm surprised to find Brad waiting for me at the front door. "What are you doing?"

There's resignation in his stance when he replies. "I'm coming with you. If I'm right, then Jeremy will be there with his Mrs." As if expecting me to argue, he continues. "Macie, I don't have his phone number. We didn't exactly exchange business cards when I caught him breaking in the other night."

Damn it, he's right. To put the plan in place, Brad needs to speak to his criminal friend. We need to force the guy to break in at a time that suits us and not the other way around.

However, I don't want Brad next to me on the drive to the bookshop, and so I don't give him the option. Instead, I unlock the driver's door of my station wagon and jump in. Despite it having been a top of the line model in its day, there's no central locking, and so I know Brad can't join me.

After starting the engine, I wind the window partway down and call out, "I'll see you there."

I then stomp on the accelerator, leaving him standing on the side of the road.

While it's an outwardly petty move, it gives me a chance to calm myself during the five minutes it takes to drive into town.

Time spent wondering how things will go, and whether this Jeremy character's wife will even attend the signing.

There's so much up in the air about all of this, especially where I stand with Brad, and what will happen when Jeremy leaves. I'm parking at the back of the bookshop when I have a realization.

When Jeremy leaves, so will Brad, and I'm not sure how I feel about that. Nor do I get the chance to examine this when, on entering the bookshop, our plan goes all to hell.

Rather than fasten the choker around Lindsey's neck and leave as I'm supposed to, the bookshop owner press-gangs me into helping. This sees me checking receipts and opening the books, ready for Lindsey to sign.

Instead of staying in the background as Brad wanted, I've got a starring role. The challenge now will be to ignore Brad when he arrives, acting like I don't know him.

BRAD

As I watch Macie drive off down her street, I have to shake my head. If she'd given me a chance, I could have explained I wouldn't be traveling with her.

I don't want to arrive too far behind her, though, which has me running back to my truck and jumping in. I'm soon tailing her into town, although I don't park behind the bookshop as she does. Rather, I park at the supermarket across the road, to further distance us.

I need to keep up the pretense that I'm simply out to rob Macie in the same way as Jeremy is. Not only will this improve the chances of the sting being a success, it'll lessen the likelihood of the bastard extorting me in exchange for Macie's continued good health.

On entering the bookshop, I can't decide what shocks me more. That it's packed to the roof with women, or that Macie, rather than having left, is up front with Lindsey. This wasn't part of the plan. She was supposed to fit the choker and then get the hell out of there.

I'm wondering how I'm supposed to hide my feelings for her when I spot Jeremy on the far side of the shop. In my favor is that he's not looking in my direction. Instead, he gazes at Holly, who's in the queue to have her book signed.

You can do this, buddy, just act like you're back inside.

This has me wiping all expression from my face, before wending my way through the crowd to join him. Despite all that, my ass being groped twice on the way has me close to losing this carefully crafted mask of indifference.

Sheesh, it was no wonder Ethan stayed out of sight at Lindsey's events like he did. If not for his warning, I'd have been more shocked than I am.

Instead, my expression is neutral when I rock up next to Jeremy. I'd learned the hard way over the years that if someone saw a chink in your armor, they were going for it. It'd kill me if my letting my guard down led to Macie being hurt.

"Fancy seeing you here?" Jeremy's opening gambit is as neutral as my expression. Strange, I'd expected him to go on the attack after I'd stopped him the other night. Could it be he's mellowing in his old age?

Or could it be that my bulking up while inside gave him pause for thought? Who am I kidding? Of course it was my added muscles.

Jeremy tips his head in Macie's direction. "And fancy seeing the chunky monkey I was visiting the other night when you interrupted me."

I have to hold myself back from flattening him. How dare this low-life talk about Macie like that? She was worth of a hundred of this guy, and his wife. There was a time I'd have gone along with him, rather than show my disapproval.

Those days are gone. Except, of course, I can't defend Macie, not without showing how I feel about her. That doesn't mean I'm falling in line completely.

"She's a hell of a designer. I'll give her that."

It's then I draw attention to the choker Lindsey is wearing. While impressive, it looks nowhere near as good as it had on Macie. "That piece of hers that the author is wearing? Yeah, well, it's worth at least five grand, and there'll be more where that came from if you give it some time."

Jeremy stares at Lindsey for a minute or two, his calculations as to the worth of the piece on full display. "That crap?" he says, not looking convinced.

"Yeah, you say that, but trust me when I say the finished pieces are worth a truckload more than the components. Macie Hart has quite a name for herself."

A glance in his direction and I can see he's not buying what I'm selling.

All this changes when his wife steps forward to get her paperback signed by Lindsey. Even from over here, it's easy to see that Holly has commented on the choker, with Lindsey's hand straying to her throat.

There's no telling what Lindsey said in response, although Ethan had promised to brief her fully. What is telling is how quickly Holly makes her way across the crowded shop to Jeremy's side after having her book signed.

A quick hello to me and she's reaching up on tiptoes to whisper in Jeremy's ear, just loud enough that I can hear. "That necklace, I want it. Get it for me. I asked if I could buy it, but she said she couldn't afford it and that it was on loan from the designer."

Rather than answer her, Jeremy turns to me. "So buddy, when are we doing this thing? You promised, remember?"

$\cdot \quad \cdot \quad \cdot$

Jeremy stares at me, disbelief writ large on this acne-scarred face. "Friday? Are you kidding? Me and Holly were planning on hitting the craps in Vegas tomorrow, not hanging around this dump."

My responding shrug is deliberately vague, as if showing I don't care either way. "Depends on whether Holly wants more than one necklace. Word is the designer is working on a collection for some trade show. It'll be ready by the end of the week."

I turn and address the rest of my lure directly to Jeremy's wife. "You'd be happy to wait if it meant Jerry boy could pick you up a couple more pieces, wouldn't you?"

Would—she—ever. There wasn't a chance Jeremy could or would say no to her after that enticement. And especially not after what she promises her husband in exchange, her voice loud enough that half the people in the bookshop hear.

Hah, once a hooker, always a hooker.

Friday morning and everything is in place for that night. As well as rehearsing our various parts for the sting, we've been busy working on finishing Macie's home studio.

Meanwhile, she's spent every hour available, and even a few that weren't, finishing more pieces for her Hart of Glass collection. She's standing in front of the newly installed mirror in the hall bathroom when I walk past, although I soon backtrack.

"It looks good on you!" In order to maintain our carefully curated truce, I'm not too over-the-top with my praise. However, if I was being truthful, the necklace looks way beyond good on her. It's spectacular, with the red heart-shaped piece of beach glass nestled in her cleavage, drawing even more attention to her breasts.

As if they needed any help in that department.

"I think this one is my favorite." She picks at the necklace, as if searching for faults, before carrying on. "I still can't believe it'll be gone by tomorrow."

Not trusting myself to comment, I instead walk out the front door, although I'm soon brought up short by a couple of man-mountains who are blocking the front path. Despite being six-foot-two myself, I still have to tilt my head back to look them in the eye.

"Can I help you boys?" I don't remember these two from the crew back on the east coast. However, it wouldn't be the first time Jeremy had called in a favor, or in this case, two. Especially with the odds stacked against him, as they are with him away from his usual stomping grounds.

They've not answered when Ethan joins me on the front path. "Brad, I'd like you to meet Heath and Josh Kendrick. They'll be giving us a hand tonight and joining the team permanently from next week."

Rather than continue to Ethan's truck to grab the back-up nail gun, I retrace my steps, helping him to instruct the newcomers on what's going down that night. They're quick studies, despite them looking to be more about brawn than brain, with me even getting a glimmer that things will turn out okay.

Still, it wouldn't be the first time I'd underestimated Jeremy. That bastard was the reason I'd ended up in prison.

ELEVEN

MACIE

Because of the time taken to move me into my studio temporarily; it's going on for six before I finish the last Hart of Glass piece.

After deciding it would be easier to corner Jeremy in the studio than out in my living room, the Lucky Break crew had moved all my stuff in here. Well, most of it, with anything of value removed from the apple crates and hidden in the garage.

As I look at the aqua glass pendant and earrings, I'm having difficulty coming to terms with the fact Jeremy will steal them later.

While the pieces in my Hart of Glass collection had started out as bait, I love them. They excite me in a more than my mainstream jewelry has in a very long time.

It might be the fakes appeal even more than my usual jewelry. Designs I'd labored over for months, rather than whipped up in under a week, to an instruction of 'have fun with it'.

Perhaps that's what was missing from my high-end pieces? Fun?

Was it this element that made the new pieces so very different from my usual fare? And yet, despite the playfulness of the designs, there's also a substance to them that is both comforting and flattering.

This will be especially true for curvy girls like me and some of my friends, where delicate pieces are all too often swamped by us. Lindsey has already put in an order for a choker like the one I'd made for her to wear to her book signing.

After removing my headphones and jeweler's loupe, I have to suppress a snort of laughter. The thought of women all over the country wearing jewelry made from old beer bottles is as funny as it is unbelievable.

And it's right then that I realize I'm going ahead with the Hart of Glass collection and that I'll show it at the gift fair. I'd be a fool to ignore the buzz I get from creating them.

There'd also been no ignoring Lindsey's relief when I could secure the choker around her neck without difficulty. All too often curvier girls were stuck using the extension chain, with this usually throwing off the balance of a piece.

I'm wrapping the aqua glass necklace and earrings in tissue paper when there's a gentle tap at the door. "Come in!"

On swiveling around to see who it is, I'm not disappointed. As I take in the man I love, I have to temper my enthusiasm. If I'm to limit my heartache, then I need to keep my defenses up.

"How are you doing?" he says, stepping closer, although nowhere near as close as I'd like. "Nearly ready?"

"Nearly. Give me a minute."

Eager to finish up, I put the tissue-wrapped piece into a gift box and close the flaps before sealing them with a gold sticker. It's only after I've slid it to the back of my workbench to sit with the others that Brad comments.

"That'll never work."

I look from the line-up of gift boxes, my brow wrinkled in confusion. "What do you mean? I always present them like that."

His frown is now a match for mine. "Macie, when have you ever left finished pieces lined up on your workbench like that?"

I don't need to think about it long, knowing the answer in seconds.

"But I don't have access to a safe here. And anyway, isn't the idea that we want him to steal them?"

To make it harder for Jeremy to do so is counterintuitive in my mind.

"Sure, but if we make it too easy, he'll smell a rat."

Spinning slowly on my work stool, I search the studio for a hidey hole. Somewhere that's obvious, but not too obvious. It's a pointless exercise, with my workbench, stool, and a few crates the only things in the unfinished studio.

My being in here is just as much window dressing as the windows themselves, with these temporarily held in place with nails. The minute Jeremy leaves with all my hard work, the team will reinstall the plywood panels.

I'm staring at Brad as if for inspiration when I hear grunting out in the living room. I only know what the fuss is about when the Kendrick boys stagger in, carrying a small safe between them.

Some deft maneuvering and they place it gently on the floor next to my workbench before proceeding to bolt it to the monolith. Now I'm confused.

"Okay, so I get we don't want to make it too easy, but if we lock the jewelry in a safe, won't that make it too hard?"

Josh Kendrick is the first to laugh, although he's soon joined by Heath, his brother. While there's no denying they're both cute, neither man attracts me in the same way as Brad.

Josh, still chuckling, slaps me on the back, nearly sending me flying. "Macie, if she thought there were brownies in there, our granny could open that safe with a bobby pin."

After seeing my Hart of Glass collection locked in the 'safe', I'm then at a loss what to do with myself. Usually Brad would have dinner underway by now, but not tonight.

I'm about to put the call out for requests on Uber eats when there's a knock at the front door. Could it be someone's beaten me to it, because I doubt that's Jeremy?

It's not. Instead, I'm greeted by Zac and Tyler, each holding a pile of pizza boxes. And they've got company, with me only getting a good look at the other guy, when he follows them in loaded down with sodas and side orders.

He's older than the other men, a lot older. However, you'd be a fool to treat him as a geriatric. Santa Claus on steroids is the description that springs to mind, although it's one I soon stifle. Call me old-fashioned, but my folks brought me up to respect my elders, even when they're as buff as this guy.

After checking to see if there's anyone else outside, I shut the front door, although I don't bother locking it. With the amount of testosterone currently swirling in my living room, there's no need.

It's when I'm grabbing plates from the cupboard that I realize Ethan isn't here. Surely he should be here, with the plan mostly down to him? On seeing me looking around, Brad instinctively knows what I'm wondering about.

"He's on his way with Lindsey. After dinner, she'll take you back to Eagle's Nest for the night."

I drop the stack of plates on the kitchen island with a clatter that stops conversations, and has all the men looking at me.

"Like heck she will. I'm staying right here!"

BRAD

When will this gorgeous woman stop surprising me? Although, really, why am I? She took me out with a tennis racket older than I am. The only problem is that it was thanks to terror rather than deadly skills.

"You're not staying here, Macie. I know you knocked me out..." I hold my hand up to stop Tyler's gibe in its tracks. "But that was down to you knowing where I was, thanks to those noisy floorboards."

On seeing her readying herself to argue, I go for the big guns, or, in this case, a Glock with the serial number filed off. "Also, I wasn't carrying a gun, whereas Jeremy will be. If anything happened to you, I'd..."

There's nothing I can do to stop myself from dragging her in for a tight hug and kissing the top of her head. The biggest surprise isn't that she melts against me like she does; it's that the others don't give me grief about it.

Get a group of guys together and it was astonishing how quickly the playground antics started up.

I'm still holding her tight when Ethan and Lindsey let themselves in through the front door. There's no missing Ethan's annoyance at finding me hugging Macie as tightly as I am.

He should be happy I've put our relationship on hold, even if it doesn't feel like it. Not with her body tight against mine, her perfume flooding my senses.

Okay, so Macie wants to stay. I can understand that. However, we'll be sticking to my rules all the way. It's time to get my life back and with no collateral damage along the way. "If everyone wants to grab some pizza, we can go through it all again. Remember. Fail to prepare..."

"Prepare to fail!" comes back to me in full force.

The team in position downstairs, and no lights on in the house. I'm right behind Macie when she walks into her closet. I have to see for myself that she'll be safe, because I've still got misgivings about her staying up here.

Never mind up here, I've got misgivings about her staying in the house, full-stop. My preference would be for her to be on the other side of town, safe with Lindsey, only she'd refused, Ethan's wife driving home alone.

Unlike me, Macie hasn't seen Jeremy when he's cornered, with the guy turning feral in the blink of an eye, often with deadly consequences.

The men downstairs have all faced that, or worse. From what Zac had said, Cole Stillman, whose background is as gray as his hair, has faced a lot worse.

After sliding the closet door shut behind us and turning on the light, Macie's pheromones head straight for my cock. I then have a thought that has me forgetting myself.

If things go pear-shaped tonight, I'll be leaving either with Jeremy, or in a body bag. If this is to be my last chance to show Macie how much I love her, then I'm not wasting it.

The briefest check of my watch and my hands are on Macie's shoulders, turning her to face me. A moment later and I'm pressing her into the dresses and coats hanging off to one side.

The subdued light from the chandelier is just enough to see that the lust in her eyes is a match for my own. I claim her lips in a kiss that bonds us as surely as if I was burying myself in her scalding depths.

I only break our kiss long enough to whisper, "I've got eight minutes and change. Shall we make it count?"

And we do, with me not even bothering to strip completely. Instead, I slide my black jeans down just enough to free my cock before lying on the upholstered bench in the middle of the crowded space.

Even better is that rather than be in jeans, Macie is wearing a skirt. After dropping her panties carelessly on the carpet, there's nothing subtle about how she takes my length before riding me like a pro.

Five minutes and change later and I come so hard that I see stars. There's something about knowing a job is coming up that gives life an edge. It doesn't matter that tonight is all for show; the effect has been as strong as ever.

Atop me, Macie has her head thrown back in ecstasy as she follows me over the edge, calling my name. Not wanting to be parted from her, I rock into a sitting position, my chest jammed against her lush breasts.

"Whatever happens tonight, I'll never forget this." I have to swallow hard before I can continue, but I need to say my piece. For her to know, in case anything should happen.

"I love you, baby." The words out, it's as if I've had a weight lifted off my chest. I've never said them to anyone before, not even my parents, especially not my bitter as gall parents.

My lips again claim hers, with me drawing strength from our kiss. Likewise, she clings to me like her life depends on it, although I hope it doesn't.

Ending our kiss wrenches at my soul, with me wanting nothing more than to stay with her, but I can't. Not if we're to have a future together.

After helping Macie to stand, I reach down and grab her panties off the floor. But rather than hand them over, I stuff them in the front pocket of my jeans, a good luck charm of sorts.

I'm giving her a kiss goodbye when I notice the tears on her cheeks. "Hey, hey, it'll be okay." I wipe her cheeks with my thumbs before pressing a chaste kiss on her forehead. "I promise I'll take care."

She sniffles before answering. "You'd better Brad McKenna, because I love you, too."

After turning off the light and making her promise to keep the door shut tight, I kiss her again before I'm on my way. Not downstairs and out through the front door, but up onto the bed. Soon after, I'm out through the window, and down to the ground via the roof of the studio.

I'm just as quiet when I climb over the fence into the neighboring property before repeating the process. I pop out onto the street half-a-dozen houses down, although I'm careful to keep to the shadows.

With all our vehicles parked around the corner, it's no surprise that the street is empty. However, all that changes when Jeremy drives slowly by in a late model BMW.

After meeting up with him next to his car, I allow him to do the honors of picking the lock on Macie's front door. I even stand back while he cracks the safe.

He's on his hands and knees, pawing through the contents when the lights in the studio flare into life and the team walks in.

If I thought Cole Stillman looked scary before, it's nothing compared to now, with him standing in front of the others. The guy exudes mob boss. "Well, well, well, what do we have here?"

While his words are conversational, there's nothing polite about the tone. This sees Jeremy on his feet with a cartoon-like speed and it's all I can do to fight my smile.

My old comrade is as quick to go for the gun in his shoulder holster, although nowhere near as fast as Zac, who immediately disarms him.

Cole takes a step in Jeremy's direction, backed up by the others. Apart from Ethan. With him having been at Lindsey's book launch, he hangs back as a precaution.

Cole glances at me before focusing on Jeremy. "So first you two bozos move in on a job we've been planning for weeks, and now you have the audacity to try pulling a gun on us. That's not friendly."

Neither is Cole. He's downright scary.

After holding his hands up to signal he means no harm, Jeremy leans in my direction, not once taking his eyes off Cole and the others. "Come on. The crap in that safe isn't worth getting killed over. The boys back home will be pleased to see you. You always were the best at getting in and out quietly."

This throwaway line has Cole moving even closer and putting his hand on Jeremy's shoulder. "In that case, he's staying here."

If I hadn't just shared a pizza with Cole, I'd be freaking out by now. As it is, my, "Nah, I'm all good. I'll head back to the east coast," comes out shakier than I'd like.

When Cole looks in my direction, I'm quick to understand the stench of fear coming off Jeremy in waves. As reminiscent as Cole is of the crazier guys in those anger management sessions, it's no surprise the effect he's having.

"And just how easy will you find it to get in and out of places after we've busted your knees?"

The edge in Cole's voice leaves no doubt that he's serious and would probably laugh while he was about it. While Tyler then brandishing a hammer isn't necessary, his timing is perfect.

His hands still up in the air, Jeremy inches slowly sideways. "Sorry Brad, looks like you're on your own." Then, not once taking his eyes off Cole and the others, Jeremy scuttles crab-like out of the studio.

We're all crowded in the entryway, watching him scamper down the front path, when a shadow detaches itself from the shrubs at the side of the property. It then sprints across the front lawn before cannoning into the unsuspecting felon.

After an 'oomph' of expressed air, and a bit of a scuffle, the words, "Chase Hunter, Bail Bonds," come through loud and clear. The unmistakable ratchet of handcuffs soon follows.

As impressive as the speed of this takedown is how quickly Ethan's younger brother drags Jeremy up off the ground and tosses him over one shoulder. A minute later, and it would be as if I've imagined the whole thing.

And if not for the BMW still parked on the other side of the road, I might have. Until Cole strolls down the front path, crosses the street, jumps into the BMW and drives away with barely a pause.

It's only then I comprehend why he'd played the part of a scary mofo like he had. There wasn't a chance any of the old crew back east would want to go through him to get to me.

As focused as I've been, it takes longer than it should to realize I've got my life back. Even locked up, Jeremy can vouch that I'd had no choice but to join my new 'gang'.

If I thought telling Macie that I loved her lifted a load off me, this is a close second.

"Okay, you lot, move it!"

I follow this up by shoving them one by one out the front door. I've no sooner slammed it behind them than I'm racing up the stairs.

There's a very special lady I need to celebrate with. Even better is that we've got all the time in the world to do so.

EPILOGUE

SIX MONTHS AND CHANGE LATER

MACIE

My studio being as quiet as it is, there's no need for me to wear the noise-canceling headphones. With three of the four walls mostly glass, often I don't even bother with my jeweler's loupe.

Part of me still can't believe how different my life is. Despite Brad and me wanting to take things slowly, he'd moved in only a month after we got together. As it was, he'd been staying over every night, with the thought of what we'd gotten up to, enough to have me grinning like a fool.

I'm putting the finishing touches to another of my Hart of Glass designs when he walks into the studio, a large glass of red wine in each hand. It's become our ritual to finish the work day like this. And despite it being Valentine's Day, today is no different.

There'll be no going out to celebrate tonight, not with us both having started the day early, and due to do so again tomorrow. The mere thought of going out to dinner at Maddigan's has me stifling a yawn. Although, I'm not so tired that we won't have fun tonight.

A lot of fun by the look of things, with Brad only dressed in faded jeans that ride low on his hips. And, oh my, there's no missing that telltale bulge.

"Give me a minute. I just need to send a photo of this latest design down to Eduardo for him to give me some production time frames."

While many designers outsource the manufacture of their pieces to Asia, I've opted for a workshop in Mexico City. This not only allows me to visit to check on production, it also lets me monitor working conditions.

I can't easily do that if I have to travel to the other side of the world. Even better is when Brad can get time off work and come with me. That's only happened twice so far with there being no let-up in the work pouring into Lucky Break Construction.

Last time I caught up with Lindsey for coffee, she'd told me that with the business doing well, Ethan was constantly on the lookout for more crew. It didn't hurt that word had gotten out that the team was easy on the eye. It had been enough for more than one woman to suddenly decide she needed an 'addition'.

According to any single ladies who'd had work done, the company motto should be "Build it and you will come." Word on the street was that more than a few had done just that.

With the design on its way to Eduardo, I take a glass of wine off Brad and clink it against the rim of his. "Happy Valentine's Day, darling."

After the smallest of sips, we both lean in to seal the deal, our Syrah-laced kiss hitting all the right places. We've not even sat on the daybed that dominates the sunniest corner of the studio, when Brad stuffs his free hand in the front pocket of his jeans.

"I know you said not to bother, but I wanted to give you something to mark the day. Hold out your hand." A moment later, he drops a small leather drawstring bag in my palm, my fingers automatically closing tight around it.

BRAD

It had taken me weeks to pull together Macie's Valentine's Day gift. As a jewelry designer, I knew I couldn't give her anything she could make herself.

And yet, it had to be special enough to show her how much I loved her.

There was only one thing she couldn't make for herself, and yet it was the one thing I could give her. Every lunch hour had seen me searching the cove at the end of the main Coogan's Break beach. Back and forth, head down, eyes peeled.

As I watch her upend the small drawstring bag, I have to hope that she's like me in thinking it's the thought that counts rather than the value.

But it wasn't just any beach glass that I'd spent hours searching for. It had to be red. Of course, the biggest challenge was that the pieces also had to be heart-shaped.

There'd been no missing how beautiful that necklace had looked on her. There'd also been no missing how reverently she'd touched the heart-shaped glass that was at the center of the piece.

I wanted her to experience that again, a thousand-fold. Well, at least fifty, of every size and shade of red. These weren't to be made into jewelry, these were for her alone.

Of course, that wasn't all that was in the bag; with her soon discovering the small gold ingot nestled there. Not wanting her to have any doubts as to the hidden message, I put my glass of wine on the windowsill before taking the small ingot out of her palm. Now holding the makings of a ring, I drop to one knee.

"Macie Hart, will you please do me the honor of becoming my wife?"

She doesn't say yes. In fact, she doesn't say a thing. She doesn't even look at me as she puts her glass of wine on the windowsill next to mine. How could I have got it so wrong? Rather than squealing with delight and yelling yes, she's now busy searching through the beach glass in her hand.

I'm thinking about getting back to my feet when she finds what it is she's obviously been looking for. She then holds up a perfect glass heart, the resultant streaks of red when the sun hits it, filling the studio.

"This one, I'll use this one."

I stay right where I am, my heart beating so hard I'm sure she'll hear it. I can hardly hear my own words when I dare to ask, "So, is that a yes?"

Macie looks from the glass heart to me, as if just now realizing I'm still hunkered down. "Of course it is." She looks confused for a moment before carrying on. "Haven't you heard me squealing, YES, since you asked?"

After getting to my feet, I sweep her off hers. I then get to hear the words I've been dreaming of for weeks.

"Of course I'll marry you, Brad McKenna. I love you so much, it hurts."

This has me dragging her in for yet another kiss. I'll never tire of kissing this woman; of joining with her and showing her I love her as much as she loves me.

For the first time in my life, I've got the start of a family, a loving family and one that'll be with me for life, not just appearances.

MOVIES

If you're looking for something to do this Saturday, the Odeon is showing Heart of Glass based on the novel of the same name by Lindsey Hunter.

Even better is that lead actress, Sasha Milroy demanded she wear jewelry from Macie McKenna nee Hart's successful Hart of Glass collection.

This truly is a Coogan's Break production from start to finish.

THANK YOU

If you've enjoyed this story, we'd be thrilled if you could take the time to give it a review on your favorite retailer. These not only give authors feedback, but they allow other readers to see if the book might appeal to them. Either way, happy reading.

ALL ABOUT HOPE

Hope believes everyone deserves love, especially curvy girls. She also likes to believe there's a welcoming town like Coogan's Break for all of us. A place where the girls are curvy and the guys hotter than hell, where opposites attract, and love is steamy and fast.

www.papersparrowsnest.com

THE PAPER SPARROW

Home to books by Andrene Low, Hope Malone, Andie Low, Sydney Hunter, and a host of others along the way.

Whether your preference is for curvy girl romances, paranormal cozies, snarky British romcoms, or something darker, we've got you covered.

Even better is that you'll enjoy discounts you might not find elsewhere. Simply click the little birdie, then your preferred genre, and you're as good as on your way.